KEEP YOUR ENEMY CLOSE . . .

She bolted to kneel on the mattress, her hands shaking and full of livid faefire.

"Angel," she said, naming him as she prepared to strike.

"That won't be necessary," Jack said. Though he could read human minds easily, Kaye's was a complete and utter blank, like all of the soulless mage-born. But he knew human nature well enough. If he remained at ease, she wouldn't burn him. Most likely.

Pillow lines creased one cheek. Her auburn hair was flat on that side as well, wavy on the other. Black eyes. Her legs were braced apart, athletic in their youth. The skirt was still rucked up high on her thighs. Her stance was full of fight, so the life she'd been leading hadn't broken her yet. Very good.

"Although historically I'm your mortal enemy—" Jack began. Mages, like the fae, had always defied Heaven. He added a smile to make the acknowledgment seem friendly. "Today, I'm your prospective employer, Jack Bastian."

Other books by Erin Kellison

Shadowman

Novellas available exclusively in eBook

Shadow Play

Shadow Touch

Published by Kensington Publishing Corporation

FIRE KISSED

The Shadow Kissed Series

ERIN KELLISON

ZEBRA BOOKS
KENSINGTON PUBLISHING CORP.
http://www.kensingtonbooks.com

ZEBRA BOOKS are published by

Kensington Publishing Corp.
119 West 40th Street
New York, NY 10018

All Kensington titles, imprints and distributed lines are available at special quantity discounts for bulk purchases for sales promotion, premiums, fund-raising, educational or institutional use.

Special book excerpts or customized printings can also be created to fit specific needs. For details, write or phone the office of the Kensington Special Sales Manager: Attn. Special Sales Department. Kensington Publishing Corp., 119 West 40th Street, New York, NY 10018. Phone: 1-800-221-2647.

ISBN-13: 978-1-4201-1897-1
ISBN-10: 1-4201-1897-8

First Printing: July 2012

10 9 8 7 6 5 4 3 2 1

Printed in the United States of America

Acknowledgments

Thank you to my husband Matt, who reads every page in every incarnation. You are *my* bastion. And to my sweet girls, who burst with creativity and magic. You inspire me every day. And to all my family, who buy my books, sometimes in quantity. To Jessica Faust, my amazing agent, for everything she does (and it's a lot). To everyone at Ken-sington, especially Alicia Condon, for helping me make my Shadow world real. To KC Klein for her fabulous critiques, support, and laughs. To Brian Anderson, my go-to resource for everything guns. Any mistakes are mine. And to Jill and Jen, who help me in so many ways, not the least of which is keeping me grounded and sane.

Prologue

Kaye Brand hid behind a fat cement pillar in the cellar, unable to wrench her gaze from the man hanging slack from his wall-chained wrists. Fear lashed her in place while her brain raced to figure out what exactly she was seeing, and what it meant.

The otherwise empty cellar was cold and musty, like old dirt, but with a sour body smell besides, which had to be coming from . . . him. Darkness seeped into the corners of the room, licking the walls, tendrils reaching for the chained man. And in the air, the hissing whispers of the fae from beyond, who watched everything that went on in the great Houses.

She hid like a little kid, one eye peeking, even though she was fifteen and basically an adult. Even though part of her mind screamed for her to get back upstairs fast, lock the door, and pretend she'd never gone snooping in the first place.

The groom's gift is in the cellar, her dad had murmured to old lady Grey, who was just arriving at Brand House for the big event. He'd used his low voice, the one meant only for the ear he wanted, but Kaye knew she had to be listening to everything that went on today, and listening good.

A groom's gift? Kaye looked it up online, since her dad

hadn't bothered to fill her in, though it was *her* wedding, *her* groom. Turned out it was supposed to be a gift from her to her soon-to-be husband, Ferrol Grey. Like the marriage, her father had arranged the whole thing and left her out of it. It was medieval crap, but that's what you got for being born a Brand with Shadow in your blood.

Of course she had to check it out, though it took all her nerve to steal Dad's keys and try each one in the cellar door's lock. She didn't quite know what he'd do to her if he caught her, which was what made her hands shake, but this was her wedding, her life. The more decisions she let go by, the more he would make for her.

Not anymore.

Kaye's *gift* was on his knees, his arms strung out to the sides, manacles chaining him to the wall. The skin of his hands and forearms was riddled with black lines from the cuffs of his bonds, like poison leeching into his veins. His bare torso was flexed, muscle caught midripple. And his head hung forward, chin to his chest, as if he were that Greek god Atlas, the one with the world on his shoulders. Even though the cellar was dark, windowless, and otherwise empty, he was somehow lit by a soft glow that kept the reaching Shadows at bay. But not for long.

The man, her *gift,* had been tortured.

In her basement.

For her wedding.

The only thing she understood was that she'd better get upstairs, and fast. Her heart was pounding as if it had already taken off and had left the rest of her frozen behind, slick with sweat.

Because, umm . . . Why was her father giving a tortured man to her soon-to-be husband . . . and from her? And why would her soon-to-be husband want him?

The questions made her feel very small and stupid. And afraid.

She had to figure out a way to say no, even if the big event *was* tomorrow. She'd practiced, but the little word wouldn't come out whenever she faced her father.

Maybe this chained guy was bad. Beautiful, but bad. He had to have done something wrong. Nobody messed with the Brands. And nobody even thought of messing with the Greys. That had to be it. The mage families never relied on human laws or authorities. Maybe this was some kind of justice. Medieval, like her arranged marriage. In which case, the prisoner probably deserved what he got.

The chained man lifted his head.

Oh sweet Shadow.

Kaye's world cracked open. She felt the change in a hot-cold shock wave over her body and gripped the cement pillar for support. Her life was over. Nothing good would ever happen to her, never ever, because she had never seen anyone so beautiful, and tomorrow she'd have to marry an old man.

Kaye blinked hard to stop her tears.

There was no way this man could be bad. Not him.

He had features like a poet: mouth full, cheekbones high and sharp, forehead smooth, with hair falling in waves around his face. His eyes were honey brown, warm, soulful, and terribly sad as he looked at her. From within, he gleamed. He was perfect. And he was also broken, a scarlet smear of blood across his jaw.

"You," he said, voice rough, "shouldn't be down here. It's dangerous."

Kaye trembled behind her pillar. It felt so stupid to hide like a kid while wearing high heels. The only thing the shoes were good for was looking her father in the eye. (Not so good if she couldn't get her *no* out, though.) But here, towering over the chained man, those extra four inches felt more like dress-up. Either she should stand up straight or run away.

"Please," the man begged, his tone clearing some. His head bobbed with the effort of looking up at her. "They will hurt you."

They'd do worse than that. They would cut her off from the outside. Cut her off absolutely this time, which would be just fine by her father and soon-to-be husband. She was a dud. She might have Shadow in her blood, but if she couldn't call fire, she was suited for only one thing. Hence the marriage, for the good of the family. She'd been promised comforts. And the Grey name would protect her from the rest of magekind. But it wasn't what she wanted.

She had to say no. Tomorrow was coming. Tomorrow was just about here. But her dad would be so angry if he had to repay Mr. Grey for all the gifts and wedding expenses when she'd agreed to the thing in the first place.

Kaye looked at the man hanging in front of her; maybe Dad was already paying Mr. Grey back. And since her name would be on the gift tag, maybe she was somehow paying too. The thought made something in her go dark and cold, like a spark turning to ash. What exactly and how much did they owe?

The chained man shivered with her, his face haggard with pain, and Kaye wondered if he was going to speak again. If she should bring him water. If she should try each one of Dad's keys on his handcuffs, as she had on the cellar door. This was trouble. Epic trouble.

She looked over her shoulder and up the dark, narrow staircase, considering. Dad would be in meetings by now, family business. If she was quick, maybe no one would know. (Someone would.) She could put the chained man's arm over her shoulder. Help him up the stairs. She could set him free. (He'd never make it off the property.)

Still . . . Only a bad person would leave him to die, because that's what was going to happen.

Her stomach twisted, panic washing through her, but she raised her fistful of keys. Unlock the cuffs, leave the rest to him. She'd just have to get the keys back to Dad's office before he found out. (Dad would find out anyway. He always did.)

"No." The chained man shook his head, gaze sharpening for a second.

Kaye startled and stepped back. The keys shook in her hand.

"Child, please. Leave while you can." His skin flushed while he gasped for air. "*Run.*"

But she wasn't a child, not anymore. The guests arriving for the wedding could say it all they wanted—*Grey's child bride*—though, *duh,* she was clearly old enough to get hitched. Old enough for what came after too.

"And keep running," he added at the end of his breath. The black lines on his arms crawled toward his elbows. The ends of his fingers went dead gray.

There was nowhere to go. Not for him. Not for her.

"Get away from here. If you are even considering setting me free," he said, slurring, "this life is not for you."

Wrong again. Kaye was a Brand. She was born to this life. Born to breed power, her father had said. She lifted her chin and let the fear within sizzle her nerves.

"No," he said, going hoarse. "Not your responsibility. Not your fault either."

Yes, her fault. The gift would be from her.

The chained man strained forward, his bonds taking his weight, arms extending farther to the sides, as if he were about to take flight. The glow around him brightened painfully, and the grasping Shadows reeled away from him. "Run away!"

Kaye flinched. *Too loud!*

She whipped to view the stairs, stumbling back, almost turning her ankle in the dumb shoes.

Someone had to have heard him. This was bad, very bad. She'd been there too long. What was she thinking? She couldn't help him. They were in the middle of nowhere. In a house full of Shadow.

She dashed tears from her eyes. *No.* She could only save herself. Pretend she'd never been here. And then hate herself forever.

The chained man sighed as if he divined her intention. Dimmed. "Go."

Kaye forced herself not to look back as she lunged upward, but she could feel the beautiful, chained man behind her, and in her mind's eye saw him looking after, watching his only chance to survive leave him to save her own skin.

If she had a soul, which for once she was glad she didn't, she'd be going to Hell. Score one for the soulless mages, though it didn't make her feel any better. Getting married tomorrow would be punishment enough. She was trapped, just like him.

Kaye trembled as she shut the cellar door behind her. Her guts and bones ached as if she had the flu. She looked left and right. Nobody in the hallway. Kitchen sounds beyond, the staff working up the night's dinner. Smelled . . . fishy, among other things.

She found the key and locked the door again, her throat tightening as the bolt snapped into place. The beautiful man was buried down there.

The keys. She had to get them back before Dad noticed. Drop them in his coat pocket before he knew they were missing. Or toss them out the window and look stupid if he asked about them.

Kaye smoothed her little black dress, reminding herself that she was the woman of the house. And a Brand.

Nothing had happened.

Please, please don't let me cry.

She swallowed to wet her mouth, forced her chin up, and headed for her father's study.

Kaye listened, forehead at the door, and hearing nothing did a quiet twist of the knob and a slow push. From the open sliver, she couldn't see anyone. So far, so good. She eased it farther, then froze at the sight of the old lady she'd met earlier today, the groom's sister. Ms. Grey was supposed to act as Ferrol's proxy in the marriage because times were too dangerous for him to come himself, which meant that Kaye had to say "I do" to her, though it meant "I do" to him.

The whole thing was screwed up. Danger even on the inside of magekind. Whispers everywhere.

The old woman sat behind her dad's new desk. Her face was deeply wrinkled like the up-down grooves of craggy tree bark, but with sour, thin lips. Her eyeballs were nested black marbles, hard and glossy, and they fixed on her.

Her dad had just turned from the bar cart with a couple of drinks. He had his usual cognac. And the old lady's drink had a toothpick stuck in a drowned green olive. Martini. Once, secretly, Kaye had sampled all the booze. Most of it was nasty.

"Kaye?" Dad sounded polite, but he had that tight look that meant she was interrupting.

"Oh, I'm sorry," Kaye said, not sorry at all. "I didn't know you were busy."

She started to retreat. The keys, out a window then. Or in the trash. Right now they felt terribly conspicuous in her hand.

"No, we're not," the old woman corrected. "Why don't you come in for a moment?" She had a broken voice that added syllables and skipped others.

Dad's lip twitched—he must be angry—but since he didn't contradict the request, Kaye obeyed.

"Sure." Kaye tucked the keys in her hand. There were more than ten on the ring. She stepped inside, sucking in her stomach and working on her shoulders. If she pushed them back, her flat chest stuck out, but any other way she stood was supposedly sloppy. Late bloomer, someone had called her.

The flames in the fireplace leapt as she entered, but then fire did that when she was around. It was a Brand thing, a *Shadow* thing, and the reason her dad had fires lit in every room—to show off to his guests what she *could* do.

Her dad's office was old-school, like he was, dark-toned with lots of new, thick furniture brought in to make them look rich for the wedding, including the hulking desk. Their family might be old blood, but those heavy antiques weren't, and probably weren't even theirs to keep.

Standing behind the old lady was one of those sad, monster people, a wraith in a suit, who was supposed to be a bodyguard or something. Wraiths were horrible but couldn't be beat in a fight. The old lady shouldn't worry; the wraith looked scary mean, but it was his funky BO that would keep everyone away.

The wraith's attention fixed on her, and his nostrils flared.

"Close the door, please," Ms. Grey said, though it was not her door.

First the old biddy sat in Dad's chair, now she gave orders?

Last time Kaye checked, this was *Brand* house. Kaye swatted behind her, and the door shut just shy of a slam.

"Kaye," her father said smoothly, but she got the warning to behave, "Zelda and I were just discussing the continuation of your studies."

Zelda. That's what the old lady's name was. A couple of weeks ago, Kaye would have been required to call her Ms. Grey or ma'am. Now it was Zelda. The perks of being suddenly all grown up.

The wraith leaned down to the grand madam's ear, whispering.

None of this boded well. Kaye was supposed to marry Ferrol tomorrow, but Zelda was the first Grey she'd ever met. And if the old lady was a crypt keeper, how old would that make her brother, Kaye's soon-to-be husband? Old. Which was probably why they weren't letting her meet him.

Wasn't fair, no matter how generous the marriage contract might be. She should just say no. It was now or never.

Zelda twitched her black eyeballs back to Kaye. "My companion says your smell is off."

As if the monster could talk.

"I was in the kitchen," Kaye explained. "They're cooking fish." She hoped it wasn't the kind where they left the inside raw. What was his excuse?

"Not that smell," Zelda said.

Silence in the office. The fire snapped, Shadows flickering. Dad paused, midmotion. Zelda's eyes glinted. The wraith looked meaner.

Anxiety tickled Kaye. The old lady knew something.

Zelda leaned forward slightly, pinning her. "You've been in the cellar."

Wraiths were known for their sharp senses as well as their hunger for human souls. He had to have sniffed the musty, sour body smell from downstairs. She must have worn it into the room. Heels. Little black dress. Eau de Dying Man.

She was caught. Her heart sucked in so much blood that the edges of the room dimmed. She looked at her father, expecting wrath. She braced to take it.

But her dad casually sipped from his glass. "And how is our friend in the cellar doing?"

Not the reaction she expected.

"You knew about this?" Zelda asked.

"I gave her the keys," he answered. To Kaye, he asked, "How is he looking today?"

Another pounding second passed before Kaye realized that her dad was trying to make it *seem* like he was okay with her going down there. Because there was no way that he was.

In weirdly numb slow motion, Kaye held out the keys to him. She was caught anyway, so why not? They'd gotten so heavy, it was a relief when her father took them.

She had no idea what to answer about the chained man, because she didn't know why he was there in the first place. "He's . . ." She went for the obvious. ". . . a little pasty."

Dad let out an odd, sharp laugh and drained his glass. Dad never laughed.

He was going to lock her up for sure. Take away her laptop, take away everything. No continuation of studies. Just Ferrol Grey's bride.

Kaye's brain filled with I'm-sorrys and excuses, but she held them back. It wouldn't matter if she was sorry. And she wasn't.

The old lady slid her beady gaze over to Dad. "I wasn't aware Kaye knew about the angel."

Angel. The beautiful man was an angel.

Kaye felt so stupid—she should have figured that much

out on her own, what with the way he seemed to shine. And his imprisonment finally made sense: Angels were supposed to hate the mage families. Light against Shadow. They were supposed to kill mages whenever they could. She'd just never seen one before.

If she'd set him free, she might be dead by now.

"They will hurt you," the angel had warned not five minutes ago.

Ironic. He was the one who'd have done the hurting. And how dumb was he that he hadn't let her undo his chains? Angels were supposed to be crazy strong. He could have fought his way out.

Wait. Then why *hadn't* he let her undo his chains?

Dad returned to the drink cart. "Kaye is a Brand," he said. "She can keep her own counsel about family matters." He shot her a look. "A glass of wine, honey?"

He never called her honey. He never offered her a drink, much less alcohol.

"Okay," she answered lamely. The yellow stuff was better than most of the other drinks on the cart.

Zelda handed her martini to the wraith, who set it aside on a bookshelf. "Ferro will be displeased."

Ferro, her soon-to-be's nickname. Kaye knew his name meant iron, like hers did fire, but this sounded like pharaoh to her. King of the world. Very magey.

Kaye took Dad's outstretched wineglass. His gaze bored into hers, full of meaning. She had no idea what he wanted.

She gulped without raising the glass. Umm . . . "Ferro won't like my groom's gift?"

Dad gave a shallow nod of approval, though his skin had gone blotchy, which made Kaye shake deep inside. His anger was usually cold and pale. This was different. Something was going on.

"You were given specific instructions," the old lady admonished her father.

"She's his bride," he answered back.

"Run!" the angel had said.

"You are not free to amend the dictates of Ferrol Grey, whether he marries your daughter or not."

"Whether he . . ." Dad puffed.

If Kaye had her way, she'd prefer not. Speak now? Or forever hold her peace?

"This is a delicate matter," Zelda continued, "one beyond your narrow understanding, and certainly beyond hers."

Zelda's condescending tone made Kaye burn all the way down to her toes. A log cracked in the fire like a gunshot.

There was no way Kaye was going to live with that old hag the rest of her life, no matter how generous Ferrol was, no matter how much the union would help the Brand family. She was going from one keeper to the next, and all because she couldn't set anything on fire. Well, her dad couldn't either, so who was he to sell her off to the highest bidder? And who was Mr. Grey, who had bought her without meeting her, who had sent this mean old woman to sit in her dad's chair? Shadow was the only important thing—who had it and who could control it.

"This life is not for you," the angel had said.

The angel might have been dangerous, but he was the only one who had seemed to know the difference between *Kaye* and *Brand.*

Family. Politics. More like control.

"No," she blurted out.

"Quiet," her father said, with a dismissive wave of his hand.

But the word was out, finally out. It had been much easier to say to the old lady than to her dad.

"I don't want to marry Mr. Grey," Kaye said to Zelda.

Her dad's skin got that strange mottled look again. "Kaye doesn't know what she's saying," he said. "You goaded her, and her temper flared. Just look at the fire. That's the Brand promise—Shadow is thick in our blood."

Sounded like a sales pitch to Kaye, but she was taking herself off the market. "I won't marry your brother."

A bright burst of light, and Kaye fell to the floor, her jaw throbbing, the room tilting at an odd angle. The wineglass lay broken, its contents soaking the rug, its fruity smell in her nose. Her father stood over her, so he must have been the one who hit her, another thing he'd never done before.

"She'll comply," he said. "She can be made to cooperate. She can be made to understand."

Before, he'd only taken away privileges, only isolated her. Kaye looked up at her father, through her tears, with all the hate and hurt she could. *Daddy?*

Her dad wiped sweat from his forehead. His hand was shaking.

She'd never seen him shake. Never seen him look like this. He'd never struck her. Why was he being like this?

Then it clicked. Her dad wasn't angry. He was scared.

The realization made the pulsing ache in her jaw worse, her heart thudding as she took on his fear.

"And this is the young woman you allowed down into the cellar, into our affairs?" Zelda lifted a brow. "I think not."

Kaye crawled to standing. She'd lost a shoe, and stepped out of the other instead of searching for the first. A kid again. She swiped at her mouth with her wrist and it came away with a smear of spit and blood.

The old lady lifted her hand, a finger raised to signal the wraith. Sighing, she said, "You may have her."

Kaye didn't understand.

But her dad lunged, shoving her backward hard, as the wraith vaulted over the desk.

Kaye hit the fireplace—the stone scraped, but the flames never burned—as the wraith pushed her father out of his way, a bony hand to her dad's face.

Dad fell back. The wraith advanced, his monster teeth extending in his mouth, which made no sense whatsoever. Wraiths fed on souls. Mages didn't have them.

What could he want from her?

"Run!" the angel's voice echoed in her memory.

Kaye flung open the door. To her left the hallway led to the warren of kitchen and pantry back rooms. Right led to the entrance foyer and guarded front door.

She took the hallway. Shouldered past the help, dodged around a corner. The wraith was after her.

Her father's voice rose in a shout behind her, but she didn't understand and wasn't about to stop now.

"And keep running."

She skittered through the kitchen and burst out of the pantry door onto the wet ice-slick of a brick walkway. The evening air was sharp, bitter, cold. The world gold and white as the sun fell.

A crash behind her. A woman shrieked, and then the sound was cut off abruptly.

Kaye took off toward the trees. Her flight was just like it would have been for that angel—nowhere to go. Nothing nearby.

Just running. Running. The cold stung her exposed skin while inside her blood pumped hot. Her feet skittered across the lawn and through the frozen brush. Scraping and cutting. *Daddy! I didn't mean it!*

The shadow gained, silent and quick.

Running. The winter woods went black, sunset turning the sky from gold to licking red. The trees were solemn black spears, stuck into the ground like the picture of the afterdeath of the great ancient battle in her childhood storybook—angels against mages.

Her breath smoked the air in broken gasps. She strained to see over her shoulder.

There. Close. Jaw hanging low. Teeth glittering.

He had to know she didn't have what he wanted.

If he worked for the Greys, he had to know. . . .

She leaned into her run, but a jerk on her arm abruptly whipped her around, crashing her into a tree and sending her into the winter-sharp growth. Pain came from everywhere, but her fear was bigger as she rolled to face the wraith.

He loomed above, monstrous, feral, his suit a strange contradiction to the devolution of his facial features.

She slapped and kicked upward, to no effect. Rocks and branches scored her back as she used her weight for strength.

"Daddy!"

But the wraith was unfazed. He took her by the head, one hand at each side of her face, and lifted her up. Her neck hurt, so she had to hold on to her attacker. His grip had closed her ears so all she could hear was the rhythmic rushing of her blood and her sobs echoing around in her brain.

"No soul!" she screamed, clawing at his hands. "No soul!"

Her feet kicked empty air as his maw opened. He tilted his face to get the kiss right, when it could never be right. She had nothing to give him.

"Please!" she shrieked. "Daddy!"

The wraith's bite clamped down on her face, his teeth spearing into the flesh and bone at her jaw. His hands at her ears kept her trapped in his grasp. Pain sharpened the moment. She was enveloped in his rank smell, yet unable to retch. The world became he and she, sharing her first-ever French kiss.

Should've been that angel. She could have kissed him forever. But she'd left him behind. Why did she leave him?

A ripple went through the wraith and his mouth flexed on hers. It was a drawing motion, a suck, a slurp, that sought deep within for what she'd already told him she didn't have.

What the old lady had to know she didn't have.

A second wave took the wraith's body, as he pulled harder at her, blistering whatever skin she had left intact.

The pain of the motion made stars prick into the gray of her vision. Warm fluid ran freely down her neck. His teeth became the nails holding her bones together. Without him, she was broken. Broken like that angel.

She didn't want to die.

She hadn't yet lived.

The kiss sent her down into herself, down down down, away from the smell and the pain and the fear. Away from the moment when the wraith would wrench himself from her lips and she would fall apart, left in the cold.

She went down into the deep of her core and found her umbra, her Shadow within, at last. It churned with darkness and beat with drums. And in the primordial depths, obscured by the circling pitch of magic, was the plume of a flame, its source, her blood, her heritage.

Brand.

She reached out to it with everything she was, with all the screams trapped in her mind, the hopes crushed by the marriage contract, the rage that her life should end now, this way. It wasn't fair! She reached to fight back.

And the flame obeyed.

It stretched up in a pillar of light, but she wanted more, demanded more. *Now!*

And the flame erupted within her, heating her twitching limbs like a volcano awakening. Like lava, the fire coursed through her veins. She was alive with it, a shimmering conflagration, a human torch.

The wraith released his kiss, flinging her away. She seemed to fall for ages, then jarred on the ground and lay slack, ravaged, blood flowing down her neck from her wounds and ears. But in her dimming vision, the wraith thrashed against her fire. He went up as if doused with accelerant and screamed his own pain as he convulsed, charring. Then he dropped into a folded heap of blackened bones.

His fire smothered quickly, and she found herself in the dark, her inner flame dimming to a flicker. The black trees blended with the night sky. The cold crept over her, and she sank, her breath shallow, toward sleep or death.

After what seemed a very long time, the world went utterly dark. Inside the blackness, there was no time. Just cold.

Until she felt herself lifted against a warm, strong chest. Felt a rolling movement like a swift stride. Someone cradling her.

See, Daddy, she thought from within the void, *I can call fire.*

Chapter 1

Ten years later

"Are you sure she's the best choice?" Jack Bastian had grave concerns about Kaye Brand.

"There are no bests here," said Laurence. "We must try everything and everyone in these dark times."

Jack shifted his gaze from the video link of his superior to the file glowing on the screen before him. Two side-by-side images of Ms. Brand headed a list of text and notes detailing the mage's life history. The first photo was of her at age fifteen, taken while in intensive care. She was unconscious. Her face, brutally damaged, was swollen and blistered beyond recognition. Wraiths were filthy beings, their bites noxious. According to the chart, in the days following her attack she'd battled a life-threatening infection with a fever that hit a sustained 107 degrees, in spite of medical intervention. But then, that's a fire mage for you.

The second photo was recent, taken at the Las Vegas Wake Hotel. Ms. Brand had a drink in hand, a man's mouth at her neck while she laughed. Jack had to admit that The Order's physicians had worked a miracle on her face. The intervention was against protocol, but every angel had been of the same mind on this point: Michael Thomas, angel and good friend, had died in the cellar of Brand House the same night of Ms. Brand's attack. His last request, sent telepathically and suddenly after a silence of some weeks, was to save the girl if possible.

Brand House had gone up in flames, taking eleven lives with it—six of which were representatives of mage families, including Ms. Brand's father; four were human, the house staff; and one was angelic. According to her feverish babble, the violence had erupted because she'd refused to marry Ferrol Grey. Smart girl.

Ms. Brand would have died in the woods some thirty yards from the house. Should have died, if not for Michael and the sentimentality of his brother and sister angels.

Jack flicked the screen to page through the file. Angels served humanity, not magekind.

And yet, Michael had thought she was worth it, but then he'd always stretched the rules where children were concerned, apparently even mage children.

Foolish: A scorpion could not stop being a scorpion. Eventually she would sting.

The girl was healed, though she never knew the nature of her benefactors. Of Michael, she professed to know nothing. She was released and, in due course, as expected, grew to live by her whims, her desires, her lusts.

And this was the woman to whom the angels now looked for aid?

Kaye swayed to standing. She realized she'd had too much to drink as she watched the conference door lever turn but managed to still the careening room with a hand to the table. She smoothed the creases in the lap of her slim skirt and did a quick upward tug of her dipping neckline.

This was not *that* kind of peep show, though her father still would have called her a whore for selling her fire.

A man entered, presumably her client, Hobbs. At least she thought that was his name. He was fiftyish, fit. He'd buzzed his balding head instead of trying to grow hair artificially, which she respected. Impeccable suit. Hard, assessing eyes. So what if his gaze lingered on her scars? Everyone's did.

The door shut with a loud, positive snap that assaulted her sensitive eardrums.

"Mr. Hobbs." She held out her hand for a shake, made him come to her. That last drink was hitting her a little hard for her to move much herself.

Mr. Hobbs went with a double-hand grasp. The hand trap. "And what may I call you?"

Kaye had to pull to extricate herself. "Merry." Because that's what she was. Happy to be there. Delighted to provide this most valuable service. Overjoyed to take his money.

She gestured to the conference table. "If you'll just have a seat." She sure wanted hers.

The table was wide, made of some beautiful deep wood. It glowed from the shifting lights off the Vegas strip, the horrible glare buffered by the concealing tint of the hotel windows. Black leather chairs with trim lines circled the table. The walls were textured, a neutral flax, easy on her mind. No city sounds penetrated the space, another relief.

After Hobbs had relaxed into one of the chairs, she took hers, keeping the table between them. That way, she was close enough to reach, yet had a barrier in case he became difficult. They always became difficult.

"So this is how it works—" she began.

He held up a hand to quiet her.

Kaye forced a smile, blinked hard to concentrate. After

all, it was his fifty grand, briefly hers, then on to the hotel to pay her debts. Her keep didn't come cheap. "Yes?"

"I would like to make you a supplementary offer."

Kaye curled her toes in her shoes but kept an outward calm. They always tried, though usually after the session was completed, when she was already on her way out the door. Getting away was the hardest part. Worse every time.

She wanted her bed. She wanted numb, black sleep.

His gaze grew steely, while his voice stayed soft. "One million for a year in my employ. An apartment, car—"

Uh-huh. Basically a nice cage.

Kaye shook her head. *No, thank you.* Not going to happen. The Las Vegas Wake Hotel was cage enough, but at least she could fly the coop whenever she wanted. Soon, probably.

Hobbs looked irritated. "Please hear me out."

She shook her head again. "Let's not argue." It would hurt her head. "I've had lots of offers to buy me. You could promise the moon, and I'd still say no."

"I could keep you safe," he said. "And comfortable."

"Not likely," she answered.

His gaze did a narrow-lidded once-over. "A woman like you . . ."

Kaye slapped the table to shut him up before he finished. He didn't know a thing about her. Prick.

His mouth thinned as he swallowed his offer. He didn't seem like the sort to give up that easy, so she took advantage of the empty moment. In Sin City, everyone took advantage.

"Ten seconds of Shadowfire for fifty thousand dollars," she said. "You'll see something in the flame—what that'll be, I have no idea. I can't interpret it for you either, so don't ask. If it's the future, it's only one version of the future, so don't worry too much either." Or get excited. Or demand something she had no power to give.

She breathed through a sudden roll of nausea. Wouldn't do to throw up on her meal ticket. What the hell was in that drink?

Hobbs rallied. "With your ability and my backing—"

"I said no." Kaye stood, leaned across the table—looked like he was going to get an eyeful of her cleavage anyway—and placed a timer before him, preset by the hotel's owner for ten seconds. She braced herself with her left arm and turned her right hand palm up in front of her client's face. "Here we go."

She concentrated inward, searching for the dark of her umbra, the source of her power, in the myriad sparks that sizzled in her blood. She focused on its draw and rush in her veins, stoking the magic deep within. Better than any booze anywhere. With a splay of her fingers, the heat flowered gorgeously in her hand. The flame, a rose rich in orange, reds, velvety black, danced seductively, and she writhed a little in her skin, responding to the flush of Shadow. It always felt so damn good.

Her client had reared back, protecting his eyes.

"You have one shot," Kaye warned and hit the timer's start button. If he wasted it cringing, that was his problem.

The man's expression went avid, and then he sat forward, staring into the flame, greedy for the vision.

Kaye looked into the wavering heat herself and almost lost the fire when she spotted Hobbs in a blurry struggle with an unseen adversary. A reach. A grab. A miss. He flailed into the air, falling off the roof of a city building. Didn't look like Vegas. No, it was somewhere the sky was as gray as the concrete. The vision followed her client down, his horror, and the abrupt, uneven strike of his body on the hood of a taxi.

That hurt her head too.

Kaye glanced over at the timer, which was beeping. The display read fourteen seconds. He could have no complaints.

She fisted her hand and the flame was doused. She spoke by rote. "It's been a pleasure doing business with you."

Mr. Hobbs flicked up his gaze, the force a smack of anger. The cast of his skin had gone sallow green, revealing an age spot or two. He was panting like a pig. "I'll pay you double for ten more seconds. A million to work for me. Five to keep me alive."

"Doesn't work like that." Kaye skirted the table. Time to get out of there. "And it's only one possible future. Just make sure you change it." *If you can.*

She was opening the door when Hobbs grabbed her shoulder. She startled with an old fear as deep as her scars. Nobody put their hands on her. The very wealthy, influential businessman got an elbow in his face. She got a wet smear on her silk sleeve.

Kaye wrenched open the door to meet Max Hampstead, the Wake Hotel's owner, and two burly security guards. Mr. Hampstead was stroking the silk of his tie. He wore his wealth in a preen too dapper to be hetero. One guard stayed behind to see to her client, now cursing furiously in the conference room. Too bad about that. The other was probably going to take her to her room. Which was a-okay with her.

"He got his time," she said to the air, hoping Mr. Hampstead heard. The floor oddly pitched upward. She had to go. Now.

Kaye didn't want the tight grip at her elbow but didn't really mind its steadying effect as she pushed out of the business suite and into the loud common area of the hotel. The hotel speaker system pumped the new pop hit "Shadow

Is My Drug of Choice." She winced against the driving rhythm, as well as the layered bells and whoops from the nearby banks of slot machines. She was so done with this place.

The guard held her upright in the elevator, though it had a gold bench, and he used a key card to let her into her room—very handy, as she'd lost hers again—then left her to herself.

She kicked off a shoe in the mini foyer, the other in the suite's living room. Untucked her blouse as she headed for the bedroom. Her vision was darkening, like she was already halfway asleep. Must have been a *very* strong drink. She managed one button on her blouse but gave the rest up and crawled the length of the bed toward a lovely, soft pillow, waiting just for her.

Beneath the last flutter of her falling lids, in the city glow at the window, she saw the shadow-shape of a man.

A sob of terror and relief knotted in her throat as thick sleep dragged her into its black depths.

No more waiting. They'd come for her. At last.

She wouldn't, couldn't run this time.

Jack Bastian regarded the wanton collapse of Kaye Brand. How the mighty Fire bloodline had fallen. The family had changed their names to start afresh in the New World—Brand—but the centuries had been hard on them. The old mages would be glad they were dead, if she was their legacy.

Her skirt was hitched up around her thighs, high enough that he could see a patch of a pink undergarment. He grabbed the edge of the skirt's hem and gave it a hard tug down. The blouse he could do little about, tangled as it was around her midriff and skewed at her shoulder and lace-covered breast. A flash of pink told him the skirt had crept up again. The woman had curves as irresponsible as her nature.

His gaze narrowed on her face. A lock of her dark red hair concealed most of her cheek, some of the strands caught in her mouth. He wanted to see the scars, so he stroked the strands of hair away. Her skin was satin until his fingertips came to fine lines gone white with time. They ran from her temple to her jaw, a cruel trophy from a vicious attack. She'd have scars on the other side of her face to match. Her survival proved she had the necessary mettle for his task. Well, maybe—she was now drooling on her pillow.

Jack checked the pulse at her throat—sure and steady—then grabbed the edge of the bedsheet, flung it over her exposed body, and strode from the room to let her sleep it off.

He settled into a chair in the main room. Head down, eyes closed, he lightly steepled his fingers to meditate.

The mind chatter of the hotel's guests filled his head. The transparent flow of thoughts on Earth was the boon and bane of being an angel. This late at night, most of the guests were contemplating or engaging in self-indulgence. Money and sex—it was always the same in places like this, regardless of the age, and he had had eleven tours on Earth to know.

In the quiet moment, time lashed his memory farther back.

A roar of wind and screams. Billows of smoke rolled across the battlefield, the smell of it heady with Shadow magic. The Brands had been the Eldr clan then and had fled under the cover of their fire. Other clans escaped as best they could. Marauders were left behind, stumbling grunts of men who were Shadow-poisoned, their minds blanked, marked by deeply gouged black Xs under their eyes. He raised his sword and cut a poor beast down, gore splattering. His arm was tired from releasing humanity from the clutches of black magic. Somewhere a mage had been left behind to control the mules they'd made of man. What clan the mage came from Jack didn't know, but he found the scoundrel, an old woman, hissing power toward the battlefield from her concealed ditch. She'd bought her clan time with her life, though she begged "Mercy!" now. Was there honor in that? Jack took her head anyway and the Shadow-possessed on the battlefield thumped to the ground.

Nearby Ms. Brand's room, an external thought interrupted his memory: *. . . drug should have put her out by now. . . .*

From the person's companion: *. . . what's Hampstead want with the woman if he's gay . . . ?*

Jack heard the lock release on the door, but he kept his seat. The two men entered, both young and strong, twin sneers curling their mouths.

"Ms. Brand isn't here," Jack said. The red of the battlefield memory still stained his vision.

Both men looked at the sprawl of limbs visible through the bedroom doorway.

"You came for her, but she was missing," Jack explained, then gave a little push with his mind. Technically, angels were not to interfere with the choices of humans, but Jack's need trumped the free agency of the parties involved—these men and the hotel's owner. "She wasn't here. You should search the rest of the hotel, however, before reporting back to Mr. Hampstead."

Hampstead's going to be pissed. . . .

Got to get out of this business. . . .

"And I wasn't here either," he continued.

What had Ms. Brand gotten herself into? More trouble,

certainly. It was time for a change . . . of venue. He was relying on her bad habits for what he had in store.

The men left. Hampstead approached the room, but he was made to change his mind as well. The hotel quieted in the very early hours of the morning. The sky paled to white, then turned a dirty blue as the sun finally crested the horizon.

When the world was bathed in light, Kaye groaned from the bedroom.

Jack leaned in the door frame and waited for the shock of a strange man in her room—unless she was used to it—to wake her completely. He hoped she wouldn't be ill. Time was wasting.

Kaye blinked, bleary. He watched as her gaze shifted to the glaring window, to the bright mess of clothing spilling off a chair. To Jack, then held.

She bolted to kneel on the mattress, her hands shaking and full of livid faefire.

"Angel," she said, naming him as she prepared to strike.

"That won't be necessary," Jack said. Though he could read human minds easily, Kaye's was a complete and utter blank, like all of the soulless mage-born. But he knew human nature well enough. If he remained at ease, she wouldn't burn him. Most likely.

Pillow lines creased one cheek. Her auburn hair was flat on that side as well, wavy on the other. Black eyes. Her legs were braced apart, athletic in their youth. The skirt was still rucked up high on her thighs. Her stance was full of fight, so the life she'd been leading hadn't broken her yet. Very good.

"Although historically I'm your mortal enemy—" Jack began. Mages, like the fae, had always defied Heaven. He added a smile to make the acknowledgment seem friendly. "Today, I'm your prospective employer, Jack Bastian."

"Get out." The blaze in her hands grew brighter, shifting to an almost citrine intensity.

Jack looked out the window at the ugly view and sighed heavily. Garish at night, the Las Vegas cityscape was hungover in the morning. "Last night the hotel's owner drugged you. Then two men came to this room intending to relocate you while you were unconscious. I think perhaps it's time to move on before it's too late."

"Thanks for the tip," she answered. "Now leave."

Jack returned his gaze to the blazing fire; he knew all too well its burn on angelic skin, yet the power and beauty of the shimmer were undeniable. "Where will you go?"

"That's my business." Kaye shrugged her shoulder and her blouse settled into more seemly coverage. The skirt remained a problem.

Jack forced his gaze back up to her face. "Will you take Mr. Hobbs's lucrative job offer?"

She smirked darkly, a flex of intent rolling through her body as she primed to hurl her fire.

No, then.

"Or will you go to Grey House?" The old clans were Houses now. "Surely its master will take you in?"

Kaye's eyes went wary, but the fire didn't waver and her body remained tense, ready to act. Also good. Emotion didn't control her. He'd need her steady.

Kaye lifted her chin. "Did he send you?"

Jack smiled, chuckling. "Ah . . . no. Ferrol Grey does not do business with angels."

Angels and mages had a long history of battling against each other, and the recent influx of Shadow back into the mortal world promised more.

Which was why Jack needed Kaye Brand, someone he could pay to be disloyal to her kind. She obviously liked money.

"So are you interested?" he asked.

"No."

He waited a beat for her curiosity to kick in. Noted the slight shift of her shoulders and head as she took a shallow breath. The subtle flare of her nostrils. The minute jerk of her irises.

"What exactly is the job?"

Never trust a pretty face, her father had once warned her. A pretty face masks a killer.

This angel wasn't pretty; he was perfect, which was something altogether different, Kaye was now learning. He had none of the soul of that other angel, none of the warmth. This angel, Jack Bastian, had fair eyes, blue probably, or hazel, though she couldn't be sure that far away. His hair was darkest brown, cut brutally short to tame a tight curl. Square face. An almost Roman nose with a full mouth to match. Though attractive, he was no model. No poet. And yet each expression and angle of his face was impossibly beautiful. Therefore, treacherous.

Angel. Memory had her throat closing. Her eyes ached as angel light filled them. She hadn't seen another, until now.

Not her fault. The other angel had said so himself. *Not her fault.* She'd been just a kid.

What could this one possibly want with her?

Bastian, who'd been leaning in her doorway, straightened. He was broad of shoulder, tall, and well muscled. Something dangerous in his bearing. Every bit the assassin. "We would need you to reenter magekind to gather information on how they are using the wraiths."

The flames in Kaye's hands diminished to a weak yellow and orange glow, as if the oxygen in the room had suddenly thinned. If she had any idea why the mage families used wraiths, she wouldn't have her scars.

"I thought you might be curious yourself," Bastian continued. He tilted his head and she could feel the stroke of his gaze on her scars. The stroke was echoed by a flutter deep within her belly. Fear, arousal—both sometimes felt the same.

"Well, I'm not curious," she said, resenting the sensation. She'd barely survived the last time. She wouldn't willingly go back. That wasn't the kind of job she wanted. "So get out of my room."

He didn't move. "You're afraid."

"Yes, I am." She had good reason to be. On the first day of every year she tried to manage the fear. She searched for a wraith, and she burned it up. It gave her just enough spine to keep going. She had three months left before she had to force herself to seek out and face another, and she wasn't about to rush it.

She drew a deep breath and forcibly regained her composure. It was too early in the morning to spend herself with fire if this Bastian wasn't going to do anything interesting. What power did angels have anyway? Or did they just stand there and pretty you to death?

Terrifying.

Run!

Yes. It was time to run. The urge was old and familiar, a knee-jerk reaction based on ten years' worth of reinforcement. Didn't matter that she hurt or was tired. Didn't matter that one angel was saying one thing in her head, and another, standing in her room, was telling her the opposite.

Kaye smothered the flames in her hands and gingerly crawled off the bed so her throbbing brain wouldn't burst. Suitcase. "And even if I weren't afraid of wraiths, you're missing the obvious."

"And what's that?"

She skirted the bed to get to the closet, staying away from Bastian. Slid open the folding doors. "It was a Grey who sicced a wraith on me. The mage families would kill me on sight."

"The mage families could kill you regardless," he said. "The point is, they haven't. It's been years since they've had anything to do with you."

She surveyed her wardrobe, considering. Her brain felt like lead from last night's drinks, making the vibrant colors of her clothes seem gaudy. But none of them were cheap. A Brand would never look cheap.

He continued, "Brand House is burned to the ground. You carry the scars of the wraith attack. Maybe they think you've been punished enough for refusing to marry Ferrol Grey."

Kaye whipped back. "How could *you* know I refused him?"

And what else did he know?

"I'm an angel," he said. "It is my business to know these things. Why did you back out of the marriage contract?"

That should be obvious; maybe he didn't know anything after all. She turned to the closet. "I was fifteen and he was an old man."

"Refusing Grey cost you dearly," Bastian said behind her. "But now you're all grown up. You've come into your power. They don't come after you, Ms. Brand, because ultimately you are one of them."

Maybe. But also because she'd kept quiet about the other angel, the one her father had captured, for a long time. She would not kid herself; that silence was everything. Out of sight, out of mind. And very, very quiet. "I've changed my answer to no way in Hell, but thanks for the offer."

"I can pay you," Bastian said. She felt him advance, a rush of white light racing across her Shadow-bred skin to buzz her nerve endings everywhere. Damn him.

Kaye could make her own money. Lots of it. Five grand a second.

The hotel cleaners weren't likely to return the laundry she'd sent down yesterday. She threw clothes, still on their hangers, from the closet to her bed. She'd have to make do with what she had here. She'd catch a cab out front, then the first flight from LAS. Go on an adventure, a comfortable one.

"I'm also offering you the kind of protection no mortal businessman like Hampstead or Hobbs can."

She turned and found him too close. A man, in her room, with an offer. "Ironically, I'd only need your kind of protection if I took your job."

"Ms. Brand, you peddle your wares at the mages' sufferance." His voice had turned authoritative, not the right tactic with her at all, seeing as how it made her blood churn that much faster, the beat in her temples even more acute. She needed some painkiller. Narcotic, preferably.

"Their power is growing, consolidating," he said. "The world is turning dark. Even you must feel it. The Age of Man is coming to an end. Eventually magekind will come for you. *Soon* they will come for you."

No. She would not go willingly back to that life. She'd been running from that life for years. That other angel had even said it: The mage life wasn't for her.

His stern mouth moved into a twist of a sardonic smile. "What about payback?"

Kaye felt a sudden tug, as if her guts were hooked on a short line. Payback, she understood. The concept had been taught to her from the cradle—how the *angels* had crushed her kind. How the mages would rise again and return the gesture.

"A wraith chewed on your face." His voice lowered an octave. "In your mage world, doesn't that deserve some kind of reprisal?"

Her face. A flash of anger swept her. Yes, that cruelty deserved something in equal measure.

Run! cried the angel from the past. He might have died in that house, but his voice followed her yet. Instinct took up his warning, signaling her to hurry. Hurry now. Get packing. Get out of there.

But . . .

Kaye looked at the spill of fabrics across her unmade bed.

She was sick to death of running. Sick to death of forcing herself to face a wraith every year when the real monster was the Grey who sent the wraith after her in the first place. The wraith who'd attacked her had been a tool, like a knife or a gun. She'd known this from the beginning. From the first time she tracked down a wraith in an alley and set it on fire. In the back of her mind, she'd always known. Or else she wouldn't be running still.

Run! Again that voice urged her to save herself. But she wasn't a kid playing dress-up anymore.

Ten years of driven flight, and she finally stopped herself in the doorway of her memory. She turned back to the beautiful ruined man who'd collapsed into his chains in the cellar of her childhood home and regarded him from the other side of time. He was owed something too. From her.

Would she choose differently now?

Would it even matter? Her angel, the one she loved, was dead and it was this Bastian who shined before her, his intensity not weakened by torture, his body not poisoned with Shadow.

She lifted her gaze to his perfect eyes and withstood the clarity of purpose that shined within them. The force of it made her ache.

"Are you a Brand, or aren't you?" he asked.

A Brand, like Ferrol Grey, would never do business with the angels.

"Kaye?"

But a Brand would use them to her advantage. She'd been gambling a lot lately. With money, with her fire, and if what Bastian said was true about Max Hampstead, with her safety as well. She was getting sloppy. Bored of her fear, if that was possible. Maybe it was time to get a little of her own back. To finally do something about that angel. That, or die. Either way, end this. She was tired.

"How much money?" she asked.

It was time for something different, starting . . . now.

"Five hundred thousand for a year of work under my direction. If at any time either of us is unsatisfied with the arrangement, the deal is off, payment prorated to the end of the week of separation."

Cheapskate. Hobbs had offered her a million, plus perks, and all she'd have to do was light fires. Give her a day and she could get a deal worth double. Maybe the angel hadn't heard: Shadow was all the rage. The very wealthy of the world were all scrambling for a bit of their own.

"One million," she returned. He had to at least match Hobbs's offer. It was the principle of the thing. The money she could do without.

"Seven hundred."

"Have a nice trip home." She was worth more. She had to be. How much had Ferrol Grey paid all those years ago?

"Eight."

"The west bank elevators run faster than the central ones," she said. But she knew she already had him. He'd pay her million, all right.

She stood fast against his battering angelic light. His beauty buffeted her sensibilities, the intensity a high, pure note she could hear ringing in the room. But his strength and masculinity bothered her more.

Treacherous, she reminded herself.

"How do I know you won't play both sides?" His gaze coolly appraised her semidisrobed state. Seemed to find her wanting.

Kaye gave him a hard-edged smile. Son of a bitch. Let him dangle. "You don't."

Chapter 2

Contrary to myth, angels were not meant to fly. Jack was sure of it, though he had to allow that the commissioned jet was comfortable enough. Soft, white leather seats, a serene view of the limitless sky, a chilled beverage in his hand, and still he preferred the sweet dirt and brambling growth of solid earth. His last tour had been conducted on horseback.

Ms. Brand, however, looked completely at ease hurtling through the atmosphere with nary a care. She wore a dress, if one could call it that, and though the blue cloth fell to her knee, it snugged her figure in a dangerous wraparound that fastened at her waist. He'd seen heeled shoes on the aristocracy of many a time, but Ms. Brand's were ridiculously high, accentuating the curve of her arches. Altogether, she had the polish of a wealthy woman and the reckless simmer of a fire mage.

The mage families would be intrigued.

Imagining Kaye Brand set aflame, he could not fault humankind for once worshipping mages as gods, but he took exception to the mages encouraging such behavior. They were as mortal as any other, though their blood was irredeemably tainted.

Smoke. Screams. Fire. Shadow on the land.

And if she did play both sides? Jack had already considered that very likely prospect. The Order would be out its million and the mages would be aware of The Order's intelligence regarding their collaboration with the wraiths. His work would be made more difficult, that's all. As always, he would persevere. There was too much at stake to do otherwise.

"So why Washington, D.C.?" Kaye took a sip from her glass. Whereas he'd asked for lemon water, she'd requested a glass of white wine. In the morning. To accompany a little blue pill.

He knew she had a headache, but this felt like more of a provocation.

He was already irritated, and they had a few more hours in flight.

Good thing he had work to do. He reached for his laptop to review a dossier on wraith capture and holding techniques prepared by the Segue Institute. Long ago, humanity could do little about scourges like wraiths upon the earth. But technology is its own kind of magic, and Adam Thorne of the Segue Institute set the standard where the Otherworld was concerned.

"We have a meeting in the D.C. area to work out the details of your reintroduction to magekind." Jack powered up the laptop and waited for the machine to blink to life. There was more to the meeting than that. Much more.

"As I'm the mage, don't you think you'd better run your plans by me first?" Her voice was a smooth and lazy drawl. She took another sip.

Jack wondered again why The Order was trusting this woman. She needed sobering. If she was going to have any dealings with her fellow mages, she needed to be sharp, smart, or at the very least, lucid. To that end, he said, "I've also arranged an introduction to a pureblood mage. We're trying to recruit him as well."

Instead she looked bored. "There's no such thing as a pureblood."

He selected his file, tapped in his password. Took on her uninterested tone. "Don't you claim one in your Brand family line?"

"Like a thousand years ago." Another sip. Careless. No, reckless.

And her line went much farther back than that.

She would set down her glass; he'd make her. "And it's impossible that another should walk this fair earth?"

The mage once known as Shadowman and now called Khan had finally agreed to the meeting that Jack had proposed weeks ago. Khan was new to the world, and as far as The Order knew, he had no dealings with magekind. He'd consented to this meeting at the request of his son-in-law. There'd been a time when Adam Thorne asked, even begged, favors of The Order. Now The Order turned to him. Curious.

"I suppose it's possible." She rotated the glass between her fingertips, regarding the gold liquid spinning in the cup.

"It's fact," he said. Text filled the screen, accompanied by thumbnail images. If he clicked on one, the image would expand to fill the screen. With such records in place, Jack doubted that wraiths or the fae or even magekind would ever be considered myth and legend again.

"So there's a pureblood," Ms. Brand said with a shrug. And another sip. "What is the essence of her umbra?"

Umbra, an old mage word for the Shadow power they wielded. The fact that they used it like humanity and The Order used the word *soul* had always bothered him.

"*His* umbra," Jack corrected. She'd set down her glass if he had to take it from her.

"His, then." She was irritated now. Not good enough. He wanted her serious.

Jack gave her his full attention for impact. "Life and death."

"I don't get it."

"Before his transformation from fae to mortal, he was commonly known to the Western world as the Grim Reaper." That ought to do it.

"You're going to introduce me to the Grim Reaper?"

"Yes." Jack smiled. He was having a little fun now. Who would have thought?

And then *he* sobered. Ms. Brand did indeed set down her glass, but not before quaffing its contents first.

Jack drove to a location just outside the D.C. Beltway, as indicated on the map provided by Thorne. The sign at the entrance to the barrow fields read NO TRESPASSING. From Jack's file on the facility, he knew that anyone who researched the land's ownership would find the business front of an agricultural research company, not a site dedicated to holding wights, the devolved form of the wraiths. Wights had little substance, so they weren't able to be contained in regular holding cells, as were the wraiths. Nor were the wights fully conscious, because their hunger and decay consumed them.

"Where are we?" Kaye asked from the passenger seat.

"A graveyard," Jack answered.

A mobile trailer had been parked to the side of the grounds. Various types of construction machinery stood at the ready, a crane now lowering a huge cylinder into the earth. That would be a barrow, according to the dossier. It would be monitored remotely, a measure that would have shocked antiquity. The premise of the structure, however, was the same: The wight would be lured into the barrow, then trapped under the earth. Buried, as if dead, which they were. The barrows were the only thing that could hold them.

And beyond the barrow was a black armored vehicle designed to be a mobile wraith cell. There would be a unit of trained soldiers present as well.

Jack parked next to the office, though the activity was across the field. He easily gleaned the command of Adam Thorne within the snarl of thoughts across the way.

Ms. Brand's footwear was not suited to the field of wet winter earth.

"You can wait here," he said.

She lowered her lids, making half-moons of her eyes. But he had to give her credit; she followed him to the construction site, picking her way through the muck, and when they met the men gathered for work, her black eyes glittered and her skin glowed against the deep red of her hair. Her scars transformed her from a merely beautiful woman—the world had many of those—to an utterly captivating one.

He could envision her in the old time, setting men ablaze with passion first, fire later, according to her whims. Felt the stir himself, and knew to be very careful with the witch.

Jack lifted his mind above the hot rush that growled through him. Too many men responding, their thoughts, though controlled, still carnal. Shadow had to be messing with all of them.

"Jack Bastian?" Adam approached, thankfully without sexual interest in Kaye. He pulled off his dirty work glove and held out his hand.

Jack shook it and was proud to. Thorne was emerging as one of the great leaders of this age. It was a benefit of angelic service on Earth to meet men such as this, when they were in the midst of changing the world.

Adam shifted his attention. “Ms. Brand?”

Kaye reached out and got a gentle shake from Adam.

“And you are?” Her voice was warm, engaging.

“Adam Thorne. I run this circus. Actually, some days it feels like it runs me.”

She smiled in sympathy at Thorne. Anyone would like her. Three words, a soft smile, and she was all charm. But then, she hadn’t wasted any at the hotel or on the flight over. How economical of her.

Adam looked back at Jack and spoke telepathically, laughter in his eyes. *Poor man, I almost feel sorry for you.*

Adam was obviously aware that angels could read human minds. Jack knew what he was getting at, some sort of affair, but didn’t credit the line of thought with a response. Adam knew nothing of the conflict between mages and angels. Jack had long experience in that arena, so he changed the subject. “How many barrows are planned for this field?”

“Twenty,” Adam answered, without further commentary. He made a large *L* with his arms, squaring off the field. “Four rows of five. We should have it ready in the next four days, but we can go ahead and inter the first wight now so you can see the process.”

The fecund smell of the turned earth was incongruous with the winter season, and yet in keeping with the nature of this meeting—the elements at odds. Life and Death. Light and Shadow.

Crawling into the darkness of an earthen mound, his angel light revealing bony fingers reaching through the dirt. And beyond, an undead creature, trapped. Him, trapped with it. A death match.

“How did you transport it?” The feat was impossible. A wight might be lured or herded. He knew from experience. But caught?

"What's a wight?" Kaye asked, her tone wary.

Adam turned to Kaye. "You've heard of wraiths?"

She nodded, shallow and short. But Jack noted how her hands flexed at her sides.

"A wight is a wraith that has been starved until it loses all semblance of humanity," Adam said.

Jack noticed that Kaye had stopped breathing. The air around her had gone still, a frigid sparkle on the morning.

"Can we take a look?" he asked. He'd posed the question to Adam, but Jack watched Kaye. She'd certainly meet another wraith if she reentered magekind. He wanted to see how she handled herself when confronted again by the kind of monster that had given her those scars.

"Yes," Adam said. "Ms. Brand, wraiths can be unsettling—you may have seen them on the news or online?"

She nodded again. Jack said nothing. If Ms. Brand wanted to share her familiarity with wraiths, it was up to her to do so. Ten years ago Jack had seen her ravaged face firsthand. He respected her trauma enough not to expose her. The story was hers to tell.

Adam must have missed the slight sickness in her eyes, because he continued. "Well, wights are similarly disturbing. Just know that you are safe. Everyone here has a great deal of experience. You okay?"

"I'm fine," she answered. Steady. Beauty flashing. She was an expert liar.

And for the first time on this tour of Earth, Jack felt himself admiring that quality. Almost always, a lie like that was twined with courage. Some liars were weak people, choosing the easy way out. Jack had known the contrary Ms. Brand for all of eight hours, but it was long enough to know that Kaye did not lie about trivial things. She would not bother herself to do so.

"Okay," Adam said. "Khan's been holding it since its capture."

Ah. That's how Thorne had captured the wight. This was exactly the reason Jack had come: The mages were somehow using, even controlling, the wraiths and probably the wights as well. There was a lot to learn here.

Adam turned to the armored vehicle near the barrow hole. "Open her up!"

A soldier spoke into a concealed mic, and the back of the vehicle opened like a razor-lipped jaw. Khan crouched within, a glow of faelight suspended in the air in front of him. Beyond, a wight was held rapt. It used to be a woman, but its naked flesh had both knotted and fallen away until it was writhing in endless decay. Its head was cocked, monstrous teeth chattering as it made a mewling sound in its throat.

Jack glanced at Kaye to see how she fared. Then stepped slowly away from her. Her hands were full of flame. Her expression had lost its polish. For a moment, a painful one, Jack saw the girl she'd been. He saw the child whom the angel Michael had begged to be saved.

Adam was going on about the process, oblivious. "We're ready, Khan."

Khan stood, inching up in height beyond the human norm, and directed the faelight slowly toward the open barrow. The small gathering parted. A tractor engine revved, ready with earth.

Ms. Brand's hands were shaking, the flames tangling with deepening color.

Steady, woman. . . .

"So we're going to compel the wight to enter the barrow," Adam continued, his back to Kaye, "and then seal it inside. Once interred, it won't be able to harm anyone."

"Thorne," Jack said, pulling mentally at Adam's attention.

Adam turned as Kaye primed her arm, her other arm extending for balance.

Adam ducked just in time.

Someone shouted.

Black and red, with licks of gold at its heart, the fire hit its target, caught, and swallowed its victim. The wight rattled as its remaining flesh fell like drops of fetid wax onto the earth. It smelled beyond foul. The mass of the creature dropped in seconds, the fire moaning, and then the afternoon was quiet again. A bit of horror on the ground smoked.

"Or we can do it her way," Adam said.

Kaye frowned at the singed cuffs of her coat. *Filthy, horrible wight.* She concentrated on the cold air against her skin to quell the rising panic attack. Her hand shook as she picked at her cuff. When she went wraith hunting, she usually wore the right clothes. The wool was ruined, though she'd heard it was supposed to be fire retardant. She'd have to shop. And that bastard angel would just have to endure it.

She closed her eyes to find composure, but it was slow coming. She'd never seen anything like a wight before. Hovering like that off the ground. The wet rattle of its bones. There had been no thought in its eyes, only hunger. It wasn't quite a wraith, so yes, it did deserve a name of its own.

"Why do you call it that?" she asked, lifting her gaze to Adam. "A wight? It wasn't white." White would mean it was clean, and that monster was filthy and disgusting. "It should be called a shiver."

Because that's what it did, and that's the effect it had too. Deep inside, she was shivering. And it had nothing to do with standing in the freezing mud.

She'd need new shoes too. Gorgeous ones. The Order could treat.

Why couldn't she stop shaking?

"I love mages," Adam said, approaching again. "Damn handy people. Come work for me at Segue. I've got lots of wraiths you can set on fire."

Kaye forced brightness back into her expression. No use letting anyone know how unsettled she was.

"She's working for me," Bastian said. He had the nerve to put his hand on her elbow. Was that ownership or comfort? She resented them both.

She fisted her hands to stop the trembling and deftly stepped out of his grasp. She didn't need anyone.

"Segue's more fun," Adam assured her, grinning. "Plus I've got Shadowy types there already."

"Not the best inducement," the angel muttered.

"Shadowy types" caught her attention. Maybe not an inducement for an angel, but for her? Interesting. All her life, there had been a hush around Shadow, a silence first imposed by magekind, which she'd kept upon waking in the rehabilitation center following her attack. It was very interesting to find a place with both answers and others of her kind.

Khan, the mage who'd cast the faelight, advanced. He was very tall, very broad. He had black hair streaking to his shoulders and wicked, slanted eyes, a deeper black still. His movements had a fluid quality, leaving a wake of danger on the earth with every step. He might have the standard limbs and features of a man, but he didn't look remotely human. A pureblood. No doubt about it. The world seemed barely able to hold him.

Kaye's mouth went dry.

And she was descended from this kind of being?

Khan didn't signal welcome to Bastian, so she guessed it was mages against angels with him too.

"How many wraith kills does that make?" Khan asked her. He had an accent impossible to place.

Kaye drew herself up to meet the Grim Reaper. "Seven. I try for one a year, but I can't always find one."

She felt Bastian's angel-gaze on her and took some pride in surprising him with her experience.

"See?" Adam continued. "It's like you've already been working for me. I'll give you back pay."

So many men trying to buy her lately.

"She's unavailable," Bastian repeated, harder.

Kaye let the chatter slide past her. How could Adam be so comfortable in Khan's presence?

Pureblood. The mage could rule the world if he wanted. No wonder there had been a war between Heaven and mages. The idea of a race of beings like Khan terrified even her.

"Seven," Khan repeated. "You must have started young."

Kaye smoothed her expression. Or tried. "I was fifteen."

"Khan," Bastian said, interrupting. "If I might have a moment of your time?"

Kaye slid her gaze over to Bastian, and she remembered one of his reasons for coming here. She almost made a fool of herself by laughing out loud: Bastian wanted to recruit . . . *Khan*? She wished the angel luck. It'd be a pleasure to watch, a scary kind of pleasure, but good nevertheless. She wouldn't miss it for the world.

"The conference room is waiting for you." Adam gestured to the mobile trailer near their parked car, and then looked to Bastian. "If you have a moment when you're finished, I'd like a word." It seemed like Adam was staying behind, though she wanted to hear more about Segue.

They reconvened in the trailer, which turned out to be

an office unit. The main space was dedicated to an office area, cluttered with computers and papers. But the back room was furnished with facing leather sofas. A large screen (now dark) was mounted on the wall. Kaye didn't think it was intended for watching television.

They all took a seat. Khan seemed to fill the room with a dark throb of magic. Bastian's inner glow pushed the Shadows aside. And she coaxed her fire hotter and hotter to try to match them. Never again would she be overlooked in a room bursting with power.

"I have very little patience for angels," Khan said. "What do you want?"

"I need you to help me avert a war," Bastian answered. His conviction permeated the room. She felt his urgency reverberate through her and even might have responded, if she were human. But she was a mage, so she refused to allow it.

Khan didn't seem interested either. "I'm already fighting the wraiths and the"—he glanced at Kaye—"shivers."

Kaye was starting to like Khan. Bastian, not so much.

"I'm referring to another great war, humanity in the balance." Bastian leaned forward, bracing his elbows on his knees. "I understand that you care for humanity now more than ever."

"I do." The irises of Khan's black eyes seemed to expand with the underlying anger of his answer. Why he was so angry, though, Kaye had no idea and she wasn't about to ask.

"Then will you help me control the mage Houses before they undermine human interests? They are colluding with wraiths to do violence." Bastian glanced at Kaye. "Ms. Brand was a victim of one such attack."

"Leave me out of it," Kaye said. Her interests were different from Bastian's; she would not allow him to think otherwise, or Khan either. Bastian wanted her to find out how the Houses were using wraiths, and now very likely the wights. And she wanted that information as well. But once discovered, then what? The question would become how she would use the information for her business with the Greys. Whatever recourse she decided to take, she was certain Bastian would not approve.

Khan shifted his attention to her. "But you've agreed to help The Order."

"I have," she answered. Her life needed to change.

"And now that you know you have other options?" Khan asked. His gaze was impenetrable. "Segue needs someone who is able to finish wraiths."

Needs someone who is able . . . ? "Bastian said you have power over life and death."

"And so I do," Khan answered. "But the wraiths and wights have no death, and so cannot die. But they can be cut from the world, as I once did with my scythe. Or burned to oblivion, as with your faefire. No mortal means can kill them, however, and I am now mortal."

"I don't understand." And she hated her ignorance. She glanced at Bastian for answers. No help there.

"A human's death is a precious thing," Khan said. "A death is transformation, from one state to another. It might be terrifying to some, but it is vital to existence. The wraiths gave up their deaths to a demon in return for immortality, for everlasting life. Without their deaths, they cannot die. The wraiths cannot cross into Shadow, cannot become something else, and so forever are consigned to their flesh."

Hence the wight's state of advanced decomposition. That made sense. Wraiths smelled awful, but they weren't that far gone. This was not an immortality anyone could want. They'd been duped.

"As the fae lord of Death," Khan continued, "I could open the way between the worlds and force a wraith to cross. I could cut them out of life with my scythe. But I am mortal now. I cannot kill what cannot die."

"But I can," Kaye said. She just had.

"Yes. Fire is by its nature *transformative*. It is a great power. A god's power."

Bastian growled disagreement.

"And the visions I see in the flame?" Kaye asked.

"Another property of Shadow—to see the possibilities of a life. To see a human's fate. I do not think you see mage futures there—we have no fate, no boundaries or limits imposed upon us." His dark expression split into a grin of victory. "We are not predestined."

"I see my fate," she said. Her breathing got tight.

Khan's brows rose. She must have surprised him. "And that is?"

"Fire." Kaye felt Bastian's gaze, but she didn't look at him. Her future was none of his business. If not for this opportunity to get answers, she would have kept quiet. "I see myself on fire."

Khan looked thoughtful, which made her uncomfortable. Somehow it seemed more prudent to avoid his notice, to avoid being the subject of his deep consideration as well. Khan was too potent for simple conversation. "I do not know how that could be, but as a fire mage, you should be protected from flames."

She tried for a smile and an affirmative nod, something with calm. She didn't feel it, though. The visions bothered her and not even Death knew why she had them.

"One of Segue's missions," Khan continued, "its primary mission, I think, is to search for understanding. You would be welcome there. It is a *good* place. The work is dangerous, yes, but I can extend your life if necessary, even preserve it in the event something goes wrong. You need not fear death while you work there."

"Sounds like the offer the demon made to the wraiths," Bastian observed.

The whites of Khan's eyes blacked until yes, he did look every bit the demon. Though angry, he continued to address Kaye. She held herself very still while he spoke.

"A mage should not trust the angels. You have no soul for this one"—Khan inclined his head in Bastian's direction—"to protect. He will not stand by you."

"I've given her my word," Bastian said. "I'd give you the same. Please help us."

Khan finally regarded Bastian, who impressed Kaye by not rearing back in his seat with the gale force of Khan's glare.

"The Order conspired to take my Layla from me," Khan said. "I will not help you. And further, I don't require the protection of an angel. Nor do I have any desire to break the mage Houses. After ages of secrecy, they are coming out of hiding and making themselves known. Room must simply be made for them on this fair earth, or the mages will take it."

"It will come to war again," Bastian said, as controlled and implacable as he'd been from the first. "And for exactly the reasons you just gave Ms. Brand. Magekind knows no limits, no constraints. You, most of all."

"You seem old to me," Khan said to Jack. "Are you old enough to remember that I was among the fae to assail the great wall of Heaven? I know war. I know war the likes of which you could never conceive. I say again, I will not help you."

Khan settled that black gaze back on Kaye. She made very sure not to flinch either. He spoke of her childhood fairy tales, Shadow rising against Light.

"Kaye, will you come?" the dark mage said.

Did she dare refuse him?

Yes.

Years ago she'd wandered from town to city afraid of everything. She would have done anything to feel safe again. And it would have been a great relief to find others like her who had no ties to the mage families.

But today? She was angry at herself for not facing the truth, when she'd always known it. She'd run for so long, for so many years, but the only thing that could ever really save her was to stop. And to turn. And to face the monsters behind her—both the wraith and the Grey who'd commanded it. She knew better now. Her monsters were not at Segue.

"I'll stick with Bastian for now, but thank you very much for the offer." Besides, the limits *she* lived by were imposed by herself. She'd said she'd do Bastian's job, and she would. That was *her* word.

Khan stood, looming dark above them. "If you reconsider, you may come at any time. You are needed."

Kaye and Bastian stood as well. That word *needed* made her feel strange, especially coming from him.

"I'll remember," Kaye said. And after matters were settled with the Greys, she just might. *Segue* meant a shift from one state to another. She needed a change, a new life. When this business was over, Segue might just be it.

When Jack left the conference room for the work center, he found Adam Thorne waiting at one of the computer stations. The screen before him showed a map—looked like Washington, D.C.—little red dots speckled throughout the metropolis, concentrated in some areas, more widely dispersed in others.

"Jack," Adam said, waving him over. "What do you make of this?"

Jack was still trying to curb his frustration at Khan's absolute refusal to work with him. But then, Jack had been among the host of angels who'd decided that the life of Khan's Layla was not worth the dangers she represented to Earth. The Order had not wanted to hurt her, but no other way had been open to them. There were never easy solutions to problems concerning Shadow.

Khan exited the trailer entirely, and suddenly the space seemed much larger, the air less static. Shadow and light did not mingle well.

Jack felt Kaye follow him to the workstation to look over Adam's shoulders at the wide display. This close, she was like a sun blazing next to him, hers a light very different from his own. Her scent, which he tried not to inhale through his nose, had the mind-fuzzing markers of Twilight, of magic. It was subtle on her, but too much of that dark stuff and he knew a man could forget who he was.

All mages were difficult, each in his or her own way.

Jack focused hard on the screen before him. A time signature at the bottom of the map said that the dots reflected wraith attacks over the past six months. Adam touched a finger to part of the city, a part with no red dots whatsoever. It was an amoebic shape of urban peacefulness where only mundane violence reigned.

"No wraiths," Adam said. Mentally, he followed with, *But why?* which Jack thought was directed inwardly, and not to him.

Very good question. Adam and Segue were never far behind The Order's own findings. There were indeed oases of safety from wraiths within several major cities, a development that concerned the angels enough to hire Kaye

Brand to investigate what was going on. No angel trusted organized peace where the wraiths were concerned.

"No wraiths is good, right?" Kaye asked. "How do they manage it?"

"We've discovered the same phenomenon," Jack said. "And we've identified at least twenty-five urban areas globally that are not troubled with wraith attacks. And yet, the neighborhoods surrounding the peace zones have a heightened wraith presence."

Adam looked over his shoulder. "The cause?"

"We believe it's the mage Houses," Jack answered. "They've begun working with the wraiths."

Not the first time in the history of the world.

"Begun?" Kaye said from behind him. "Wraiths have been around mages for more than a decade at least."

"In what capacity?" Adam asked her, turning, surprise in his voice.

"Bodyguards, security," she answered. "Anything that needed brute force."

"And no one was concerned?" Adam shook his head in disbelief. "They're hungry predators. No one is safe with them around . . ."

Adam's sentence trailed off, but the train of thought continued. . . . *except, of course, someone who doesn't have a soul.*

"That's right," Jack said. Adam understood now.

Jack saw Kaye glance over, as if suddenly aware of the telepathy. She narrowed her eyes at him, but he remained impassive.

Adam sighed hard. "Well, this bears some serious reflection. I can't believe I hadn't considered it before. I guess I just couldn't fathom that anyone would accept, condone, and use monsters that feed on the souls of humankind. It's beyond cold-blooded."

"The wraiths are only a weapon," Kaye said, voice smooth. Too smooth for truth. "Like any other that takes a life."

Adam sat back in his chair, his thoughts roiling with interest.

"A weapon? If you've killed wraiths before, you must have seen how they feed," Adam argued. "They are much more than that."

Jack let them disagree, though he had no idea what had set Kaye off. No . . . he thought he knew. The "cold-blooded" comment about the mages. And she was set on proving Adam right. On owning the description herself—though there was no way Kaye would ever be associated with the word *cold*. Kaye burned.

"I've seen how they feed." Kaye smiled. "How do you think I got my scars?"

Adam's eyes widened, horrified. "Good God. You survived a wraith's bite?"

"The mages are a race apart, Adam," Jack said. "And they are no longer hiding in their Houses. They are taking steps; using wraiths was just one of many. The peace zones are another."

"But the peace is a ruthless kind, isn't it?" Adam looked at Kaye. Jack knew he saw her scars more clearly now.

Kaye's expression went aloof. And suddenly Jack knew that was how she coped with appraisal—making herself remote, above, beyond anything that sought to reach her. People looking all the time. But it wasn't the real woman. Heaven help him when he met the real Kaye if he was already running hot for this one.

"I take it you're supposed to figure out what the mages are doing?" Adam asked her. Jack was glad Adam didn't renew his offers of employment.

"Yes," she said.

Jack didn't miss the glint that came into her eye, and neither did Adam.

"And then what?" Adam asked.

Jack intended to curb the rising power of the Houses before it came to bloodshed. He wanted to quash any attempt at a new hegemony of Shadow on the world, putting humankind under mage dominion. But Kaye did him one better.

Her skin took on that seductive, almost solar glow. "And then I think there will be fire."

Certainly no more offers of employment today. A hundred years ago they'd have burned her at the stake.

Jack gave Adam assurances of cooperation, and then, ladies first, he and Kaye exited the mobile trailer and started down the outside steps. The clouds hung low, turning the sky white, but he did not think it would rain and compromise the open barrow across the way.

"You couldn't have thought Khan would cooperate," Kaye said over her shoulder.

"No, but I had to try. With little effort he could have upset whatever plans the mage Houses have. It would have been fast and complete, one danger among many averted."

"And my role?" She turned back to watch the steps, minding the icy footing.

"As a mage yourself, you have a good chance of being invited past the wards on their Houses," he said to her back. "You know how the families work, the underlying politics."

"You want the mages hobbled. From the inside."

Not his preferred choice of words. "I want the threat managed."

"Khan said your Order had acted against him." She reached the long rubber mat over the mud that led to the pseudo parking area.

Jack stepped around Kaye, got another headful of her soul-drawing scent, and opened her car door. She stood within his outstretched arms, waiting for him to explain, and he had the impulse to step forward, step closer. He *wanted* something from her. Badly. Shadow again, had to be.

"We did act against him." His breath smoked the air between them, curling toward her while he forced himself to keep back. "Khan was Death then, and he'd forged a gate to Hell. The thing had to be destroyed, even if that destruction also meant the death of his beloved Layla. She lived, however, but Khan still won't tolerate The Order."

Her breath reached too, and tangled with his. "That *would* put you at odds. What House does she come from? Her connection to Khan is easily the match of the millennium."

"No House. She's human," he said. "Khan works tirelessly for Segue. I hoped he might expand his scope."

An eyebrow arched. "A human woman lies down with Death?"

Yes. Just like an angel is tempted to embrace Shadowfire. The universe was insane.

"Dark times," he reminded her. He angled his chin toward the waiting seat, and she turned and slid inside the car. He shut the door and rounded the vehicle, taking lungfuls of the cold air to clear his head of woman and magic. This would not do. Once he was inside, she had another question ready.

"So now what? I might be permitted inside the Houses, but I can't exactly knock on a front door. A mage never begs for favors."

Jack had hoped it wouldn't come to this, but without Khan's support . . . "What about Grey? The marriage contract provides an ideal opening."

Kaye smiled warmly, so he knew she'd refuse. "Last

time I spoke with a Grey, a wraith was set on me. Brand House burned to the ground."

"Eventually you will meet him face-to-face. You can't let your history compromise the work that we have to do. Grey will at the least be curious. And once he sees you . . ."

Jack didn't finish. She got the point: Use the same fire that was even now reminding Jack that he was a man before he was an angel.

"That's one way to go about it, I guess," she said, composed. But Jack could sense the light tension pulling at her lovely features, her scars slightly whitening.

The conversation turned sour in Jack's mouth. The work was just beginning, and already he felt world-weary. He did not like his part in this, dangling a woman in front of a dangerous man. Even if the woman was dangerous herself. "The question is, how do we get his attention?"

She nodded and shrugged, world-weary too. "With that bad business at the Wake, it would be reasonable, expected even, for me to move my business elsewhere. It's what I was going to do anyway."

Immediately Jack knew where she was going with the idea. "And Washington, D.C., would be an ideal choice—where politicians would pay handsomely for a glimpse at their future. The move would show ambition, which the mages would respect."

She brought her gaze back up. "Arouse their curiosity. Make them come to me."

"It could work," Jack said. "And we have a good start. I've already arranged a house for you in Georgetown. I had something a little more spectacular set aside for Khan, but I think it's too much for your purposes."

"I like hotels," she corrected with a lazy shake of her head. "The Hay-Adams."

"You'll live in a house this time." He put the keys in the ignition.

Her color warmed. "That's not my style."

"A hotel is not an option," he said. "What if your treachery is discovered? What of the hotel's other patrons?"

She flushed.

Angry? Too bad. The whole point of this venture, for him at least, was the preservation of humankind.

"You'll need a client right away," Jack pressed on. "Any ideas? I'd prefer not to coerce anyone to use your services." He'd known the line between right and wrong would gray many times before this business was over. He hadn't anticipated that it would begin so dark.

"I have someone I can contact, a senator," Kaye answered, still displeased. "She's used me before." She paused, those heavy lids lowering a little. "And where will you be during all this fun?"

Jack could have explained, but a demonstration would work better. He held his breath to get it just right. He focused on the cells that made up his body: the tissue, bone, and fluid. And from all that matter, he withdrew his angel's light, his spark of divinity. He stuffed himself down inside his core and bottled it. Put a stopper on his soul.

Kaye's eyes widened at the effect, and he knew what she saw: a regular man with his features, his dark hair, blue eyes, his slightly crooked nose. Just a man. No one, not even a mage, would be able to tell he was an angel.

Where would he be during all this fun? He started the car.

"Right by your side."

Chapter 3

Upon entering the library, Ferrol Grey spotted the naked woman—Gail Meallan, a tempest mage—lying in a provocative sideways twist on the red settee next to the fireplace. Flowing ebony hair, ruddy tits, interestingly hairless at the juncture of her legs. Since it was his library, he assumed she was waiting for him. The ambush was brazen, considering his house had other guests for the upcoming Council meetings. Finally, the good stuff was happening. The waiting was over.

"Excuse me," he said, retrieving the mage history he was after, and exited.

No seductions today, thanks. House women came in three sorts: viper (Ms. Meallan), broken (under the thumb of her House), and honorable (stayed clear of House politics, therefore stayed clear of Grey House).

Once upon a time, he'd been married to an honorable woman. Penny's support had made his strong House stronger, hence the rise of the Greys. He did not begrudge her memory that triumph. Credit was due. He hadn't known what he was doing to her until it was too late. Hadn't known that it would leave him without heirs as well. His next wife would have to be stronger. Much stronger.

However, in this, his second life, the honorable mage women declined his advances. It seemed cold iron was as anathema to them as it was to the fae, though he was descended from those beings himself too. He wanted little Greys running around and stirring up Shadow. At least the Council meetings would be an excellent opportunity to gauge prospects. To show the honorables that he really wasn't that bad. And if he was, he'd embrace their better influence.

Honor was power, as true as the iron of his House. One couldn't trust viper or broken.

For damn certain, his children would not come from the womb of Gail Meallan. If she thought that seducing him would make him blind to the business in Galveston, she was mistaken. Meallan could not have Galveston; it was promised already in the parcel allotted to Wright House, and not for two years yet.

He moved back down the hallway to his private office, glancing at his watch. Twenty minutes to spare. The Shadows swirled as he passed, lifting those ever-present, incomprehensible fae whispers to his ears. They were watching; he knew they were. Could feel it on the back of his neck.

Ferro raised his chin in hello to his secretary, Camilla, and entered his office, the thick tome detailing the history of his kind under his arm. Fortunately, he had the Gordian Knot of the Houses well in hand. Like Alexander the Great, he held the mages at both ends of the string.

Humankind, however, was a mystery. The difference between the two races was subtle at first, as if they were parallel lines in the course of history. But a negligible divergence of trajectory forced the lines farther and farther apart. At a distance, they were clearly at cross purposes.

Therefore: There is only one world. Humanity has had its time. Now rise the mages.

Ferro dropped the history book on his desk, picked up the television remote, and seated himself.

Reality television intrigued him, this idea of looking into a house, just like the fae who looked in on his. This particular program featured twelve young people confined together, their goal to find a way out either through their ingenuity (of which they had none) or through clues they earned performing certain tasks. One million dollars was at stake, but these people seemed more interested in having sex with one another and crying at the camera.

What did this human generation, *his* new generation, want? How could he give it to them and take what he wanted as well?

The show was Ferro's homework. A lesson in human nature via their entertainment. One per day to keep his sensibilities current, his mind, like his body, young. At one hundred and two, he needed it.

Some fifteen minutes into his work, a polite knock sounded at the door. His appointment. Early.

"Enter," he said, but didn't shift his gaze from the screen. A blond girl on the show had walked right by a concealed doorway in the mazelike house. *Right there!* Her gorgeous breasts were admirable. Her attention to detail, lacking. She reminded him of Gail Meallan.

"Miss Darshana Maya and her father have arrived to see you," Ferro's secretary said from the office doorway. "Her father brought his wraith."

Ferro went inside himself, deep inside, and sought the umbra echo of the Grey House ward stones that protected the building from entry. He allowed the Mayas to enter, but refused the wraith, which would stink up the whole house with its decay. "The wraith will wait outside." A moment's thought. "And have her father wait"—the fool had caused him too much trouble— "in the *library*. Just send the girl in."

"Yes, sir," his secretary said.

On the show, a young man made himself a peanut butter and jelly sandwich. He'd taken to wearing only swim trunks, probably in the event that he needed to use the Jacuzzi at a moment's notice.

Shana shrieked her fear from outside the office door, and Ferro heaved a sigh.

The father bellowed to match.

And on the show, the girl with the breasts *leaned* her back on the concealed doorway. This was agony. Ferro willed the girl to turn around, but she struck up a conversation with the boy in the swim trunks, who was ogling her assets.

The hidden door. Was. Right. There.

"Miss Maya, sir," Camilla said.

Ferro looked away from the TV. Shana Maya, eighteen-year-old scion of Maya House, stood two feet inside his office, body held tense as if only force would move her farther. Her gaze darted around his office—touched the windows, the grouping of comfortable chairs, the flat-screen TV to the left of his desk. There was no way out, and so her gaze came back to him.

"Do you watch *Mad House*?" Ferro asked her.

Shana just stood there, white-faced. Her straight black hair had a jagged urban cut, longer in the front, short in back. She was petite, like all the Mayas, and dressed in some kind of Euro-chic jumper with too many zippers. Or were zippers the new trend? Hmm.

"*Mad House*," Ferro repeated.

She shrugged. He couldn't tell if that meant yes or no.

And here he'd been trying to make friends.

Better get it over with. Ferro reluctantly picked up the

remote and turned off the TV, then stood and rounded his desk to approach the girl.

"The first time a mage is indiscreet using Shadow," he said, leaning back against his desk, "I allow the House to handle it. The second time, I personally touch base with the Head—your father assured me that you would not repeat your behavior. The third time, the errant mage comes here."

Damn, he sounded like an old man. It was one thing to think like one, another to act out of touch.

Her eyes shined, but her face was too tense to quiver. Poor kid. She'd gotten herself into real trouble this time, and now she had to see the dreaded Mr. Grey.

"Miss Maya—"

His phone buzzed in his pocket, interrupting. He pulled it out and looked at the number. "Yeah?" he answered amiably. He'd seen a young man in a hot nightclub answer that way. Just "Yeah," no "Hello." *That's* how the young sounded.

Shana's chest hitched for breath. Ferro threw her a smile and a wink, then turned a little to the side to concentrate on the call.

"Sir, Kaye Brand has moved again—she's living in Georgetown."

"Here? Why?" The woman, one of the broken, never stayed in one place long. She was a boozy, scarred wreck. But to move here while the Houses were meeting had to mean something. Yes, this news was worth bothering him with. An interesting development. "What is she up to?" Was she here to finally say her *I dos*? Had to be. The smartest thing she could do was ally herself with Grey. Too bad she was far too late for the party.

The question was, did he want her? At least Ms. Brand,

unlike Shana, was extremely selective about how and when she used her Shadow.

But no, he'd pass. Kaye Brand had no spine. No one weak could bear the Grey name. Or bear him children.

"Keep me posted." He'd have to make certain there wasn't some collusion afoot. He ended the call and tossed the mobile on his desk next to the mage history book.

Darshana now. "I trust your father explained where you went wrong?"

Silence. The girl had stolen merchandise from a shopping mall jewelry store by confusing the minds of the staff. The theft wasn't the problem, however.

"Answer me, please," Ferro said.

Her chin dimpled with anger, but she recited by rote. "My illusions work on humans, not security cameras. I can still be caught using Shadow in public, and then magic and magekind would be exposed in a negative light and popular opinion could turn against us."

She'd clearly heard the lecture many times before.

Magic and magekind were already exposed, but not to the general public, not quite yet, and certainly not with convenient video proof. Only some human elite knew—those in positions of power and those with great wealth. The rest of the world heard only rumors, rumblings of trouble. For now. The day would soon come, however, when that would change. And when it did, magekind would be seen as saviors, demigods, not petty thieves.

"Cameras are everywhere." He gestured toward the television. "Your generation should know that better than any."

Her expression went sullen as she anticipated her punishment.

He lifted the book, *her* homework. Funny that he studied

the present, while she needed to remember the past. The future he would write as he went along.

"Miss Maya, *Darshana.* Do you know what happens when mages are discovered by the masses and, by extension, their guardians, the angels?"

Silence again.

Perhaps a visual aid. He gestured to the painting over the fireplace to his right. "See that?"

Ferro couldn't be sure, but he thought he might have caught her attention.

He tried for a bigger reaction. "That painting is worth more than your House's combined wealth. Doubled."

Her gaze flicked up, held.

"That's our history, Miss Maya."

Ferro looked at the Rubens through her fresh eyes. It had been commissioned in the early 1600s by graymage Lloyd Trahaearn to depict, in the artist's lusty frenetic style, *The Fall of Magic*. Angels, in their perfect beauty, bore down with mighty swords on the naked flesh of magekind, who writhed in myriad angry agonies. And throughout the melee, the immortal trees of Twilight reached into the sky as silent, still witnesses to the scouring of magic from the earth.

It had happened more than once.

Ferro glanced back at Shana, hoping for understanding. A flicker of anything in her eyes might spare her.

But no. The very real threat of angelic discovery had yet to dawn on her. *His* discovery would have to be enough. Pity.

"Okay, one more thing and we're done here." He loosened the ring on his index finger; it was a little sweat-stuck. The ring was iron, the backbone of Grey House. A circular rim was its only decoration, as if it had once held a stone, but now only the setting remained. No stone had been lost; the ring had always held Shadow.

He was about to earn his reputation. "This is for your own good, the good of your House, and magekind. And it's *temporary*."

Shana made a little noise and backed away from him. He respected her instincts.

"You'll be all right." Eventually. "But you won't be trouble for some time."

He backed her to the door. He took her hand in his—her nails were short, painted black—and turned her palm upward. She trembled in his grasp, and though he was sorry for her discomfort, he didn't regret what he had to do. She had to learn somehow, and through her, perhaps a few other careless mages, just coming into their power, would take note. And think twice. Or think at all.

He pressed the top of the ring into the center of her palm.

Shana's eyes rolled back in their sockets, and she shook against the closed door. He felt a curl of her Shadow enter him, sweet, sharp, and potent. It mixed with the darkness already gathered in his blood. Magic. With it would come the Maya House's gift of illusion. For a little while, at least.

Color fled from her face, and when she fell to the floor, her weight took her hand. A circular welt had been scorched into her palm, but at least it didn't bleed.

Eventually Shadow would thread through her system again, quicken her umbra, and she'd be able to wield the magic that had brought her this unwelcome attention. How long that would take varied from mage to mage. But the scar would remain and would remind her to be very careful.

Ferro nudged her fallen body out of the way with his foot and shin. Then opened the door and exited.

"Camilla, have Arman Maya come collect his daughter.

Give them a room here in Grey House until she is well enough to leave." He handed Camilla the book on mage history. "And see that her father gets this too. Miss Maya is to read it before I see her again. Thank you."

Camilla stood. "Mr. Maya said that he wanted to speak with you when you were finished."

"Arman can see me at the dinner tomorrow," Ferro said. "I have other work to do."

Ferro kept tabs on every mage—but apparently, today was all about women. Darshana Maya, Gail Meallan, and Kaye Brand. But where, if it please Shadow, could he find one of his own?

Jack was not surprised that the senator didn't like the future she witnessed in Kaye's Shadowfire. She'd paled, the press of her lips highlighting the deep wrinkles around her lipsticked mouth.

The oil and gas lobbyist Kaye and Jack saw two days later struck at the fire. Tried to strike Kaye, which Jack intercepted.

And the congressional aide this morning broke down in tears, hurling hoarse threats, as if Kaye had anything to do with his future. All three saw doom, yet another proof that the world was darkening once again.

Jack had seen it all before: Kaye's visions of the future looked very much like the reality of the distant past. Shadow grasping at ankles as the angels laid siege to warded temples that spread a twisted gospel: Please the gods, and they will protect you; anger them, and meet your doom.

Kaye stepped back as the session with the congressional aide unraveled, her eyes jaded, her fingertips trembling. "I want to go home."

The aide had collapsed, weeping at his desk, and Jack

knew his thoughts were bent on leaving D.C. The D.C. of the future was a frightening place, a colder, singular power in place of the squabbling one of the present.

They took the elevators, a modern contrivance Jack didn't care for, and exited the building onto Constitution Avenue. The air smelled like snow, blown on the breath of the city. Dirty, icy slush was piled along the side of the sleet-blackened road. He'd parked a block down.

Only a few people were out, puffing air before them, their internal dialogues revealing random pieces of their lives.

A secretary who had just bought herself lunch.

A young man who had interviewed for an internship.

A prophet tolling the end of the world: "Darkness comes!"

And then there was another man, who strode right by them, his mind a blank, a vacuum. His gaze lingered on Ms. Brand, and though her beauty often drew attention, this notice felt like something more. Excellent.

They were being watched.

Jack yanked open Kaye's door and helped her inside the black leather interior, then walked casually around to his side.

"Are you ready?" he asked, slamming his own door shut. She'd better be.

Kaye looked over in a return question. Black, beautiful eyes. Magic so close.

"We passed a mage on the street," he answered, eager. "This may be it."

Kaye sighed and leaned back in her seat. Alone. Vulnerable.

To keep it simple, he added, "One step at a time. I'll be right there every moment. More likely than not, they just want to get a look at you. See if you are willing to be approached."

A twist in his gut told him that this wasn't right, that

he ought to get her away and quickly. That they'd taken the wrong course.

No. He shook off the idea.

That he was thrusting her, ill-armed, onto the battlefield in between two armies bent on war. Instinct, a thousand years old, told him to take up his sword and *protect* her instead.

"Oh, I'm willing," she told him, low and determined. Like a mage.

And the twist eased. He was left with disquiet, his constant companion since he'd met her. Everything about Kaye was wrong. Beautiful, and scarred. Unfeeling, and frightened. She was made of too many contradictions to be trusted.

Go back. Rethink. Not right.

Too late. They were on the brink of contact.

Jack took Rock Creek Parkway back to Georgetown. A car followed them, but instead of returning to the luxury town house The Order had leased for Kaye's use, Jack headed for The Quick Fix, an upscale coffee shop off M Street. They'd been there every afternoon for her midday chemical stimulant, and for good reason. He'd wanted to keep Kaye predictable and accessible. Anyone who was watching them could easily guess where they would head. Jack didn't deviate now.

The place was busy, the clientele dressed conservatively, the women of this age styled too much like men, with the exception of Ms. Brand. A few patrons had their laptops open, screens shining bright on their faces.

"You find a seat. I'll get you a drink," Jack said.

"I'll take a double-shot mocha latte, skim milk." Kaye was already unbuttoning her coat.

He gave a curt nod, though by now he already knew her order. Just like he knew that she took off her shoes under the table. That she played with her jewelry when she was nervous, usually discussing the client of the day. That her little square napkin would be carefully shredded while she drank. That she'd flash him her best smile when he was the most irritated. A little over a week in D.C., and he already knew too much about her.

Get her out of here. Not too late.

She selected a free table surrounded by upholstered and padded chairs. Always comfort. He spoke to the boy behind the counter, then glanced back at Kaye. She'd removed her black coat, her slim-styled dress a flash of cobalt heat in the midst of black, grays, and navy blue. No matter what color she wore, she was always on fire.

Stay the course. Too important.

Jack retrieved the drink, and when he turned a second time, he found that a man had joined her. The lack of thoughts streaming from the newcomer meant he was a mage. Kaye was playing with the stone at the end of her necklace, though her expression was a creamy bloom of interest. She was a born actress.

Here we go.

Jack approached and set the coffee in front of her, hating that he'd missed the opening exchange and introductions. To the man, he asked, "Can I get something for you?"

The man glanced up with a "no," and Jack got his first good look at his face. Early thirties, mild coloring—medium brown hair, brownish eyes. Good muscle on a narrow frame. Of all things, friendly. Something . . . *likeable.*

Jack didn't recognize him, but that was fine for now; The Order didn't have files on all the mages. Jack retreated a few steps and took up a standing, though relaxed, guard position, close enough to protect, if need be. But most important, close enough to hear.

"And he is . . . ?" The young man's gaze didn't leave Kaye, but Jack knew the question was about him.

"Security," she answered.

The man made a worried face. "Does he know what you are?"

"Yes," she said, shrugging. "But I wasn't the one to tell him. Before me, he subdued wraiths with some task force, and he learned about magekind there."

Our cover story. Good.

"Wraiths, huh?" The man put a hand to Kaye's chin, turning her head so he could view her scars. That she allowed the intimacy made Jack tense. She hated people touching her. Who was this man that she didn't slap back? Should he intervene? He wanted to intervene.

When the man pulled away, Kaye continued. "He's safe enough."

The man looked sympathetic. "I understand why you'd want wraith protection. The attack must have been brutal. It's a wonder you survived. The wraith's strength alone should have killed you."

"But wraiths don't want to kill their prey. Wraiths want a human soul. I just didn't have what he was looking for, and by the time he figured it out, he was on fire." A lick of Shadow flame appeared in her hand to demonstrate. The light danced for a moment, and then she made a fist.

The man covered her hand with his. "Not here, Kaye. All the world is watching. In fact, that's one thing I wanted to discuss with you. Using Shadow among humans requires special dispensation from the Council."

"I'm very selective," she answered with a curl of her full mouth. A pause. "But of course I appreciate your advice."

Smart girl, Jack thought. *Play it right down the line. Give nothing or they will crush you.*

"Somehow I don't think you'll be asking permission to continue practicing." The man sat back in his chair with an affable smile, admiration in his eyes.

Hold your ground.

"No. I don't think I will." She sipped her coffee. The motion highlighted her gorgeous cheekbones. And her scars. "You can, however, count on my discretion."

God, she's good.

"Not using your power in public is a rule, and one that it is my job to enforce." The man looked at her over a charged moment, twisting an ugly gray ring on his finger, as if considering something. Jack would've loved to read his mind. A crawl of tension went up Jack's spine.

Then the mage lifted both hands in a good-natured shrug. "Kaye, I have to say, a few minutes in your company, and I'm smitten. I mean, of course I was curious when I heard you were in town, but"—that grin again—"I can't be more delighted how *well* you are. You seem so *strong,* so vibrant, . . . so lovely."

Jack hadn't expected a flirtation. Kaye did her job expertly. Whatever business had brought the man had been abandoned in favor of something else.

Kaye gave a throaty laugh, smiling with pleasure. "You flatter me, Mr. Grey. Please continue."

Jack was surprised again. Grey? The old man had a son? Jack had thought Penelope Grey had died without bearing any children. Why didn't The Order know?

"Call me Ferro, and I'm being sincere." The man looked at her with appreciative male awe. "I mean . . . wow. I wish I hadn't torn up that marriage contract."

Jack's belly hardened into stone. No, it was Ferrol Grey, the man himself. Kaye would have thought twice about slapping *him* when he'd touched her.

Damn it. Jack had known this was a mistake. They were in too deep, too fast, but there was no going back now.

Her eyes narrowed prettily. "I still can't quite believe it's you."

"Shadow." Grey sat forward again, glowing with youth. "There I was aging toward the end of my life, not fun, by the way. And then it started to slowly reverse. Took me about five years to be absolutely sure it was happening"—he barked a laugh—"that my hair was growing back. Must be something in the Grey bloodline. We've always been long-lived, but I admit this is a little extreme." Another happy, natural grin. "I'll take it, though."

Jack bet the reversal had begun about thirty years ago, when Death sent Shadow trickling back into the world. The trickle had become a flood, and among other things, it quickened the darkness in the mages' blood. No wonder they didn't have a recent photo of Grey. He wouldn't have looked like himself.

Jack had to make some calls.

"I have to ask," Grey said, "are you here to honor the contract? To put it before the Council? I don't know that I'm opposed." Said with heat, with happy lust.

In too fast, too deep.

Kaye flicked absently at the stone on her necklace. She was nervous. "Ah, no . . . I'm not. I find I prefer my independence, especially after what happened—the fire, losing my father. You tore up the marriage contract?" She sounded like she wanted confirmation. A chink in her armor.

Ferro Grey brushed her worry out of the air. "The marriage contract was a mistake. I had reservations from the beginning." Again, he placed a hand over hers on the table. His thumb stroked what Jack knew was smooth, silky skin. "I'm so sorry for the distress it caused. And I am so sorry for your loss. Your father was a great man. I can't imagine how frightened you must have been. Why didn't you come to me for help?"

Kaye gave a wry expression. "My father had been very

strict. When I recovered from the attack, I grieved, but I was also wild with my freedom. I didn't want the confines of another House, and I understood you were older than my father."

"Well, I am."

"You don't look it." Now she smiled appreciatively, looking pleased with Grey's attention. She leaned slightly forward and to the side, as if she knew her best angles. As if she knew the warm light of the coffeehouse would honey her skin. Of course she knew.

This was a problem.

"He can't take his eyes off you." Grey glanced at Jack.

Kaye laughed again and looked over her shoulder, bringing her Shadow-black gaze to Jack's. "He's not supposed to."

Jack fought a hard pull in his chest but couldn't name the feeling. Something . . . possessive. Her Shadow working on him.

"So you're here to stay?" Grey asked. "I hope to hell you are."

She returned her attention to the mage. "Yes. I think the area suits me."

"Have dinner with me tonight," he said, almost pleading. "At my home. There are so many things I'd like to discuss that *aren't* in the public mainstream." He made a lazy gesture in Jack's direction. "Your guard can come too."

A week and she had done it. With so little effort, she could catch anyone on fire, even Ferro Grey. Jack didn't know why he was surprised; he'd known as much from the beginning of this wretched mission.

Kaye delicately cleared her throat and took a hesitant breath. "I'm sorry. I don't think so."

Now what game was she playing? Getting inside Grey House meant acceptance by the other mage Houses, and therefore access to information on the wraiths. This was the job. Didn't she want her payback?

"We've just met," she continued, with her soft smile. "While I'm interested, I'd like to proceed slowly."

"I don't understand."

Jack didn't either. If she turned Grey down, no one from any of the Houses would approach her. She was as good as done. One did not flirt with Ferro Grey, and then play hard to get. Tease.

"As a *mage,* you should," she answered. "Dinner would be lovely, of course, but I want a seat at a very different table."

"As a mage," Grey repeated in a murmur, respect dawning in his eyes. "You're referring to the Council."

"I'm all that's left of Brand House. A seat, by rights, is mine. I intend to have it. Before dinner with you, I must make my way back into magekind on my own merit. I think you know that. The seat is my priority."

Jack almost swayed on his feet. This was too far. A seat on the mage council. The other Houses would fight it. Fight her. She hadn't discussed this insane tactic with him. She was gambling with her life. Again.

Ferro cocked his head, as if stretching away a momentary discomfort. "So much like your father. You're a formidable woman, Kaye. I'll bet you're well worth the effort. I hope you survive the rite of passage."

She smiled.

How would Jack ever keep her alive?

"My House will be stronger than ever," she said. "I'll do whatever it takes."

"I must say, you've surprised me."

"I hope in a good way." Again that low, smooth voice. All confidence. All sex.

"You have no idea." Grey rose, took and kissed her hand. "Until we meet next, then."

"I look forward to it," she said. And if Jack wasn't mistaken, she pushed a little fire into her skin so that she was luminous in the quiet lighting of the coffeehouse. A siren.

Grey winked his good nature at her refusal and moved toward the door. He stopped and turned back to address Jack. "What wraith task force?"

Jack kept himself level as he lied, something that didn't come naturally. "Segue for three years." He'd have to get Adam Thorne to cover for him. Grey would be thorough.

Grey made a noise at the back of his throat, then exited. Another man rose, a mage whom Jack hadn't noticed, and followed Grey out the door. Still another crossed the street outside to join the pair. Mages everywhere, hiding among the human patrons, and Jack had had no idea.

Hooves pounding the ground. Screams. Bullheaded black clouds overhead, flickering with unnatural lightning. Rain in his breath. Mage-contrived winds driving against his sword arm, his strikes and slashes going awry. Unseasonable hail pelting.

Jack turned back to Kaye, frustration a living, writhing snake in his blood. She'd pushed too hard, too far, and in so doing, she'd endangered both herself and their mission. Promising sex with her looks and leans. Then angling for a seat at the Council? She might as well have asked Grey to kill her outright.

This was a mistake from the beginning. He'd known it all along.

Kaye had stood as well and was donning her coat. He was too late to help her on with it and was left empty-handed, her scent in his nose.

Like Grey, he wanted to speak with her in private. He had a few things to say.

Aaliyah Cook had kept her face angled down to her laptop, but she couldn't help watching the exchange between the couple in front of her, both with such cold black eyes that she'd wanted to put on her sweater.

But it was the candle flame that had appeared in the woman's hand that made Aaliyah shiver.

Thomas had said that all the shit that was happening—the monsters in the alleys, the darkness everywhere—was because of an alien invasion. That even the government had to know about it. She'd rolled her eyes, but had kept smiling, hoping he'd kiss her.

But, now, looking at the witchy woman with the red hair and the scars and the fire thing. Yeah, those people weren't from around here.

When the couple stood, Aaliyah darted her gaze around to see if anyone else was noticing too.

And found another pair of black eyes, belonging to a man on her left, this time fixed on her like a threat.

Aaliyah brought her gaze quickly back to her laptop screen, shaking as this new man rose and stalked by her. She prayed that the darkness in those eyes and on the streets at night would, please God, pass her and her family by.

Chapter 4

Kaye went for a bottle as soon as she was inside the town house door. She left the cold blasting in behind her. Felt good. Her coat fell on the foyer floor. She needed a drink to fuzz out the burn of that first meeting. Oblivion would be even better.

She veered into the living room—some uptight person had decorated it federal style. Antiques with skinny legs. Striped, tea-colored sofa, as hard to sit on as it looked. Bland, pleated curtains. And, adding insult to injury, in the corner a bust of some bulb-nosed man. This was Hell.

Her heart urged her to grab her bag and run. She rifled through the liquor cabinet instead, found the whiskey, and flinched when she heard keys hit the table behind her.

"What did you think you were doing? A seat at the Council table? Do you want to die?" Bastian said as hard and cold as only he could.

Kaye turned, the bottle under her arm. "I'm going to my room." There was color in there. Shadow too, with the curtains drawn. Grey had *touched* her. She wanted to wash her face, no, her whole body. "I'm tired after pulling fire this morning."

"No. We're going to come to an understanding." Bastian jerked his chin toward the sofa. "Sit down."

"I can't talk now." Really, she couldn't. Facing Ferro had been more than enough. She didn't have it in her to revisit or explain. Bastian would just have to wait. She made for the hallway.

He took her arm. "I'm not done, which means you're not done. I hired you for a job."

The fire leaped within her, begging for fuel. "Get your hand off me," Kaye warned. She wasn't above a demonstration when pushed. And legend had it that Shadowfire loved angels.

He released her but blocked her way. "What were you thinking? Leading him on, then asking for a *seat*? Our business here is probably over, thanks to you."

Kaye snorted. How just like an angel to take things at face value.

"Or did you see a good thing in Ferro Grey?" he pressed. "Young, powerful, and seduced by you? Did you decide to go for it all?"

She yanked her arm free. "Mister Perfect Angel Man, let me tell you something."

"Listening," he snapped.

"There's no such thing as a good thing." It was the best advice she could give him, and in her mind, the statement encompassed everything and everyone, including angels. Including Jack Bastian.

Asking for a seat at the mage Council was a desperate resort, because there *was* no turning down Ferro Grey. What he wanted he took. Kaye remembered the way her dad had looked that terrible night in his office ten years ago. His blotchy skin. The lightning strike of pain as he'd struck her.

"You said you could handle Grey, and you sure did,"

Bastian countered. "The dinner tonight sounded perfect. You were back in."

"Too perfect. Too easy," she said. Another wisp of Shadow in her blood caught fire, compelling her to continue. "Too nice. Too charming. Too young."

He took a small step, right in her way. "So you didn't—"

"—buy his load of crap?" she finished. "No. And neither was I going to gift wrap another angel for whatever the hell he'd use you for." She pushed Bastian out of the way and headed for the stairs. She groused under her breath, "Take you to dinner like some twisted hostess gift: Here's another angel."

Stupid. What had Ferro Grey said? *Your guard can come too.* The thought made her sick.

She was three steps up when Bastian responded. "What do you mean *another angel*?"

That strange, quelling vibration of Heaven on her skin stopped her. Years ago she'd run up another set of stairs, an angel below her looking after.

"Kaye, what do you know about the angel Michael Thomas?" Bastian's voice had gone dangerously calm.

Halfway up the stairs, she turned around to find Bastian, not her poet. Dark hair. Penetrating eyes. He looked like a man, but every molecule of her flesh knew what he was. In any incarnation, he was beautiful. But there was no compassion in *his* eyes.

"I don't know anything," she answered. "He'd been tortured, and rather than escape himself, he told me to." Could have been different. "Told me to run, which I've been doing ever since. That's all."

"How tortured?"

"I have no idea." She remembered the chains, the dark matter leeching through his skin. "I think infected with

Shadow. I saw him for less than two minutes when he was chained up in the cellar." And then life as she knew it had ended. "I won't deliver another angel into Grey's keeping. I swear I won't do it. Not even you."

Bastian flinched. "I can take care of myself. It's you who needs protection. You should have told me this in the beginning."

She turned again and headed up the stairs. The conversation was over. Her guts hurt. Her eyes ached but wouldn't water. She drew in air, but it didn't clear her head.

"You should have told me about Michael," Bastian called.

Kaye slammed the door to her bedroom. The oval mirror above the antique dressing table shuddered in answer. She hated this house. Hated the furniture. Wanted room service.

What in dark Shadow's madness had she done?

For an absolutely necessary distraction, she drew out the bottle and unscrewed the cap while wetting her lips. The fire within was out of control. Then she froze when she read the label: Jack Daniels.

Jack.

The man was everywhere. She hurled the bottle at the mirror, but the shattering glass didn't remotely satisfy.

At the bottom of the stairs, Jack stared after her. A door slammed. Then a crash sounded from above. Glass breaking.

He wanted to roar, *Do not run away from me!* His body demanded to pelt up the stairs after her. To enter her bedroom. To slam the door behind him.

And then what?

His angel mind blanked there, but his blood knew exactly what he wanted. A thousand years had passed since he'd been a man, but *yesss*, he knew this rising, determined heat.

Instead he paced like a dog and tried very hard to think. She'd flirted with—no outright *seduced*—Ferro Grey in that coffee shop. And apparently she'd done the same to him.

Fine.

God damn her to Hell, but fine.

Not to mention, she'd known all along about Michael. Of course she had. Duplicitous to the core. At least her story gelled with the events of that night ten years ago. Michael had died, yes, but seemingly not before urging Kaye to run away. And then he had sent a telepathic message to save the girl. She'd been little more than a child then.

And Jack *had* saved her. *Lifting her slack, almost weightless form from her collapse in the wet and frozen wood, and carrying her to safety while his angelic brother burned in the warded house behind him.* Just another memory Jack couldn't escape.

And now—*total insanity*—she intended to protect him to honor the memory of Michael. This made no sense. Jack glared up the stairs. If she was unwilling to take him past the wards into Grey House as her guard, then how, pray tell, was *he* supposed to protect *her*?

Shadow. Woman. Both inclined to madness.

Not that any of that mattered now, because by refusing Grey's invitation, and by asking for a seat on the mage Council, of all things, she'd effectively made herself a target, rather than a subtle spy for The Order. The Brand seat meant power, and the other mages weren't just going to let her take it.

The job was a wash, and yet, he couldn't very well leave that walking catastrophe of a woman to her own devices after she'd aroused Grey's interest while working for The Order. For him.

Jack gripped the stairway banister at its terminating curl. A strange, pressing kind of feeling was working its way up his throat. It had to be a good feeling, because he was smiling in spite of everything. It was a vicious kind of smile, but a smile nonetheless: Ms. Brand, *Kaye,* was protecting him. She'd refused the likes of Ferro Grey to protect him.

Why that made him so satisfied—angry still, but satisfied—he didn't know. And he wasn't about to think about it too much either. Or he would follow her up those stairs.

He had work to do now, anyway—a report to make to The Order and a call to make to Segue to cover his lie. He'd have to make sure Adam Thorne had only bad things to say about him, or Grey would grow suspicious. There was a known connection between The Order and the Segue Institute.

The sun had long since set when Jack heard movement upstairs. A door opening. Closing. Then nothing. A door opened again. Then a few minutes later, footsteps on the stairs.

It was time for a calm discussion. They'd make a new plan, clearly delineated, with objections settled beforehand.

When Kaye appeared, she was dressed to work out. Leggings, he thought they were called, that revealed every smooth plane and curve of her lower physique; a sweatshirt; cuffs rolled to her forearms; and running shoes.

"I didn't think you owned sensible shoes," he said in a bid for levity. And she was in head-to-toe black, another first.

"Yeah, well, this body that you like to look at so much requires maintenance."

Jack was rendered speechless. Kaye was very good at that.

"I need to go for a run," she continued. "I'd like to do it alone, but I'm guessing you'd have a problem with that."

"I would," he said, his brain turning over her earlier comment. Rise to the bait or let it pass? Either way, he couldn't win. It was better to admit the truth anyway—he did like to look at her.

She gave him a once-over. "So are you going to change?"

"We have to talk first."

She tilted her head to the side, a bit of inner exhaustion showing. "The talk would go better after a run. Take my word for it."

Jack fought the impulse to insist on speaking first. He'd spent the last hours working out what he'd say, and just how to say it. He wanted to control the situation, as he tried to control himself. But this late at night, the delay was harmless, and her cooperation essential. Besides, a run would do him good. His blood was stirring again.

He strode across the foyer to get away from her and was just approaching the stairs when a faraway scream reached him. Female. And then another woman screamed.

Women in trouble. He denied the sudden instinct to protect; his duty lay here.

Kaye stepped into the hallway, frowning, and looked from him to the front door, a "what was that?" question in her eyes.

Then, closer, the shrill, piercing monster cry of a beast in pursuit—a wraith screech.

The sound was a thousand years old in his mind. The wraiths had been wiped out ages ago, he'd hoped for forever, but they were back these thirty years.

Their numbers had stopped growing, but it still seemed like the soulsuckers were everywhere.

When another wraith's voice lifted to join the first, Kaye closed her eyes, her head bowing, as if weighted with knowledge.

"What?" Jack demanded.

A third screech rose from another direction, and Kaye bent farther to brace her hands on her knees, hitching for breath and swearing. Some mumbled words, of which he only caught ". . . so soon . . . !"

"Kaye!"

She lifted her head. Her face had gone white. "Grey sent them. I'm sure of it."

"The meeting went *that* badly?" Yes, she'd refused a dinner with the man, but it didn't deserve an attacking army of wraiths.

"No." She straightened, hands covering her face. Stress tensed the long lines of her body.

She was right to be scared, considering her history. She was right to be scared, regardless.

Another screech filled the air. It sounded as if the wraiths were calling to one another, organizing.

Kaye dropped her hands, but her expression was guarded. "No, the meeting went superfantastic, I'd say."

Jack flung a hand toward the door. "He sent wraiths to kill you!"

"It's an invitation," Kaye said, with a sick and twisted smile. "An invitation to show off."

"I still don't understand."

Kaye rolled her eyes at him. "Because you don't understand mages. It's a trial. I came to D.C. and went into business with Shadow, asked for a seat. Well, now he wants to see me do my thing. To prove myself." She shook her head, and a light grew within her, the flame burning brightest in her palms. "He wants a demonstration of power."

"In public?" Jack was incredulous.

"Wraiths are common knowledge already. The rest is up to me to control."

A shriek lifted just outside the door.

Jack stared at Kaye, working it over in his mind. In the old days, the mages had required a difficult initiation in order for postulants to join their Councils. Only the most powerful joined that table. And hadn't Grey mentioned some kind of trial at the coffeehouse? Times had changed, but the practice obviously hadn't. What better test than to make Kaye face her demons?

Jack's throat constricted with the awful realization that this was no simple information-gathering mission, and for Kaye, it had probably never been. "What have I gotten you into?"

He should have paid attention to his reservations, found another way. He should have gotten her away from this, in spite of The Order's need.

"Open the door." Kaye's hands were ablaze now. "And don't forget you're playing human, or we're both dead."

A woman's scream—*Jodi?*—brought Tom Peterman from his sofa to his feet, the newspaper sliding from his lap to the floor. He'd heard his daughter scream in fear as a child, but never as a grown woman.

Heart in his throat, he strode to his town house door. While he unlocked the dead bolt, another woman's scream ripped through him—Marianne, his wife. After thirty-two years of marriage, he was absolutely certain to whom that voice belonged.

He flung open the door. Descended the short flight of

stairs that led to the street. Searched left and right for any sign of them. "Marianne!" he called. "Jodi?!"

They'd gone shopping. A girl's night out while Jodi was on a rare break from her residency. Said they were going to spend his money on something extravagant. And he'd asked, "Why *my* money?" His wife made more. Which was a point of family pride—Marianne's recent promotion to partner. Everything they'd worked for was finally coming through.

He saw two slight figures and started running toward them. Oh, God, his girls. He moved to collect them in his arms. "What's go—"

Another figure, a man, appeared behind them, moving fast. He was half a block away, but Tom could see his elongating teeth. The man opened his mouth nightmare-wide and let out a monster shriek.

Jesus.

"Inside," Tom said, dragging Marianne and Jodi.

He'd seen news reports and screen captures of creatures like this, but not here. Not in his neighborhood. Not after his family.

What was happening to the world? The explanations on the news were all bad, all unbelievable, all terrifying. But were they true?

The three of them tripped up the steps to the house. Slammed themselves inside. Marianne and Jodi babbled through tears and broken breaths. ". . . came out of nowhere . . . almost got Mom . . . mace did nothing . . ."

Tom was shaking too. Monsters in the night, coming after his girls.

Not his girls.

He went for his shotgun.

* * *

Kaye braced as Bastian flung open the door. She watched as he shifted his weight to the side and kicked the wraith ascending the front steps. He'd have to work on the human thing; that kind of force took something more. The creature fell backward, Bastian's foot gripped at its chest. They hit the brick steps together with a dull *whump*.

On instinct, Kaye leaped on the sprawling limbs to free Bastian.

He hollered at her touch. Fire. She'd apologize later.

The wraith shrieked, its dagger teeth bared, but it was pinned just long enough for Kaye to lay her hands on its yellow skin and make the monster—a woman, by the looks of it—burn. The sound in the creature's throat went wraith falsetto as the flames caught. But it was the stench of the decay that made Kaye lose her fire. The wraith burned before her, its silhouette a human engulfed in Shadow flame.

"You should run," Bastian was saying. "You didn't sign up for *this*."

Kaye laughed out loud. *Run*. Now he told her.

She watched two more wraiths glide down the street toward the town house. Sirens wailed a block over. Help coming, as if they could do anything. As if law enforcement wouldn't shoot the woman wielding fire too.

"There's nowhere to run," Kaye said, recovering her equilibrium. She should know; she was the expert. "There's no way out of this . . . but *through*. And I really need to be through with it."

"The host can be here in five minutes."

"And then Grey would know I was lying." Out of the corner of her eye, she spotted another wraith spider-walking down the side of the building. "And he'd have to come after me."

"Then we're going to fight?" His gaze flicked around the scene.

Kaye snorted yes.

"Don't try to protect me this time," Bastian said.

"Don't worry."

A wraith dropped behind Kaye. Jack grabbed the thing by its throat and used his weight to push the creature off balance. The wraith's stringy hair went flying, and its noxious smell smeared through the air. In the lurch of movement, the wraith brought two clasped hands down on Jack's arm—the bone cracked as it broke, but the real pain came from Kaye's accidental faefire burn, roaring on the underside of his forearm. The bone would heal quickly, the scorched skin, never.

Kaye grasped the matted hair of the wraith, and the creature ignited, screaming agony into the frigid night as the wick took and the wraith's candle flesh stretched into a fiery plume.

. . . *Assistance is on its way. . . .* The thought, angelic in origin, wafted through the air.

. . . *No* . . . Jack pushed back. *This has to be just us . . . but delay the police.*

. . . *We could pick off the rear wraiths. . . .*

. . . *No* . . . Jack insisted. Not if this really was some sort of test. He could handle it. He knew battles against creatures of Shadow. Every thrust, kick, strike was recorded in his muscle and bone. That's why he'd been called for yet another tour of duty on Earth.

. . . *Goddamn motherfuckers* . . . This time a human source. . . . *going after my girls* . . .

The blast of a shotgun abruptly brought Jack's attention

down the row of houses where a man had emerged to fight. A wraith tottered, half its face missing.

A ratchet sounded as the man cocked the shotgun. Another swift aim. . . . *stink like yesterday's garbage* . . . Blast.

A shivering wight, a wraith beyond all humanity, darted from the sky toward Kaye, blurring with speed. Jack flung his good arm out, got the monster in the neck, but the wight still sent Kaye tumbling to the sidewalk. She snarled and threw fire.

Jack dodged her bad aim. One burn was quite enough.

"Get inside!" he called to the man, the neighborhood's wraith vigilante.

"I have to do something!" the stranger yelled back. Ratchet. Blast.

A good effort, but a wasted one. Nothing mortal could kill a wraith, just slow it temporarily. If the wraiths weren't bent on Kaye, the man would be dead by now. And the man was in danger from more than wraiths, too; he was a witness.

The wight had collected the floating debris of its body, made itself as whole as possible. Though it had mass, it lacked solidity. It lunged again, and Jack ducked, putting a little nonhuman force into a strike that planted it face forward in the street, its dusty tissue again coughing into the air. Unclean things.

This fight was too familiar—the smell, the sounds of fear. He'd battled these creatures a hundred times before, but never alongside a mage woman. Jack wished his damn bone would heal so he could have the use of both arms. The pain of the burn put an edge on his mood.

He looked over his shoulder to see Kaye scramble up.

"What do you want to do?" he demanded. He didn't think she wanted to kill the wraiths one by one, though he'd be willing to set them up for her if she'd burn them each into oblivion.

"Fire," she said. She was glowing again, but not illuminated from the inside like the white-bright of a soul. No, Kaye was a flame, the fire itself, just trapped in the shape of an incomparable woman.

She lifted her hand to the gloomy street and lit the night.

If Jack needed proof that Shadow had seeped into every nook and cranny of mortality, Kaye's show of power confirmed it. Darkness coursed from every void, swirling and eddying into spinning devils of magic. They churned together, rushing, sparking, and taking on molten hues of color in a river of faery flame. It carried the scent of Twilight, dark and intoxicating, soul seducing, even to an angel. Certainly to this angel.

The fire flooded the length of the street, tumbling waves fed by ready magic. Two wraiths were caught immediately by the tide. The fire climbed their bodies and clawed them down into death, their screams strangled by the deluge. Another two had yet to finish regenerating from gunshots and were swallowed in a silent final reckoning.

From Jack's place on the steps, he forced the thrashing wight into the flow. It went down with an almost human keen of fear.

The man with the shotgun had attempted to scale another townhome via the decorative iron railings covering the lower windows and now clutched the exterior like a child afraid to come out of a tree. He was terrified, but the names of two women were foremost in his mind.

The fire licked at the pavement, and then flickered and sparked back into darkness. Heaps of wraith flesh remained wrapped in the burnt remnants of their soiled clothing.

A police car finally turned down the street, trolling slowly, its strobe wheeling. Too late, yet just in time.

Jack almost forced the vigilante down from his perch, almost altered his memory to forget what Kaye had done. Almost, but no. Grey might need a witness to believe what happened here. A single witness, hardly problematic to magekind, to make the lack of public exposure plausible. The rest of the neighbors had been smart enough to hide deep in their homes.

Kaye's clothing was falling to pieces of char and dust, revealing the dip of her waist, the swell of her bare breast, her exposed thigh. Smudges of black marked her smooth skin. She passed him by on her way back to the town house. Faltered.

Jack swept her up into his arms.

"I don't want to talk to anyone," she mumbled.

The vigilante scrambled down to meet the police officers, pointing toward Jack, his mind full of images of fire, his words tripping to describe it. The officers looked over, but Jack mentally rebuffed their interest, recasting the vigilante's words as the ravings of a madman. No matter what the man said, they would not bother Kaye. Besides, the officers had a wraith mess to clean up; he nudged them toward that duty. Reports of tonight's events would be convoluted at best.

Jack carried Kaye inside. Locked the door, though he knew it wouldn't do any good. What was one bolt against Shadow? Nothing. Against wraiths? Little more than nothing. Against mages? She was completely vulnerable.

Which was why mages lived in warded Houses.

An angel's tour on Earth regularly brought him into danger. And with darkness encroaching, the dangers were compounded infinitely. Fae, wraiths, wights, and mages—

they were only the beginning of Other creatures that imperiled humankind. The Order was stretched thin, and would be more so as this new age deepened.

But this was not what Jack had expected during his work with Kaye. Though he'd anticipated some tight moments, he had never intended to make her the object of a direct attack.

Wasn't supposed to be like this.

Had never been like this.

He laid her down on the sofa, and she curled into herself, spent. She seemed numb to her nakedness. Numb to the world. Her skin was ashy, with dark circles under her sunken eyes. Her lush lips had paled and dried. Her breath was shallow, expression slack. He'd never seen her so vulnerable. He'd done this to her, just as much as Ferro Grey had.

He knelt at her side. "Kaye?" And cursed himself. He checked her pulse, wondering if it would become habit, and released a breath of relief when he found it.

Then he put her to bed, drew a chair to the side. Waited.

The vigilante, whom Jack learned was named Tom Peterman, was taken from his home late that night by mages—Grey's people, Jack was sure. Peterman would tell Grey what he saw Kaye do.

She slept through the next day, and she couldn't be roused for food or drink. Her skin seemed thinner, her lush body hollow. Jack felt hollow too.

Mr. Peterman was delivered back to his doorstep, dead, one of the first casualties of the war. Jack decided not to tell Kaye anything about it. More darkness on his soul, compromises made that couldn't be helped.

When Kaye didn't stir on the third day, Jack appealed to The Order for aid. They sent an angel by the name of Custo Santovari.

* * *

Kaye cracked an eye. The brightness of the room made her close it again. She had the weirdest sensation of being like dead weight, and yet strangely bodiless as well. She didn't like it, so she grunted.

"There she is," said an unfamiliar voice.

She wet her lips with a gluey tongue to answer, but decided talking would take too much energy.

"Kaye, can you drink some water?"

Hands lifted her into a sitting position. She begrudgingly opened her eyes. There was Jack Bastian, frowning as usual, and a strange-looking man—angel, if his perfectness spoke true, but with gray veins and an animalistic kind of intensity.

Bastian nudged her mouth with a glass, and just in case he tried to pour water down her throat himself, she took it from his grasp. Sipped.

"You've been out for almost three days," Bastian said.

She recalled the wraiths, the fight, her river of fire, and the overwhelming weakness that followed.

"I was tired," she answered. Still was. If they'd just leave her alone . . .

The other angel chuckled. "We've been steeping you in Shadow. You were completely spent, but we finally got some color back in your skin." The strange angel slid his gaze over to Bastian, then back to Kaye. "He was very worried you'd never wake."

Bastian's expression hardened.

The other man's face grew more mobile as he grinned hugely. "And he thinks you're pretty."

They had to be doing the angel mind-reading thing. Thanks to Shadow, her mind was her own. How did the angels stand it? And she already knew Bastian thought she was pretty, just like she knew he thought she was pampered, weak, and self-indulgent. So what? Maybe she was.

A muscle twitched in Bastian's cheek. "This is Custo Santovari, part angel, part fae. He opened a way to the Shadowlands and filled the room with its darkness. He brought you back."

That made her sit up straighter. The Shadowlands, or Twilight, was a legendary place among the mages. But the description of Santovari was even more surprising, "A fae who's an angel?"

"Not quite," Custo said. "I'm an angel first, with a fae trapped within me. I can't ever shutter my light, like Jack here, or the beast will take over. I'm more like a cousin to you mages."

Unbelievable. This man, this angel, had Shadow magic coursing through his veins. Weren't the angels bent on casting magic out of the world? "The angels don't kill you?"

"Oh, we want to," Bastian said. "Believe me, we want to. I'd do it myself with pleasure."

Custo ignored Bastian and furrowed his brow in concern at Kaye. "Don't get so close to the edge again. Burn your Shadow out, and you will die."

Kaye felt like she'd come close. Custo's tone made it sound as if he was leaving, but there was so much she wanted to know. She had so many questions.

"Do you have to go?"

Custo nodded. "It's not wise to have an unrepressed angelic light in this house. The mages will discover it and wonder."

The mages would know her for a traitor. Yes, he had to go, and right away. "Thanks for . . . everything." She wet her lips—still so dry. "And when you have time . . . if it's okay, I mean . . . I'd like to talk to you about Shadow and about the fae."

She had only what her father had told her to go on. He'd said angels would murder her if they got close—and she'd come into contact with two, and both of them had done the exact opposite. And now here was Custo, someone who was of Shadow and Order. It made no sense, and if she was going to do this mage thing, she needed answers.

"Absolutely," Custo said. "I'd like to learn something about magekind."

And then he shocked her breathless when Shadow pulsed and converged around him, as if summoned, and he stepped out of the world and into a realm of color and music that made all of her ache. Heart thudding, Kaye dropped the glass of water, drenching her lap, and reached after the velvety darkness, her core vibrating with longing. But as soon as the glimpse of Twilight appeared, it was gone.

She was left with a gnawing emptiness within.

"Don't worry," Bastian said. "It's always there, on the other side of the veil. Doesn't help when he keeps going in and out, though, and letting more Shadow into the world."

Kaye turned, furious and helpless at the same time. Tears welled and blurred her vision. "You couldn't possibly understand." It was Shadow, the *source,* it was the stuff in her blood, yet she could never, ever cross into it herself because she had no soul.

"I'm sure I couldn't," Bastian said, that all too familiar clip back in his tone. There had been a moment—had she dreamed it?—when he'd spoken to her differently. Like they'd finally reached an accord. She guessed she was wrong.

He turned and picked up something. "While you were out, this was delivered."

He held out a crisp, square envelope, an invitation. Kaye's name was scrawled in black, by a masculine hand. The seal on the envelope was broken, Bastian's work no doubt. She pulled out a white linen card, the words hand-lettered in careful, modern calligraphy.

> *Ferrol Bartholomew Grey*
>
> *invites you to a formal reception*
> *honoring the triumphant return of*
>
> *Kaye Ilona Brand*
>
> *January 12, 8:00 pm*
> *Grey House*
>
> *Shadow only*

"He's throwing you a party," Bastian said. "It's unfortunate that you're too ill to attend."

Kaye stared at the invitation. The dark lettering grew starker as she contemplated its meaning. Ferro Grey was throwing her a party. That had to mean that her show of fire had met with his approval. And now he was presenting her to magekind.

He was both her tormenter and her sponsor, but that was mage life for you.

"Oh, I'm going," Kaye answered, though the prospect sent terror screaming through her.

"You can't even get out of bed." Bastian rose from a chair at her bedside and paced the length of the room. "Count the days, and you'll figure out that the event is tomorrow and you're still as weak as a baby." He stopped and faced her, expression furious. "And you look like hell."

The man actually seemed worried.

"There's no choice here," she said. Bastian had to see that. "He's throwing the damn party in *my* honor. It would be an unforgivable insult not to attend." She pushed the wet bedsheet away and found herself in a T-shirt, not hers, and underwear. Fantastic. "The repercussions would be terrible."

Bastian leaned forward and grabbed the card out of Kaye's hand. "Look here." He pointed to a line on the card. "Right here. It says, Shadow only. Which means I cannot accompany you."

"I wouldn't want to take you anyway," she mumbled, trying a little weight on her legs. "I thought we already covered that." The shift to standing made her heart pound like a drum.

But Bastian was at her side, his arm under her shoulders. Solid. He smelled of sweat, as if he hadn't showered in days, but still, disturbingly, good. "He sent ten wraiths to test you. I'm not letting you anywhere near magekind, especially not when you're this weak."

"Bathroom, please," Kaye said, taking a first step. "I have a whole day to rest, but I *am* going. This is the opportunity you wanted for me to join Grey's circle, to gain his trust." She tried for humor, patting his hand when they reached the bathroom door. "You can come next time."

His body filled the door frame behind her, which he gripped as if he could hold his ground in the argument by remaining steadfastly at the threshold of the bathroom. His angel's light was still missing, but the glower of his frustration was just as intense.

She must have really scared him.

"Of course I'll need something to wear," she said to distract them both. And there was little time to have anything altered to fit. Shoes too. And jewelry.

"You don't have the energy to shop," he returned, biting.

Her heart had kicked up again, making her breathless, so she leaned nonchalantly against the counter. It was either lean or pass out, which wouldn't help her cause. She had the sense to lift a feminine smile. "I *always* have energy to shop."

His expression went mean. "What about fire?" He stepped inside, too close for comfort, and looked down at her like a bully, or a lover. "Show me a little Shadowfire to prove you can handle yourself."

She stuck up her chin, met his glare. "I'm pretty sure I've already proven myself. Or do I need to demonstrate one more time?"

Tension hung in the air. Bastian's jaw finally twitched and he stepped back. "You'd probably spend yourself again, and that wouldn't do anyone any good."

No, it wouldn't.

His gaze bored into her, and she knew the argument was far from over.

"I'll be out in a minute," Kaye said. When he didn't move, she added, "If you please?"

"God damn it." His ferocity made her drop her smile. The man was angrier than she'd ever seen him. Maybe it was better not to push just now.

Bastian turned and closed the bathroom door with chilling control, but his question remained. Kaye lifted her hand, palm up. She closed her eyes and searched for a spark within, sought a little heat in her blood, that dark twist of ecstasy, and pushed.

Nothing.

She tried again for Shadow, harder this time, made the room tilt and stars prick into her vision.

But still, nothing.

Panting for breath, Kaye dropped her hand to the counter and wracked her brain for what to do. It was as if she was fifteen all over again, and at a total loss. Bastian's opinion was clear.

She shook her head. No, that was not an option.

She had to attend, or she'd incur Ferro Grey's wrath. For all that he'd seemed so friendly at the coffeehouse, the mage had still sent ten wraiths for her to prove her mettle. Shadow bred ruthlessness.

Right.

There was really no choice, not unless she wanted to run away. Or hide among those self-righteous angels, a fate worse than death.

Her mind reached back to the suffocating press of power among the gathering of mages, the other ceremonies she'd attended as a child. The seduction of the darkness, the cruel illusions cast to trick and test and torment. She was a grown woman now.

She would attend her party, with fire, or without.

Chapter 5

Ferro descended the great hall's sweeping staircase while surveying the space below. Decorations were in place—candles and sconces everywhere, as yet unlit. Shadow roiled on the floor and gathered in the corners, whispering. At the turn, he caught sight of Alistair Verity, ankle deep in magic. Alistair was frowning into his jowls like a bulldog, his head thrust forward as if he were already refusing. The collar of his tuxedo shirt must have been strangling him.

Ferro checked the clasps of his cuff links; he'd dressed for the formal reception quickly. But no, he was ready, just nervous, a welcome jittery feeling in his belly. A little excitement for once. *Kaye.*

"You summoned me?" Alistair growled.

Alistair Verity didn't have the luxury of refusing. Ferro had a need; Alistair would meet it. And so it would be until Alistair's son took head of House, at which time Ferro would come to terms with him too. How else did they think they got the Florida Panhandle? And how did they think to keep it? The arrangement was very reasonable.

Ferro came to the landing and approached, his hand out to seal the bargain.

Alistair got red in the face. "You'll leave me defenseless."

"That's not true." Ferro pulled back his hand, soured. "I am your defense."

"Too much and you'll kill me."

"I'm careful."

Alistair spoke through gritted teeth. "You're a vampire."

Ferro went as cold as his House iron. He'd been called many things behind his back, all foul, but this—he breathed through his sudden anger—this he was going to like. If only he had that one vampire characteristic that eluded him. He'd regained his youth, yes, but immortality still escaped him. Vampire. There were worse names; he could own this one.

Besides, these days everyone loved vampires. Especially old ones wrapped in young bodies.

"That's why we're such good friends, Alistair," Ferro said, the rest of his ire evaporating. "You're all about the truth, while the rest of us stick to the Shadows."

It was a House Verity trait.

"This is against my will." Alistair Verity did not, could not, deceive.

"You'll of course be excused from the party tonight." Ferro made a beckoning gesture to hurry things along. "Your hand? Or would you like a fresh spot?"

He had to know if Kaye's intentions, however ambitious, were true.

Alistair's hand came up, an old circular scar at the center of his palm. Ferro moved quickly; she'd be here soon. He touched the Shadow setting in his iron ring on the spot and closed his eyes to conceal the eye-flickering rapture of Verity Shadow entering his being. Did it make him bisexual to enjoy Alistair so?

Bisexual was popular too.

Ferro opened his eyes, his gaze inadvertently on the man's jowls. No.

Alistair fell, gasping, to one knee, his hand smearing the floor with a streak of blood as he tried to catch himself from falling all the way. His resting position was not unlike the deep bow of a knight before his liege. Their relationship was not much different.

"Sir Verity?"

Alistair drew a shuddering breath. He seemed beyond humor just now.

"Do you want help leaving?"

"I want to kill you," he said.

A bright echo, like harmonics climbing a major scale, sounded within Alistair's words, and Ferro knew—*knew*—that what he said was true.

That was the power of Verity Shadow.

When the Bentley pulled up to the receiving portico at Grey House, Jack immediately slid out of the car. Though he'd accompanied Kaye in the backseat, rather than driving, they hadn't spoken since they'd left the house. She sat like a queen in her deep red slip of a dress and dark wrap, her gaze hard, jaw set, though her complexion lacked its customary warmth.

An attendant in Grey livery reached to assist Kaye, but Jack raised a *stay back* hand. No one would touch Kaye while he was present. And since he couldn't enter the main house—*Shadow only*—he intended to at least deliver her to the front door.

He turned back to the car to find Kaye rising gracefully into the night. He'd have preferred to help her, but as always, she didn't need anyone. She adjusted her wrap so that her upper arms were covered, but not her bare shoulders or neck. Her hair was swept up, her scars on display, which reminded Jack of the last time a party had been held in Kaye's honor, and how perilous that had been.

"Deep breaths," he said. He'd already given her instructions for the evening. Attaching names to faces, who spoke with whom, general dynamics of the group.

"I got it," Kaye murmured.

Why was he returning her to a world of danger and treachery? His mind fought with the question. His spirit rebelled too, straining against his control. But underneath the personal melee, he knew the answer—to discover the role of magekind in the wraiths' reorganization. Danger on the streets, power consolidating. If not Kaye, then who could discover what was going on?

She walked a step ahead of him, up the stone walkway toward the main door. The path was lit by fat, white candles, and their flames stretched at Kaye's approach. The sight made the tension collected in Jack's chest even more acute. The Shadowfire welcomed her. It leaped at her approach, a mage coming home. And the only solace he could take was that her power was returning. She would not be completely unarmed.

The arched double doors to the main house's entrance opened, though Jack and Kaye had several yards to go. Quiet within, but it was early yet. Ferro Grey himself came to stand in the doorway to await his companion for the evening. He wore a smart, trim tuxedo and a smile of anticipation. When Grey reached out *his* hand, Kaye answered with a reach of her own—pale, gorgeous skin, a band of diamonds at her wrist. They clasped, and Grey drew her to his side, twining her arm in his.

"You're breathtaking," he said.

Jack hated him.

"You're dashing," she answered.

Jack hated her too, until she glanced over her shoulder in farewell. Her face gleamed with its polish, but in her black eyes lurked terror.

"I'll be waiting," Jack said. He kept the words short, useful, but hoped with everything he was that she understood he would be near, straining for any indication of trouble. Nevertheless, the Grey House wards would prevent him from entering. She was all alone.

She arched a brow and replied with seductive mirth. "It'll be a long night."

Ferro Grey laughed as the doors were shut in Jack's face. And all Jack knew was that a bright light, not so different from a soul, had been swallowed by Shadow.

He knew on every level of his being that her presence in Grey House was wrong, the kind of wrong he'd dedicated his existence to fighting.

And he knew that he'd been the one to put her up to it.

Kaye stood at Ferro's side in the massive foyer of Grey House to welcome guests as they arrived for her reintroduction party, each mage in elaborate evening finery. French doors were open to both sides of them. The chatter of early party conversation was just rising, a girl with a low-key band crooning a jazzy version of that pop hit about Shadow. Deeper still into the foyer, another set of doors. More talk. A staircase swept up from the right. And if she went very still and listened very closely, she could hear the maddening undersigh of Shadow whispers.

"It's so nice to meet you," Kaye said, clasping hands with yet another guest. This one was furtive and nervous, barely meeting her gaze. His head was bowed, shoulders hunched when he took Ferro Grey's hand.

Ferro said only, "Arman," like a reminder, although

whatever business they had, it seemed to her that Arman remembered just fine on his own.

Kaye didn't want to know the particulars.

And yet, the jagged edge of the interaction was familiar. Everything was familiar. The party raised the sensory specter of her childhood: Candles covered the marble foyer tables, their flames flickering in a bouquet of fire. Tall floor sconces flanked the doorways, fire dancing there too. Those flames nearest to her brightened and stretched in response to her proximity, the shadows moving as if alive, layered and elemental.

In the open rooms beyond, the shifting glowlight promised more fire. Ferro was honoring her with her element everywhere. All this for her. What did he want?

She didn't have time to figure it out, not as the guests approached to greet her. Some faces she recognized, but it took Ferro's gentle, sometimes humorous, reminding to put a name to them. "Reynold Heist," he said. Then under his breath, "who cheats at cards." Her laughter was feigned at first, but after a while, begrudgingly genuine. How strange, and typical of Shadow, that she should laugh with Ferro and fear him simultaneously.

His presence at her side required each attendee to stop, take her hand, smile, and wish her well, a courtesy she hadn't expected. She knew that she and Ferro appeared to be a couple, which many remarked upon with a silent shift of their gazes, a question in the sly stretch of their smiles.

"Raiden Terrell and his son, Alex," Ferro said as a man stepped up with a teenage boy who stared openly at her cleavage, his face reddening.

"I'm very happy to meet you," Kaye said, remembering Raiden. "I think my father said you owed him money."

He winked. "Or was it the other way around?"

The boy's palm was a little damp.

And so it went on.

"Lorelei Blake," Ferro said. His mouth thinned as he regarded the tall woman in blue satin. "Don't touch her."

Kaye didn't take her outstretched hand, and the guest passed by, slighted.

"Why?" Kaye asked as she tracked her progress through the French doors and watched everyone curiously step out of the way.

"She's a lure. Her touch will make you want to follow her," he said. "Make you want to do as she says. One touch and her umbra will overtake yours."

Ah. A chill swept Kaye's skin. She'd been too long away from magekind and too sheltered when among them. And now she had to depend on Ferro Grey, of all people, for safety. The realization made her very uncomfortable. "Thank you for the warning."

"But of course." He turned to her, searching her gaze for something. He seemed earnest when he said, "I would never let anyone harm you."

"You are very kind." Kaye smiled warmly at him, thinking, *If he wanted me harmed, he'd see to it himself.*

The great doors to the house closed, shutting out the night. The guests had all arrived, and either lurked in the doorways, watching Kaye, or added to the rising din of the party. And under it all, those incomprehensible whispers, slithering over her bare skin to find her ear, yet only speaking nonsense. It had been a long time since she'd heard them, these almost imaginary friends of her childhood.

"I think we're done here." Ferro opened one arm toward one of the larger rooms; his other arm fitted low on her waist. "Let's get you a drink."

"That would be lovely." Though there was no way Kaye would be drinking anything. It was one thing to dull the edges on her own, and another to be careless around magekind, taking drinks from people who did not wish her well. She'd learned her lesson in Vegas.

Ferro led her to the first of the French doors, which opened to an enormous room. The ceiling was made of clear glass panes, so that starlight looked down on them. And tall candle pedestals stood throughout the space, waist level, so that no one could mistake the fire for mere lighting. Ferro was making a point, but to whom? The guests, who had to navigate the flames? Or to her, but why?

Kaye's nerve faltered when she saw the beverage of the night: Black Moll. The high alcohol content would spin any room, but its use was usually reserved for ceremonial functions. Only a drop had ever touched her tongue, when she was ten and Brand House had sworn fealty to Grey. She wasn't about to swear anything tonight.

She took a crystal goblet of the stuff, wondering what its purpose was here. More importantly, how could she get rid of it without drinking?

"So let's see some of that fire!" a woman called.

Kaye turned toward the voice, her heart leaping. Party talk lowered as her gaze swept the faces of those nearest to find the source. Beyond, the singer didn't miss a note, swaying on a raised dais before the band. A nearby group of people shuffled out of the way, looking over their shoulders for gossip.

"I want fire!" the woman all but shouted.

There. The woman wore a black evening gown with a concealed corset, its boning pushing up her blue-veined breasts. Black hair, black eyes. She obviously hadn't figured out that there was such a thing as too much black. Her mouth had the lines of someone who was disappointed all the time.

A goblet full of Moll and a challenge for fire—the moment couldn't be worse.

"Gail," Ferro said in warning.

The woman weaved forward, awkwardly dodging the lit candles, and the other guests backed away into a thick crowd to let her have her moment. Only those tall candle pedestals of fire stood between them.

"We're here," Gail said. "He made us all come." She swiped the air with her arm to encompass all the guests. She was a little drunk, must have started early. She forced her voice over the music. "Let's see what she can do!"

Kaye felt the other guests turn their eyes on her, expecting something.

"Gail!" Ferro was stern now. The song dribbled away to a lost beat on a snare. The room grew silent.

But Kaye would not have him protect her from any of them. Not again. It was too dangerous to be dependent. Dependent was stupid. Plus, she was a Brand. *A Brand.* She'd been taught since birth that her name meant something. Her name should command respect, not the derision of being challenged at her own party.

She had to answer, had to do something. Magekind was waiting. And how ironic that there was fire everywhere yet Kaye didn't have a spark to work with. Sweat prickled at her nape, but her heart kicked up to a vindictive rhythm. She knew the drill: Someone strikes? You strike back harder. Yes, she was home.

"Kaye," Ferro said, "simply ignore her. She's suffered some recent disappointments, that's all."

Ignoring Gail was the wrong thing to do. Kaye couldn't start by losing ground. Not to that weak woman. They were all insulting her. If she failed here, she'd be invisible. She'd be an outsider. No one would mention wraiths or anything important in her presence. Not to Ferro Grey's pet.

When was she going to be finished proving herself to people? Jack, then Ferro, now this? Enough.

"Well?" Gail said, lifting both arms.

First Kaye sent Ferro a narrow look: *I can handle myself.*

And he nodded slightly, a little amused, as if giving her permission to proceed.

She didn't need permission. But as long as she had it . . .

"You want fire?" Kaye asked. Anger laced her words.

"Bring it on," Gail said as if she knew Kaye was tapped out.

"Fine." Kaye held tight to the stem of her goblet, but she flung the dark, liquid contents toward the bitch. The alcohol skimmed the candle flames between them, igniting. And so with almost no effort, Kaye sent a fireball snapping through the air like a baby dragon.

Maybe not Shadowfire, but Brand fire all the same.

Gail screamed and ducked, shielding her head and hair with her arms. The fire didn't catch, but it must have singed, because Gail whimpered and sniveled, choking on cries, while holding shiny, chapped arms away from her body as if they hurt her terribly.

Kaye cast her gaze over the rest of the crowd, as if seeking another challenger.

No? Okay then. She put the empty glass on the tray.

She turned back to Ferro, whose eyes were lit with excitement and some other emotion she couldn't quite place. . . .

The party, the candlelight, the Black Moll. Then this bit of trouble. His turn. "Why am I really here?"

* * *

Jack stood across the street, watching the mansion from the cover of earthly shadows. The lower levels were obscured by distance, and foliage, and the tall iron fence around the perimeter. The upper floor's Tudor half-timbers and sloping attics were visible, massive wings falling back out of sight. He doubted that Kaye would be in those rooms. She'd be below, with the other guests. Among her kind.

And in his chest the urge to drag her from that place clamored like a devil. She was so close, but behind the House wards, absolutely out of his reach.

And yet he couldn't contemplate any other course of action. Her entrée into magekind was necessary. This party was ideal. And her connection to Grey, the emerging leader, was beyond fortuitous.

There was no turning back now. What had Kaye said? No way out but *through.*

A soft *pat* of a footstep sounded far behind him. Too far for human ears to pick up, and he was still supposed to be acting like a human. Wraith stink hit him next; two distinctly foul body odors. Still far off, only teased on the air. A scuff of a heavy step. Three of them? He had no choice but to stand and wait out the approach.

If it was bad out here, what was it like at the party?

What if one of the screams echoing in his mind should belong to her?

Finally, movement darted into his peripheral vision, and he backed into the street as a wary man might. His defensive posture was real, however, as was the pounding of his heart.

"Who's there?!" he shouted. Was this a random attack, or more? More.

A wraith finally emerged fully from the trees. He was built like a mountain, but dressed rich and crisp, rather than in the foul rags most wore. He looked newly made, which was impossible. The demon who'd created the wraiths had been killed a few years ago by Adam Thorne's wife, Talia. Either this one had had a plentiful diet of souls, or something even more foul was going on.

Jack thought of Kaye as he felt the other wraiths come up behind him, their stink wrapping around him. No human man could take on three at once, and few unarmed angels. Regardless, he had to remain passive or risk discovery, and then Kaye would be discovered too.

"We want you to deliver a message to the Little Match Girl," the near-human wraith said.

"Who?" Jack played stupid, but he knew the fairy tale. Knew that it didn't end well for the girl who saw visions in her fire.

"The message is for Kaye Brand."

She'd drawn more than Grey's interest.

"And that is?" Jack returned.

"She never should've come back," the wraith said. Part of Jack agreed with him. "She's to leave town and never conspire with the Houses again. The Brands are as good as dead."

"And if she doesn't leave?"

"Then the Brands *will* be dead. All of them. This is a mercy warning."

Mercy. Magekind couldn't fathom the meaning of the word. "Who do you speak for? Or does the mage cower in the dark?"

The wraith adjusted the neck of his coat, then threw a glance at his comrades behind Jack. "Explain it to him."

A blow to his spine sent him sprawling at the feet of the near-human wraith with a shock of starburst pain that blackened his sight for a moment. The roar and screams of the battlefield filled his ears—his mind didn't know what time he was in. Nevertheless, an answering tingle told him he was already healing. He found himself belly first on concrete. The wraith put a boot on Jack's already burned forearm, and Jack yelled. The pain of Kaye's accidental Shadowfire burn never subsided, and the wraith's pressure drove the constant sear to a blistering intensity until Jack heard the bright, hot crack of the bone, the second time in this life that it was broken. Another wraith kicked Jack hard enough in the belly to jackknife his prone body and make him cough blood. He panted in a loose fetal position and hoped the blood was enough to fool them into thinking he was human.

The pain would pass, he told himself. His body would heal. This was not the time to defend himself. He didn't matter at all in the great scheme. He had to let this happen.

"If she remains in the area, I'll feed on your soul and I'll kill her," the first wraith said.

"I could feed on him now," one of the others offered.

"Wouldn't send the same message," the first said.

"What's the damn message then?" Jack gasped from the ground.

"That this warning comes from a friend."

Ferro shut the door to his office, his mind racing to find the right words. Kaye Brand was a goddess—power, beauty, intelligence. She wasn't broken, as he'd thought all these years. One couldn't break a woman like her. If it were possible, the wraith attack ten years ago would've done it. But that violence had only made her stronger, and she'd been a child then. Look at her now, throwing fire in Gail Meallan's face. He about burst with pride to have her on his arm.

Kaye could have his children. He was sure of it.

The flames in the fireplace roared approval.

There was no better partner for him during the remaking of the world. None compared. And to think she'd almost been his. Brand fire, he'd known he needed it from the beginning.

Now all they had to do was trust each other, the reason he'd borrowed Alistair Verity's Shadow. Thus far during the party, she'd only delivered polite lies, revealed by an atonal dissonance under her *it's-very-nice-to-meet-yous*. He couldn't fault her for the lies of pleasantries and manners. He didn't like most of his guests either.

"I know Shadow is infamous for concealing true intentions," she began. The black of her eyes churned with temper. She wore a deep red dress that skimmed her body, dipping deliciously at her small waist, then loving her hips in a straight fall to the floor. Effortless grace. He'd marry her now if she'd say yes. "But I am more fond of light," she continued. "Why have you gone to this trouble, when you can't possibly want to give me a seat at the Council table? Why do you serve the Moll, when I will *not* swear my House to yours?"

Only an honorable woman would defy him to his face. This was love.

"You say you want to know my intentions." What a perfect opening. They were already working in tandem. "Then let's each make ours clear. Are you colluding with any other House or stray mage against me?"

She stood for a moment, unblinking, seeming to wrestle with her anger.

He stopped breathing in anticipation.

Then, "No, I am not."

Spoken with the harmonic of truth. She would be his, then.

But just to be careful . . . "Have you had any contact with magekind since you ran away at fifteen?"

"No." Not even the brittle delivery could mask her truth.

"Are you an agent of a human interest in magekind?"

"No." This said like the concept was beneath her. Amazing woman.

One last try. In her own words. "Why are you here, then? Why did you come back?"

Her lids lowered halfway, but her glare grew stronger. "I came back to see to and advance my *own* interests. Beyond that is none of your business."

Again, she spoke true. Finally—an upwelling of relief threatened to unman him—he'd found someone whom he could trust. A woman, and a formidable one. Her motivation was ambition, just as he'd hoped. And who better to further her interests than he?

Ferro grinned. Kaye Brand was the woman for him. He was in pursuit, and for once *felt* young again.

"Your turn," she said, low and silky. Dangerous. "Why am I here?"

He opened his hands as if he were opening his heart. "I'm courting you."

She flinched.

"I'd like you to be my lady."

Her expression went stony, emotion throttled. The flinch was more authentic.

"A feeling you apparently don't return." *Yet.* Maybe she'd heard the vampire thing. Or maybe the Black Moll had been overkill. But Moll was rare, and Kaye was rare—both full of Shadow. Serving it tonight had seemed symbolic, a tribute to her return, and to the start of their future together.

"You said you'd torn up the marriage contract."

"And so I did," he confirmed. This seemed a very important point to her, curiously so since mage children were raised not to romanticize marriage. Something important had to have happened the night Brand House burned. He'd never known the particulars, since no one but Kaye had survived. All was turmoil afterward. Mages who had gone to attend the ceremony were dead, the girl had disappeared. It was time he learned what had happened. "The contract does not exist. I would be happy to draw up papers to that effect, if it would ease your mind."

"It might." All ice. Yet the leaping fire three paces away attested otherwise.

"Consider it done." He approached her slowly. "Now tell me why."

Her gaze did not falter.

Neither did he. "Why does the contract matter so much? Or more specifically, why didn't we marry?"

"My House burned." A subtle dissonance there, so that wasn't the real reason. She was lying.

"Before that. Why did your House burn?"

A subtle shift and her expression likewise went mean. Her chest heaved slightly, as if she were aching for air. Certainly in distress.

"Let's have it." He tried to sound kind. "What happened that night?"

Her pretty tongue went to her upper lip, a little tell that she was thinking. But whatever lies she'd been concocting were pushed aside by the very old anger she'd held in check.

"What happened?" Her breath puffed out flared nostrils. "You gave me these scars," she said, turning her face slightly to the side so that her jawline shined, the scars going white. She didn't take her gaze from him.

The sound of truth in her voice meant she believed it.

The fire snapped and crackled, a violent sound. And he knew he was in imminent danger of being lit up like a firecracker. She'd carried this pain for ten years, hating him all the while. He didn't blame her; he'd seen a wraith at its prey before.

Besides, he liked the way she made his old heart pound.

"I wasn't even there." He tried to remain affable. He had to be man enough to stand her tempers if he hoped to have her. What would she be like in bed? He'd have to be man enough there too.

"Your sister, Zelda, was, in your name."

Zelda was supposed to have been his proxy in the ceremony. Ten years ago, relations between the Houses had been strained, everyone ready to put a dagger in someone's back. Each had been coming into the fullness of his or her Shadow. His aging had started to reverse, his own abilities heightening. It hadn't been the time for him to appear in the open. The alliance with Brand House first, via marriage, and subtle deals with others—Maya, for illusion, Wright, for the making of tools of power, Terrell, for storm—a consolidation of resources and strength.

But he'd always intended to be good to his young bride. Her youth was everything, just as her fire was now. He'd wanted the children Penny wasn't strong enough to bear. A girl of fifteen, and of fire, would have the strength Penny lacked.

"Go on," he said. "That day should've—*would've*—been the happiest of my life. What went wrong?"

Through her dark eyes swam troubling thoughts, formless thoughts, until her mouth took on the shape of a sneer. Her hands flexed at her sides. "I refused you."

Truth again. "You refused."

He took a moment to assimilate that information, while his heart went *flutter-boom flutter-boom.*

Of course she'd refused. Why did it make him happy? Because Kaye, child or woman, would never be malleable or obedient. It was a wonder her father hadn't warned him about the possibility for catastrophe when they had drawn up the marriage agreement. She'd probably burned her own house down in her rage. Breathless, he asked, "And then?"

"My father struck me."

"I'm sorry." And he was. No one touched his Kaye, not even her father.

"And your sister set the wraith after me." Her beautiful head, scars crawling, tilted to the side, a predatory, feline movement. "Which reminds me of a question I've been longing to ask these ten years."

"Go on." He gulped to find his mettle. Blood beat at his crotch. He wanted her. One hundred and two and he was getting hard.

"Why would she send a wraith, a soulsucker, after me?" Her next exhalation had the low quality of danger. "When we mages have no soul to suck?"

Ferro considered his answer. "I think, maybe . . ." And then he opted for only half the truth. Had Kaye been doing the same? Speaking half-truths? Troubling thought. Though . . . she had not hedged her answers at his most important questions—she was not colluding with any mage or human. If she had subtler interests, he'd simply have to learn them over time. The main issue was clear: she blamed him for her attack.

"You think what?" she prompted.

"I think that she was insulting you and therefore the Brand name."

Kaye's forehead gathered slightly. "Insulting, how?"

Damn Zelda. "By sending a wraith, she suggested that you were . . . *human.* Or no better than a human. Or not good enough for a Grey."

There was more to it, he was sure. Back then, Kaye hadn't yet manifested such a facility with Shadowfire. Yes, there had been confirmed passive signs of magery within her, not unlike the now quickening blaze in his fireplace. But nothing like the river of fire she'd created a few nights ago. Obviously, at fifteen Kaye hadn't finished developing her full adult power with Shadow. Likewise, she'd been rail thin, the awkward type. Even in photos—which was how he'd seen her—she hadn't seemed to know what to do with her elbows. Zelda could have deemed her power too weak. Yes, too close to human.

And for those House-born more akin to humanity than magekind, death by wraith was accepted practice. The Houses couldn't have any among their number who sympathized with humans, who, Shadow forbid, might even have a soul. They couldn't have that soul crossing into the Hereafter and taking mage secrets, willingly or not, to the angels.

A soul was a dangerous liability. A fatal liability. He was so glad that Kaye didn't have one. Her fundamental interests would always align with those of her kind. And now, soon, as fast as he could convince her, they'd align with his.

"I'm not good enough for your House?" Kaye held on to that insult as tightly as she could. She had to find a way out of responding to his declaration of interest, and "not good enough" seemed like an excellent way to be outraged.

The old man had asked all the wrong questions—because he feared magekind and humanity. One day she would laugh in his face and ask him, as if he were a child backed into a corner, whom did their kind fear the most? Who would gain the most from his House's destruction? Heaven. The Order. *Angels.*

She bet that he'd somehow found a way to divine truth from lie—an unusual property for Shadow. Bastian had warned her about that—to speak only the truth, unless absolutely necessary. They'd argued on a few points, specifically the truth that she hadn't wanted to marry an old man, but Bastian had been right. Truth had power. Lies got awkward quickly. And apparently, she'd passed the test. She'd kept only one thing back.

Because no mage, ever, had cooperated with angels. For a mage, it was beyond thinking. It was a betrayal of self. Heaven had no interest in the fae or its human castoffs, the soulless mages. And when magekind used its magic, vying for dominion over the mortal world, the angels struck them down again and again in favor of humanity. No mage colluded with the angels.

Yet here she was.

She'd come tonight expecting a continuation of the flirtation Grey had started in the coffeehouse, but she hadn't considered that his interest would be earnest. He wanted her to be his lady? Who said that these days?

"Zelda was a blind old woman," Ferro argued, "and while she acted on behalf of my House, she didn't act on *my* behalf."

"She was sent to say *your* 'I do.'"

"No." He shook his head. "She was sent for Grey House. She wasn't there for *me*."

Kaye stopped cold. His point went deep, and . . . hurt a little as it resonated within. The distinction between herself and her family had been the impetus that had started her nightmare ten years ago.

"I am not my House," he pressed. "Do you get that? Can you understand?"

She didn't want to, but his claim was too familiar to reject. She understood, and worse, she related. That conflict had been in her heart all her life. To discover they *shared* the feeling was very strange. To realize she couldn't blame him personally for the wraith attack was stranger still, because she couldn't—the whole arrangement had been House business. How surreal to see him morph before her eyes, not in appearance, but much more dangerously—in character.

"Kaye?" he pleaded.

"Yes," she allowed with difficulty. "I remember thinking something similar the night Brand House burned, about the difference between Kaye and Brand."

Did admitting it give him power? What was his power anyway?

He stepped forward, wary, as if taming a wild thing. "Kaye, I'm happy to help you reclaim the Brand seat at the Council table. Your power is too great not to have you among us, as you demonstrated so ably in your trial. There will be trouble with some of the other families, but that's to be expected. Eventually we will prevail."

It was hard to maintain her ferocity when his words were going in, not bouncing back. *The difference between Grey and Ferro; Brand and Kaye. I am not my House.* He'd support her bid for a Council seat. It was as good as hers.

Bastian's information on how the mages were using wraiths was essentially hers as well. What was the catch?

"And the old marriage contract is void," he continued. "I'll get you papers to that effect immediately. Because I don't want a marriage contract, an agreement between Houses."

Kaye braced herself.

"I want a *marriage.* I want a partner. I want a lover." His voice roughened. "I want a *wife.*"

She shook her head. "I'm not interested. There are many other prospects here for you tonight."

"You don't know me well enough to refuse." Under his control lurked harsh longing. "Give me a chance."

"I don't want a relationship. They just complicate things, and right now my life is complicated enough."

"Let me try. Let me take you out."

"No." She sold her magic, not herself. That was not the job.

"I swear I will harbor no expectations of a romantic commitment from you. I just want to earn your trust."

"That's not all you want."

"Your trust is what I want most. I will work for it. Let me work for it."

Kaye was so cold she was shaking, the air too thin for a real breath.

He wanted to date her. And that was just for starters.

His handsome face was a lie, so friendly, a little weary around the eyes. Most would think he was attractive, charming. She had to remember that everything about him was a lie.

Not everything, her inner voice said. *He is just a man. And he wants you. Use it.*

His face lit up, as if he had an idea. "Bring along your wraith fighter."

She startled. "Excuse me?"

"Your wraith fighter, from the coffeehouse," he said. "I'll need to take a wraith anyway, House security, so I want you to be comfortable."

She shook her head at the sudden absurdity. "So our date would be a party of four, including my bodyguard and your monster?"

He grinned. "If you'd like."

Kaye was momentarily speechless as a vision of their group eating popcorn at a movie flashed in her mind. In the vision, Bastian watched her with hot eyes.

"How's Tuesday?" Ferro asked carefully.

She came back to reality and shook her head. "I have a client that night."

"Ah." He seemed stricken, disappointed, as if her answer had been a version of "I'll be washing my hair."

Don't lose this chance, the inner voice said. *There may never be another. He's met your demands, and then some.*

Costs too much. And a seat on the Council is not what I really want.

Then why are you here?

She remembered the feeling of Michael's angel light behind her as she'd fled the cellar to save her own skin. And no one was selling her this time, either. This was all her decision. A little merciless maybe, but she was a mage after all.

Right. Deep breath. "I'm free Wednesday, though."

The light flashed again in his eyes. "Wednesday."

"This is not romantic."

"Not romantic," he agreed. But he couldn't have been smiling wider.

"And I'm not touching any Moll."

"Certainly not," he said gravely. "Foolish of me."

Charming. She arched a brow and played a slow smile of reluctant humor across her face, as if amused. Inside, she was breaking into pieces.

He offered her his arm, the old-school gentleman. "Shall we, my lady?"

Chapter 6

"A meeting with Grey?" Bastian said. "Why didn't you tell me this before?"

"You were too busy going on about someone beating you up," Kaye said as she took a sip of her coffee. Dark goodness. She was sure coffee originated in Twilight, which was why the world was so mad about it. Funny that it was Bastian who made such a mean cup of something so seductive.

She watched him unpack a bag of supplies, just delivered, including medical tape, a plastic arm brace, and what she thought was a sling, though it was only folded cloth right now. "I thought you were all better."

Last night, after accepting a light kiss from Grey, she'd summoned her car to leave. Bastian had been hunched in the backseat, blood all over his shirt and dried on his cheek and neck. She recalled the surge of fear and concern—a sickening combination—that had shot through her. He'd told her to get in quickly, and only when they'd departed did she understand that he wasn't hurt. Or not anymore. That the blood was left over, and that he was whole and well. She'd gone from panic to anger as he delivered his message from the "friend" who wanted her to go elsewhere and leave magekind alone, lest she meet the same fate as the Little Match Girl: death via burnout.

"Yeah, but your 'friend' doesn't know I've healed," Bastian said. "If they'd hit me in the face we'd be in real trouble. I'd try makeup, but it'd have to pass close inspection. I doubt we could approximate swelling. More likely, you'd just get another angel to watch over you."

Kaye chuckled. "I'd like to see you in makeup." But really she was relieved he hadn't been hit in the face. She didn't want anyone else. She needed someone hard behind her, like a wall she could trust at her back. And Bastian was cold and implacable; he might get beat up, but he would always stand. And the Little Match Girl thing had scared her.

"When is your meeting with Grey? You have a client this evening." Bastian pulled off his cotton T, right there in the kitchen, which made Kaye grin into her cup in spite of everything.

Bastian's stomach was flexed, muscles delineated. He had the kind of body hair that speckled across his chest, concentrating between his pecs, then thinning to a line that disappeared at the end of his ribs, only to reappear at his belly button, leading straight down to the fastening of his pants. The sight made her happy for some reason. Bastian, half naked.

Threats seemed very far away in the kitchen of this house, with him near.

He opened the tape and started to wrap his torso, and she had to wonder for whom he planned to remove his shirt. Was this attention to detail necessary? Not that she was complaining.

"The meeting with Grey is tomorrow night," she said, watching the left-right flex of muscle with his circular motion. "He'll have a wraith present, and I'll have you."

She really didn't want to think about Grey's intention to court her, so she concentrated on the aroma of her coffee, the warmth of the mug in her hands, and the man in front of her.

"Where, damn it?"

His mood was foul, however.

"All I know is he'll pick us up at seven," she said. "He's planning the evening's activities."

Bastian frowned, cutting the tape and tucking the end under one of the bands of white. "That's not an appointment."

"It's a date." She had to force the last word out of her mouth. "He wants to court me. He talked about us trusting each other, getting to know each other."

"And you're going along with it?" Bastian's motions started to get sharper, brusque. He attempted to start on his forearm, but the wrap wouldn't stay put. He needed two hands.

"You're the one who suggested that I use the marriage contract as an opening." She put her cup down and took the tape from him. "Let me do it."

"I'm rethinking that strategy," Bastian said, holding out his arm. "The salve first."

Salve? For a fake injury? Kaye turned his forearm slightly and saw a large wound on the underside. The blistered white and red flesh screamed pain. A burn. She flushed when she realized that she'd been the source. Had to be. And she remembered when: the night of her trial, on the steps, with the wraiths surrounding them. "I'm sorry," she said. "I wasn't careful."

"It's fine," Bastian grumbled, clearly angry at her.

But when she looked up, it wasn't quite anger she saw in his expression. The air was hot around him. Between them.

Her mouth went dry. "Why didn't you heal rapidly from that too?"

"Shadowfire," he said, by way of explanation. "It was an accident. It doesn't bother me."

Words collected in Kaye's mouth, but she was too ashamed to sort them into the right order. Truth was, she'd taken his well-being for granted. Her childhood was riddled with stories of the strong and terrible angels. Bastian had been beaten brutally, but the one hurt that remained, she'd given him.

"I don't want you dating Grey," he said. "It's too dangerous. I was wrong to suggest the marriage contract was the way to go."

"Means to an end," she said. They both knew it was too late to back out. She was right where she needed to be. So she spread salve on the wound and wrapped his arm carefully. Tucked the end of the cloth. All the while breathing in his smell, feeling the air beat between them. His head bowed over hers.

"Revenge?" he growled.

Yes. And no. "I don't want to run," she said carefully, without looking at him. "And that's all there is left. I have to be strong among them. Magekind is my world. I've always known it. And they trampled on me."

She had to be inside Grey House for good reasons.

When she was done with the bandage, she glanced up at him while reaching for his shirt to help him on with it. Buttons meant he had to flex that wrist and arm. "Can I . . . ?"

She stalled midmotion.

Bastian still looked down at her, and the slight reach transmuted to a different, deeper movement. She was pulled beyond the blue-green-brown flecks in his eyes into a fuzzy, dangerous space, a pocket in the universe they'd made by accident. Particles of energy zapped between them, and she knew if she stepped closer, the particles would accelerate. They'd been reaching like this for a while now.

"You're shorter," he said.

She liked his mouth so much.

"I'm not wearing heels." Didn't need to around him.

"You have to get out of the date," he said, his voice getting lower, his expression hard. Her Bastian, begging.

He really needed to put on that shirt. Even if it hurt.

It was everything Kaye could do to wrench her gaze away. "You know I can't."

The trouble with being an angel on Earth was that he was still a man.

He got hungry. He thirsted. His lungs clamored without the draw of air.

And for this woman, the only one in a thousand years, his body and soul ached.

The trick was to will his mind to ignore the Earthly sensations, as he'd done so many times with pain and trouble. Desire was no different, a call of the flesh. He could divide himself—acknowledge the lust, but act on intellect.

But see, the trouble with being an angel was that he was still a man.

The receptionist at Kaye's client meeting opened a set of double doors and stepped back for Kaye to enter what appeared to be a large conference room. Four men and one woman dressed in smart, expensive clothes gathered at one end of a long, narrow table. They represented the partners of Ballogh & Johnson, a law firm specializing in international trade. Something about the group reminded her of dark birds with sharp beaks.

Bastian entered behind her, and when the partners' gazes fixed on his cast, his arm in a sling, Kaye explained neatly, "Wraith."

One of the men circled the table, his hand outstretched, but before he reached her, Kaye continued, "I only see clients one-on-one. The rest of you will please leave."

The man slowed while she spoke, then resumed, undeterred. "Yes, of course. Horace Ballogh"—he gestured to the patriarch of the group—"will be having the actual session with you. But first we were hoping you'd answer a few questions about your services. About Shadow."

"I'm not here to educate," Kaye said. Talking about the nature of Shadow with a human was too dangerous.

The man opened his hands. Friendly. "We only want to know how the session works."

"Mr. Ballogh can describe it to you after," she answered.

The man didn't waver. "The future is the specialty of your House, is it not?"

Oh. This was a fishing expedition. Goody for them that they knew about the Houses—the knowledge would either save their lives during the turmoil to come or end them sooner. The future, however, was not her specialty—that was only good for humans and no help to magekind at all. Shadowfire was her power. But she still wasn't going to correct him. "Either I begin now, or I leave."

"We have clients interested in making a deal," he said, ignoring her once again, "similar to the one Urlich made with one of the Houses. Can you facilitate the contact for such a venture?"

So they knew *of* the Houses, yet were not in contact with any. The arrangement with Urlich? She had no idea what he was talking about and didn't want to.

She smiled. “I’ll reimburse your fee.” Then turned to Bastian and said, “Let’s go.”

She stepped forward just as Bastian moved to the side to let her pass, and they almost collided. The sudden close proximity sent an electric current zapping between them. They’d been doing this awkward dance for the past two days. You first. No, you. It was driving her crazy. Him too, if she had to guess.

“Ms. Brand,” the man said behind her. “Forgive my questions, please.”

She turned, waited for his cooperation.

“We’ll leave you and Mr. Ballogh alone immediately.”

“Thank you.”

The room cleared as she and Bastian approached the old man, who had seated himself at the far end. He had sparse white hair, a quaver in his swollen joints, but his eyes were sharp. His gaze flicked to the side of her face, then back. “Ms. Brand.”

Bastian placed a timer on the table at her side.

“Mr. Ballogh. I’m going to cast a fire and hold it in my hand. You have no reason to fear; I’ll make certain that it doesn’t burn you. Look into the fire, and you will see a vision of a possible future. I cannot interpret it for you. You will have a full ten seconds. My associate will start the timer on my mark. Do you have any questions?”

“Yes,” he said, direct and certain. “What is Shadow?”

Kaye looked the wily old man in the eye. “You’ll know the answer when we are finished.”

She closed her eyes to search for the spark in her blood. And felt it answer in a shock wave awareness of Jack Bastian’s presence, just to the left and behind her, his banked light simmering on her skin. She flushed against the surge of coarse desire for him, for his touch and his strength and the soul in his eyes, and pushed the feeling into a molten bloom on her palm. She cracked her lids to find the Shadowfire had flared to life and danced in an erotic shimmer before her. Her eyes filled with tears at its beauty; they soon skated down her cheeks, only to get caught in the riddle maze of her scars.

Nothing ever felt so good, so why, *for the love of Shadow,* did she want more?

"Magic," the old man said, answering his question.

"Yes," Kaye said, with the last of her breath. She paused, then ground out, "Start the fucking timer."

Bastian reached around her and the sensations intensified. *Beep.*

Figures were already appearing in the flames. Kaye prepared herself for an advance preview of the world's destruction—the desolation, the collapse of buildings, the furtive misery that would be this man's life in the years to come. But the Horace Ballogh phasing in and out of the firelight seemed calm, wealthy, salting his dinner at a table laid with good food. The dinner guests were scattered at intervals around the table, but there were blurs of darkness warping the vision at the empty chairs, especially the one on Ballogh's right.

Beep.

So Kaye knew his future, even as she fisted her hand and killed the flames. Unfortunately, her clenched hand didn't kill the fever inside.

She knew Ballogh would find the Houses he sought. Why did that frighten her?

"What was that?" he demanded, standing. His hands were trembling harder.

And she knew he would make a deal like that Urlich the other lawyer had mentioned.

"Fifty thousand dollars to see myself at dinner!"

"Looked delicious," Kaye said, also rising. And in an

undertone, “Bastian,” to signal the time to leave. She wanted to be out of there. Get her out of there.

“I demand another,” Ballogh said.

A steady hand on her elbow. Safe. A one-winged angel at her back.

“You know where to reach me,” Kaye answered as Bastian escorted her toward the doors. She had a lot to think about.

The blurs around that dinner table, the dark warp in the empty seats, could be only one thing. And considering the pointed questions of her client’s partner today, she knew exactly what the visual “absences” had to be.

Mages.

With the exception of herself, she could never see the futures of mages in her Shadowfire, and today was no different. Not that she would inform her client what he was missing when he looked at his future.

But the mages were there, in the warp of darkness and fire. She was sure of it.

And they were cutting deals with humankind.

Horace Ballogh stilled his quavering hands on the conference table. He wanted a cup of tea but was too preoccupied to walk to the conference door, open it, and ask. Shadow—the word had confounded his team. It was used in too many contexts and ways for him and his colleagues to reliably define, until now.

Shadow was magic.

Magic was real.

And that woman with the scars could wield it—though there was nothing dark, shadowy, about *her* magic. Horace could still see the flames, though the woman had left.

The trembling that had beset his hands these last few years now spread to the rest of his body.

Houses? He still couldn't define that one. Were they political groups that controlled different kinds of Shadow? Or was Shadow more of a genetic trait? House, meaning heritage?

The door opened, his partners reentering for a report.

There was only one recourse left. He didn't have to like it. This was survival. The paradigms of the world were shifting, and only a few were privy to that knowledge. The masses would be crushed under such power—Shadow—but he would not be among them. "Make the call," Horace said.

"Don't tell me you believed her," Linda said. "She's a fortune-teller, a scam artist; she's supposed to be persuasive."

"Men like him will burn in Hell," Mark added, referencing the person Horace wanted him to call.

Horace put a shaking hand over his face. He'd been involved in some unpleasant business over the years, hence his connection to Urlich, but magic, Shadow, fire—that Horace could hire Ms. Brand in the first place, take a meeting with someone like that—meant that he was probably too late to the game already.

He looked up at his partners. Still saw the wild fire. "You don't understand," he said. "The world is already burning. Make the call."

Jack kept close behind Kaye as they headed for the elevator. He considered the details of the meeting and the thoughts he'd fished out of the lawyers' minds. Yes, they'd paid for Kaye's services, but they were really trying to network with the mages, an ignorant, foolhardy endeavor at best. They had no idea whom they were meddling with.

The known interaction between magekind and humanity had just ratcheted up several notches. Even Kaye seemed unnerved. "Terrible place."

The word *Houses* used in this context was like a pebble hopping down a dangerous mountainside; soon awareness would avalanche, all eyes would turn in fear or awe toward magic, and its reemergence would demolish the current structures of government and order. He'd seen it happen before. In five years, what would the world look like? He already knew from the visions in Kaye's fire.

He'd lived it before.

Jack turned to the fast *clack* of female footsteps.

. . . message for Ms. Brand . . . From the receptionist's mind, he got a quick flash of a delivery boy, as well as her signing a clipboard. "This came during the meeting."

He and Kaye had to have been followed to the appointment. Someone was tracking their movements, which was expected, but still of concern.

"Thank you." He took the envelope and stepped inside the elevator. The doors closed, and he handed the missive to Kaye.

She opened the flap, pulled out a card, and after a moment looked up at him. "Hirshhorn Sculpture Gardens."

Jack frowned. "It's a couple blocks from here, toward the National Mall. Mage?"

"That's my guess. It's not signed. We have a thing about names."

"You're getting popular." Magekind was eating her in one big gulp.

"That's the point, right?" She looked at the card again. "We don't have to go. It could read like a summons, which I would ignore."

He smiled at her temper and felt a little better. "Or the mage could merely be cautious." Which meant a possible connection, possible information. And it was highly unlikely it had anything to do with Grey.

She sighed. "All right. But I'm not dressed to fight wraiths." Her dark gaze darted to his arm. "And you still look too busted up for anything athletic."

"Well, they'd better not try me." *You can, though.*

As they moved briskly through the lobby, he was aware of angels at a distance forming a lookout. The driver had the car waiting outside. All very quick, very efficient.

"Interesting vision," Kaye said once she was settled inside the backseat with Jack. "Mr. Ballogh was having dinner with mages—we just couldn't see them. I'm sure they were there."

"We've been tracking suspected human-mage connections," Jack said, thinking of Urlich. "But none lead directly to a House. If humans are negotiating deals, they're buffered from the real identities of the other side. Grey knows that The Order will suffer no mage dominion of humanity."

And Jack was there again, creeping through a wood toward a clearing. Sacrifices on dark altars to the fae on the Other side for more power, more Shadow, more seduction. Daggers of black. He'd been focused on human thoughts, so when the wolves jumped him, ripping his flesh, he fell.

"I'll mention the vision to Ferro tomorrow night. See if he says anything." Kaye looked worried. "Though it'll do no favors for Mr. Ballogh."

"Ballogh and his partners are actively looking for trouble anyway," Jack returned. The past and the present weren't lining up right for him anymore. It was all a jumble. And the war was beginning again. "We need the information. The sooner this is over, the better for all involved."

The car traveled a few long blocks and slowed to a stop at 7th Street and Jefferson. The evening was overcast, the colors of the buildings, streets, and trees creating a drab pall, which made him uneasy. They walked the half block to the opening that led them down into the sunken garden. Bronze sculptures, most anthropomorphic, stood at easy intervals, their patinas darkened to graphite black. They passed a naked woman, arms extended. Two modern seated figures. The human forms all seemed alive, yet trapped in metal skins.

Kaye, gleaming in the sullen air, peered at the art as they strolled down the pathways, her lips parted in wonder.

Though the space was enclosed and landscaped, it felt eerie, bare vines crawling the white walls. And though the cloudy sky cast no shadows, darkness pooled in every corner and under each statue.

An angel communicated, *Two soulless just ahead of you.*

Mages were here. Of course they were. It was he, the angel, who seemed to be trespassing in this little bit of their world.

They approached Rodin's *Burghers of Calais,* a gathering of six life-sized men, each with a somber and defeated aspect as they walked to their deaths.

Before the raised area of these statues, two black-eyed mages stood—an old man in a wool coat and scarf and a young one in only a jacket—awaiting their approach. Jack flexed his hands to keep himself loose. The Shadowfire burn seared.

"I'm cold," Kaye said to the elder. "But I like this place."

Which didn't surprise Jack. It was melancholy and beautiful.

"I like it too," the older man said. "I feel a little stronger when I visit."

"Seems like there's Shadow in plenty here," she answered. Jack agreed. "Maybe we can linger for a while."

She tilted her head in his direction. "This is my associate, Mr. Bastian. He's human, but loyal to me."

Yes, loyal. He would keep her from harm, if she'd let him.

The old man's eyes crinkled. "With your beauty, any man would be loyal. Even an old one."

"I think we're going to be friends." She shifted to the younger. "You have the same eyes. Grandson?"

"Son." The young man's short delivery was less flattering.

So, of course, she switched back to his father and his compliments. Jack almost laughed at how predictable she could be.

"Your wife is a lucky woman," she said warmly.

"Have you made an arrangement with Ferrol Grey?" the young one said.

A soft warning from the elder. "Marcell."

Kaye bit her lip, looking closely at the old man. "I don't recall meeting you at my party."

"We weren't invited," he said. He held out a business card. "Sigmund Lakatos."

Kaye took the card, glanced down at the text. "House Lakatos?"

"We were forced to disband," Marcell spat. "We're all that's left."

Jack wondered what form their Shadow talent took. Lakatos. Locksmith.

"We were once loyal to your father. The mages of Brand House were our patrons. But when your House burned, we fell on hard times." Sigmund didn't look well. "And times have only become more difficult."

She glanced back at the young one, Marcell. "Then you're astray?"

Jack had encountered this once before, ages ago. When

a House grew weak, its numbers few, they lost status among their kind. Their House would not be recognized until they reclaimed power and prestige, as Kaye was now doing for Brand. The remaining members of a fallen House were considered stray, again as Kaye had been for the past ten years, and were often preyed upon in the mage world. Occasionally, a stray made other arrangements—by marriage or indenture—to be absorbed into a greater mage Household.

"I'd rather die," Marcell said.

Rather die than what?

Sigmund cleared his throat, but it still took him a moment to speak. "We would be open to discussing an arrangement."

Marriage? Poor Marcell, Jack thought. He could never hope to match Kaye Brand. He had to have known that the moment she came around the corner. This was as close as Marcell was ever going to get to ecstasy.

Kaye was silent a moment, then, "You honor me."

Her way of saying no.

"She's in with Grey!" Marcell said. "He threw a fucking party for her. What do think she's going to do with us?"

"She's just being cautious, son."

Not as cautious as Jack would like.

She grinned at the old man. "If *you* were fifty years younger—"

"Grey is more than thirty years my senior," he said. "But that is not what I am suggesting. I've come to—" The man halted briefly as he lowered himself awkwardly to his knees, then looked up with respect and deep sadness at Kaye. "I've come to beseech Brand House to take us in once again. We would serve you faithfully, as we did your father, and add our wealth to yours." A rueful smile. "Triple your numbers."

Shadow thickened on the pavement, smoking at the old man's knees. His expression was resolute and proud. Tears streaked down Marcell's angry face. He fell too, but he wouldn't look at Kaye. His head was bowed and turned to the side.

Kaye stared, fixed in horror. She suddenly came to and reached forward to help the old man up, but Jack grabbed her arm and held her back, kept her on her feet, so that she wouldn't touch either Lakatos. Could be a trap.

So many traps.

"Get up," Kaye said thickly. Jack still held the balance of her weight.

"We have a facility with locks," the old man continued. "We can get you in and out of anywhere, a talent—"

"Get up before I throw up."

Jack could feel her shaking. This was not what either he or Kaye expected. Clearly they hadn't thought matters through well enough. They knew Grey's patronage would make her a target for suspicion, even violence. But this?

"The Dark Age is upon the world," the old man said. "Please. We need your fire to protect us."

"Well, with your talent, rob a bank and set yourself up," Kaye returned. "You can fend for yourself."

Jack had to say something. "Or try to earn an honest living." Always an option.

Sigmund ignored him. "The world doesn't have that long, and you know it. A House is refuge from the coming storm. Heaven itself will fall on magekind while the flood of Shadow drowns humanity. Take us in and Lakatos can be strong again."

Very clever, if desperate. If Grey were joined to Brand, and Kaye had taken these two under her wing, then the Lakatoses would go from outcast to inner circle in one deft move. They would indeed be saved by her greater strength.

The Houses had to know this. Others would follow. Or act to stop it.

"I can't," Kaye said. She'd regained her balance and taken a step back from the pair, up against Bastian's chest. Her scent, especially here, ensnared his mind. Why fight it?

"We're yours," Sigmund said.

"No." She shook her head. "I don't want you. The weak are meant to die."

Her voice was so cutting that not so long ago Jack would have bought it. But this was the same woman who had dared to offend Ferro Grey to protect Jack, her angel employer, an angel she loathed. She was lying, hardening her heart with a show of cruelty. And now Jack understood where that came from as well. And that it was a lie.

Because she'd never be so weak as to feed these men false promises, not even in return for information. If Bastian were to suggest she use the Lakatoses to glean what they knew about happenings within magekind, he knew she would tell him to go to Hell. She would not endanger them if she could help it. But she couldn't take them in either.

"Let's go," said Kaye over her shoulder. To Sigmund, on his knees, "Don't approach me again."

Jessica Becker saw the red-haired woman turn her back on the kneeling old man, a young man bowed beside him. Manners urged her to hurry forward and help them up—her mom would expect her to—but she'd promised her dad that she wouldn't go out alone anymore. Not even in the middle of the day. Not even for a class project, even though her grade depended on it. She hesitated, clutching her charcoal pencil, as the younger man helped the old one stand.

The whole thing was weird in the first place. Did people

actually kneel before other people in this day and age? Would she ever have to kneel to someone? The thought made her tight inside.

She watched as they followed the walkway back to the stairs. Waited for them to go, the sculpture garden growing colder by the moment, then whipped her sketch pad shut, her drawing of the Maillol nude forgotten, and hurried away herself.

Chapter 7

A white gift box was delivered to the house first thing in the morning. Jack signed for it and turned to find Kaye descending the stairs, curious. She wore a deep blue silk robe, belted around the waist. No cosmetics. Her thick hair was sleep wild, the whites of her eyes red; he hoped not from drink. She hadn't wanted to talk or eat after her encounter with Sigmund Lakatos and his son.

Now she looked vulnerable and soft, the woman who saw visions in fire. He had his own vision of himself drawing her close, parting that robe to look upon, to stroke, to feel the weight of her breasts. His face would go into that hair and he would go mad for a little while. He was half mad already from his long service. And in a wilding part of his mind, he was beginning to think that maybe the advent of Shadow on the world wouldn't be so bad. Because Kaye was of Shadow, and if her blood pumped that dark stuff, then maybe a reckless world would have its own glories.

She held out her hand. "I'm guessing that's for me?"

A tag on the lid was addressed to the Little Match Girl.

"Let me check it first." Jack brought the box inside and set it on the kitchen counter. It was shaped like a pie box and had a sturdy lid, which slid off easily. Inside was a photo album covered in cartoons of fairies with wands making magic.

Jack opened the cover. Yes, the album was for Kaye. The very first picture showed the death of Mr. Hobbs, her last client in Las Vegas. He appeared to have fallen from a great height, crushing the windshield and hood of a car. The mess of his head and face made him near unrecognizable, but his name was scrawled in the memory lines to the side of the photo.

Jack turned the page and discovered how Max Hampstead, the Wake Hotel's owner, had met his end too.

The rest of the pages were empty . . . no . . . they were waiting to be filled. Another threat.

How many clients had she seen since then?

Eight. He needed to find out who'd hired the delivery service and if possible discover where the album had been purchased and, even more unlikely, by whom.

"Well?" she mocked from her position leaning in the kitchen doorway. "Is it deadly?"

Jack closed the book, not trusting himself to speak without revealing the depth of his rage.

"Yes," he answered with forced calm. "It's poison."

Kaye sat at a spindly antique desk in the living room, her head bent over a paper, but her eyes not focused on it. It had been a couple of hours since the package had arrived. She'd dressed and set herself up to work but still felt as if she had a hot coal burning in her belly. A couple weeks ago she'd seen Hobbs's death in her fire. The thought that she had inadvertently been the cause made her feel red inside.

The Little Match Girl. Yeah, the story applied to her, though she hadn't heard it since she was a child. It was an old-fashioned tale: The Match Girl had been sent out by her father into the winter chill to sell matches and feared returning home without any money to show for the day. She'd lost her shoes and had finally huddled in an alley using her matches' fire to keep her warm. And in the tiny flames she'd had visions—though the girl in the story had seen only good things—while she'd slowly frozen to death.

Not all fairy tales ended happily ever after.

Kaye was afraid.

"Are you in the mood for a visitor?" Bastian asked, coming into the room. He was using his efficient voice, so she knew the package still bothered him as well. He'd reminded her that the Match Girl had been defenseless and friendless, both of which Kaye was not. And then he'd even tried to make a joke about her being far, far from penniless, which wasn't the case for the Match Girl.

But all Bastian had accomplished was to make Kaye want to rest her head on his chest, just for a little while. People had died because of her. And she was caught up in a story of ruin. She knew it would end in fire.

She'd been trying to concentrate on a list of House names. Most were familiar, but she could remember little about which ones Brand might have been doing business with when she was young. Her father had told her next to nothing.

She set the paper aside. "Who is it?" Pretty please someone she could fight. She had to have a clear head for her date with Ferro Grey tonight and she was nowhere near it now.

"It's Layla Mathews." Another strange note in his voice.

"Who—?" Then Kaye remembered. *Layla*. Had to be Khan's woman, the one Bastian and his fellow angels had tried to kill once upon a time. The human who'd inspired Death to love.

Yes, Kaye wanted to meet *her*.

Bastian must've seen her interest because he scowled. "Her car's coming up the street."

Had to be the angels' telepathic network again, which she imagined was like birds hanging out on telephone wires watching the world below them.

Kaye stood and smoothed her slacks, grateful for the distraction. She needed distance from the knowledge that two people she'd known, however horrible they had been, had died because of their association with her. Were more to follow? The thought strangled her. Did she dare strike any more matches?

A black sedan pulled up outside. A woman got out of the driver's side, light brown hair whipping over her face in the wind.

"No security," Kaye observed to Bastian.

"Oh, she's secure," he said. "I have no doubts about Khan."

The bell rang as Kaye was already opening the door.

Gray eyes, like a cold breaking ocean. Sweet narrow face, hair settling in a mess of layers. Trim black coat, gray fitted skirt, black skinny boots with a nice heel. But nothing so outrageously remarkable to be paired with *him*. Khan's Layla was . . . human.

Layla's eyes sparkled with a return appraisal. She grinned, which transformed her plain features into unrestrained humor and vitality, and the force of it smacked the breath out of Kaye. She was transfixed, as if gravity were stronger immediately around Layla's person.

"Well, you look fae, that's for sure," Layla said. "Which is to say, gorgeous."

"You've seen the fae?"

"I have," Layla said. "And you're a mage?"

"Yes," Kaye answered. She finally remembered to close the front door and then led Layla into the living room. "I'm sorry. None of the furniture is comfortable." She looked over at Bastian, who was still so angry. "It's his taste, I'm afraid."

The tension tugging at his forehead eased a fraction. She didn't want to think about how she knew the increments of his moods. And how she'd like to smooth her thumb over that last forehead wrinkle.

Layla settled onto the hard sofa. Rocked her hips back and forth slightly, as if seeking a soft spot and finding none. Then she too looked over at Bastian. "Cozy."

His tension cleared entirely for a moment, almost a laugh, and then he was back to his stony self.

The smile Layla got from Bastian made Kaye like her immediately. "How can I help you?"

"I want to learn about the Houses, specifically how to get an audience with the Council."

Kaye went very still inside. "I understood Khan wasn't interested in magekind."

Her heart thumped as she considered the ramifications: He who used to be Death leading a magekind army. The angels raising their swords to defeat them, only *this time* to be struck down themselves. Magic would win. Heaven would fall. The world would go dark and the mages would rule forevermore. It was the mage fantasy.

"Khan isn't involved," Layla said, sighing. "He remains firm about that. He will not cooperate in any way with The Order. Nevertheless, Segue's primary research focus is Shadow, its denizens, and their relatives. We'd like to begin a dialogue with the mages."

Kaye shook her head. This was crazy too. "Um . . . I'm not on the Council, and my relationship with the other Houses is nonexistent."

"Can you tell me whom to contact?"

"No, I can't." Layla asked the impossible. "Naming a mage is punishable by death. Not to mention, it would endanger the work I'm doing, even if you kept your source a secret."

"But I have it on good authority they're reaching out to high-profile people already," Layla argued.

"As usual, Segue is never far behind The Order's intelligence," Bastian said dryly. "But Kaye is right. For her safety and yours, she can say nothing. Rest assured, however; I'm certain that the Council will turn its interest to Segue. They can't allow an independent organization to delve into the secrets of Shadow that they've carefully protected for so long. My guess is that you can expect them soon. But they won't come to chat."

Layla's gaze went steel sharp. "Then how can we prepare ourselves if we don't know how they are organized? How they work? How can we avoid a conflict?"

"Conflict is inevitable where the mages are concerned," Bastian said. "Take your personal history, for example—Khan created a gate to *Hell* to get what he wanted."

Layla leaned forward, expression sharper. "And why did he do that?"

"For you."

"No." Layla shook her head. "He did it because there is only one place among the three worlds where he and I can coexist. Earth. Here, now. The mortal world is the only place where anything matters, and every living thing knows it. And yet, the fae and The Order won't recognize their common interest. I'm guessing the mages won't either. And humanity is only semi-aware of the crisis. Soon it will be too late. It might be already. Khan has told me this: There is no way to stop the flood of Shadow now. The world is changing, and everyone will change with it. Magic is here to stay."

Kaye smiled halfway. "In our storybooks we call it the Dark Age."

Layla cut her gaze to Kaye. "I'm sorry if providing me with a name endangers you, but I need it anyway. There must be some kind of dialogue, even if it's just between humanity and the mages. The Order can go to Hell."

"Your judgment is clouded by your past history," Bastian said coldly.

"No, my judgment is clouded by my pregnancy, the life I carry, the future." Layla jabbed a pointed finger at Bastian. "*You* are the past, dead, just like the wraiths, but you just don't stink as bad."

Bastian looked aghast, which almost made Kaye laugh out loud. The expression was so foreign to his face.

"On the other hand, Layla," Kaye said, shrugging, suddenly feeling amiable, "maybe you and the Council *will* get along. Just lead in with that last little bit about the angels being dead."

Bastian stood, his chair cracking to the old wood floor. Where was his sense of humor?

"I'd like to point out," Kaye said, "that it's the firemage in this room who has the cool head."

"I need a contact," Layla said, apparently not amused.

Kaye sighed. "Khan will protect you?"

"You were hired for a job, Ms. Brand," Bastian said. She liked when he got that uptight tone in his voice. Made her want to mess up his hair.

"Khan will not let anyone harm me."

"Unbelievable." Bastian brought his hands to his head as if to help his brain.

Kaye ignored him, observing to Layla, "You realize you could start a war yourself, and so very easily."

"How?"

"Well . . . let's say you misspeak; then the mages will strike at you, Khan will strike at them, and magekind in force will then try to take down the baddest motherfucker of them all, lest they be under his absolute rule."

"But you don't fear Khan," Layla said.

"Why should I? He likes me." She glanced over at her angel; their gazes caught. "He loathes Mr. Bastian, though."

"Whom do I contact?" Layla pressed.

"He will punish you," Bastian said to Kaye. His voice was rough with feeling.

"Who will punish her?" Layla asked.

Kaye was stuck on the intensity of Bastian's forbidding expression. He should learn to give her a little credit—she wasn't going to actually say a name. It was a farce that the three of them should be in a room together—human, mage, and angel. The Dark Age was coming. Kaye and Bastian had both seen it in her visions, so Layla was right. The only thing Kaye could do was what she advised her clients: change the future by taking a different course. Her photo album required it. Besides, one day she just might want to make Segue her real House. Didn't hurt to help that along.

"Give me your card," Kaye said to Layla. "I'll see that the man in charge gets it."

"And who is this again?" Ferro asked, his fingertips turning the card over and over, as if it were of no interest to him at all. Just Kaye and the reason she'd handed it to him.

He wore a dark suit with a touch of luster to the cloth, the collar of his white shirt open. He seemed to be going for a young Hollywood look, the flawed, sweet "every guy" so popular in romantic comedies. But he actually skewed more pretty-faced horror. Fine line there. There was a menace beneath his surface; he was too still, too mild about the Segue business card he now held.

Which was why Kaye found herself leaning back against her seat, closer to Bastian, who stood behind her. If Ferro was a strong forward current, taking and pulling and wanting, Bastian was an anchor, keeping her steady. If Ferro was cold iron, Bastian was light—and she needed very much to stay warm.

"Ms. Mathews works for Segue," Kaye said, picking up her fork, "and she wants a meeting with the Council of Houses."

Ferro had gone trendy and expensive in his choice of restaurants, the kind with a celebrity chef who served dollops of deconstructed whatnot alongside her branzino.

"Why would you be speaking to a human about the Houses?" A kind, baffled smile.

"I told her nothing, merely accepted the card," Kaye said. "You said you wanted to earn my trust; well, how about you start by trusting my judgment."

It was brazen to challenge him, but more dangerous to show weakness. She took a bite and tried not to swallow the mass whole. Ferro Grey would probably take her apart bone by bone for pushing him so.

"Segue," Ferro said, sliding his gaze up to where Bastian stood behind Kaye. "I've done some checking on you."

Kaye's heart stopped, but her mouth didn't. "As long as we're on the subject, one of my clients also inquired about contacting the Houses. Wanted to make a deal. That's twice in as many days. It is not *I* who is indiscreet." Another small bite. Swallow. She went for it. "Word of the Houses has gotten out, and since hundreds of years have gone by since magekind moved in the open, I can only conclude that that public knowledge of the Houses is deliberate. I'd go even further"—now she was really going to die—"and guess that *you* are behind it. What's going on?"

Ferro pressed his lips together, considering. Then his

eyebrows darted up in a facial shrug. "We are going public." He set the card aside. "It's happening more quickly than I'd like, but there it is."

"Public how?"

"Very carefully." Ferro covered her hand with his. Possessive. He still wore that ugly iron ring. "Take your business, for example. You cater to only clients who can pay. They witness great power in a controlled environment. And they are left desperate for more. That is the reason you've been allowed to continue. It serves the Council's purpose. Power. Discretion. Yet aloof."

How did he know the way she worked?

"Your approach is exactly in line with my own," he continued.

"In all honesty, I'm more mercenary." She didn't want to be in line with him. "I didn't seek to further the Council's ends, just my own."

Ferro smiled, handsome. "And now that I've put in my sponsorship of your bid for a seat before the Council?"

She affected an avaricious kind of smile. "You did?"

"Your interview is tomorrow."

"So fast?"

"Well, I do sit in the big chair." He withdrew his hand and picked up his fork. "Would you like one by my side?"

Kaye's head swam. She had to force herself not to look behind her to gauge Bastian's reaction.

"Is the chair's location a condition of regaining a seat on the Council?" She had to ask.

Ferro actually looked hurt. "No." He took a bite. Swallowed. "But I hope that soon you might consider my company bearable." He paused again. "I'd like to make you happy."

"You can't fault me for being on my guard."

"No," Ferro said. "I remind myself of that fact every

minute or so. A formal arrangement would be easier, I think. House to House. But I don't want formality."

Kaye remembered: He wanted a marriage. A wife. Was that so bad?

"And yet times are changing quickly," he continued. "We've just met, I know, but I'm giving you all you ask, and as quickly as I can make it happen."

"I'm new and shiny and you decided you wanted me on the spur of a moment," Kaye countered. "Because you don't *know* me at all."

His voice was low and harsh when he answered. "I know enough. One look and I desire. One conversation and my mind quickens. One show of power and my ambition is satisfied."

Such passion, yet all Kaye felt was Bastian at her back. He probably had that impassive, stony look on his face again. The one that hid his thoughts. What would it be like if she could make the angel desire, quicken, and be satisfied? But Bastian couldn't be seduced and he sure wasn't interested in her ambition or her House power. All those he treated with contempt.

"What if I'm a romantic?" she tried, lightly touching her chest.

"You'll find I've got a heart too," Ferro said, too serious, "and I would be more than happy to dedicate each beat to you."

Damn. She looked away, searching for a way out of this conversation. "I'm not ready for this. I've had two death threats recently."

Ferro followed close behind her shift in conversation. "Come live at Grey House. There will be more danger. I can protect you."

Apparently every topic led to a union between Grey and Brand.

Kaye used the opening to turn and look at her current protection. Bastian didn't even flick a glance down at her, but his jaw was tight, hands clasped in front of him.

"I'll make a bargain with you," she finally said, turning back around. "How about we have a pleasant evening, and I'll agree to consider your proposal, but for now we leave it at that?"

Ferro smiled slightly. "I'm still going to try to hold your hand later."

Kaye smiled back. That would be fine.

"And I've been practicing a deft move to get you into my arms."

The smile on her face faltered.

He must have taken her expression for encouragement. "And you'd better believe that every second I'll be calculating how and when to kiss you." He speared another bite with his fork. "But by all means, let's leave off and have a pleasant evening. How's your fish?"

The driver sped them home. The wet night rushed by the slick windows, but all Jack could see was the moment Kaye's hand went up to the back of Ferro Grey's neck as she returned the mage's kiss. A glare of headlights, and Jack saw Grey's arm around her waist, the forward list of her body. The press of their mouths.

Jack couldn't breathe.

The ten seconds had lasted ten minutes. Ten hours. Would be in his mind for ten years. At the very least.

Kaye did her job too well, but Jack couldn't blame her for it. He'd set this in motion. What did that make him?

A kiss today, deeper tomorrow. How long before she was in Grey's bed?

Jack's chest, lungs, heart, shoulders ached viciously, but

from no wound or magic. Not the Shadow kind anyway. Kaye was strong and fast and agile, but it was still miserable not to be able to protect her from Grey.

Jack couldn't even look at her, though she sat three inches to his left. And there was nothing to say. *It was just a kiss.*

Like hell. If Jack had done the same, it wouldn't be "just" anything.

The car stopped in front of the town house. Jack got out and held the door for Kaye. She brushed by and left the lingering scent of Twilight in her wake. The wet night misted around her, like steam to her fire. She was doing her goddess thing, above it all, untouchable.

When she'd just. Been. Touched.

Just.

He was strangling with the little word.

The house was dark. He slammed the door behind him.

She flipped on the entrance hall light. Took off her coat. Put it over her arm. Regal. Her act. Liar. Couldn't believe a thing the woman did or said.

Her mouth was moving. ". . . suspend meeting with clients . . ."

But the sounds were warped. The tilt of her face shifted slightly this way. And slightly that. Her tongue artfully shaping sounds that made no sense.

". . . can't very well continue when . . ."

She tucked a curl behind her ear.

Just.

". . . for a little while . . ."

Touch.

". . . not when Ferro . . ."

And then Jack was kissing her. Because she couldn't say that name again, not one more time tonight, or tomorrow, or ever again, in his presence. He had to kiss all knowledge of it out of her and leave nothing but himself behind. He was a moth to her flame and he didn't care.

His hands gripped her upper arms, but when she opened her mouth under his, her body saying yes, he made a grab for all of her. Hauled her up against the wall.

He trapped her there, his hand at her breast, his tongue rasping against hers, wild and wet. A bolt of lightning heat went through him, as if God struck, but Jack held on to Kaye and for once refused to care. His groin beat dark and needy, while he gripped the fabric of her dress and ripped because he couldn't begin to think about zippers or buttons.

He felt a flutter of movement at his waist. Her bare hands found the skin at his navel. And he made an inhuman sound of longing.

She pulled out of the kiss to *shhhh* him, comforting, while she stroked and peeled off clothes to get them closer. Coat. Suit jacket. A tug and yank at his shirt.

"I'm here. I'm yours," she said, answering the need he couldn't have put into words if he'd tried.

But he had to know it. Needed to prove it. Had to kiss her more deeply. More absolutely than any before.

His shirt opened and the skin-to-skin contact darkened his mind. Mouth to neck. Kisses to breast. He ripped cloth as he went down to his knees, his mouth claiming. He stroked that waist, circled the knot of her belly button. He found a band of lace across her pelvis. His hands were busy, so his teeth yanked downward at her underwear. Above him, she cried out. Then his tongue found a paradise all Kaye in scent and taste.

Her hands were in his hair, trembling. Her legs parted; heeled shoes kept her way up high. He gripped her perfect ass. He was determined to get a real reaction out of her, a response she couldn't fake. A kiss that truly claimed.

She gave a high sound, as if afraid, but he held her and

wouldn't stop because she was everything he wanted, all his lives, forever. Shadow could have him at last. He used his teeth and tongue and mouth, angry and hungry, to consume her until her body acknowledged with deep, surrendering shakes that she was his.

When he stood again, he was shaking too. Tears had left pink trails down her cheeks, but he didn't care about that either. Her eyes were wide and bright, breath still coming fast. Her exposed body was glorious.

"I love you," Jack said, the taste of her still on his tongue. He finally sounded like himself. The himself from eons ago, and not the soldier he'd become.

"I know," she answered back. "I didn't know what to do when he kissed me."

"I do. Burn him," he bit out. "You're done with this job."

Her head dropped to his shoulder, and the abrupt ecstasy of holding her in his arms knocked the breath out of him.

"I can't quit," she said to his neck. "I've been caught in this all my life. I have to be done with it. I can't just run. Not anymore."

"You're fired then." He turned his face into her hair. Tightened his hold because she felt so right.

She laughed weakly against him. "You're missing the point."

"I think you are."

"Are we going to argue?"

"No more Grey," Jack said again, pulling back to find her eyes. That one thing had to be clear. "And I'll protect you from the rest."

"No more Grey," she repeated. Promised, and he'd hold her to it.

"All right then." Jack picked her up and threw her across his shoulder. *Mine.* She shrieked and laughed a protest, but suddenly he had the strength of a hundred angels, though he wasn't quite sure if he was one anymore.

A hand at her ass balanced her weight. The other tamed her kicking legs. Faker. He carried her up the stairs to her bedroom. He'd have dragged her to the closest soft surface for what he wanted next, but she was right: the couch was as hard as hell.

When Bastian tossed her onto the bed, Kaye had a pang of worry. She was molten with need, had been wanting him for so long now, but . . .

"The angel thing?"

His beauty was beyond human, beyond her race even. There was something old and frightening in his eyes, but she couldn't help the way she needed him. She was greedy, desperate to lose herself, to be consumed by him, her enemy, her lover, dangers ignored for lust. Magekind would kill her if they knew. And yet, there were a lot of ways to die. She figured riding Bastian into blind ecstasy was as good a way as any.

A swift movement, and he dropped his unfastened shirt onto the floor. "What about it?"

"Are you going to Hell for this?" Though that might have been okay with her. She was burning; why shouldn't he be too?

"For loving you?" His pants and underwear dropped simultaneously. He was huge, straining skyward, the sight forcing her to squeeze her eyes shut because she couldn't find the will to shift her gaze.

"Yes," she said. But maybe Hell was just fine for both of them. "I can think of only bad things I want," she confessed, a little miserably. "Real bad."

"Good," he said, stroking a hand up the inside of her calf and higher. "I've got a few in mind myself. First up, torture."

He flipped her over. She turned, willing, shaking in anticipation, arching her hips for him. She was wired, ready, tingling for the sense of fullness pushing inside her. Bastian was exacting and thorough in everything he did. She was counting on it. Panting for him.

His hand found her sex, and she ground herself into him, encouraging. But instead he kept his palm there, hot, pressing, claiming. Then with his other hand, he began a deep massage of her thigh, her hip, the small of her back. She strained her hips to tell him what she wanted, to make him feel the wetness of her arousal, but he kept his hold firm. And then continued unlocking the tightness of every strand of muscle. His assault was devious: This was no sleepytime massage; she was aware of every second that his hand was at the juncture, hot and sure. If he'd but massage just there, she would shatter. "Please," she begged.

"Not on your life," he ground out. So she knew that he was tortured too, that his hand was keeping him from his fulfillment as well.

She writhed against the bed as he stroked her back, her shoulders, her neck. And the second she started to relax, he flexed the hand between her legs, teased his fingers against her swollen flesh. Had her trembling with need all over again. She was limp and blind for a release that had been stretched and folded over and doubled. Never had she wanted so much. That hand, her punisher. Her severe angel, schooling her in patience while he coaxed her inner burn higher and higher.

She was all sensation when he finally shifted. Time ceased to have meaning. His mouth grazed the slope of her neck, his breath arousing goose bumps down across her skin. She was lost in a red haze. His body slid over her, hulking behind her, his heat seeping in to feed hers. That hand on her hip, a touch and she arched, couldn't help it. Her body obeyed him now.

He entered her slowly, setting each nerve flaring, and then seated himself deep within. She'd forgotten to breathe, so it came in chokes and gasps for air. He surrounded her, his chest to her back, arms braced near her shoulders so that her world was him and the bed and sex. And when he began a relentless motion, an unhurried stroke that took her over and over, she gripped the top of the mattress and knew that he'd go on forever. He knew forever. And it was wonderful and terrible. Ecstasy.

Only when she wept did he move faster, and each time they locked together she cried out his name. A small shift, his hand again between her legs, his mouth at her ear. "I've got you," he comforted, then stroked and thrust and the world came apart as she shuddered with pleasure in his arms.

Her vision was bleary when she finally became aware of the bed, of him holding her, still deep inside. And she was glowing like smoldering coals in a fire. He'd done this to her. She turned in his arms and found an expression of fierce satisfaction on his face. He knew no man had come close to finding that kind of pleasure and possession with her.

She pushed him flat on his back and could see her reflection in his eyes. The flame straddled him, took him inside her again. His vision went cloudy. Her breasts peaked and he reached up to cup the undersides with his hands. She rolled her hips, went hazy herself.

And applied the lesson he'd just taught her.

Chapter 8

"He's not going to try anything," Kaye said as she watched Bastian pace in front of the bed. He'd put on his pants, but not his shirt, and his muscle-defined torso was flushed with his argument. She, on the other hand, was being very reasonable from within the tangle of covers. "And if I can get on the Council, then I can get our information. I hate wraiths." She paused for effect. "*Hate* them."

"But I can't be there." Bastian halted before her.

She loved how his shoulders flared when he had his hands on his hips.

"I can take care of myself." She'd only said so fifty times since dawn. "It's just an interview. And then I'll say I have a client and come right back here. We can have dinner at home. I'll even cook."

His expression went deadpan. "You can't cook."

"I'm going to learn," she vowed. She might even go into a grocery store. It would be fun. "And I'll start tonight. Will you still eat it if it comes out badly?"

Bastian moved fast, crawling onto the bed, forcing her onto her back. His weight was pure pleasure. She couldn't stop smiling.

"You make me dinner, and I'll eat every bite."

Her body was going warm again, and considering the look in Bastian's eyes, his must have been too.

"Our first date," she said. "Everything will work out." Hope was making her dizzy.

"I don't like this," he said. "I've had reservations about this assignment for a long time now."

"It'll be over soon." She didn't want to think about or ask what would come next. Would Bastian go back to his Order? Would she be left to her clients? But she wouldn't ruin the moment. Because she was happy. Truly happy. For once.

"And then what?" he demanded, asking that very question.

She shrugged, as if the future didn't matter. "I was thinking of Segue. Making it my House."

Bastian's jaw worked with an internal conflict. "Do you think they'd have room for an errant angel? Adam might take me in, but you said it yourself: Khan doesn't like me."

She couldn't help the burn of tears in her eyes. "If they don't have room, we could go somewhere else." She choked on a laugh-cry. "I have a little money coming to me." The Order's money. "We'd be all right. We'd make our own House."

"Together, yes?" he demanded. "Forever."

She was too full of tears to answer, so she nodded her answer. They'd probably fight every day, but she would never ever be afraid again.

"And you'll call me Jack?" His eyes crinkled as he smiled.

Kaye shook her head no, and pushed through the sobs to answer. Because he had to understand this. "You're Bastian, because you're my safe place. My stronghold. My bastion."

What a House should be.

His crinkles smoothed as he put his forehead to hers. "I guess I can live with that."

Jack had to let her go again. A few more days, that was all. Every moment carefully played. A reward like no other when the mission was completed.

Though he'd warded his thoughts during his time with Kaye, still the angels knew that his loyalties had shifted. He was no longer a servant of Order. Or not only.

His superior, Laurence, had been summoned. Probably an intervention was planned. To save his soul?

He'd already given it away.

They would claim Shadow madness.

He'd embrace that too.

And he'd counter the rest of their arguments with one single truth, a constant, a creed: free will.

Kaye Brand, fire goddess, Shadow mage, was his.

Just a few more days . . .

"Ms. Brand, the Council is ready for you," a stocky troll of a man said. He opened the great door that led to the Houses' meeting room.

The fire was snapping within Kaye, and every nerve in her body felt wonderful. She'd worn a serious suit, fitted, a sapphire blouse, the most conservative ensemble she had.

Bastian had only rolled his eyes and said, "Nice try," for which he'd gotten a kiss.

Kaye had been picked up by a car late in the morning. The backseat windows had been blacked out, so she'd had no idea where she was going. The drive had lasted hours, and then she'd been led, blindfolded, into a cold, echoing building. She was permitted to refresh herself with a light lunch, beautifully prepared. She'd retouched her hair, drawn away from her face so that her scars were clearly visible, proof that she had no soul. Ready.

"May Shadow be with you," the troll man said.

She strode through the oversized door and into a cavernous, long room, concrete and windowless, like a bunker. Shadow was thick here. She was glowing, and she knew it. Dark tendrils kicked up around her ankles with each stride, crackling with magic.

At last she reached a long, wooden table, situated perpendicular to her advance. Nine mages sat along its length, both men and women of the Houses, all with black eyes. Ferro sat at the center; his chair was indeed bigger than the others'.

"Good morning, Ms. Brand," Grey said.

"Ferro," she returned in greeting.

From the darkness at the side of the room, a wraith emerged, metal folding chair in hand, presumably for her. It was an insult, so she dropped her purse on the seat and resolved to stand.

Which made Ferro grin. He liked her when she was difficult. She intended to be exceedingly so.

A woman spoke from the end of the table, Martin House, if memory served. "Kaye Ilona Brand. We are gathered today to hear your petition for a seat on this esteemed Council. What say you?"

Her father had never taught her any special words—never taught her anything important—so she addressed the group with basic formality. "Council of Shadow. Fire has always been represented among the first of magekind. I have ably proven to be a master of this element, rivaling even my ancestors of old. I come to claim my father's seat once again for Brand House." She hoped that would do the trick.

"Will any among us sponsor this request?" Mage Martin asked. She was from one of the war houses. This had the sound of ritual.

"Aye," said Ferro, loud and clear. "Grey House sponsors Brand."

"Any dissent?" Mage Martin prompted.

"Aye," answered the rest of the group in chorus.

Kaye let her gaze slide down the row of mages, meeting the gaze of each, and awaited the first of their questions.

"Ms. Brand," the head of Webb House called out. The Webbs were storytellers, their power rumored to be subtle but unmistakable. "I say your House is dead. There is but one of you. One mage, however strong, does not make a House."

"One is a beginning," Kaye responded. "I intend to expand my numbers as Nature and Shadow permit."

Ferro was gloating. He must have thought she referred to bearing his children, as was intended by her father. The thought of herself at fifteen, given over to an old man, made her shiver again now.

"There is also the matter of your practicing fire in the presence of humans without dispensation from the Council," another said.

"A mage has to make a living," she answered. No apologies. "And I make an excellent one."

"And what about your association with angels?" Arman Maya asked. Illusion, if Kaye knew her names.

The question struck Kaye like a blow. Bastian. How could they know?

"I'm sorry, I don't understand," she said. Which was the truth.

"You have a worrisome connection with the Segue

Institute," the mage continued. "Your bodyguard hails from there and you had a guest, one Layla Mathews, visit your residence and even ask about this Council. We've since discovered that Segue is associated with The Order."

"I don't know anything about that." True, again. And a relief. This was about Segue.

"We could question her bodyguard," Ferro said, smug, as if he'd been waiting for an opportunity.

"I trust Jack Bastian implicitly," Kaye answered coldly, as if to say, *This is as cold as our bed will be if you cross me.*

Ferro sighed. "Well then, the Mathews woman." But the look in his eyes said that he was not finished where Bastian was concerned. "She wants to meet us anyway. We could question her . . . at some length . . . thereby sending a message to the Segue Institute at the same time."

Kaye chuckled, and the sound echoed weirdly in the Shadowy cavern. "You don't want to do that either."

"You protect this human as well?" Ferro asked, her sponsor now the inquisitor.

"By all means, bring her in," Kaye said. "Just make sure your House business is in order because you will not leave this room alive."

"You threaten us?" The Martin woman again.

"Not me, no." Kaye raised her hands to ward off any involvement. "But her . . . uh . . . significant other will undoubtedly take offense. I suggest that you agree to meet with Ms. Mathews and that you are very polite with her."

"Why?" Ferro asked. "Who is this fearsome 'other'?"

Kaye wondered what she was doing talking about Khan. Not that he or Adam Thorne or even Jack Bastian had prohibited it, but merely thinking about him too much seemed dangerous.

If she was going to die, she might as well be thorough. "A few weeks ago a pureblood mage by the name of Khan approached me with a job offer and a welcome at Segue. He wanted me to work with him there. His power is controlling life and death, which he said he would employ on my behalf. In his fae incarnation he was the Grim Reaper."

Silence.

"You lie," Martin spat.

"I have Verity's truth," Grey said, proving Bastian right. Grey had been testing her. "She believes everything she says."

"Layla Mathews is his human lover," Kaye finished. She smiled for her summation: "I got the distinct impression that he won't allow her to be harmed. Your call, of course."

"A pureblood?" Mage Martin gripped the arm of the mage to her left. "Shadow is rising at last!"

Ferro leaned forward. Kaye couldn't read the strange expression on his face. "The pureblood wanted you for his House?"

"Something like that," Kaye answered. Her clout had either just soared or plummeted.

"And you had the gall to refuse this most frightening mage?"

By now Ferro had to know something about her gall.

"He understood my preference for independence." Kaye opened her hand to concede. "But the offer remains open."

Ferro looked like he was about ready to climb over the conference table to get to her. "Tell me everything you know of him."

Soared then.

Kaye shifted her weight. Locked her knees so they wouldn't shake. "My shoes cost a small fortune, but they aren't comfortable while standing for long periods on concrete." She flicked her hand downward. "And this chair isn't to my liking."

"The pureblood," Ferro urged.

"A chair," Kaye answered back. She knew an opportunity when she saw one.

Ferro's gaze burned cold and black.

"Arman," he said, not taking his gaze from Kaye's. "Please offer Ms. Brand your seat."

"I will not," the mage responded, his fist thumping the table.

"Now. And drag it round the other side so that we may see Ms. Brand while she gives her testimony."

The silent rebellion lasted less than a minute. The chair, intricately carved, beautifully upholstered, was brought round. She seated herself, crossed her ankles, and angled her legs to the side. Arman returned to the table, then stood in his spot, like a placeholder.

Too bad, she had the chair. She wasn't giving it up. Ever. Five minutes and she was seated at the Council.

Then she began: "I know that Khan created a gate to Hell, now destroyed. I know that The Order massed against him, and even attempted to kill Ms. Mathews. Ms. Mathews herself went so far as to liken angels to wraiths in her one conversation with me. Something about both already being dead, and that Shadow was the future. Khan hates the angels, so if Segue has some relationship with them, it is unlikely to be a peaceful one."

Truth again. Adam Thorne must have to negotiate those interactions very carefully.

"A gate to Hell?" one of the mages asked. "Is it even possible?"

"It's said when Death was fae, he fought at Heaven's wall."

"Why does he not challenge the Council for a seat himself?" another asked. This mage flicked a glance at Ferro

Grey, who would have to cede his own chair to the greater power, Khan.

"My impression," Kaye answered, "is that he is uneasy with this world. He said he is not interested in magekind." He was not interested in helping The Order. "It's *Ms. Mathews* who desires a dialogue."

Ferro didn't look the least bit appeased.

Jack could almost feel the progress of Laurence as his superior navigated the freeways and thoroughfares and side roads to the town house. Jack kept his own mind locked down; his thoughts were full of Kaye, echoes of seeing her beneath him, the sound of her pleasure, the things he'd whispered into her ear. These memories were so much better than the others that crowded his head.

He'd made his decision.

Nothing Laurence could say would sway him.

Now if only she'd return, safe and sound.

A car door slammed outside, and Jack went to meet the argument head-on. He waited in the open doorway, then closed the door behind Laurence after he entered.

"This isn't necessary," Jack said as Laurence divested himself of his coat and slung it over the banister.

"I've been called," Laurence responded. "And by no less than fourteen of the angels assigned to Ms. Brand and her protection. Reports indicate that you've been compromised."

"I love her," Jack said, and realized he sounded like a boy.

"I've known you for how long?"

"Long time."

A sense of swift movement. A clash of blades. Breath heavy, uneven. A friend at his back.

"And you've never weakened to sentiment." Laurence was smiling. Why was he smiling?

"I'm different now," Jack said. "Everything's different."

"That it is."

"So what are you going to do?" Angels sometimes married. It wasn't uncommon, and then there was Custo, living in sin with that ballerina while they planned a wedding.

"I'm here to save you," Laurence said.

"I don't need to be saved." Jack stepped back from Laurence for the first time. He'd fight him if he had to. Jack had dedicated his existence to The Order for lives upon lives. This one life was for him.

Laurence instead strolled into the formal living room, sat in a chair, leaned back, pretended to be at his ease. "Damn it, Jack, nothing so terrible."

"Then why are you here?" Jack demanded, following.

Laurence lifted his gaze. His eyes were sad. "Because I think very soon you're going to need a friend."

"What do you mean?"

"Nothing with the mages ends well. I hope this does, would love to see you happy as you haven't been for an age, but I don't trust it."

"You don't trust *her*."

"More like I don't trust Shadow. If you love Kaye, she must be extraordinary."

"I do and she is."

"Which is why I am here. Because eventually—and I don't know how or when—this love will break you, and I refuse to let Shadow squander your soul."

* * *

"You'll kindly take your hands off me," Kaye said. The interview was over, the Council members departing to confirm, scheme, and wonder at the news that a pureblood, and a dark one, walked the world again. Only Ferro Grey remained, and he was rabid. He'd pushed her into a dark corner and spoke in strong whispers.

"Why didn't you tell me about Khan before?" he demanded.

"I know how to keep my mouth shut," Kaye answered. "I didn't give Ms. Mathews your name for the very same reason. Mages do not name each other."

Ferro puffed air out his nostrils like a bull. "He wants you?"

"I think we've covered that."

"But why you? Why not approach others among magekind? Is not my iron as powerful? What is he doing? What is his game?"

"I don't know," Kaye said. "Please recall that I refused his offer."

"I still don't understand why you would do that."

"Because I want my own House!" With Bastian at her side.

"Come," Ferro said, drawing her into a long passage. "We've got to move. Got to think this out."

Kaye yanked her arm free, then followed him as he jogged the length of the corridor, though her coat was in the meeting room. The revelation of Khan's existence had had quite an effect. And at the perfect time. This couldn't be better: Ferro's leadership seemed at risk. A nudge and he might actually start spilling those secrets about controlling wraiths and why and how. Today, this afternoon even, her mission could be complete. She'd have done something to get her own back, to take her stand, and then she could start her new life.

They exited into a wide courtyard, winter stark. His Maybach was waiting. He gestured for her to get in, while he answered a ring on his mobile phone. He listened intently, then scooted in next to her. Since he was talking, she pulled out her own phone to let Bastian know where she was. Or at least with whom.

But Ferro put a hand on her arm again—always touching her—signaling her to wait. When he finished his call, he asked, "Just to be clear . . . if you had accepted Khan's offer, would you have been subsumed under Segue, or would you have been allowed to maintain Brand House?"

"I think he was under the assumption that I was stray." Like the Lakatoses. "The 'Brand' part of me was not interesting to him. Just the 'Kaye.'"

Ferro grinned. "That pesky House versus mage question again, but in reverse. We know about that."

"I guess so." They understood each other on some level.

The car pulled onto the main road. No blindfold this time. No secrecy. Not when Kaye knew the Grim Reaper. She noticed a street sign—HARPER'S FERRY ROAD—and a larger sign showing mileage to the next town, Sharpsburg. A useful bit of information for Bastian. The Order would know where the Council gathered. She was doing her job magnificently.

"And Brand House would also be assumed under Grey if we were to marry," Ferro continued.

The word *marry* jolted her, but the custom of taking on the male spouse's name and House was a relief—yet another handy reason to get out of this tangle, if her goal was to stay Brand. "Yes," she said, though slightly hesitant.

"What if I were to offer you better terms?" he said. "What if Brand and Grey were to stand as equals?"

Kaye could only make a "Hmmmm" sound. She wanted out of the car.

"You could maintain your own accounts and personnel, within reason," he began.

"You're giving me permission?" Kaye asked, amused. As for personnel, he was, of course, referring to Jack Bastian.

But he either didn't hear her sarcasm or wasn't ready to answer it. "In addition, I would be willing to agree that any of our children who lean toward iron will be under my House, any to fire under yours. Brand House will stand if you side with me."

"Very equitable," Kaye said, but she made certain that her tone was not completely engaged. That she'd have to think about it. That she had options to consider.

She looked out the window to watch winter-bare farmland rush by.

"But . . ." Ferro led. Was he grinding his teeth?

"But I'd have to know what you have," Kaye said, going for it all, "or think you have, that someone else does not."

And then she could be free. This was it; she had to control the sound of her heart so Ferro wouldn't hear how it sang. The muscles in her face ached to draw into a beaming smile. She wanted to say, "Yes . . . please Shadow . . . just tell me!"

"How do you think I hold my seat among the Houses when each is vying for the prize?"

"I couldn't say." She shrugged, but kept the tone mellow so as not to insult.

"I will show you," Ferro said, "and it's a power to challenge even a lord over life and death."

* * *

Jack read the text message from Kaye on his mobile phone:

Will be late for dinner plans. Can you pick up champagne?

Then he lifted his gaze to his friend, whose expression matched his own spike of concern. *She says she'll be late.* The only part of the message that mattered.

I'll have every free soul start looking for her immediately, Laurence said.

"You shall see," Ferro said to Kaye. He reached across the seat and took her hand in his. Raised her fingers to his lips.

Marriage was the answer. Union with Brand was the key. And as soon as possible.

She was not allied with any other House against him, not even the pureblood. Her Shadow was strong. She glowed with youth. What more could he possibly ask for?

Kaye looked over, her scars etching her cheek in the harsh light. He loved the faint, jagged lines, loved that he had his mark on her already. The last Brand, claimed.

She smiled, extracting herself. "Where are we going?"

"Grey House," he said. "I can't wait to have you with me there."

"With you?" Still edgy, on her guard. He liked a careful woman.

"Well, you need to be in a warded House." That went without saying. "You'll be beset by angels or humans if you remain where you are. And after you conceive . . . really, there is no other option. A warded House is necessary. And I happen to have a comfortable one."

Her expression went remote, though he already knew she wasn't eager. That bodyguard was sleeping with her, and worse, she'd developed an attachment to him. The guard had come to her with inside knowledge about Shadow and had therefore been a companion as well as trained protection.

Had she considered the possibility that Khan was using the guard to get to her?

Enough was enough. The affair would be put aside.

She'd do her duty to her House, and Ferro and she would both see to it that there was no speculation about who fathered her children. Loyalty came first; affection would follow with time. And he wanted affection. Wanted true love, because among the Shadow-bred, true love was not myth. True love was magic, and they breathed magic every day.

"Let's not get ahead of ourselves," she said. "I understand that the news about the pureblood mage has startled the Council, but nothing has changed for me."

"Just wait," he said, with a smug smile. "I'll change everything." He reached forward and tapped the driver on his arm. "Faster."

Ferro had known this was coming. Had to be coming. Supposedly no one born to the mortal world could understand the whispers within Shadow. In fact, an old magekind lullaby warned against listening too closely, *lest you go mad, lest you go mad*. But every once in a while he'd let the chatter into his mind. The language of mage progenitors was irregular and lacked cohesion, but if he stopped listening with his ears and brain, he could almost *feel* meaning in the sounds.

The news that a great fae had become mortal was

only a verbal confirmation of what he'd somehow already understood in an upside-down dream. Other creatures of Twilight had been known to cross into this world, but none in recent history had been a pureblood mage. No, the great power of mages had been consigned to story for hundreds of years. Some stories went back millennia. When Shadow coursed into the world, the mage Houses grew strong and ruled over the lesser humans. When Shadow weakened, so did the umbras of the Houses, and magekind was forced to labor alongside humanity. Never again.

The drive home was too long, Kaye's composed silence a needle in his mood. She'd been resistant to his advances from the beginning, and now he knew why. His ambitious woman wasn't going to settle. When they arrived home, she was checking the time, as if she had somewhere else to be and was anxious to get going.

"I have a client this evening. . . ."

She wasn't going anywhere. He could make Brand House strong.

He shrugged off his coat and handed it to Gerard, one of the house staff. Then turned to help Kaye off with hers, only to find that she wasn't wearing one. Her blouse was lovely, but too thin for the weather. He paused, hands midair.

Her black eyes glittered. "We seem to have left mine behind."

The criticism implied smarted, a bad beginning, but this—*this*—would make up for it. "Follow me."

Ferro led her beyond the formal rooms of the house, past Camilla's desk and his office. He turned into a small, comfortable receiving room for visitors, though no visitor had ever waited upon him there. At the opposite end was a door, always locked, with one key, which he kept in his pocket.

The door opened to downward-leading steps. Shadow

was dense there, flood deep, the whispers fully audible. The fae enjoyed looking into the great Houses for entertainment.

He started down the first several steps, only to turn and find Kaye hesitating at the top. Her face had paled, and her scars were whiter still.

"I'll wait here," she said, her usually smooth voice now thready.

"Don't be silly." He turned and continued down. "Come see the future, the iron behind your House. Once I explain, you'll have no reservations whatsoever."

Her footsteps were ghost light, childlike, as she descended to the cellar floor. Her eyes were so big, he'd almost think she was scared. Maybe she didn't like tight places. He could use that.

Her whole body stiffly rotated to see the contents of the room. Ferro had the strangest impression that if he touched her now, she would shatter. Curious.

Kaye had to look, but she didn't want to see. Her heart pounded so hard, it sent percussion ripples out into the soupy Shadow of the cellar. Whispers teased her mind; she refused to hear the voices, which only made them louder.

. . . *you knew already* . . .

. . . *what else could it be?* . . .

. . . *you belong in the dark* . . .

. . . *a brand in the dark* . . .

The moment Ferro had opened the door, the moment she'd seen the stairs falling into darkness, she'd known. Time had whipped her back in a parabola that was too Ordered and perfect to be anything other than angelic in origin. The cellar door was the zenith of the whiplash arc in her life. She was back at the beginning, just older. No wiser.

The angel before her had collapsed, immobile and gray, in a heap on the floor. No glow pushed Shadow back. The smell approached the stink of a wraith. The figure was slight, the fine bones and softness of a woman. Her gummy eyes were open, sightless. Lips parted.

"Did you know iron is an excellent conductor of Shadow?" Ferro nudged the form with his foot, and the angel rolled onto her back, whimpering. Alive.

Kaye was fifteen years old again: angel, imminent marriage, House business looming, the cellar, indecision and despair.

Why did the angel have to be alive? The whimper might as well have been a chain attached to a puckered red sore, perfectly circular, on the angel's breast. The iron links dragged through the darkness and clasped Kaye around the neck. She would never be free of this.

Iron conducting Shadow—it was an old bit of mage trivia that sounded familiar, but Kaye couldn't recall the context of learning it. She didn't answer Ferro, and damned her father for her ignorance all over again.

"It means I can acquire and employ the more active powers of the Houses, of other mages." Iron gave him all the powers. "Of course, some are more useful than others."

"And the other Houses tolerate this?" Kaye couldn't believe it.

"They do, but then I'm as cautious as you are." He was twisting that ugly ring. The one that fit the bloody mark on the angel's body so perfectly.

"Not cautious if you have *that* in your House." Kaye gestured toward the abused angel.

"Risk has value too," Ferro said, "And when you talk to me in that tone, I can only believe you understand its merits, though perhaps not its shortcomings. I risked everything that first time I took an angel's light into myself."

"You . . ." Kaye looked from Ferro to the fallen angel and back again.

"I was old anyway, nothing to lose, everything to gain. Angel light worked so well to sustain and renew wraiths, as it should, since wraiths consume souls, and what is angel light, but an undiluted soul? I decided to see if I could take the rejuvenating power into myself as well."

"Didn't the light consume your Shadow?" Had to. Angel light and Shadow magic were always at odds.

"No," Ferro said, smiling, cheerful. "I discovered that the two can coexist most harmoniously if given the opportunity."

Kaye felt her heart clot with the truth of that—she knew intimately just how well angel and mage came together. And now, once again, how very far apart they were. Bastian.

"Light also makes me persuasive, commanding," Ferro said, shrugging. "I am never passed over. I use light to master the Houses for our collective good."

"And you kill angels to do this?" How much of Ferro's good humor, good looks, good mood belonged to someone else?

Her father had known, Kaye was sure.

"They've killed us." He turned the angel's face with the toe of his shoe. Another whimper. "And besides, they're recycled people. They've already lived one life. Why should they get a second, or third, or fourth when our first is imperiled?"

His logic was revolting.

"You're essentially eating souls, like a wraith." No, he was doing more than that.

He smiled broadly, opening his hands to accept the

noxious idea. "Angel light renews wraith bodies, as it does mine. That's where I got the idea."

Kaye had the broad strokes of Bastian's answers, only to be replaced with questions more bitter than she ever could have imagined, and on a scale that confirmed the desolation revealed in so many of her visions.

"And all the Houses do this?"

Her own dreams were ashes in her heart. She wouldn't be making Bastian dinner tonight.

"No, but they should," he answered. "And once you get over your fear of wraiths, you will too."

Because war was not brewing between magekind and The Order; the war was in full swing—Shadow had struck first. As soon as he knew, Bastian would fight—but he couldn't get past the wards. The angels would fall on the Houses, as they had in ages past. But this time, Shadow would win. Had to win. The world was covered in it.

Kaye gulped. "Where do you get your . . . stock?"

Ferro shrugged. "Here and there. We bait traps. Isolate them. Transport them to where they are needed. An angel lasts many feedings, so their diminishing numbers aren't as apparent as humans. The Order is being more careful, but we are managing just fine."

"Until they discover what you're doing." And they would; Kaye had been hired to tell Bastian.

But what then? The Order might fight magekind, but they couldn't win this time. The Houses would eventually rule. That was a simple truth no one could deny.

Therefore, the change had to come from inside. Someone had to change the future. Isn't that what she counseled her clients?

"We are strong," Ferro said. "And we're securing the cooperation of humanity. It's in humankind's best interests to side with us."

"If you have all this in place, why are you so worried about Khan?"

Khan. Maybe he could stop this. If he were seated in Grey's big chair, maybe he could enact rapid changes. Wasn't that what Ferro was afraid of? That Khan would take over?

Except Khan hated angels. He had no reason to save them. They were dead already as far as he was concerned.

Kaye shook inside and had to force control upon every muscle.

Ferro laughed and clenched the air with his fist in victory. "Khan can do nothing. Exactly the point I wanted to make by bringing you here. Now is not the time for an inter-House squabble for power. There is enough to go around, even for the pureblood mage. Plus, dissent would give The Order an opening to challenge us. Unite with Grey House. Marry me."

Oh, please, Shadow, no.

"You have that Council seat you wanted," he continued. "You took it right out from under Arman Maya. Put your fire behind Grey House, and not even Death can challenge us. Together we can make the future."

No. Not this way.

"You're proposing to me in a crypt, with a dying angel at my feet." Her distaste was real, her belly rolling. But someone had to make the future . . . good.

No. When she was fifteen, she'd worked so hard to say that word to her father, to refuse the marriage. No. Ten years and she was still struggling with it.

"An offering," he said, gesturing to the angel with an amiable smile.

"I prefer jewelry."

He twisted the iron ring on his finger.

She stepped back quickly. "Not that ring."

"I'll buy you a fat diamond," he promised. And with a gesture, he compelled the Shadows to condense into a bright and glittering ring. An illusion borne out of some other mage's stolen power. "Just say yes."

This life is not for you, the angel Michael had said.

Ten years ago, she'd refused Grey and her life had burned. She'd run away, a child's solution. But she was an adult now and angrier than she had ever been before. Layla Mathews was right. This had to stop. The mortal world was the only common ground angel, human, and mage shared.

She had a seat on the Council. And an angel lay dying at her feet. Michael was already dead. Would Bastian be next?

There was but one choice that would honor her House, though Bastian would hate her. She'd promised him. *No more Grey.*

Bastian was everything.

Run away, then? Leave this angel to die?

No. She said the little word to *herself,* the one person in this equation who could do something right. Perhaps she was feeling Bastian's influence; Shadow knew no right and wrong.

But this time she would make the right choice. She'd returned to magekind. Now she had to go all the way back inside it. And take it apart brick by brick. Rebuild it better.

An ocean of feeling rose within her, threatening to lay her secrets bare. That she hated Grey and loved an angel, and that she'd set the world on fire if she didn't get what she wanted. Kaye first.

No.

There was no Segue in her future. Never had been. That was a fairy tale, and fairy tales were for children. Kaye understood the opportunism inherent in Shadow. And this was opportunity way beyond the revenge she'd set out for. This was redemption.

"I will marry you," she said to Ferro, but she was looking down at the angel. She would not run away this time, though she was frigid inside. She would not run. Not when she could do something.

Ferro came up behind her. Put his hands on her shoulders; his touch seemed to sap her strength. "And I'll give you everything you can dream of."

Not likely.

Kaye was more interested in the gray cast to the angel's skin. How much time did she have? Could she heal if Shadow didn't envelop her so completely?

"This one's just about dead," Ferro said. "I'll have to throw her out soon."

If Kaye was going to do this, that angel had damn well better live. "I don't know. If she can moan like that, I bet she's got more in her. And we have to be careful where The Order is concerned. Get every last drop." Kaye stooped down, slapped the angel's face, light but sharp, then spoke into her semi-roused eyes. "You endure, damn it."

And Kaye would too.

Chapter 9

Jack was on the sidewalk in front of the town house when two long black sedans pulled up. The driver of the first, a wraith, got out and opened the rear door.

Within the vehicle, Jack caught a flash of pale skin, red hair—Kaye was all right. A wave of "Alive" went through the angels stationed nearby, Laurence recalling those who'd been dispatched to search for her.

Jack was relieved—visions of the worst had tormented him through the long night—but the feeling was quickly turning sour with alarm. His whole body buzzed with it.

Kaye took the monster's hand and allowed it to help her out. Her expression was haughty, hair swept back in a twist. And she wore a dead animal for a coat—not her usual style.

"Jack," she said, in passing, which staked him through his gut to his spot on the sidewalk. He was *Bastian* to her.

What did she mean?

A small entourage of wraiths and mages followed her inside. "My things are upstairs, in the first room on the right," she was saying. "If anything is ruined, I'll be very unhappy. Each pair of shoes must be individually boxed."

Jack forced himself into the house, as if his limbs didn't really belong to him. Activity bustled inside, mostly upstairs, but he felt as if time traveled slowly for him, only him. He could almost see the time-lapse ribbons of movement streaking through the space. Each second was measured in pain. He spotted Laurence in the arch to the dining area. His angel light was buried, his expression solemn. Jack wanted to punch it off his face.

Camilla, Grey's secretary, stood at Kaye's side, a clipboard in hand, taking direction.

"Ah, yes," Kaye finally said to Jack, addressing him as if he were one more matter to take care of. Her hands were clasped on front of herself, a block of ice hanging off her ring finger. "I have good news! I am engaged to Ferro Grey."

She might as well have clubbed him in the chest. Shards of bone blistered his lungs. One more injury he'd never recover from.

"What happened?" Which Jack knew was a stupid question. She couldn't speak candidly now.

Camilla glanced up at him, then back down at her board.

"Aren't you going to congratulate me?" Part of her act.

"Where were you?" he demanded. This she should be able to answer.

"Grey House, of course. Where I'm moving." She put on a slightly pained face. "I'm afraid I'm going to have to let you go."

Go where?

"Ferro has his own security; magic you wouldn't understand. I have no place for you."

"What are you talking about?"

The wraiths and mages were taking things to the cars. So fast. So efficient.

Another pained expression twisted her features. "It's just that Ferro is the jealous sort. He feels strongly where you're concerned, and we both know he has reason to. It *has* to be this way."

How dare she use that smooth, sexy voice on me now.

How dare she after . . . when we . . . when I . . .

This is a time to think, not feel, Laurence said to him telepathically.

I love her. I'd do anything for her. I've embraced Shadow, Jack returned.

Think.

His brain didn't want to.

What could've possibly prompted her to accept Grey? She hates Grey.

Think, Laurence commanded again. *She's in danger right now.*

Something very bad must have happened.

Yes.

Very bad to make her accept him. All night long. Did she sleep with him?

Don't go there.

Jack's arm burned, his chest burned, and now the rest of him did too. But he used the punch of fury brought on by the thought of Kaye in Ferro's bed and hauled himself together. Felt the armor snap back in place.

"Are you sure this is what you want?" he asked through clenched teeth. The pain was like nothing he'd ever known.

He watched for one flicker, one silent entreaty, for him to stop this. One bat of her eye and he'd get her away from there. Maybe he would anyway. He could imagine no circumstance in which it would make sense for Kaye to marry Ferrol Grey.

"It has to be this way," she repeated, harder.

"No, it doesn't."

Listen to her. She's in danger.

And Grey's not dangerous? Jack demanded of Laurence.

"Trust me," she said, patting his burned arm. "I'm doing the best thing for both of us."

Jack heard the emphasis on "Trust me." Saw the directness in her gaze. The conviction that robbed him of further speech. Almost brought him to his knees.

"All ready?" Camilla asked.

"I'm going to do a quick check upstairs," Kaye said, "and then be back down."

If you follow her, the mage will too, Laurence said.

I know, Jack answered. But it was damn difficult to wait when he knew she was alone, and so close. When he could shake the answers out of her.

Kaye returned waving a silk scarf. The one Jack had used to blindfold her during a particularly erotic part of their night together.

"Let's go," she said. The mage followed her out the door.

Suddenly the house felt echoingly empty, as if someone had died.

Jack looked out a window while Kaye climbed into one of the cars, watched her pull away.

Then he pelted up the stairs to find the note she'd surely left for him. She'd have left a message that explained this swift, drastic turn of events. She wouldn't leave him hanging after what they'd shared.

He found it under her pillow, a scrawl written quickly, but it confused as much as it informed:

> The Council of Houses meets off Harper's Ferry Road near Sharpsburg. Look for a building with a courtyard. Conflict over news of Khan. Grey feels the challenge to his power. New wraiths are not being born. Old ones are being renewed. Will try to meet you at Lincoln Memorial at noon tomorrow. Brand has a seat. I'm building my House.

Jack crumpled the note in his hand. His angel's calm crumpled too.

He didn't notice Laurence standing in the doorway until he spoke. "She walks a fine line between her loyalties—to report against her kind and work for a place among them."

It was easier not to speak aloud when overcome by betrayal. *I'd thought she'd chosen.*

"Oh, she's chosen something. How about you? Will you stand by her to find out what she's decided?"

"Darling," Ferro said, entering the large room that had been dedicated to Kaye's wardrobe. Racks had been set up, and the clothing she'd retrieved today from the town house was hanging on a few. He had no doubt she would fill them all.

"Yes?" Kaye sat at a beautiful desk, concentrating on a laptop. She wore a midnight silk robe. A long, bare leg was visible, and he remembered just how her legs softened at the round of her thighs and ever so slightly at the juncture of paradise.

He held up two ties. "Which is better?"

She flicked up her gaze for a fraction of a second, then lowered it again. "Neither."

"I was told they were on trend." A little shiny perhaps.

"For a twentysomething model who plans a trip to the moon, maybe."

Would Kaye always bite? Penny had been very accommodating. But then she'd been taught to be.

Ferro throttled his irritation. He wouldn't quash in Kaye the quality he valued most in her. "I look twentysomething," he pointed out. Kaye knew his physique as intimately as he knew hers. He was perfect.

"But you're over a hundred. Go classic, not ridiculous."

* * *

Kaye bit her tongue. Damn. No use antagonizing him just because she was angry. And scared. And alone.

Where was Bastian? What was he doing? Just how much did he hate her? Shame and sorrow burned in her breast. It scorched like no flame of Shadow or Earth could. The rest of her was slowly turning into white ash. She was beyond tears, even private, silent ones. The shame would burn until all of her was slowly consumed. Vital organs first please, so her heart wouldn't ache quite so badly.

But still, she couldn't think of any other way. And at least with this course of action she had a purpose. There was an Order to her return, a symmetry, and that at least Bastian had to understand. Even if she couldn't tell him.

She smiled in spite of herself: Bastian had gone crazy, and she was acting with purpose. Now there was symmetry.

She glanced at him again; Ferro was still looking at his ties. "I hadn't thought of them that way. Ridiculous." He spoke carefully, which Kaye knew was dangerous.

"I apologize," Kaye said. She tried to push a spark into a warm smile, but it fizzled on the way to her mouth. "I didn't get a lot of sleep last night."

Heavy on the hint. She was tired all the way to her bones. And in her heart. And, strangely, even in Shadow.

She looked back down at her laptop screen, to tell Ferro that she had to work. And she did have a meeting to arrange with a client—it was important to maintain her flow of income, and therefore independence—but it was the business card she'd hidden under her laptop that interested her.

Lakatos.

"I'm sorry you aren't feeling well." Ferro sounded genuinely concerned.

"No, I'm sorry. You'll find that when I'm tired, my temper snaps," she said.

"You need your strength. I completely understand."

Did he? And what did she need her strength for? Weird thing to say.

He turned to leave, but then looked back. "By the way, your news about the pureblood yesterday had a curious effect among my houseguests visiting for the Council meetings. Webb packed and left while you and I were enjoying one another's company. They are now traitors to Grey and Brand; we will recognize them no longer."

She felt her temper snap again. She'd decide who was a traitor to her House, not Ferro.

"And a couple others asked to stay over a few days to get to know you, which I approved. Remember not to touch Lorelei Blake, the lure—she won't harm you, but she might like to play with you a bit."

Kaye shuddered but kept her fire high.

"And if Raiden Terrell approaches you about your father's debts, remand him to me. Nothing from your past will follow you into our new life. We begin anew."

"I can pay my own debts," she said.

He made a funny smile and winked. "I wouldn't hear of it." Then continued, "And beware of 'accidents.' I can think of at least two remaining here—Gail and Arman—who wouldn't hesitate to help you down the stairs. And thank you for the advice about the ties. I know I can depend on you."

He left, taking his trendy ties with him.

Kaye stared at the empty doorway, marveling at how threats and cautions could come out of the same mouth at the same time, and how many ways there were for her to displease him, or to die.

And it seemed to her that the other mages and Houses, like players in a game, moved in tandem with each step of

Ferrol's, for or against him. Grey House was full of traps; the mage who could navigate them the best won everything.

She had better set her own. Lakatos.

She dialed the number on her mobile. The phone was almost dead, but she'd been careful to keep it with her since the Council meeting. She was paranoid Ferro would tamper with it.

The ring warbled in her ear.

The old man, Sigmund, answered. He'd said hello twice before she finished wrestling with a fresh pang of indecision. If she did this, there was no going to Segue, no calling it her House. No Bastian. She'd be taking on dependents, making a vow as serious and binding as her name. If she did this, she'd be once and always Brand.

"Hello?" he said again.

The decision was made already; she'd made it in the cellar yesterday, looking down at the angel, and she'd affirmed it before, during, and after being with Ferro last night.

She was building her House. If her plan had any chance of succeeding, she had to make it strong.

"It's Kaye Brand," she said to Sigmund. "I've reconsidered."

A pause on the line. Had they found another to take them in? Was she too late?

"It's our honor to serve Brand, and always has been," Sigmund said at last. "And may I congratulate you on your recent joy."

Less than twenty-four hours and even he knew.

"We need to meet as soon as possible," she said, "to make this formal. But I'd rather not tell Mr. Grey just now. This is between Lakatos and Brand alone."

Another pause while he considered his loyalties. Then,

"I imagine there are a number of matters a lady might keep from her intended."

Very diplomatic.

"If we do this then you answer only to me." That had to be understood. She was not a gateway to Grey. Lakatos would be hers.

"If I'd wanted Grey, I would've approached him instead. He likes people on their knees." Which she knew was a warning to her too.

"All right, then." This was crazy. "Our meeting. Tonight."

"I'll come to you, Lady Brand."

"Come here?" Her pulse leaped.

"It's the easiest way." He spoke with a tone of experience.

"How will you get in?" Impossible. "Even if you have a key, the wards will keep you out."

"Lakatos is just our modern name, my lady, and locksmith the modern way we ply our trade. But our power is really to cross boundaries that shut others out."

Cross boundaries. "You've been into Twilight."

"Yes, I have."

"With that power, how could you possibly have been stray?" He was playing her. "Any House would take you in. Why mine?"

"I didn't want just anyone. We've always been loyal to Brand."

Nightfall. Jack looked at Grey House from the same spot he'd observed it the night of Kaye's party. Where he'd been beaten as a message to her, the Match Girl with visions in her fire. Now she was selling her fire again.

He'd been eager for her to access her Brand roots. He'd been a fool.

Where is she? Is she safe? Is Grey touching her?

A roar of fury built within him.

Laurence, at his side, shook his head. *I'm sorry, friend. You could choose to ascend to the next circle, and with it gain knowledge. It gave me peace.*

Too high up and the seraphim go silent, too much knowledge. I belong on the ground.

But Laurence was right. He couldn't go on like this anymore. *This will be my last tour.*

There was too much trouble in Jack's heart to contemplate another. Something was wrong with his soul. Had been, long before this assignment. Secretly, he hoped it was Shadow. No, he knew it was Shadow. He'd had too much of it over the centuries. Madness wouldn't be so bad. It was better than thinking.

I guessed as much, Laurence returned.

A flash of shame overtook Jack. He should probably ask to be replaced, but he wouldn't. Not now. No. Some curse had turned him into stone and forced him to stare up at those windows. The Order couldn't drag him from here if they tried.

What is she doing? Is she safe? Is Grey touching her?

Laurence turned to him and smiled with warmth and pity. *Shadowman ripped the veil open for love of a woman, and so shall the world fall.*

And Jack knew he was utterly doomed. Doomed and damned and ripped to pieces. His soul was lost, the future bleak, his passion turned to rage. Because after eleven tours among humanity, he'd learned a few things about human nature.

Love was the most destructive force of them all.

Take him, for example.

* * *

Kaye headed to the kitchen to get herself a drink, but really she was walking the house to become familiar with the layout. The place was massive, with no regularity to anticipate what might be around the next corner. Formal rooms up front, still littered with candles. Some spaces beyond the foyer on the main-floor midsection were open, where Shadow deepened in the corners, strange patterns moving within. Ferro had a pool table in the middle of a pillared great room, with upholstered benches and high-backed couches. A nook highlighted the electric guitar of a mage rock star forced into retirement by his popularity.

She actually could use a little of that *bow-pow sexxxx* driving beat right now. She'd thought the walk would get her blood moving, but she still felt low, sad, frightened. She kept moving.

That way led to Ferro's offices and the basement below; that way to the workout center, pool, theater. An alternate staircase was tucked behind that recessed door, a side exit, due east.

. . . come come come come . . .

And fae everywhere.

They were the voices of her childhood, imaginary friends and tormenters, out of sight like hide-and-seek. They'd kept her company day after day, listening to her complaints and outrages. She'd never seen a fae head-on, not even in the darkest rooms when she'd begged them to take her away. But they'd also gotten her into trouble. And no one, not even her father, had believed her claims that "the fae did it." Everyone knew the fae couldn't cross. She wasn't so sure.

. . . come come come come . . .

As she had in the past, she followed the whispers. "This way?"

Not that they would answer. She had to imagine a response for them.

. . . won't let anything hurt hurt hurt you here . . .

Exactly what she wanted to hear. They knew she was scared. "I missed you."

. . . missed you missed you missed you . . .

She rounded a corner and found a side hallway blanketed with dark. Interesting. Faint electric glows made a shoulder-high landing strip down the passage but didn't illuminate. She lit a fire in her palm and proceeded anyway.

. . . can't can't can't . . .

She passed two figures, her light reflecting off their eyes, but their identities concealed by Shadow.

"Can't let her . . . childless . . . can't let him . . . get an heir on her."

Their black gazes followed her as she passed. She hoped she didn't give Grey an heir either. Hope was the worst form of contraception. Extreme body heat, however, had always worked well for her.

. . . this way . . .

The Shadow thinned to nighttime murk. She entered a series of side pantries superstocked for some kind of Armageddon. A couple of large boxes stamped WHEAT had been recently delivered, dolly waiting. POWDERED MILK. Four big boxes. Kaye could guess why it wasn't stored in the cellar. And she thought that if the world was to come to an end today, Grey House was where you'd want to be.

A flapping door led to a massive stainless-steel kitchen that could have served a hotel. Nothing stylish here. This area was for staff and utility.

Kaye halted when she spotted Gail, the woman who'd challenged her at the party. She was wearing jeans and a slouchy sweater and reading the paper at a scarred worktable. Bulky long sleeves covered her arms, bandages visible at the wrists. She had a red carry-on at her feet, coat flung over the handle. A nice bag hung off the back of the chair.

"Going somewhere?" Did Ferro know?

Gail glanced up, then retreated a fraction in her seat. "I don't want any trouble."

"I'm not the one who caused trouble in the first place."

"I'm leaving. You don't have to worry about me." Gail made a face, as if conceding a point. "Not that a woman like you ever has to worry."

A woman like you . . . Kaye felt like burning her again.

. . . burn her burn her burn her . . .

Shhh, thought Kaye. Not yet.

"I've been called home," Gail continued. "I'll be out of your hair as soon as the cab arrives. I did my best. Truth is, I'm just not sexy. You, on the other hand . . ." Her eyes went wide, eyebrows up. "Anyway . . . my House thought I had a chance since my Shadow has some unusual properties. But Ferrol just wasn't interested." Another face. "I also talk too much, especially when I'm nervous. So don't mind me. I will read the paper and giggle at how hopeful the news is. Can they not see the Shadow everywhere? I swear humans are blind. And then there're the mages who—"

"Wow," Kaye said. "You do talk a lot."

"No filter," Gail said. "Which was why I was so rude at your party. I'd just been chewed out pretty bad by my great aunt and then some stylist put me in that horrible dress and I couldn't breathe, but I still managed to drink . . . and so that's what I did."

"The Moll?"

"Made me stupid."

Gail was supposed to have seduced Ferrol for her House. Kaye got it, the trap the woman had been in.

"Moll is dangerous stuff," Kaye said.

"I have the scars to prove it," Gail said, lifting her arms, then flushed with embarrassment as she flicked her gaze to Kaye's cheek. "Sorry."

Kaye walked over. Dragged out a seat. Lowered herself like an old woman, she was so tired. "I'm not sorry, not anymore. My scars scare people, make them think twice. If you wear yours right, they'll do the same thing for you. Show them off like you're a crazy bitch who doesn't give a shit as long you draw blood."

Gail's throat worked in a gulp. "Dang. You're twisted."

"A wraith had at me," Kaye explained. "Are you going to be okay? With your House? Your aunt? Can I help?"

Another face. No filter or control there either. "Why would *you* help *me*?"

Kaye shrugged. "I like a distraction."

Gail pressed her mouth into a frown, considering. "Look. You might be a good person, I can't really tell, but if you are, then really . . . this place"—she shook her head—"it's not the most fun I've ever had."

"I'm not here for fun"—Kaye smiled—"or couldn't you tell?"

She got a return grin from Gail.

Headlights flashed before a roll of tires sounded on the pavement outside. Cab. Gail stood and put on her coat. Relaxed and casual, she was beautiful, not like the caricature she'd been the night of the party. And she was getting out; anywhere would be better than here.

Gail shouldered her bag and pulled out the handle on her rolling suitcase. She stood there looking conflicted, then leaned in, eyes skating left and right to the doorways looking for eavesdroppers, and delivered a warning: "Girl to girl, you should know that he can take your Shadow."

"The ring thing." Kaye had already seen its effects.

"He doesn't need the ring to do it," Gail said, then bit her lips. Probably to keep everything else she knew inside.

Kaye's heart thudded. "Thanks." Her turn to swallow. Then, "Sorry I burned you."

She hadn't been sorry before. The fire had been self-defense and it had won her the respect of Grey. But now . . .

"It's my fault." Wry smile. "When I'm done healing, I'll wear the scars like I mean it. Thanks for the tip. I needed a little badass anyway to make up for my lost dignity."

"Hard way to come by it." Kaye knew from experience.

Gail pushed open the door to the rear drive. She looked back over her shoulder. "Luck." And then climbed into the cab.

"You too," Kaye said as the car drove away, wishing Gail wasn't going. There were fae whispers everywhere, mage talk in dark corridors, a castle ready for war, and now Gail. She and Kaye were the same, which was the strangest thing Kaye had discovered so far.

A taxi circled around from the back of the house, by Jack's count the fourth vehicle to leave. None arrived, so this felt like a slow exodus, a reorganization based on an upset.

It was late, Shadow above and below, like black sky on water. This was the long wait before lines were drawn. And then blood.

The thick smell of smoke meant Shaw was near, though Jacques couldn't see the fire. He had to be here, just hidden from view within Shadow. Leaves and brush crackled as wolves surrounded him, ears pinned, jaws ready, growls rolling. Close.

"A game?" Jacques called. The wolves awaited the command of their alpha, the mage. Jacques knew he couldn't take them all, unarmed as he was, but this was worth the risk. A different approach. A parley. Just the two of them.

Shaw stepped out of Shadow, a woodsman with wiry

branches for hair, pebbles for teeth, sooty holes for nostrils. He was earthen with his magic, black-eyed.

Jacques held up a cloth bundle that contained the game pieces.

"Aye," the woodsman told him. Shadow receded and Jacques found himself one step from the fire. The woods were the mage's home, unwarded by stones but well protected by the beasts who lived with him. The Order stayed clear of this place—too much like Twilight—but Jacques had ventured in, played for and won his life.

The stakes were higher this time.

Shaw and Jacques sat on the ground, and the woodsman cleared a space of loose earth, twigs, and bugs with his hand. The dirt smelled good. Jacques laid out the cloth along with the carved bone pieces. Picked them up, tossed them in the air, caught all but one on the back of his hand, tallied. Shaw followed, catching all of them, and so the game went until Jacques was losing by half.

"And here I'd hoped to cheat you out of battle tomorrow," he told him. Jack had been an idealist then.

If just one mage could see reason. If just one would hear terms and agree to the strictures set out by The Order for peace, then maybe there'd be hope no blood need dampen the earth come dawn. If just one would say no. Shaw was the wildest of them all, and stayed out of the politicking and schemes of the clans. He could choose to live in his woods.

"Shadow will gather me up with the rest when it's time," Shaw said, "whether you win this game or not."

Would Shadow take Kaye as well when the time came? Had it already taken her?

He shook at the futility of it all. The only thing that had changed was that Shadow had taken him.

* * *

Kaye's fatigue seemed to really concern Ferro, but it took actual vomit for him to back a step away from her. She had practice bringing up bile from her drinking days and put the skill to good use now.

Not so sexy tonight. Plus, he'd had her already. And he would again soon; she wouldn't lie to herself about that. But Ferro could wait. He'd have to wait.

Kaye had snagged a bottle of Ferro's Black Moll, a sharp knife, and a wineglass. Then she waited in the dark, her heart beating in time to the seconds as they passed. Waited, listening to the whispers.

. . . wanna play . . . wanna play . . . wanna play . . .

Kaye's private rooms had once belonged to Ferro's dead wife, Penelope. The apartment needed renovation but was lovely in its outdated way. She'd been partial to mellow golds and golden greens, colors that washed out Kaye, literally and figuratively. But with the lights off and Shadow rising, the shimmer and dramatic stretches of fabric reminded her of trees, magical ones that swayed and moved and were inhabited by whispering fae.

Ferro came by again to "check on her." How like a man.

She communicated in no uncertain terms that she was not available.

The hours stretched; whispers rose.

. . . not yet . . . not yet . . . not yet . . .

And still she waited.

Kaye knew Sigmund Lakatos was smart. She just hoped he wasn't clumsy. Shadow confused wraith senses, and if he kept to the darkest bits, he might have a chance. Every mage child learned to navigate the pitch and cling of magic. But he'd lived most of his life in the near absence of Shadow. Had he figured out its secrets later in life? Had he practiced?

She heard someone outside the door.

She braced, though her heart galloped.

No . . . someone just passing by.

This was insane. She should have found a way to sneak out. She hated waiting; it gave her too much time to think.

Seconds and minutes collected. Kaye wondered about Bastian, how he must hate her and if he'd go to Segue and if they'd ever really talk again. And if the gaping hole in her chest would ever stop aching. But she didn't regret loving him, and didn't regret the ten years of Hell that it took for him to find her, and didn't even regret the wraith attack that destroyed her life at fifteen. All of it had prepared her for this. And Bastian had taught her the conviction that would see her through. This was her life. She was needed here. She could make something better here.

She thought of Michael, who'd saved her so long ago, and who'd been wrong about what to do and where she belonged. And she willed strength to the angel now sunk in darkness below the house. If she could just hold out a few more days . . .

It was past three AM when her door opened, and Sigmund Lakatos entered, without stealth, as if he lived there. "I'm sorry, my lady, to have kept you up so late. I had to wait until the house was still."

Kaye hurried across the room to him, a question burning. "Do others know you can get past wards?"

"If others knew, I wouldn't be standing here."

"No, you would not." Kaye's head pounded at what came next. She was in the position of power, yet was agitated. She wrung her hands as she whispered, "We'd better get to it, then."

"My lady."

Were there special words for taking on vassals? She didn't know.

"So"—Kaye swallowed hard—"I'll arrange a settlement and purchase a residence for your bloodline. In the event of war, I will arrange with Grey for you to stay here, within his wards, for protection. And I'll see to it that the name Lakatos is honored. Your quarrels will be mine, our fortunes entwined."

"I thank you for your generosity," Sigmund said. "Lakatos is your servant."

Kaye turned to locate the wineglass, but Sigmund stilled her.

"I believe it is customary that you stipulate a sixty percent tithe on anything my family earns through labor or investment."

"Sixty percent!" Kaye whispered. But she did kind of remember that the families within the great Houses gave a portion of their earnings. "That's robbery."

"It's tradition."

Well.

"You keep your money," she told him. "I only want loyalty."

"Again, you are very generous." Sigmund bowed. "You have my loyalty, my life, my Shadow." He smiled a bit. "Your quarrels are mine, our fortunes entwined."

Kaye made a face. "I rhymed there, didn't I?"

He shrugged. "I liked it, though."

"My first time."

"You don't say."

"So now we seal the deal." She led him to a table. Poured the Moll into the wineglass, then lifted the knife. "Archaic," she muttered, then drew the blade across her palm. He did the same as she let her blood drip into the glass. Then she staunched the flow with cloths she'd set aside for the purpose. Drops fell from his palm as well.

Shadow and blood swirled in the glass though no mortal physics had encouraged the minivortex. The words were formal, but this was binding. Magic. This made them part of a whole.

She took a deep breath, reminding herself that she was Brand, and drank deeply from the glass. It roared down her throat and dispersed, hot and cold at the same time, into her system.

Sigmund solemnly did the same. When he put it down on the table, he said. "Lakatos is yours."

Great. "Can you make me a key?"

He jerked slightly in surprise. Then immediately recovered. "Certainly, my lady. What do you want it to open?"

"That I can't tell you."

He frowned a moment. "Ah. Of course." He said it like he'd known there'd be a catch to her sudden acceptance of his family. "You're asking for a skeleton key."

"Is there such a thing?"

"There is."

"And do you know how to make one?"

"Yes."

He seemed disturbed, but Kaye couldn't do anything about that. The problem was much larger than Sigmund or her. And this was the only way she could think of to get to the angel. Once upon a time, ten years ago, she'd stolen keys. Every decision she made would be different now.

"I need it right away. How long will it take you?"

The diffused light made him look pale and older. "Can you meet me tomorrow afternoon? Where we first met? I'll be bringing my son; the two of us together can't make it into your rooms here."

Kaye didn't think Ferro would leave her alone tomorrow night anyway. "In the sculpture garden."

"Yes. Come whenever you can. We'll be waiting." He turned to leave, and though Kaye was terrified of discovery, she secretly wanted him to stay. He was a nice old man. He made her feel . . . not so alone. If he sat by her bedside, she might even be able to sleep. He was of Brand House now, that's what this feeling was. And she needed that: Twenty-four hours in Grey's home and she was already exhausted and heartsick. Not so strong.

"A question," he said, turning. "So I don't mistake anything."

"Ask." Though she didn't know what was safe to tell him.

"Why is your old bodyguard waiting across the street, watching the house, and not inside with you here?"

A flame burst within her. She resisted the urge to dart to the window. To fling herself across the lawns and sob in Bastian's arms.

He had *stayed*.

"Is he still loyal to Brand?" Sigmund asked.

The inner flames crackled, feeding her better than water and food and sleep and comfort. She felt herself growing strong again.

Her throat clogged with feeling. Was Bastian loyal to Brand? "Apparently so."

Chapter 10

Work was all that was left until they could meet. Eleven tours, a millennia of service, and Jack could barely get through the sixty seconds that comprised a minute. And the sixty of those that made an hour. And so on and so forth—the prospect making his teeth clench and his nerves snap. Shadow might be insanity, but the mortal world was no different. And The Order? Might as well be Hell. There was no place left for him.

Work. Urlich was the only lead he had. The rest would have to wait for Kaye. *Noon. Two hours from now. One hundred twenty minutes. Seventy-two hundred seconds.*

Work.

The Gregory Building was a stately block of brick and plaster left over from the last century. It was a quiet building, expensive, its apartments primarily let by foreign dignitaries and businessmen visiting the D.C. area. Often the apartments remained empty, at the ready, but hushed.

Jack entered through the tall double doors, immediately turning the security cameras away, a critical measure for angels in these modern times; leave no record of The Order behind. The lobby was black and gray marble, cold. Shadow clung to the corners like translucent cobwebs.

A security guard stood sentry by the elevator. No weapon was visible, but Jack knew he had one just inside his jacket. Jack distracted the guard's mind as he approached, then cracked his skull against the wall.

This was what he was good at. This was what he was on Earth to do.

One hour, fifty-nine minutes before he could see Kaye and demand an explanation.

Jack punched the button for the elevator.

Another guard stepped out from behind a concealed counter, rifle raised.

Jack flicked a hand his way, yanked hard on the man's consciousness, and the guard slumped into oblivion.

How many breaths did he have to take until then?

The twenty-sixth floor was also guarded, this time with semiautomatic rifles.

As Jack advanced, he was tempted to turn the guards on each other. Oh, how he wanted to, but instead blanked their minds, rendering them both unconscious as well.

He wasn't supposed to meddle with humankind, but there was no use warning Urlich he was there.

Urlich, the human who'd cut a deal with the mage Houses, the deal that Kaye's client Mr. Ballogh had wanted to mirror.

The Order's intelligence had finally located and identified this waste of a man. Wealthy, connected, the mastermind behind a carefully planned system of human trafficking. Urlich didn't value human life, which made him a perfect candidate for a mage deal. He'd established a government of his own that didn't recognize political boundaries or laws. His was an underworld organization, a world unto himself, with channels for commerce, transport, and access to arms.

The mage-Urlich deal was actually quite inspired: Once

the dominant governments toppled, another was already in place, entrenched and functional. Global markets would turn to black markets. And humanity, desperate to survive, would buy in, therefore strengthening the dominion of the Houses.

This was no Shadow-based claim to power; this was a multilayered, systemic undermining. Coupled with the flow of Shadow, the Houses really couldn't lose.

Jack stalked through Urlich's large suite looking for his prey. He could sense him just ahead by the muck of his thoughts.

There.

Jack kicked in a door. Urlich, half-dressed, was mid-grunt, mounted on a woman, beads of sweat on his forehead. The woman's mind was fuzzed by drugs. She'd have to be stoned to have sex with that monster.

Urlich stopped puffing and drew out his prick, pushed the woman out of the way. Jack's death was on his mind.

Once upon a time, Jack would have carefully used reason and patience to compel answers. He would have kept himself out of reach of the atrocities littering Urlich's mind. But a little bit of Shadow had infiltrated Jack's heart, and the burn on his arm—all Kaye, of course—put him in a bad mood.

Which was why he had his hand around Urlich's throat. He used his angel's strength to lift the man and braced his body on the bedroom wall.

The man was lizard lean, with sparse black hair and old pockmarks. Big nose. He didn't look the least bit afraid.

The woman limped away, oblivious to her nudity. No need to wipe her mind; she was doing that herself.

"I'm going to ask you some questions," Jack said to Urlich, whose face was going purple. "And you're going to answer me. I can tell when you lie, so don't even try."

Jack let go and Urlich fell to the floor. Urlich gasped and sputtered for a moment. He brought his head up only when several soldiers burst through the door behind Jack.

Kill him, Urlich thought, while he still choked on sound.

Jack didn't even turn as he pushed into the soldiers' minds and ripped out the violence. They staggered back, collapsing, eyes rolling up.

"Mage," Urlich said, raspy. "I have protection, eh, from your Mr. Grey."

How cute. This soon-to-be devil thought Jack's strength and abilities came from Shadow. Well, Shadow did have something to do with it.

One hour, forty-seven minutes. Kaye.

Jack took the lid off his light. Let whatever divinity Kaye had left behind unfold within him. Burn into his cells, his bones, his sight. And once again he was an avenging angel of old, terrible in beauty, swift in strike. His expansive soul filled the room with his fury. The dazzling blaze narrowed Urlich's pupils to black specks.

Urlich finally trembled, raising a hand to protect himself or to beg.

"I'm no mage," Jack said. "I am of Order, and I'm here to destroy you."

"Can't very well travel with her like this," came a man's harsh whisper, carried on the shallow drifts of Shadow down the hallway outside Kaye's cracked bedroom door.

Kaye hesitated, her bag and scarf in hand. Bastian might be waiting for her even now.

Bastian. Her heart had been battering her inside since waking.

A woman murmured in response, but Kaye couldn't make out her words.

"You can't be serious," the man whispered back.

Kaye really had to go, but instinct told her to investigate. A fast check. Better to see how the house was run and who lived there than go on in ignorance.

She looked both ways down the hallway—red carpet, wide moldings—and then traveled the passage to her right until she turned into a narrow gabled corridor, less elaborate in decoration, but still in keeping with the richness of the house. At the end of the hallway stood Arman Maya, the mage she'd unseated at the Council. And he was whispering to Ferro's secretary, Camilla.

"Mr. Grey says you can't stay here any longer," Camilla was saying.

"She can't be moved—" Arman Maya broke off when he spotted Kaye.

"Who can't be moved?" Kaye asked, approaching.

Camilla was undeterred. "Might I suggest a hospital? You have his message." The secretary turned to leave. Upon passing, she said, "Ms. Brand."

Kaye didn't answer. She couldn't risk shifting her gaze from Arman, who looked ready for violence.

This meeting was good. If he wanted to fight her, now was the time. She was still feeling a little iffy, but she could take this guy. And she'd make quick work of it. Didn't matter that she didn't remember how his House used Shadow.

Kaye was prepping to warn him in no uncertain terms not to cross her—that she'd burn him like lightning—when someone screamed from inside the room.

"Shana!" Arman opened the door in a blur of panic.

Kaye sputtered with her threats as she looked after him.

Inside the room was a girl, a starved-looking teenager, and she was struggling on the floor against an unseen adversary. She had black, scraggly hair, which accented her pallor. The room smelled of sweat and bad breath. The girl rasped as she craned her head away from whatever was attacking her. In the brightly lit room, no danger was apparent. Mentally ill?

Arman tried to comfort her, but the girl fought him too.

"It's only in your head," he was saying. "Sweetheart, there's nothing here. Just Dad."

The girl clawed the air, thrashed, thumped her hips up and down.

"Honey, it's just me." He tried to stroke her hair. "These are *your* illusions. Not real."

Damn it. Now she had to like Arman, a father who was so tender.

But she didn't have to show it. "What's the matter with her?"

"Nothing," he said. "Go away."

He reached to slam the door shut in Kaye's face, but she stopped it with a palm, dropped her purse and scarf to push the door open again, and entered.

"It's on me!" the girl screamed. "Shadow!"

"Nothing's on you, honey," Arman said. "I swear there's no Shadow in here."

Kaye knew there was Shadow everywhere, especially in this house. The room might be filled with light, but it wasn't angelic light, which was the only kind that could push Shadow back. All light was not created equal; thinking that it was equal was like believing shadow and Shadow were the same. And just as with anything else, light's quality varied. So simple a concept, yet even a Council member didn't understand.

Kaye lifted her palm, Shadowfire in hand, the better to *really* see.

Arman gave a primal, defensive shout as he grabbed the

girl roughly and dragged her away from Kaye. His torso hulked over his child in protection.

"I'm not going to hurt anyone," Kaye muttered. "At least not yet."

Fire was a different kind of light too, and it was good stuff, like gold—ageless and true. Kaye crouched to brandish the flame about, and sure enough, a faint outline of something skittered back, but she couldn't make out what.

Shadow was indeed everywhere. The room was webbed with the stuff.

"Illusion!" Arman spat.

Kaye looked up at him. "Not my thing."

She slowly moved forward, made her intention clear that she was going to approach the girl. Arman tensed protectively again, but then relaxed his grip so Kaye could bring her fire close.

A little gremlin cringed into sight, its planes and contours going hyper-black next to Kaye's fire. He had his skinny fingers on the girl, but like a squirrel, the creature went from sudden stillness to a flash of movement as he fled into obscurity.

There! She'd seen it. The fae *could* cross into the world.

"What was that?" Arman demanded.

The girl began weeping, turning against her father's chest. He gathered her close to him again.

"I don't know." The thing reminded her of an intelligent rat. "My guess is it was a pest taking advantage of her weakness."

It made sense, though. If Shadow could cross, more and more of it by the minute, then its creatures would find a way as well, even the least of them, like the gremlin. Nosing through fissures, sneaking through gaps in the veil—the pests would be the first to come. To nest. To breed.

"Why would it attack a child of Shadow?" Arman sounded angry.

As if Twilight didn't have its parasites too.

"Why do mosquitoes bite humans?" Kaye snapped back. "*Now,* will you tell me what's the matter with her?"

Arman's mouth closed up tight, but he took his daughter's wrist and showed Kaye the girl's palm. A circle was burned into its center and red streaks radiated from the wound.

Kaye closed her eyes. She knew what that circle meant.

"Don't ask what you don't want to know," Arman said.

She felt angry again, which pushed her energy back up to a blaze. "I take it that your daughter's Shadow has been depleted," Kaye said diplomatically. One did not name mages. "That her magic has been stolen."

And the mages let Ferrol Grey prey upon them because the angel light, among many other things, gave him some kind of magnetism that drew magekind to him. She understood now: Ferro was their leader, their Order, their pharaoh.

"Then you do know." Arman's contempt was back again. "This was her punishment for using illusion to shoplift."

Kaye shuddered in revulsion. "Why do you have her in this shitty light? She won't heal this way."

Bastian and Custo had steeped Kaye in the deepest, purest Shadow when she was ill. That's what this girl needed.

"She's afraid of the dark," Arman answered. "Sees things, which isn't unusual for one with our power."

A mage who was afraid of the dark? Poor girl. Stupid, if caring, father.

"Still. She can't heal this way. And she was probably weak to start with because she's refused Shadow her whole life." And if Kaye's tone suggested Arman was partly to blame for allowing the behavior, she wasn't sorry. The man should have taught his daughter better.

"You just saw that thing on her!" he argued. "And you want me to put her in Shadow?"

"The world is turning to Shadow," Kaye said. "The number of predators will grow."

"They don't bother me," Arman said.

"Probably because she's more of a mage than you."

He looked taken aback.

Kaye wasn't going to apologize. "You were born before Shadow started coming back into the world. She's lived with it all her life."

"You're saying I can't protect her."

"She's got to learn to do that," Kaye said, thinking of herself too, as a teen. "Instead of shoplifting, she needs to learn to fool the fae. Make herself appear as the greater threat."

Kaye was inwardly quaking. Who was she to educate a Council member on Shadow?

A thousand years since the last rise and maybe now all of magekind was ignorant of what this advent of darkness meant. Ignorant mages plotting in their Houses against humanity and Order, when the fae were drawing closer. What then? What would the fae do with their lesser brothers and sisters?

"I had no idea she was in danger. Yes, she needs to learn," Arman said bitterly. "That is, if she survives her punishment."

Kaye sighed. Bastian was just going to have to wait a little bit longer. "Turn off the light; let Shadow come. I'll sit with her while she rests. My fire will keep the pests away."

For a while at least, until she drew the attention of something bigger, meaner, and madder. What then?

Ferro stooped to touch a vacant-eyed soldier on the threshold of Urlich's apartment. The soldier was alive, breathing, but stupid to the world.

And deeper inside, he found Urlich dead, though no wound was apparent. He wasn't wearing pants. Looked like he'd died of fright.

At his side, mage Minqua, who was from a house of stealth, said, "Do you think it's the Eastern Houses? Urlich had ties with them too."

Ferro shook his head. The setting was too bloodless, too serene. "This is Order. They've struck their first blow."

Minqua looked grim, though he had to have known it was coming. "What now?"

Ferro smiled, excited, though the timing was difficult, what with the news of the pureblood mage causing friction in the ranks. "Call Terre House. We strike back."

12:47 PM. *Now she shows up.*

Jack had started shaking at five minutes past the hour. He was ragged with anger now. He stayed seated on the steps to the Lincoln Memorial, though he'd spotted Kaye's approach. If he stood, he might do something, something like grab her or overpower her. Put the bird in a cage.

He darted a glance since he wasn't safe, not near safe enough to look at her fully, and saw only the red halo of her hair and her black eyes. "Does your fiancé know where you are?"

He shocked himself by sounding mild when he felt so bitter.

"I don't think so. I was followed, of course, but I lost them." She towered above him for a moment, a shadow on the white steps, then lowered herself all the way down beside him. Her scent circled his head again, made him want to find where her scent darkened and grew more potent. The thought made him hot with lust for a woman he'd refused to ever touch again.

A group of schoolkids in coats and hats was being led up the steps in a messy line. Thank God. He wouldn't do anything dumb in front of children. He hoped he wouldn't.

"I'm sorry I'm late," she said. "Couldn't be helped. I hope you haven't been waiting long."

"Three days, four hours"—he checked his watch—"fifty minutes."

He couldn't breathe.

"I'm so sorry, Jack."

He had nothing to say to that because sorry couldn't remotely cover it. Not remotely cover the damage she'd left in her wake. How magelike of her. "Are you safe?"

Let her be safe. So he could have at her.

"I think so," she said.

"Are you sleeping with him?"

Silence, which was answer enough. Jack had already known—Ferro would've demanded it and Kaye was quite the performer—but the silent admission still made heat roar over his skin. Only a kiss before. Now only sex? People had sex all the time for lots of reasons. But Kaye, under Grey's hands . . . Dear God. Laurence was right: *Don't go there.* His mind would break for sure.

"Please understand," she said.

"I'm working on it." He looked away to find some relief, but the grounds around the memorial didn't have any peace for him, misty as they were with darkness. Violence was rising within him again; he'd better get this over with. "So you wanted to meet," he prompted. What information was so valuable that she had to climb into bed with Ferro Grey?

Another long silence, but he wouldn't look at her. If she had something to say, now was the time.

"Are you missing angels?" she asked.

"Yeah." Still wouldn't look at her. "A few."

"Go out in groups. Don't let anyone do anything alone."

"Why?" Angels did what was required of them. Avoiding danger was counterproductive to their cause.

"Ferro and some other mages are trapping angels and feeding them to wraiths. That's how the wraiths are being renewed. They can think more clearly afterward; the hunger doesn't rule them, so they are useful. They follow orders."

So the war was on. Of course it was. It had been on forever. Yes, he would warn the others, though they wouldn't alter their missions to save themselves. More likely The Order would soon command a direct strike. And Kaye was on the side of Shadow.

"Some catch you've got there," he said, sickened all over again.

"You set me up for this," she shot back.

"I thought we'd decided on a different course of action."

Silence again. She was so close, he could feel himself circling his arms around her and pulling her tightly to him to protect her. He was afraid he might do just that without thinking. Lock her in his arms here, forever. Until they became stone *together*.

"And there's some uproar over Khan," Kaye continued. "Ferro feels his position is threatened. He doesn't like Segue, suggested action against them. They need to watch out too. You need to warn them."

"Khan doesn't care about Grey."

"Still. Ferro's knee-jerk was to go after Layla."

"Then all our problems will be solved. Ferro will be dead." And Jack would be finished with this, finished with her.

"This is bigger than that. It's not just Grey, Bastian," Kaye said.

"Don't call me that." She might as well burn him again. "What bigger problems?"

But Jack had an idea, considering what he'd found in Urlich's dirty mind. The plans were vast and so well guarded that The Order hadn't had a clue.

Jack needed to get inside Grey House. Find the next layer, destroy it too. And then the next and the next and so on until he wasn't angry anymore.

"If Ferro's gone," Kaye was saying, low to his ear, "others are ready and eager to step into his place. There's a plan at work. You should have seen how excited they got over Khan."

"Will you screw them too?"

Silence. Good. The wind whipped up the steps and the children babbled at Lincoln's feet.

"I need to get inside Grey House," he finally told her.

Her voice was distant, removed. "No. I won't allow it."

Was she trying to protect him again? No thanks.

He finally looked her in the face. She was all washed out, pale. Cold-looking. Hungover? "I'm not asking. I need to be inside, and you will get me in. That's the job you were hired to do."

"How do you propose I do that?" Circles under her eyes too. "I'm not the man's wife yet."

Good strike. It stung.

"You'll think of something." Just like that they were back to their old dynamic. Fire and ice. "Invite Segue to

Grey House as a gesture of goodwill. The Shadow types can size each other up, and I'll come along."

She blinked, considering. Her scars looked starker in her bloodless face. "Segue. I don't know."

Jack stood because he was finished here. Had to be. "Make it happen." He started down the steps. "And Ms. Brand, lay off the drink."

Ferro breathed deep for calm as he listened on his mobile to Minqua's report on his new fiancée's activities. "As you requested, two followed Ms. Brand today: one wraith and myself."

Kaye had gone "shopping" this morning. He'd assigned her security and staff to assist her, but she'd complained bitterly upon leaving with the group, and so it was no surprise that she'd sent them away at her earliest opportunity. Which was why he'd required two to follow her regardless.

"And?" Ferro prompted.

"The wraith is a pile of stinking barbeque."

Ferro closed his eyes to control his reaction; Kaye's temper was lit, but that didn't surprise him either. He could feel a little bit of her Shadow licking within him. Every time he touched her, he couldn't help but take a little bit of her Shadow. How did she stand the sizzle and burn day in, day out?

"This happened in public?"

"In a dressing room stall."

He was sure she would defend her actions vigorously, without a moment of contrition. And he'd have to assure his other wraiths that they would not meet the same fiery end.

She was supposed to be his helpmate, not a liability.

"And did she lose you too?"

"No, sir. She's on foot, heading across the National Mall."

"What has she been up to all morning?"

"She just met with her old bodyguard, Jack Bastian."

"So good to see you again," Kaye said upon approaching Sigmund and his son, Marcell. The ground of the sculpture garden was thick with Shadow. Why did it feel like she was being watched?

Shadow was playing with her mind. She was here for a key, crafted by her new vassals. But Marcell was still frowning even though they were now basically family.

Her smile faded. There was no pleasing him.

"I wasn't there last night for your ceremony," Marcell said, "but you had better believe that I'll be paying every cent of your fucking sixty percent."

Kaye was tired of his unrelenting hostility. "All I want is the key. If Lakatos doesn't want to be associated with Brand, I'll find a way to release you." She had no idea how that was done now that their bloodlines were bound by Shadow.

"No," Sigmund said to Kaye. "You pledged protection for Lakatos. A place for Lakatos in the new world."

Kaye held up a hand toward Marcell. "If he doesn't want . . ."

"We are bound!" Sigmund said.

But Kaye was looking at the old man, really looking for the first time since approaching them. Sigmund's skin was sallow, looser even, as if fat no longer softened his skull. His hair was thinner, greasy, and his eyeballs were bloodshot. The old man was wavering on his feet.

". . . that I'd take *money* for the life of my father," Marcell was saying, his voice ruined with sadness and anger. He shook his head back and forth and back and forth in a forever refusal. "No."

Something tightened within Kaye in response, the *no* echoing in her mind. "I don't understand."

"Let's finish this," Sigmund said. He opened a shaking hand to her. In the center of his palm was an ugly thing, bone-white, nubby, streaked with black. Shadow fuzzed its surface.

"The skeleton key?" It looked dirty. She didn't want to touch it.

Marcell put his arms around his father and seemed to brace himself, though it was Sigmund who seemed in danger of falling over.

"Take it, my lady," Sigmund said, putting his free hand on his son's arm. Comfort. "And do right by my son."

"No." She stepped back. What had she done? What had she asked?

"I'm an old man already. And there's no going back," Sigmund said. "Best you take what you wanted. Make our Houses strong."

His son heaved soundlessly.

Understanding was coming slowly and reluctantly. Kaye knew that the key—the key to opening anything—had come at a very high price. Way too high, by the looks of Sigmund. And she knew it had something to do with her dismissal of the 60 percent tithe. The son had vowed to pay her regardless.

She'd only been trying to be different from her greedy forebears. She didn't need her vassals' money.

Had the Lakatoses thought she'd bought the key with false generosity?

. . . *that I'd take* money *for the life of my father* . . .

Oh, dear Shadow. All the fathers were protecting their children today.

What about her father? Had he ever tried to protect her like this? Arman Maya, so gentle with his girl. And Sigmund Lakatos, holding out the bone of his life to raise up his son.

Her father, Aidan Brand, had died in the midst of a deal having to do with her.

Had her father seen the dark turn of the world? Had he taken steps, bitter ones, so that she would survive the fall of man? Did she owe him forgiveness?

"Why didn't you stop me?" she asked Sigmund.

"You'll see to it that Marcell will rise," he answered. "That he'll have power. That he won't be lost in the war. You'll use your fire to protect him."

"You knew I didn't know," Kaye said. "You used me."

Sigmund smiled. "We used each other."

She should have demanded the damn 60 percent. She should have honored tradition—there was protection in ritual, in the ruthless schema of the Houses—and not waved it away so carelessly.

"Take it now, please," Sigmund repeated. "I'm very tired."

Kaye rode the edge of her revulsion. Reached out. Grasped the key.

Son of a bitch.

"Love you, son," Sigmund said, and his body gasped into a cloud of dust, his clothing dropping to a heap on the ground. Fine particles lingered in the air.

Marcell was left with a collapsed embrace where his heart had been. When he angled his chin toward Kaye, she blanched at the hatred in his eyes.

"You heard him. I didn't know," Kaye said. Shock numbed everything.

So when the strike came out of nowhere, taking her at the jaw, she felt only a jolt. She fell backward onto the concrete, clutching the bone key in her hand. Her legs were splayed, bag was spilled.

Marcell leaped onto her—heavy—and struck again. She blocked with one hand; the other was pinned.

A park visitor, human, yelled, "Call the police!"

Footsteps running.

Kaye tried to deny it again, tears blurring her eyes—*didn't ask for his life, not his life*—but the sounds were knocked out of her mouth. Her head started to *boom boom*. She struggled, then lashed out with a whip of fire.

Marcell screamed, falling back, flailing to rip off his blazing coat.

A witness screamed too.

Kaye kicked her way free of him, a heel leaving a red gash along his jawbone.

A blur of movement. Onto Marcell jumped a figure who attacked him with vicious strikes to his face. One. Two. Though Marcell was already limp in the angel's grip.

"Stop!" Kaye shouted. Marcell was House. No one would touch him, not even Bastian. Sigmund had seen to that.

Bastian hit Marcell again, sending him in a bloody arc to the pavement, unconscious.

"He's mine." Her Shadow expanded within until her eyesight darkened. *Mine!* "He belongs to me." Sigmund had bought her with the key.

Bastian stepped over Marcell's prone body to help Kaye back to her feet. He threw her personal items back into her purse and retrieved her scarf. The key, she clutched in her hand.

"Mr. Grey will be angry," he said. Her angel had blood on his hands. "Sloppy work. You *were* followed. Grey will know you were with me."

Shit. If Grey knew that she'd met with Bastian, it would be bad. Grey was so jealous. But if Grey knew about

Lakatos, then her plan to save the angel would be wrecked.

"Another wraith?" She'd killed one this morning. She had to find the other fast, and kill it too. Where was it?

"No wraith. A mage."

Oh. Hope was knocked out of her. It was over then. She'd done all this for nothing. And Sigmund . . . She was going to be sick.

"If you'll excuse me," Bastian said, so angry, "I have to get rid of the body."

"He's dead?" Had she killed Marcell too? Her legs gave, and Bastian caught her at her arm and waist. His hold was too tight, painful, but wonderful all the same. She wanted to stay in his grasp, even if it hurt.

"No, the mage," Bastian corrected. "Snapped his neck to save yours." He angled his chin Marcell's way. "That one will hurt. A lot. But he'll live."

A mage, dead. At Bastian's hands.

Marcell Lakatos okay.

"And the witnesses?" A semidispersed crowd looked on.

Bastian forced her to take her own weight. Stepped away from her like she was dangerous.

"They won't remember anything," he said. "I wish someone could do the same for me."

When the dark-haired man turned his gaze his way, Gary Shultz retreated, putting his wife, Becca, behind him. But the attack was more insidious, a grip on his mind and a flutter within it. Gary felt a deep inner command to forget.

They'd seen the commotion. Seen that young guy hit the red-haired woman, and then jump on her to hit some more. Becca had said, "Help her," as if it were she, long ago, under the angry fists of her ex, and not some stranger in the park. And so Gary had run forward to save both women, because now, finally, he could.

Wait. Save whom again? Becca!

But the dark-haired man had gotten there first and had whaled on the guy until he was a bloody pulp.

Oh, God, who was a bloody pulp? Where are we? Why couldn't he remember?

"Gary?" asked Becca.

He turned and saw the panic in her eyes.

"What's happening?" she pleaded, raising a hand to her head.

"I have no idea," he answered, putting an arm around her to usher her away. Far away. "But it's not safe here."

It wasn't safe anywhere anymore.

Chapter 11

"You met with your guard," Ferro said. He didn't care that he sounded jealous. He was.

But he kept himself moving toward the in-house theater. Made her follow *him*. He'd cued this upcoming holiday season's blockbusters. The films were all about epic disasters and special abilities and romance. He would give humankind all of that, and soon. Already the public clamored for mages.

Although now he was rethinking his attire. "Classic, not ridiculous." And Kaye should know; she was from this generation. He'd go black. Shadow black and be a hero.

"Jack Bastian and I had unfinished business," Kaye said, entering behind him and seating herself in the padded chair at his side, the angle of her body pitched toward him. She had a mark on her chin, as if she'd been struck. She still looked too pale as well.

Regardless, he'd take her tonight. He had his pride after all. And he wanted to celebrate what would happen tomorrow. It was a big day.

"You mean your relationship isn't over," Ferro returned. Had that Mr. Bastian raised a hand to her? Ferro would kill him. He'd kill him regardless. Should have already.

"No, it's over." She leaned over, took a pretzel from his bowl. Gave him a peek at her cleavage.

The Verity Shadow was weakening in Ferro's blood, but he could still hear the major harmony of truth in her words. The relationship was over. Why didn't he believe her?

"Is it over for him as well?" The human was holding on to Kaye. Ferro would cut him off at the wrists if he had to.

She looked irritated at the question, but the expression turned to resignation. Seemed like she agreed that Ferro deserved an answer. She took a nibble at her pretzel. "Yes. It's over for him as well. This meeting was strictly pertaining to a job I was hired for."

"What job?" Why did she need clients anymore, when he had enough wealth and influence for both of them?

Never mind. Tomorrow she would stick close to home.

"It was regarding a client." She took a second to examine her manicure, then returned her attention to the pretzel. "I like the pay, and I have a house to buy for Brand."

"You live here. I won't have you living anywhere that isn't protected by wards." She'd take other lovers if she had her own place, a woman like her. Hot all the time. Ready all the time.

Kaye shook her head, crunching the last bite. "That was not our agreement. I have my own House to think of, and it requires a separate residence. I won't compromise."

She would, but he'd let her believe what she wanted for now. He was more interested in the rest of her day.

"Where did you go after that? You've been out a while." Ferro hadn't heard from Minqua. There was one call about her meeting with Jack Bastian, then nothing. Someone was lying. Had to be Kaye. But how?

"I took a walk around the monuments, spent most of my time in the sculpture garden. Lots of Shadow there. If my visions are true, everything will soon be rubble."

She was right.

"I lost a wraith today," he said. *Deny that.*

"I killed him." She didn't sound apologetic. She even took another pretzel. "We're going to have to talk about you using wraiths in any capacity that has to do with me. In spite of your . . . dietary assistance to them, they're still too violent and they still stink."

A diversion. "What about the man I had assigned to protect you?"

She lifted a brow. "I never saw any man."

Truth and truth and more truth. The only lie she'd ever fed him had followed his earnest question, "Was it good for you?"

She tilted her head, a feminine movement. "The walk gave me time to think."

Here it comes. He picked up the remote so it looked like he didn't care.

"I believe you may be taking the wrong approach with regard to Khan."

He sneered at her. "Did your Mr. Bastian say so?"

She smiled in return, with a little seductive arch to her back. "Mr. Bastian would prefer that I work at Segue, and that I count Khan as an ally. Which I still do."

Grey went very still. "You prefer Khan?"

"I didn't say that." She turned fully in her seat to face him. She was beautiful, more so with her scars.

"What *are* you saying?"

"That I agree with Bastian's approach to be friendly with Khan. I think you should consider it too."

"Consider what?"

"Inviting Khan here."

"Bring the pureblood into my House?" What kind of bald duplicity was this?

She remained impassive. "Don't you think it would be

smart, both a gesture of goodwill and an opportunity to size them up? I'm on good terms already. We could use that."

Now she used "we." Only when it suited her.

"No." There was too much going on at present, especially with the loss of Urlich. Tomorrow the world would know that the mages would not be ignored. At this moment his plan was being put into place. "Soon enough I'll make Khan come to me."

"Ms. Mathews, his lover, *did* reach out to you, though on behalf of Segue," Kaye pointed out. "And you must have concerns that one or more of the other Houses has contacted Segue. We have an advantage; let's not waste it."

All true. And yes, the other Houses could be moving against him.

Their continued loyalty hadn't bothered him *before* Kaye and her atom-bomb report that a pureblood walked the world.

Urlich gone. Tomorrow a strike. Ferro couldn't afford trouble from the Houses as well. This was his moment, his time to seize the future. His plans were thirty years in the making, too intricate to be thrown off by such a potent variable as a pureblood.

Kaye claimed—*believed*—that Khan liked her. All men liked her.

The Shadow whispers hushed, as if the fae were watching him make this decision, a great reward in the balance.

"What do you have in mind?"

"A meeting. Here, not so formal as the Council table. I think we should keep it friendly, but with a little home-field advantage." She leaned in, closer, like a sensuous cat. "This timing is critical: Ms. Mathews made an overture. Ignoring it might be dangerous. Plus . . . another House is going to approach them. Probably already has."

"Yes, yes, you're right," Ferro finally said. And what time would be better than when the Earth was reeling.

"I'll arrange everything myself," Kaye said.

Funny. "No, I don't think so," Ferro said, lifting the remote. First up, a natural-disaster movie. "Camilla will handle everything. You've done quite enough."

Ferro snored a deep, shaken bass tone. He was naked, though still semihard, and had kicked away the covers after declaring her too hot beside him. He smelled a little funky, but then, he'd exerted himself for more than an hour.

Kaye eased off the bed. Then stood at the side, watching him, to see whether he could feel the weight of her gaze. Shadow slid over her nude skin, a stroking, cool embrace of magic, reminding her that this was where she belonged. She belonged in Shadow.

Deep snores. In and out. The sound of a sated man.

Okay.

The darkness parted and rolled as she crossed his bedroom, and the whispers rose from a quiet sigh and soft breaths to the words of some foreign poem about danger and pursuit and *sex, sex, sex.*

She kept to the darkest patches, kicked away a scurrying thing—mortal or Otherworld, she had no idea—and made it with stealth to her suite. Not very dangerous, considering there were any number of reasons she'd want to return to her own rooms, a shower topping the list.

She peeked inside. Empty. Closed the door. Ran across the room to the hidey-hole under her bed. Grasped the skeleton key, which hummed in her hand.

Did the angel still live?

The next part was not so easy, and each step after that, even worse.

She exited her suite, heart pounding. She felt as though she was watched, but in a mage House, it wasn't an unusual sensation. She knew how close the fae really were. How long before they could reach out and touch her?

The hallway extended to her left, and she walked down its center as if she had nothing to hide. She paused in the darkness.

. . . not this way . . .

She didn't trust it either. She turned.

A little farther. A door. She placed her hand on the wood, as if that would help her divine what lay beyond it. All she got was "flat."

Screw it.

She turned the knob and opened the door to find blackness. She held fire before her and descended. Exited onto the main floor. One look to see if the coast was clear and she smothered her light.

She kept to the deepest Shadows as she came to the main foyer. A wraith waited near the front door. It was a man, big, looking uncomfortable in his suit and tie, a silly getup that reminded her of the security surrounding the president.

. . . see see see see . . .

The fae had been right. If she'd come down the main stairs, she'd have been spotted.

She went as far as she dared to the entrance to the office wing. Any nearer, and the Shadows weakened slightly in the moonlight.

She could set the wraith on fire, hope he didn't squeal.

No, that would cost her in explanations and suspicion. What she needed was patience. Angel patience, the kind that didn't respond to the quickening licks inside that wanted her to move fast.

She had to be still, a slow burn. Really not her thing.

Kaye waited. Felt the night reach its full deepness. Saw a shift. A gleam of hunger madness. The wraith paced. And then he prowled in a wider circle.

His back finally turned, and Kaye glided to the office entrance. A keypad blinked green next to the door.

She had a key but no code.

Wasn't a code just a different kind of ward? Lakatos had said his real talent was to get past impassable boundaries.

She had to try anyway.

But how did the bone fit into a slim modern lock? How did Shadow disengage the technological device? Not that she doubted. But how did it work?

She started to touch the lock, and a Shadow hand emerged from her skin—a long, skinny-fingered limb, both feminine and graceful. Fae. Its movement smoked the air, reaching. The light on the keypad went out. The ghost hand turned the lever.

The door opened.

Fast.

Kaye closed herself within and hurried into the little receiving room, pleasant when lit, a mouth of darkness in the night. She lit a fistful of Shadowfire, used the skeleton key to open the cellar door, and rushed headlong down the stairs.

The angel was still there. Still collapsed.

Still breathing.

Kaye crouched and shook her hard.

The angel mewled and curled into herself.

Kaye leaned over, her mouth to the angel's ear. "It's time. We've got to go."

"Please, no."

"Jack Bastian sent me," Kaye said, trying a lie for cooperation. "He sent me to save you."

The angel closed her eyes, shutting herself off. Refusing to listen.

"Believe me."

"No mage would save an angel." The woman was resolute, resigned enough to death not to fall for games and tricks.

"But an angel once saved a mage," Kaye said. She swallowed hard, because she was suddenly fighting tears, remembering how she'd once held her keys out to a chained man. And how he had refused her. "I'm Kaye Brand, and Michael Thomas traded his life for mine."

Help. Come.

The voice, angelic in origin, was weak in Jack's mind. Weak, but nearby. So close. He came to full attention, concentrating. There were no other angels positioned in the vicinity, just Jack. The rest had been reassigned when Ms. Brand chose to leave The Order's security. Her loyalties, and his, were in question. Didn't matter that Laurence believed when the others all doubted. They readied for war.

Come. Please.

Jack's gaze zeroed on Grey House, across the street from him.

Huge edifice, expansive lawns, gated.

Somewhere on the grounds was an angel in peril. Rage burst within him as he recalled what Ms. Brand had told him: that the mages were feeding his kind to wraiths.

Was it feeding time?

Please.

I'm coming, Jack answered. He streaked through the wintery trees from his vigil place. He kept his inner light shoved deep down low but used his strength to vault over the high fence. *Where?*

He circled to the left of the building. Kept to the trees to round the perimeter. Streaked across the lawns. Avoided the wraiths that prowled the grounds so as not to lose time with a fight. Rounded a corner.

And found a side entrance tucked under an overhang. All Shadow. And the slight blue soul gleam of an angel. A dark figure clasped the angel—a mage or wraith since its mind was empty. The two struggled against each other, the angel collapsing.

Jack would not have it. He dived into the fight, grasped the attacker by its hair and threw it out onto the walkway leading to the door.

The angel slumped down. *Mage.*

Yes, mage. Jack had killed one today. He'd be happy to dispatch another. Feeding souls to wraiths. The mages were as corrupt as they'd been a thousand years ago.

Jack lifted his hand for a killing blow. Aimed for the neck behind that mess of wild red hair.

And then all strength left him.

Kaye turned, her face contorted in pain. Her garment had opened, so her naked body was revealed to the stars. Creamy skin, round breast, the maddening slope of her waist. His heaven.

Jack reared back.

He looked at the angel, who'd raised her arm to say stop.

Looked back at Kaye, trying to push herself up.

"What is this?" he demanded. The wraiths on the lawns would hear, would smell. They would be coming.

Kaye was all reckless danger and sex.

She got me out. The angel's legs buckled and she slid

down the brick wall of the house. The angel was very ill, her light so dim, her body so weak and parched. Her eyes were bloodied by burst capillaries. She'd come very close to her end.

What had Kaye done? Jack swung back to Kaye, now just getting to her feet. She wrapped her robe around herself, held it closed at her throat. But would not look at him, not even as she passed on her way back to the door.

He didn't understand. "Ms. Brand?"

Just now she had an ethereal quality, like a fine-boned sparrow in winter.

She stopped, back proud, but still clutching her shiny, dark robe around her. "Ferro agreed to meet with Segue. I believe he's planning it for tomorrow night."

Jack felt himself breaking again inside. He was helpless . . . so angry, so frightened for her. His eyes and heart burned.

She told me to call you. Said you'd be near. The angel's jaw had gone as slack as her body. He had to get her out of there, get her to help immediately. But . . .

"Kaye!" He moved to grab or hold her, but she stepped out of his reach, her features contorting slightly with constrained painful emotion.

"Come away from this," he begged. "Please."

He didn't care about the Houses' plans for a doomed world anymore. Let Shadow take over. Let darkness rise. If only he could keep her safe.

A wraith screeched as it approached. They would be found in moments.

"I have to go," she said, opening the door again. "Ferro might miss me."

* * *

"You look like Hell," Adam Thorne said, shaking Jack's hand.

"I'm in Hell," Jack returned. No use denying it.

They met at the rear entrance to the Segue Institute, the huge building evoking more expansive turn-of-the-century hotel than paranormal research center. Jack had left the D.C. area at dawn, flown by one of The Order's private planes, and landed on a strip in the West Virginia mountains.

He'd heard the story from Ava Bennerman, the angel Kaye had rescued from Grey. She'd been captured in Nova Scotia and transported in a sealed crate to Grey's cellar. Ferro Grey had used an iron ring to extract light from her seven times. She was fed irregularly by him, what looked like scraps from meals. The only other visitor to the cellar had been Kaye, just once, when Ferro had offered Ava to her as a wedding gift.

Which hollowed Jack out. That had been the day, the moment, that changed everything.

Considering Kaye's history, Jack knew that the sight of Ava in that cellar had been enough for Kaye to make a drastic decision. The fullness of that decision, he couldn't guess, but now at least he knew a part. And he held on to that part with the entirety of his soul. Eleven tours on Earth and leaps of faith were still agonizingly difficult. This one, like grace, transmuted his rage to renewed, singular purpose, as sharp and cutting as a blade wrought by The Order. From that moment on, he might question Kaye's methods, and question them deeply and violently, but he would not doubt her reasons.

He'd almost killed her for saving one of his kind.

Ava explained that Kaye had told her she was repaying a debt to Michael Thomas, but not even Ava believed that was all there was to it. Ava was afraid for Kaye, spoke from her heart when she said that Kaye was a light unto herself, and that Grey would eventually notice and take it too.

Laurence, listening to this report, pointed out that four trusted angels now had thought Kaye Brand extraordinary, trustworthy, precious; and the woman had only ever met four. The Order was at her disposal.

"And how is Ms. Brand?" Adam asked. But Jack read his thought: *Now there's a man sick in love.*

"In danger," Jack answered.

Jack felt Adam regard him for a long moment, deciding how forward he could be with an old, old angel when Adam was so young in comparison.

"I'm listening," Jack said. He'd been a blind idiot where Kaye was concerned. Adam, for all his comparative youth, was far beyond him in experience. Jack should have listened to him in that wraith interment field a few weeks ago when Adam had pitied him. Jack should have asked for help.

"From one poor fool to another"—Adam put a hand to Jack's shoulder—"danger comes with the territory of loving a woman of Shadow. I've never felt such fear as when Talia is in trouble. And the thought of my boys with what's to come?" *Agony.*

"I've never had children." Never would. And hearing this, he knew his soul couldn't have taken fatherhood. Not if his fear about Kaye alone shuddered him at every turn.

"I hope you have ten kids," Adam said, grinning. "For starters. Gray some of that angelic hair."

Jack felt the burn on his arm and was grateful for it. Because in a way, she still touched him. Always touched him. "Will you help me get close enough to strangle her?"

"You bet." Adam punched a code in a connecting entrance, and they entered a long hallway with doors off to each side, what Jack presumed to be offices and research areas. The architecture here was distinctly modern, minimalist, and favored technology. Not a place Jack would've thought was haunted, and yet Segue had a reputation for just that.

They ended up in Adam's office poring over two strange communications that Layla Mathews had received, both of which were from mage Houses seeking to ingratiate themselves with Khan.

One message was a declaration of obeisance to the pureblood via his human mate. They offered up the strength of their House to aid Khan's eventual domination of the mortal world.

Very disturbing. But not the Grey invite Jack was looking for.

The second was a cryptic invitation on behalf of several mage Houses. Layla was named, but it was clear Khan was its intended recipient.

Was a coup afoot? Ferro Grey must be going out of his mind. But still not what Jack wanted.

"We got both messages yesterday within an hour of each other. Around ten in the morning."

"Khan's response?"

"He muttered that Layla was responsible and took her off to discuss the gravity of her actions. I don't think they reached a resolution, however," Adam told him dryly. "Frankly, this mage business worries me as much as it does Layla."

Jack was thinking about the timing. "The day before yesterday, Kaye stood before the Council of Houses to claim a seat for Brand. She never came home. And now she's engaged to be married to Ferro Grey."

Oh, you poor son of a bitch, Adam thought.

Jack continued, anger and worry surging again. "Before

the Council meeting, we'd planned to come here together after all this was over. I'd leave The Order. See if we could work with Segue."

Always welcome here.

He paced to stop the anxiety riddling his muscles from cramping him up and forged ahead. "Last night Kaye said Grey had agreed to inviting Segue, Khan in particular, to a meeting. She thought it would be tonight."

Which is why you're here.

"Yes."

"But we don't have any communication from Grey."

"Sure we do," Layla said.

Jack whipped around to find Layla Mathews in the doorway to Adam's office. Her expression said she had news.

"When?" Adam looked at Jack as he beckoned her inside.

But Jack was already picking through her brain to discover the answers. He didn't care that he shouldn't invade another's mind. Didn't care that Layla had a right to privacy.

"Just delivered." She held out a card, the calligraphy of which was similar to the one celebrating Kaye's return to magekind. "We are invited to Grey House to celebrate and discuss the advent of the Dark Age."

"I'm going," Jack said. He could say he was Segue security or whatever.

"I need to be there too," Layla added. "I approached Kaye in the first place, and this is an important step toward establishing a relationship between the Council and Segue."

A trick of perception, and Khan stepped out of a sudden lift and whip of Shadow, like an inky blur in the pristine doorway. His black eyes were tipped with menace. This party was made for bloodshed.

"So you can cause more trouble?" Khan asked Layla.

Layla smiled broadly and patted Khan's arm. "You don't scare me."

"I'd better go as well," Adam said. Jack knew he was thinking of his wife and boys. He'd be sizing up the mages as potential threats or allies.

Jack turned to glare at Khan. "It's addressed to you. Will you be attending or are you still staying out of this?"

Khan's eyes went full black, a warning, but his tone was even. "My presence will suggest I intend to play games with these mages. I don't play games. I don't negotiate for power. I say we don't go."

Layla looked thoughtful. "Considering the other invitations, I think you might cause more trouble and divisiveness than good."

"You're not going without adequate protection," Khan said.

"I'll have Kaye on my side," Layla returned. "Adam, Jack . . . what if we added one more to mix it up some? I think I'll be covered."

Jack dived into her brain again. Found the name she wanted to suggest. Dismissed it out of hand, then reconsidered. The addition would make things interesting. Set Grey off balance. "Yes," he said. "Let's bring him."

The same name turned Adam's mind too.

"The dog." Khan looked satisfied.

So everyone was on the same page, though technically it was a feral wolf of Twilight that Khan referred to, and not a dog. And it was that fae aspect that would compel Ferro to allow this final addition to the Segue group inside his house.

Jack nodded. "Custo comes too. Let's see what Grey makes of the angel-fae."

Adam looked at Jack. "And we'll take our cues from

you regarding Ms. Brand. You and Custo may enter my mind freely to help manage the evening. I have a feeling things may get very interesting."

"Mine too," Layla offered.

And then Khan's arms went protectively around her, Shadow rising like a blast of smoke.

Jack felt the disturbance too, a slight imbalance under his feet. And heard it in the simultaneous rattle of small objects, light fixtures, and furniture all at once. The wraiths in the underground containment facility lifted eerie screams audible in the main building. The earth was trembling. A family photo on Adam's desk fell over.

"What is this?" Khan demanded.

Jack and Adam in unison replied: "Earthquake."

Jenn Ripley held her cell phone between her ear and shoulder so she could use a ready wipe to clean the yogurt off her daughter Emily's face while keeping one eye on Ben, toddling around the playground's sandbox.

"Mom, you'll love him," she said of her boyfriend. "And he has a little girl of his own."

Ben squatted to dig with his shovel. She'd already checked for old cigarette butts. "All done," Jenn said to Emmie, who ran back to the sandbox, allowing Jenn to get a look at the sand-crusted yogurt smear on the side of her pants. Baths, first thing, when they got home.

"Yes, he's met them, but not like that," Jenn argued. Her mom questioned everything. The paranoia on the news. The men she dated. "We had a playdate, and it went great." She couldn't stop smiling about it. He might just be the one. "He even—"

The ground lurched, and Emmie fell back on her bum in the sand. She giggled.

"Wait," Jenn said, standing. The sippy cups fell on their sides and rolled off the bench. The ground seemed to roll under her feet. Her heart stopped beating. "Earthquake."

In D.C.?

Ben's face was getting red, a prelude to a cry. But it was the leaning wooden structure of the fort slide, its shadow growing over the sandbox, that had Jenn stretching into flight.

Chapter 12

"Kindly remember, I was with you last night," Kaye said from her chair opposite Ferro's desk.

Ferro watched her for signs of deceit. She was striking in black. The lightweight cashmere sweater covered her up to her collarbones, but the cut glorified the sensuality of her body. Her pants were slim and long, and she wore bright blue shoes, so high they made her long legs longer, even seated. Her hair was knotted off her face, her composure cool.

He was getting hard again for the woman who thought she could betray him. Verity's Shadow had dwindled in his blood, so he didn't know for certain whether or not she was telling the truth. Resolving the issue of his missing angel didn't require too much effort, however. Only he, Kaye, and Camilla knew about the prisoner in the basement. And Camilla had been loyal for more than twenty years.

"You want me weak," Ferro said to bait her. "You plot with the other Houses against me."

But she looked bored. "What good would that do me? I'm curious. Enlighten me why I should bother myself about an angel and why I'd want you weak when I could have set you and this house on fire while you were sleeping. And how can I be plotting with the other Houses if they are loyal to you? Or do you have doubts about some of them too? You're paranoid, and that irritates me."

He. Irritated. Her? "Do you have an alternative explanation?"

"Maybe it's Shadow," she said. "Have you considered that? Just ask Arman Maya. His daughter was attacked by a creature from Twilight just yesterday in your very own house."

Ferro felt his mind pause, as if his train of thought had just met an unexpected switch in the tracks.

A creature of faerie in his house. Absurd. "What do you mean?"

"Don't worry, Shana is just fine." There was some kind of judgment in Kaye's tone.

But he wasn't about to pretend he cared about the girl. "Go on."

Kaye sighed. "The creature was about the size of a squirrel or some other nasty rodent. Fortunately for *me*, my Shadowfire scared it off. But if that thing can cross, other creatures from faerie might be able to as well, especially in this dark house." Now Kaye smiled satisfaction. "For example, if a mage child attracted that freakish rodent, I'd imagine an angel's light would hook something a bit bigger. Your angel might have easily been carried away by the fae."

This was too bald a story, even for her.

She huffed. Lifted her hand and lit a bright faefire. Instantly the room filled with cobwebs of Shadow, but gray and white and layered and strange.

"Ferro." Kaye's eyes were big.

He turned his head and fell off his chair. A naked creature stood next to him, human in proportion, alien in features. And the eyes . . . It reached a four-fingered hand his way, but some distance must have remained between their realms, because Ferro couldn't feel its touch.

The fae crossing into his House? The thought made him giddy-scared.

This one was very close. So beautiful. So foreign to his understanding.

"See?" Kaye said.

With her fire, Ferro could. A fae had taken the angel away. Kaye was still loyal. He preferred her loyal. And why shouldn't she be, with all that he could give her?

And now this. He wanted her by his side.

Fae in this world. The ever-present watchers joining the game.

"Are we done?" Kaye asked, fisting her hand over the fire. The room returned to its usual murk. "I have to get my nails done and be back in time to prepare for our meeting with Segue. You have no idea what it takes for a woman to get ready."

He laughed outright. "Oh, I remember. I was married for forty years." Nevertheless. "You're not going anywhere."

At least in the chaos of the next few days, another angel should be easy to find, one with bright light to take into himself and make him strong.

Another huff from Kaye. "This isn't going to work if you doubt and control my every move. I'll tell you that right now."

He eased his tone, tried to pull from the angel light he still had, tried to infuse the sound of reason into his voice. "It'll be dangerous out in the world today. Order whatever service you need to come here. If they can make it."

"How dangerous?"

So smart. If she was loyal—and it was possible that she was—then he might still be able to love her.

Ferro checked his watch, then smiled broadly at Kaye

as the earth began to jerk and move and lurch. A rattle on the wall brought his attention over to his painting, *The Fall of Magic.* Never again would magic be under the sword of Heaven.

Terre House was right on time.

"Shall we turn on the news and watch the pandemonium as it unfolds?"

And so it would begin. A warning shot before the first strike.

The current infrastructure would be strained. Soon it would break. Though Grey House was set back from the road, he thought he could imagine the faint sounds of sirens.

"You're doing this?" Kaye looked horrified. Dear Shadow, her eyes were tearing up.

Did she care so much about humanity? Did she have some twisted moral concern for humankind's welfare? It would be a problem if she did. The race was about to endure a mage-styled end of the world.

She was on her feet. "What about our meeting? I was to sit in my Council seat today."

So not humanity.

Yes, definitely, he could love her.

"Why should the earthquake have anything to do with it? I will be here. And you will be here. And the Council Houses as well." He smiled smugly. "And if this Khan and his Segue are as powerful and connected as it seems, then they should have no trouble either. Humanity will suffer, but we will go on as planned."

Adam got off the phone, but Jack had the information already from his head: 6.2 on the Richter scale. The epicenter of the quake was the National Mall in D.C. Most quakes originated from deep within the strata of Earth's layers. This came at ground level, more akin to the impact of a bomb, if not for the extended time the motion had continued.

But that was not the worst of it. Paris, Hong Kong, and Abu Dhabi had also experienced city-centered quakes. This was not a geological event. This was an attack.

The members of The Order would be dispersing to help where they could and to minimize the loss of life. At Segue there was very little damage. Broken glass. A knock or bruise. Its wraith containment had held.

Adam turned on the massive view screen in his office and selected "TV." Got news anchors at their desks concentrating on their earpieces while reporting what Jack already knew. The reports were too early for on-site footage, but Jack had no problem seeing the damage. He'd witnessed it time and time again in Kaye's visions. Rubble. Darkness. Smoke and fire. Cracks in the white buildings and monuments. Over the coming weeks and months and years, they would all fall.

"You don't look surprised," Adam said.

"I've had a preview of what's to come," Jack replied. "This is only the beginning."

The sound of helicopter rotors seemed to beat against Kaye's chest. Or maybe it was her heart going wild because a helicopter meant a new arrival. And since everyone else was gathered—the Council and selected heads of other Houses—the arrival could only be the group from Segue.

Kaye liked Layla, who had a point of view that resonated with hers. Angels, mages, and humanity—there had to be a dialogue on equal terms.

And though Khan frightened Kaye, he seemed to respect her. He'd issued no threats, had made no attempts to intimidate (more than his presence already did), and most of all, he'd given her a choice to work with him, and wasn't angry when she'd refused.

How Khan would get along with Ferro was another matter.

She and Ferro stood in the grand foyer, side by side, surrounded by the tall, lit candles. The other mages gathered in a great semicircle behind them to witness the approach of the pureblood. Shadow misted the floor, whispers rising.

Movement beyond the windows. A group approaching.

Ferro took her hand, and she could almost feel the pulse of energy go through him as he released the wards so each of them could enter.

The double doors opened to welcome the new arrivals.

Adam Thorne, handsome in a dark business suit. Layla, with her magnetic smile.

And—Kaye inhaled hugely—that angel who was also a fae, Custo. He gleamed while his gray veins pumped Shadow.

He moved to the side just enough for Bastian to come into view. Then Kaye couldn't breathe at all.

No Khan.

"Kaye?" Ferro said in a low voice.

But Layla was already stepping forward with her hand outstretched.

Kaye returned the grasp. It felt like a lifeline.

"Kaye," Layla said as if they were old friends, "it's wonderful to see you again. Thank you so much for inviting us this evening. And congratulations on your engagement. Did the earthquake affect you at all, so close to the epicenter? Anyone hurt? Any damage?"

"Layla. No, we're all good here. I'm glad you could make it. Handy having a helicopter when the roads are so bad."

Kaye turned her body slightly toward Ferro. "This is my fiancé, Ferrol Grey, High Seat of the Council of Houses."

Layla's handshake transferred to Ferro. "So nice to finally meet you."

"Likewise," Ferro said, with all his charm. Kaye saw how his gaze moved to the three men in her group, paused long on Bastian, then came to rest on Custo.

"Is this your . . . ?" Ferro began.

Layla laughed. "No, no. I'm so sorry, but Khan elected not to come. We were given to understand that his presence has caused tension among the Houses. Yours was the third communication we received, so he decided it was sensible not to attend any at this time."

Ferro's charm withered somewhat. "Sensible? One who used to be fae is *sensible* now? A pureblood cares what others think of his decisions?"

Layla chuckled. "I should've known that you, being so well acquainted with Shadow, might see through that excuse. Okay, the truth: Khan is profoundly uninterested in anything political, organized, or polite. How's that? I decided the event *I* would attend, and he is satisfied with the men who accompany me."

"He sounds scarcely human," Ferro said, which Kaye knew was for the benefit of her and the other mages, to show himself the better leader.

Layla's expression was threat serene. "Scarcely human at all, but as ever, a dark lord of Shadow."

Kaye blinked extra long, imagining Grey's inner displeasure. And the Council watched from the circle behind them. This was a disaster. Where was Khan?

Thank Shadow that Adam stepped forward, holding out his hand. "Ms. Brand."

Kaye gave him hers. "It's so nice to see you again too, Mr. Thorne."

"Adam," he corrected. "My wife, Talia, sends her congratulations. She would have attended as well, but the fae have taken an interest in our boys and she won't leave them for anything. 'Course it doesn't help that the boys take an interest back."

Ferro's attention snapped from Layla to Adam. "You're married to a mage?"

Adam shifted to shake his hand. "Talia is half fae. She's Khan's daughter from before he made the transformation from fae to mage."

Ferro shot Kaye a look, which she interpreted as, *Why didn't you tell me all this?*

"I had no idea," Kaye said to Adam, answering Ferro at the same time. "And of course, I'd love to meet her. We had a bit of trouble here with the fae too, so I understand why she'd want to stay close to the children."

Adam's brow furrowed. "That's one more thing for us to talk about, I think. The fae, even the ones I love, are *all* trouble."

Custo stepped up to Kaye. Gray-veined, wild-looking, yet shining in angelic glory. She wondered what the group assembled thought of him. An angel in this House. Was everyone at Segue crazy?

"You need more Shadow," Custo said. "I thought I warned you about that."

"In this House, I'm surrounded by it," she replied. "I have to admit, I didn't expect you, but I'm glad you're here."

Custo shifted to look at Grey. They stood eye to eye, each regarding the other.

"Darling," Kaye said, with a hint of warning in her voice, "this is Custo Santovari. He's both fae and *angel.*"

"Angel," Ferro said. Flat voice.

Custo cocked his head to the side. "Most of The Order want me dead, if it helps."

"And fae," Ferro continued.

"Wolf, to be specific," Custo offered. "Shadow in every cell and drop of blood."

Kaye forced herself not to show exasperation with all the problems each person presented Ferro. Each was a wild card, and Bastian, her former lover, was up next. And this was supposed to be a good idea?

"Forgive me"—Ferro retracted his lips in some kind of smile, not a friendly one—"but how could this come to be?"

Custo was affable. "Possession."

The smile aged to a grimace. "And are you more angel or more fae?"

"Angel," Custo answered. He held out a hand to shake. A dare. "Barely."

Everyone watched and waited for Ferro's response. The smart thing to do was shake and make nice, and then decide later if anyone, including her, needed to die. At least with Custo present, Ferro would be distracted from Bastian. But really, how could she have known that Adam Thorne had a half-fae wife? And why on earth would they bring Custo, unless it was some gambit to demonstrate that Order and magic could coexist? No, more likely, they just wanted to throw Ferro off balance, gain an edge for the night that they'd lost when Khan had decided not to come.

No big bad Death at the party. But take this angel-fae freak as consolation. And outside Grey House, the leftover difficulties of a Shadow-induced earthquake.

Ferro held out his hand to Custo, now true charm flashing in his smile.

Why was he so happy now?

Wait . . . Kaye thought, remembering what Gail had

said. Connecting her fatigue to that outstretched hand as well. Her plastered smile fell as puzzle pieces clicked into place. Ferro didn't need the ring to draw from anyone.

But Custo was already in motion. The circumspection in his gaze mellowed somewhat from dare to wry acceptance as he reached back.

Kaye moved to intercept. Too late.

Ferro and Custo gripped hands.

Jack watched the exchange from the back of the group. So far, everyone was on his or her best behavior. He kept one eyeball on the major players, shaking hands and making nice. One eyeball on the dark semicircle of observers, representatives of the mage Houses. He matched faces to those on whom The Order had information. Terrell, Martin, Wright. Some serious wealth and power in the room. And still others he didn't recognize.

But his heart was fixed on Kaye, a slender flame in a matte silver suit. Her eyes were made larger by heavy kohl on her lids. Her deep red hair was down. She'd glanced at him when he came in, flushed slightly, but hadn't looked at him since.

Custo was keeping two conversations going, pleasantries with his tongue, commentary in his mind. *Smug piece of shit, isn't he? Boo, he wanted Khan and not me. Is he going to pout all night or suck it up like a man?*

To which Jack didn't respond. And then the internal monologue went strange, fragmented: *Hunt. Kill. Blood.*

"Custo," Adam said sharply, which was when Jack knew something was very wrong.

A deep growl knocked around Custo's chest, his shoulders hunching.

When Custo turned his head, Jack saw the wild faelight

in his eyes, the slight morph of his facial features into those of a beast.

The wolf was ascendant. Hungry. Angry.

"Kaye, get back," Jack commanded in a mild tone, so as not to startle the wolf.

For once, she did as he said, and backed up a few steps. Grey, the coward who had loosed the fae beast, followed suit, amusement in his eyes. What a fool; this wasn't entertainment.

Adam ranged to Custo's left. *You take him on the right,* Adam said telepathically.

"Everyone just stay calm," Layla said. She was backing up as well to give Jack and Custo room. Her thoughts were full of *What just happened?* questions.

Jack had those same questions himself.

Jack flanked Custo, concerned at the cording of the angel's neck, the bulking of his shoulders. And the angel had been big to start with.

"Your lead," Jack said to Adam.

"What is going on?" Grey demanded, as if he wasn't to blame. "What's the matter with him?"

Custo's hands were changing as well, nails lengthening to sharp, black claws, the better to rip flesh. *Rip out their throats. Gorge on their bellies.*

Easy, Adam thought. *Slow approach. We restrain him and decide what to do from there.*

"Can I help?" Kaye asked. If she was scared, no one would know it.

"No," Jack said.

He'd had no idea just how close to the surface the wolf had been within Custo. He must have to battle with it every second of every day. Jack knew what an undertaking it had been to master the wolf in the first place, and how close Custo had come to failure and rabid violence. There'd been a time when almost everyone had wanted Custo put down. And seeing him like this, Jack wasn't so sure he'd argue against it.

"What game is this?" Ferro shouted.

Jack knew he'd started it somehow. But how?

Now, Adam said to Jack's mind.

Jack moved in swiftly toward Custo, grabbing at his arm and twisting it behind him. Adam moved in, kicking at the back of Custo's knee to knock him off balance so Jack could take him down. But Custo was too fast. He leapt into the air, striking back at Adam, and spun around to Jack, who got an elbow to his face and found himself colliding sharply with the wall behind him.

Adam was sprawled on the floor, face forward. *Too strong. So fucking strong.*

Layla stepped into the fray. "Custo!"

And got a backhand from the beast that sent her flying. She hadn't been there the first time around. Hadn't seen how Custo had almost strangled the life out of his love, Annabella, before the angel overcame the beast trapped within and stopped the madness. Layla had thought to reason with a wild animal. Not possible.

She fell back too, all thought knocked momentarily out of her mind.

Now Kaye was moving to intercept.

"No!" Jack shouted. The other mages retreated to a mass at the back of the hall, but he knew Shadow was stirring among them. And Ferro just watched, a satisfied leer on his face.

The wolf growled, lips pulled back to show sharp, elongated teeth. He was crouched to leap with his bulking hind legs. Ears pinned.

"Stop!" Kaye cried. In her hands she held a great bloom

of faefire. Golden bright, with feathers of umber, orange, and hot, hot red, the fire both fed and illuminated the darkness.

"Down," she said to Custo, one fistful of light brandished his way. In her light, each smoky tendril of magic encircling her was revealed. And so too were the faery voyeurs lurking about the foyer, watching with keen, glowy-eyed interest the dramas of magekind.

Custo's growl lowered, and he cowered from the light.

Jack felt the outward push of Kaye's power. He was ready to become an angel again and face Custo himself, if need be.

But how could he when Kaye was incandescent in the blackened hallway, keeping Custo's madness at bay. Jack was not afraid for her. Not this glorious woman with courage in every pore. The fae looking on were just as entranced.

"Leash the wolf," she commanded Custo.

And Jack could feel the angel's intellect battling the violence. Angel and fae circled each other within one body, but the Shadowfire made the wolf draw back just enough from the flame. Just that little bit within the angel. And it was enough.

Custo sat back on the floor, his head in his hands, the wolf mastered again.

With the danger passed, Kaye was like a candle in the darkness, her light on the faces of the gathered party. And then the Shadow dispersed, dim electricity taking over. With reality came murmurs from the other guests.

She clenched her fists, smothering her fire, turned, and took in the state of the group. She opened a hand toward an inviting drawing room. "I think we should discuss the fae first."

* * *

Ferro quaked on his spot at Kaye's interference. She smiled into his face, eyebrows raised to urge him back to reality. "What would you like to drink?"

But he turned away from her without answering to take in the chaotic foyer.

Every man needed a wife, but not one who made him look small in front of his guests.

The woman, Layla, and Adam Thorne, were on their knees making much of Custo Santovari and the human, Jack Bastian, on the floor. The high mages gathered in the foyer were whispering like the fae, and all Ferro could hear was the name *Kaye, Kaye, Kaye*.

He forced himself to turn back. "You were splendid, darling. Absolutely dazzling."

One half of her mouth pulled upward. "I like to make you proud."

Ferro could have handled Santovari. How dare Kaye step in front of him. How dare she show off in Grey House.

"A whiskey, please," she said to the staff.

Adam Thorne brought the angel-fae to standing; Kaye's lover was still sprawled on the floor.

"Please excuse me, Mr. Grey," Santovari said, again more angel than fae.

Ferro noticed he did not approach. At least there was one person here who knew whom to fear. Not Kaye. Fear Grey.

Ferro was flush with well-being and strength. His angel in the basement was missing, but she'd never given him anything remotely like the high he'd gotten off one tug of angel bliss from this monster.

"I don't think I'm fit company this evening." Santovari tilted his head at Kaye's lover. "And I may have injured Jack as well. We'd best be going." He glanced around the foyer. "You all enjoy the rest of your night." Then to Kaye,

"Thank you for your help. And congratulations again. I wish you every happiness."

Kaye nodded, with a tight smile. At least she had sense enough not to approach Santovari or her former lover.

She needed to learn her place.

Santovari and Thorne stooped to help the human up, shoulders under arms, the angel-fae saying, "Come on, old man."

Thorne stepped away just as Shadow blossomed inky beautiful into the foyer. Santovari had the power to cross into Twilight. The fae lurking in the darkness reached, the trees of Twilight moaning under the weight of their magic. A heady scent beckoned. Music dripped like dew from the jewel-toned leaves.

Ferro's heart seized with longing as the angel-fae carried that, that *human* into wonderland. That the human, Kaye's lover, got to linger in those ancient trees, and not a graymage, was an insult Ferro would not bear.

"You have interesting friends, Kaye," Ferro said. Friends with gifts she had not fully disclosed.

She angled those pretty scars his way. "Let's make them your friends as well."

Jack rode Shadow into Twilight on a plunging, drowning surf of magic. He had a moment in the trees, the color, smell, sigh, before Custo was dragging him back out again. His head was muddled, but he could have sworn that a tree was on fire. And that the fire took flight . . .

We've got to be fast, Custo said, heading for Ferro Grey's desk.

Jack took a second longer to get his bearings. They were still inside the Grey House wards and, more specifically, inside Ferro Grey's office, as they'd planned. But how they'd gotten there was definitely not the agreed-upon arrangement. At some point during the evening, the Segue group, with Kaye's help, was supposed to facilitate Jack getting into Grey's office to search for some indication of what was to come. Earthquake, then what . . . ?

What did Grey do to you? Jack asked Custo. He found the computer hibernating. A nudge of the mouse and the screen lit. Jack ignored the grasp of Shadow around him, put aside the whispers filling his mind. He didn't know the language the fae spoke, but he knew that they were taunting him to go back and take her. Take her. Take her.

I don't know what the bastard did, Custo answered. *But I was weakened enough for the wolf to take control. If that happens again, seriously, someone needs to kill me. Khan will do it, if no one else will. He knows not to flinch when someone's time is up. If the wolf hadn't been afraid of the Shadowfire, I don't know that I could have reclaimed control.*

Jack pulled out a silver USB flash drive and plugged it into the computer. Immediately the drive uploaded a decryption program designed by The Order's IT sector to bypass all known security systems. In seconds the program had rendered all of Grey's files visible and decrypted. E-mails, images, folders, all these he zipped up and loaded onto the drive. That this was so easy proved how much Grey relied on his House wards to keep out those he didn't trust.

Not going to happen, my friend, Jack said as he worked. *Even those who don't like you would agree that you're too much an asset to kill. You'll have to suffer your presence along with the rest of us.*

The files transferred quickly. Jack disconnected the drive, glanced up at Custo, and was taken aback at the angel's stricken expression. This time Jack answered carefully. *You hurt no one tonight. And you were surrounded by strength.*

Shadow curled and stretched between them.

But I lost myself in a split second. What if I had been with Annabella?

If you had been with Annabella, you wouldn't have needed Shadowfire to dominate the wolf. Your heart would have done it.

Custo's expression shifted. *How's* your *heart?*

Jack concentrated on the computer, positioning the mouse just so. *My heart's not mine anymore. Let's get out of here.*

Jack moved toward Custo, brushing aside Shadow as if it were old, sticky cobwebs. Hopefully, they could piece together elements of Grey's plans and his networks from the computer files. There would be a team waiting to parse and cross-reference. They would not let another "natural" disaster occur if they could help it.

Jack surveyed the office one more time and paused when he spotted a painting, one he'd seen before, a long time ago. *The Fall of Magic.* Angels with raised swords were striking down mages in a bloody reckoning. The world was covered in Shadow and fear. During another tour, a couple hundred years past, Jack had pondered the painting as he did now, and then as now, he had looked for himself among the host depicted.

It will come to this again, he thought. He could still smell the smoke and hear the screams. Still feel the weight of the sword in his hand. Still feel the flex of the downward strike as it met flesh and bone.

Custo came up beside him to look at the painting as well. A moment, then he growled low in his chest. *I would be fighting against myself if it does come to war. Shadow and Light.*

And I would be fighting Kaye. Jack's arm burned already. *Would it be so bad to go up in her fire?* No.

You're on an edge yourself, Custo observed coolly.

Jack flinched. Should have shuttered his thoughts.

Perhaps it won't be necessary. Custo leaned in to look at the painting more closely. *Humankind is stronger now. They have their own weapons with which to battle darkness. Thorne, for example, is far from helpless.*

Jack looked over at Custo. He'd never have taken the fae-ridden angel for an optimist. *The earth moved this morning,* Jack reminded him. *What was the death toll?*

Custo pulled back. Frowned.

And in spite of the turmoil just outside their houses, the mages are scheming.

Custo stepped away. *Point taken. Then tell me, so I can protect the ones I love, what does the future hold?*

Jack pocketed the flash drive. He'd lived it in another time, and had seen the future version in Kaye's visions. *Scarcity. Chaos. And worse. Until Order collapses and Shadow reigns. Can't you feel it happening? The future is now.*

Chapter 13

"We still haven't decided what we're doing about the fae," Kaye noted.

Ferro watched as she spun his tie caddy and selected a smart blue in a woven silk. She intended to make him look good, as she should've done before as the dedicated, if not loving, fiancée. Who cared that yesterday he'd coordinated massive destruction? "This one."

Kaye sat on the end of Ferro's bed. Bedroom banter was what he needed, even as outside the world grappled with terror. The feeling was surreal. They'd been up all night—Kaye had seen to it—discussing last night's meeting, impressions of people, possible plans with or against Segue, as well as her tendency to grab the spotlight, for which she'd apologized. He'd said, "Of course," but that was not "Forgiven," so she knew he'd make her pay.

Ferro looped the tie around his neck and started on the knot. "If *you* could hold off a wild fae, I think we'll be fine."

He'd said little about Custo but she knew the angel-fae's ability to cross into Twilight bothered him deeply. She felt the ache in her own breast just thinking of that place, the true home of her umbra heart, Shadow calling to Shadow, frailty to forever.

"I'm going to raise the topic at the Council of Houses," she said. "Have there been any motions to research the fae? Has anyone examined faelore to discover the best ways to protect ourselves from them?"

"The Council is occupied with other pressing matters," Ferro said, affixing his cuff links.

Kaye's throat went dry. "Another earthquake?"

Grey shrugged on his suit jacket, a smile of pleasure on his face. "First you wake the world, then you show them the sun has risen, or in our case, darkness. Not a good time to bring something else up, but by all means, I have the manuscripts in my library. You're welcome to them." He fitted his iron ring to his index finger. Paused. "Now that I think about it, maybe you *should* look into the fae. Keep you busy."

"I'm already busy," Kaye said, standing also and retrieving her scarf and bag. "But I think it's important enough to make time. I'll let you know what I find."

Ferro stopped her with a smirk. "Where do you think you're going?"

"Client meeting," she said. "Adam Thorne mentioned it last night at dinner. He wants to see his future." It was smart of Adam to arrange it with Ferro present. It helped forestall any objections.

Adam might want to see his future, but Kaye was desperate to know whether Bastian and Custo had found what they needed to stop Ferro's dark revolution. They'd gotten past the wards when they'd entered the front door, and even though Custo was shaken by his almost transformation, and Bastian professed to be beaten up, there was no way they'd have left without their information.

Ferro did a *ha!* puff with his chest. "Thorne's future is contingent on whether or not I decide to do business with him. I'm not convinced we're suited to be partners."

"With his half-fae wife, he'd probably be motivated to come to a generous agreement." It would be a relief to have members of Segue around. People she could trust. Bastian. "I've heard his Segue is an armed fortress for her protection."

"But Segue is not a warded House," Grey returned. "And that's a vulnerability. No one is really secure without wards. That goes for your plans to build too."

She pressed her lips together to show mild irritation. "I'll go cutting edge, which is good enough for me. Brand House can't reside within Grey and still be considered independent. You know it doesn't work that way."

"You're such a traditionalist," Ferro said as if that were a bad thing. "Our generation makes its own rules. We live by our own whims. I want you here, where you can be completely safe."

Our generation? He was a hundred and two.

"I'm safe enough," she said. Then softer, to change the subject, "Will I see you tonight?"

"You're barely safe at all." He looked her full in the face. "Take a wraith with you to your client meeting."

She smiled. "In the words of our generation, *not going to happen.*"

Now he smiled, bitterly. "This is not a negotiation. I have a staff member, Minqua, who is still unaccounted for. He was assigned to your protection. So today it'll be one wraith or two wraiths, you can choose. I don't want either killed." Ferro walked to the door as if the conversation were over. "And give my regards to your human lover, who, no doubt, will also be at this meeting."

Kaye had been waiting for Ferro to say something, especially after Bastian had turned up at Grey House last night, another insult.

"Tell him if he touches you today or ever again, my wraiths are instructed to eat his soul."

She had to pick her battles.

The sky was early blue when Kaye left Grey House. She'd opted for two wraiths to show Ferro that she'd risen over her fear and that he couldn't scare her that way, even though it was a lie. Upon seating herself in the car, she'd demanded all the windows be cracked and forced herself not to gag at their smell, their closeness, the thought of what sustained them.

Though Ferro had only threatened, Kaye knew he was going to kill Bastian, or have him killed. His ego demanded it. She'd warn Bastian all right, but she also knew he'd dismiss it out of hand, even though Ferro traded in slave angels. A sense of foreboding made her want to run again, run with Bastian just to get him away, but she knew it would never be far enough from danger now.

The images on TV showed the uneven collapse of office buildings, the square-shaped platform pieces of a fallen bridge, the sideways pitch of an overpass onto a freeway, and cracks in the national monuments. The other cities had fared no better, some worse. Politicians named wraiths as the new terrorists—close, but not quite. Seismologists argued geology. And prophets walked the streets ringing bells to usher in the apocalypse.

And every radio station seemed to be playing songs about Shadow.

Her appointment with Adam Thorne had been moved

outside the Beltway, since power in the city had yet to be restored. The highway exit said they should head north, to Fairfax, but the wraith at the wheel took the south exit.

She rapped on the shoulder of the driver's seat. "You're going the wrong way."

He glanced in the rearview mirror. His face, which she'd avoided looking at closely, was misshapen and brutish, as if he'd had his angel food too late to avoid looking like a mashed-up monster. "Your friend has given me other instructions, Match Girl."

Thorny fear uncurled in Kaye's breast.

The companion wraith, a passably human young man, looked over at him quizzically but didn't comment.

This detour wasn't Grey's doing. The "friend" who'd beaten Bastian and killed her clients had caught up with her again.

Kaye sat back, fear pricking her deeply, and considered how bad the accident would be if she were to light said match and start a fire in the car. Could she grab the wheel in time? Could she stop the car before it hurt anyone else on the road?

Or instead, should she face the author of Bastian's brutal beating, and of the deaths of Hampstead and Hobbs, photographed for her benefit?

Who and why? The car slid along the road smoothly, while a whole bunch of emotions gripped her. Helplessness. Anger. Fear. This "friend" who delivered such violent messages was powerful enough to reach inside Grey House. Damn. She guessed she was going to have to reach a little deeper then too, for courage, because she was just about out. And there was no Bastian beside her.

Luckily, her dregs of courage were enough. All she really had to do was look out the window and let herself be taken.

They drove a while in the country, through small towns that used the highway for a main street. The air seemed extra thin, as if the atmosphere had little resistance to their progress. They went up into the mountains and looked down upon empty farmland. They came to a field in the midst of a stand of dense trees and undergrowth.

When the car stopped, Kaye got out and looked for a murderer. The cold made her skin feel tighter. Fear did that too.

She found her kidnapper leaning against the hood of some kind of classic muscle car badly in need of a paint job. A Camaro, maybe? On the ground before him was the heap of a body.

Oh please, Shadow, make me strong.

Kaye approached, steeling herself. The ground was frozen hard enough for what Bastian would have called her inappropriate footwear, but her ankles still wobbled. The wraiths followed close behind, leaving a trail of stink.

The man ahead looked like he was in his thirties, dark haired, with the black-black eyes of a mage. He wore jeans and boots like a cowboy, but hunkered into what Kaye knew was a very expensive leather jacket. He had a pump-action shotgun at his side.

The body on the ground had its back to her, very still, very dead.

"You'll want to put fire to that one," the mage said, raising his chin to the second wraith. "Or Grey will know we're meeting."

Kaye looked at the wraith in question, now struggling in the grip of the driver wraith, and then back at the mage. "Who are you?"

Whom did you kill this time?

He cocked his head. "The wraith first. I'd like to see that fire for myself."

No. Grey was suspicious and angry already. He'd explicitly told her to bring both wraiths back alive. "I can't."

"Oh, well." The mage shrugged, lifted the shotgun, cocked, and shot the wraith in the face. Blood, bone, and gray matter splattered.

Kaye jerked at the blast, then shivered with nausea at the muck.

He winked at her. "That gives us what? Five minutes until it regenerates. I'm Mason, and I've brought you here today so that I can figure out if you know what you're doing or not."

But Kaye was fixed on the dead body before the mage. "Who is that?"

Mason glanced down. "That's Horace Ballogh. You read his future last week."

The old man from the law firm. The last client she'd seen with Bastian.

"He's the one who *lived*," she argued. Ballogh was the client who'd been feasting with the mages in the vision.

"Well, mages don't abide by Fate," Mason said. "Ballogh needed to die."

"Why are you killing my clients?" It was a weird feeling of responsibility that made her ask, because she didn't necessarily like her clients. Their individual deaths didn't affect her personally, but her connection made her their too late defender.

"I've only killed the bad ones," he said with a smile. "They know enough about Shadow to take advantage of your fire and enough about magekind to support Grey's efforts. But not enough to know that they are destroying the world by helping him." Mason waved his shotgun at Ballogh. "He recently facilitated the import of illegal cargo. His last shipment may have even fed that wraith there."

The wraith stirred on the ground, and Mason shot it again. More splatter.

Kaye turned and took a step away, her hand over her mouth.

The other wraith just stood there, watching his brother bleed.

Mason was a hypocrite. "You're obviously engaged in the same practice if you employ him."

"That's not a wraith," he said, his eyes twinkling. "That's a golum, a mudman made of clay and animated by my umbra. I must have done a pretty good job if I fooled a wraith hunter like yourself."

As if she'd believe that. "He doesn't smell like mud."

Mason laughed once, hard. "No, he smells like what—or rather who—was in the mud I created him from."

Kaye took another step away. She was going to throw up for sure. "Nice."

"No, necessary." He furrowed his brow. "You understand 'necessary'; I know you do if you're engaged to Ferro Grey."

Kaye went still. What did he mean?

Mason twinkled again. "You freed Grey's trapped angel, his superjuice, with a Lakatos skeleton key." He pushed off the car and approached, tall, lean, in need of a shave. "And you stole a seat on the Council—impressive. And then there was last night's meeting, your interesting friends from Segue. Khan."

Kaye drew herself up. Since Mason hadn't been there, one of the guests had to have reported to him. There was a spy among the Council of Houses. Someone working against Grey. But how did Mason know about the rest?

Lakatos had *bound* himself to her, so how could he be a traitor and inform *against* her? Shadow would not have permitted it.

"So, again, you've got me wondering," Mason said, looking down at her, watching every blink and twitch of her face, "whether or not you know what you're doing. You're up to something interesting, that's for sure. If I had to guess, you're in the revenge business, 'cause you're sure as hell not *helping* Grey."

Kaye glared back at him. He could just as easily point that gun at her and shoot. "I'm building my House."

"Girls who play with matches shouldn't build anything."

"Girls who have fire in their blood don't burn."

"And Grey? He can squash you like a bug."

"I am a Brand, old and rich in Shadow." She looked at him eye to eye, strength to strength. "You have no idea what I'm capable of. And neither does he."

The grin that split Mason's face went all the way to his eyes. "Excellent."

He turned and strode back to his car, gun lowered. Opened the front door and reached deep inside, vulnerable to attack. Was he mocking her?

When he reemerged, he held the rope drawstring of a dull cloth sack that appeared heavy. He approached again. "A gift."

"I don't want it." She would not touch it. "I don't like your gifts." The last had been a photo album.

"You'll want this." His deep, lazy drawl was getting on her nerves. "And I apologize for the other. I was trying to scare you away on behalf of a friend."

A friend. "The same 'friend' who had my bodyguard viciously beaten?"

"Yep. That one. My friend has been very worried about

you." He loosened the rope until the bag opened and held it out so she could look inside.

Kaye let her gaze drop. Grayish, whitish oval stones. Then she looked closer, a strange, numb exhilaration suddenly flowing through her body. Stones.

"You've made my friend change his mind. He'd rather you get the hell out of Dodge while you still can, but if you won't, if you're determined in this course—"

"I am." Her heart pulled and pulled until she didn't think she could breathe.

"—then he wants you to have these."

Kaye was going to cry. She looked away, off into the dry, brittle field and the dense growth of the trees in an attempt to compose herself. Another gunshot, and she burst with a short, undignified laugh. She wiped her wet eyes, trying to clean her mascara at the same time. Then gazed into the bag again.

Oh Shadow come and Shadow drum, Shadow make the whole world hum.

She put an arm into the bag, wrapped her hand around a sooty stone, and felt a deep response in her marrow, and in her umbra, and in the *thud* of her heart. Then she drew out and looked upon a Brand House ward stone. The splatter of a tear made the white dust run and the gray stone darken.

"How?" was all she could say. With these—*these*—she could do something. The stones were her legacy and her future all at once.

This changed everything.

"They were collected from the rubble ten years ago and kept safe for you, Little Match Girl. You can't build a mage House without wards."

A happy sob finally escaped her. She should have

known it from the first. For in the story, who had sent the Little Match Girl out to sell her fire but her father?

"How is he?"

She'd concluded he was dead. She'd been told—by whom? she couldn't remember—that he was dead. He'd never had an active power with fire, but his Brand umbra must have protected him anyway. If she never burned, why would he?

She had to remember back. What had happened that night? What had happened . . . *after*?

"You have more supporters than you know," Mason said. "And vassals sworn to Aidan Brand seek now to align themselves again under his heir. They want to become yours in every way that Lakatos has."

Supporters. Vassals. Mages allied against Grey. But no one was like Lakatos, her first.

"And as you're a Council member, you're also now the Head of your House."

Mason handed off the stones to her. The bag was awkward, heavy, but Kaye hugged it to her like a precious treasure. The bitter smell of ash floated up to her nose.

"Why didn't my father come?" The man who'd slapped her, then stood in front of a wraith while she ran. So many feelings there. Conflicting memories. Maybe it was time she examined them.

"Your old man is biased," he said. "And I'm trusted to do what needs to be done."

Ah. The shotgun. Mason had good aim.

"And Lakatos . . . ?" But now she thought she knew.

"Has always been loyal to Brand. He just swore himself to the new generation."

"But he died for the key."

"He died so that Lakatos would flourish in the time to come. So that you'd make his son powerful. He wants a great House. Listen: We understand you want revenge against Grey House for what they did to Brand. Well and good, payback is warranted. Your father wants it just as badly and is proud of all you've accomplished so far to weaken Grey."

Kaye's high dropped a notch. They wanted something from her.

"But even your father agrees that you're too well positioned to waste on a single feud."

"You're saying my father wants me to marry Ferro after all." Why did that hurt when she'd already decided to do so herself? Brand before Kaye.

"I'm saying not to do anything that would jeopardize what you've accomplished. The war is on. Shadow will win this one, there's no doubt about that, but we want to be strategic about how we proceed."

"Meaning?" The ward stones were getting heavier.

"Meaning, if you waste yourself by bringing Grey low, then none of the Houses that support him will trust you. But if we know their plans, we can make sure that our Houses survive the turmoil. Let them take the brunt of The Order's assault. And when it's over, Brand House will be among those that still stand."

Kaye's coat wasn't warm enough for this conversation. She was chilled all the way through.

"You have responsibilities, Kaye. Others who are bound to Brand. Do not fail them for personal reasons."

"But I don't want a war with The Order," she said in a low voice.

He laughed. "Don't tell me that you, who held fire in the face of a fae, are afraid of the angels. You saw how weak and frail they can be when you got rid of Grey's pet."

"I'm not afraid. I just don't want war."

"History repeats itself, but at least this time the outcome is assured in our favor. The Dark Age is coming at last."

The Dark Age was here. But this gave her a lot to think about. Her father. Supporters. Stones. No matter what, however, she would do whatever the hell she wanted.

Her arms ached. "How do I reach you? How do I get in touch with my father? I want to see him. I demand to see him."

Mason sighed. "Too dangerous. So far you've been magnificent."

She usually loved flattery. But she shook her head.

"Shit, okay. But it has to be tomorrow. Battle Park outside Warrenton."

Fine. In the meantime, "I'll consider what you've said."

He ratcheted the gun. Shot. "You do that."

There was no way she could bring the wraith back now. And the golúm made from the mud of dead people couldn't come back either. Grey would find out eventually, and she would be implicated.

Picking battles.

A spark was easy to find while embracing the ward stones; the fire within licked every pulsing nerve. A clench of an inner muscle and the wraith exploded in flame. She lit the golum as well, to make a point, which seemed to make Mason's eyes go even blacker, hungry, impressed.

She turned on her heel, wobbled, but kept her shoulders back anyway, then started for the car. "And stop killing my clients."

Chapter 14

"Fiefdoms," Jack said suddenly, examining Adam's demarcated maps of North America.

Adam had taken over a small Colonial inn near a historic battlefield in Fredericksburg. The place had an independent generator and sufficient amenities to dive immediately into parsing the information from Grey's office. The Order was also working on the same elsewhere.

"Fiefdoms," he repeated, surer now. The wraith-free zones were shaded like topography, the center white. Adam had added a sideways triangle icon common to computer-generated data to identify each one, but to Jack the triangles looked like pennants. And pennants were hung to show unity behind a team, or a fraternity, or long ago, a noble family.

Of course. That's what Grey was doing with his Houses. It was brilliant. The mage was corrupt, but he had vision.

"Excuse me?" Adam said.

"He's put in place a feudal system underneath your democratic government. See here—" Jack pointed to a zone near the Georgia coast. "Hall House makes its home here." He pointed to an area. "Webb." There were so many. "Martin." And another. "Wright." He continued, "And Grey House is here, lording over them all."

His gaze skated over the map again. "And considering that they intend to hit power hubs next, yes, I'm almost certain that they intend to rule and protect at the same time. It makes perfect sense."

He glanced over at Adam. "You don't believe me?"

Adam shrugged. "People would never stand for it. Not today. Kids learn about the horrors of tyranny in grade school. No one would recognize some guy, no matter how powerful, who thought he could lord it over people."

Jack shook his head. Adam lacked the scope of time to see it clearly. "You don't understand the benefits of the system, why it worked for so long, and you're not remembering the first priority of humankind. While yes, the population of an area would be under the thumb of a lord, or House in this case, and through it, a king (or Ferro), they could also expect in return *protection* for themselves and their families. Safety, peace. Shadow *will* continue to deepen on Earth.

"Grey knows that the future will not be governed by politicians who speak carefully worded rhetoric on any number of controversial subjects. The future will be governed by those who have the power to manage Shadow, to keep it out, to fight the monsters, and to keep food and medical supplies moving. An infrastructure." Jack was certain that Urlich had provided part of that service. "The Houses do not rise in strength by wealth and cunning alone. They have real power. They know they have it."

"Then The Order should take over," Adam concluded, as if this were easy.

Jack smiled. "That's just a tyranny of a different kind."

Adam threw his stylus onto the map. "So you *agree* with what Grey is doing?"

"No," Jack answered. "I'm acknowledging the issue and the viable solution he's found and put into place. No mage is going to wait for people to vote on how he or she should handle a problem presented by Shadow. You never waited for permission to act. And in a way, Segue is a little kingdom too. Think about it."

She's arrived. Drove herself, came the report from a bird's-eye vantage.

Jack's heart jumped.

Movement outside drew him to the window. The rolling grounds allowed them to see anyone approaching, like now. A Mercedes was climbing the drive, one of Grey's.

"She's here," Jack said. He clenched his fists, anticipating the victory. He couldn't believe Grey had let her come unattended, or at all. Not after the angry way he'd looked at her last night amid the commotion. He must think she was absolutely loyal.

Jack knew that she was. The worst was now over, though his blood rushed to the beat of danger. Adam Thorne would be her last "client." The assignment was officially over. It had been far worse than he'd predicted, and for reasons he never could've anticipated.

Adam glanced up briefly at the news, but then went back to the map rolled out before him, expression haunted by their conversation. At another desk, Layla Mathews was on the phone, listening and nodding, as if the person on the other line could see her agreement.

Far off, Jack heard the door close, the sound of Kaye's heels. He loved that sharp rap on the floor—it said, *I am strong. I still burn. I'll burn you if you cross me. I might burn you anyway.*

He held himself back, jaw clenched, while Laurence ushered her into the salon where they'd been working. "Ms. Brand, please come in."

Kaye entered, one hand loosening a scarf around her neck, the other clutching a heavy sack. She flushed when she spotted Jack, gaze to gaze, heartbeat to heartbeat, but then swallowed as she looked around the room and took in the other occupants.

Laurence put a hand to her elbow, drawing her farther inside. "I've been looking forward to meeting you properly."

Jack didn't trust himself to get too close. He didn't know what he'd do specifically, but it would embarrass everyone but him.

"You're an angel," Kaye said slowly, her posture going wary. "Where have I seen you before?"

Laurence nodded confirmation. "I was at your town house in Georgetown when you returned to collect your belongings. I was worried about Jacques, my old friend, who'd gone and fallen in love on the job."

She flushed deeper. "Oh." Her gaze found Jack's again. Held. "Oh."

"Please have a seat," Laurence said. "I'll get you some tea to warm you up."

Tea wasn't Kaye. "She takes coffee," Jack said, looking into the Shadow in her eyes. "As sweet and creamy as you can make it."

There. Her scent. Magic. He swayed on his feet toward her. If he took one step, he wouldn't stop until he'd gotten her out of the state, the country. Farther.

She broke eye contact again. Found Laurence. Lifted a nice smile. "Thank you. If it's not too much trouble, coffee would be lovely." Then she slowly lowered herself into a chair, her drawstring bag at her feet. What was in it? Not her clothes. A truckload of those little bags might handle her wardrobe, but not one little bag. Good thing he'd taken care of that.

"So how'd we make out?" she asked.

"We got everything." Jack moved to the sofa beside her. "We know what Grey will hit next—power hubs. He's looking to go medieval for a while. Adam's working on safeguards now."

Adam still stared at the map.

But that wasn't all they'd retrieved in Grey's office. Not nearly. "And we know about Grey's deeper networks. We are more careful than ever tracking our angels. We know who is accounted for, who is missing—and why. We know why the wraiths are stronger and smarter, and we know how Grey intends to use them. You're done. You've done it all."

She still gripped the cloth at the top of the sack, though the weight of it rested on the floor.

"This is good," Jack told her. In case she didn't get the point.

"My father's alive."

Jack was silenced, the room a vacuum.

"He sent these to his Little Match Girl."

Little—?

He took the cloth from her grasp and opened it. Eleven tours on Earth, including one bloody annihilation of magekind's power, and he'd never looked upon ward stones. Until now.

Gray and white, smooth and oval, this was old magic. Powerful magic, and rare among her kind. How could Jack tell her that he'd been among the host that fell upon the warder's House and decimated that line so that there would be no more sanctuaries for Shadow?

And yet . . . his blood pumped relief. Relief and treasure and miracles. He'd never believed until now. Miracles were for humanity, not angels. And he'd just been handed one.

"Ward stones," he breathed. The foundation of a mage castle of her own.

Kaye could be protected, if only it was built in time. He'd build the fortress of safety around her that she'd once named him. She just needed land. He'd find her land.

"And there's another faction of Houses," she continued. "Less inclined to wage war on angels or humanity, I think, but very happy to reap the spoils."

Jack's head came up. He felt Adam and Layla's attention narrow on Kaye's news as well. He would not look at Laurence, who would counsel caution.

"I've been given instructions not to squander my position," Kaye said, with an ironic kind of laugh in her voice. "Ten years and I'm right where my father has always wanted me."

"No." She was finished with magekind. He wouldn't let her leave the room until she was convinced.

"Don't worry," she said. "I'm way more selfish than he gives me credit for." But she looked to the side, her expression full of thought. "I've been trying to remember that night."

"What night—?" Jack was trying to follow.

"He carried me out of there, I think. He took me to a hospital. He made arrangements for my care. Why didn't he come back for me? Why aren't I part of this other faction of Houses?"

"Carried you out of where? Brand House?"

She nodded absently. "I'd wondered who did that, since

I thought he was dead. Someone told me he was dead. But I can't remember."

"You were delirious, in and out of consciousness. How could you remember?" Laurence put a steaming mug before her. "We thought everyone was dead, which is what we told you. Michael asked that you live, so we did our best to save you and repair the damage done to your face."

She looked at Laurence, eyes widening. "You . . . ?"

When those black eyes of hers looked back in question at Jack, he confessed. "Your wedding would have been a key alliance among the Houses. We were sent to observe and listen. To learn what we could."

"You were there too?"

"I was, yes, with a few others." It had taken awhile to find her body when there were no thoughts to follow. When the house was on fire. "We couldn't get inside the wards to save anyone else. Not even Michael."

"What happened?" Her voice was gut raw.

He should have told her before. He should have told her the first day he met her. That he'd seen the damage to her face firsthand. That he'd been there the night Brand House burned.

"We were watching the house. I was concentrating on the thoughts of the kitchen staff. Someone important had arrived—"

"Zelda Grey," Kaye said. "I was to marry Ferro by proxy."

"We wondered how he'd survived." Proxy. Romantic.

Jack felt Adam and Layla draw close to listen, forming an irregular circle.

"The thoughts in the kitchen flashed to terror; a wraith rampaging. A human life was lost in one quick moment, but the wraith passed over the others and left the house."

"He was coming after me."

Again, Jack saw the child she'd been in her eyes, as if some part of her had frozen in time while the rest of her grew up. That night was present in her every day; he could feel it himself in the isolation of her words.

"We heard sounds of a struggle in the woods, and then the house exploded into flame." Everyone in the room could guess the source of the fire.

"It was me." Her expression changed color. "I set my own House on fire when I found my umbra. I was the one who burned down Brand House."

"It's not your fault," Jack said. "Grey sent the wraith after you. You found it within yourself to fight back. You were strong."

"Umbra?" Layla murmured. Jack could feel her interest shift.

"A darkness within," Laurence explained, as an aside. "Mages occasionally use the word as we do *soul*."

Jack reached for Kaye, who'd gone inside herself to think, where he could not follow.

But Adam wasn't satisfied with an aside. "I thought mages didn't have souls."

"They don't," Laurence said brusquely. "An umbra is the source of their power in mage cosmology, the intimate Shadow from which they draw."

"But if she called upon a source of power, then there's something there," Adam argued. "They aren't empty inside."

"Not now," Jack said through gritted teeth. Kaye seemed upset.

"Yes, now. My wife is sick over this no soul thing. Our boys. Do the fae, or the part fae have an umbra?"

"An umbra is not a soul," Laurence said. *I'm sorry, Jack. I should've realized Adam would be angry.*

But Kaye's eyes were shining like she finally understood something. She looked at Jack, really looked, and for some reason he was uneasy. "So it's always been you. You got me out of there, took me to safety, and then returned me to magekind to save me all over again. You and you again, on both sides of my story. Is that Order?"

Jack's heart was breaking. He'd never intended to save her. He wished he had. He liked her version better. Would he lie for it? Where was the Order in that? "I—."

"My children have umbras, Shadow souls," Adam said to Laurence. "How did we not know this? Even when I worked with The Order, why wasn't I told?"

Laurence had raised his hands to hold Adam's arguments back. "You misunderstand."

Jack was spared responding to Kaye's misguided epiphany when she looked over his shoulder at Adam. "Mages don't use the word *soul* either. We don't like it and it really doesn't fit."

Laurence closed his eyes and muttered a low thank-you.

"I don't remember much of the lore," Kaye said. "I was a bad student. But every mage child knows that the umbra is our darkest self, and manifests the power of our House. We don't answer to Fate, so our umbra is unbound and can be harnessed and used, as I do my fire. Just today, I met a mage, Mason, who can animate matter with his inner Shadow, his umbra. He made a fake wraith to mix with Grey's others. Totally pulled it off."

"And where do umbras come from?" Adam asked. A child's question.

"It's supposed to be a bit of our faery progenitor—though only a few Houses still know who originally sired them. Brand certainly has no idea."

Jack squeezed Kaye's hand, reminding himself that he had plenty of time with her. That he was not leaving her side. That these questions had to stop eventually.

Adam turned to Layla. "Does Khan know all this?"

Layla drew a big blinking breath. "Umm . . . I've never heard him say the word *umbra*, specifically. But we did compare the idea of passing along DNA to the passing along of Shadow and its traits, as his affinity with death passed to Talia."

"But is the umbra *unique* to a mage," Adam said, heading into soul territory again. "Is it conserved?"

Layla shook her head, her shoulders rising, indicating she didn't know.

Adam whipped back. "Kaye?"

"Oh . . . well . . . there are books on the lore, which would tell you better. Grey has them all, I'm sure. What I do know is that the penumbra is supposedly our foregoing intention, how we intend to act—there's a House that can sense that. And the antumbra is the trail our Shadow leaves through time. Where we've been, what we've touched. There's a House that sees that too and could follow me here. So my sense is that my umbra is mine, is me, but I don't know if I go on after I die, if that's what you're asking."

Jack and Laurence made no comment as an answer to that. There were no mages Beyond.

Adam stalked back to his schematic. Stress lined his features; deep thought hardened his gaze. "I should've been told about this."

"I'll get you something from Grey's library," Kaye offered to appease him.

Jack startled. He didn't understand.

"He's encouraged me to look into faelore, so it would be no trouble. And really, I'm not very good at this existential stuff."

The salon went quiet for a blink while everyone processed her words. Kaye thought she was going back. Jack had a wild impulse to laugh. She was joking.

"Thank you, but no," Adam said carefully. "It's good to know resources are out there. I can find them without your returning to Grey."

"Online," Layla interjected with too much energy. "Bet you something's on eBay."

Adam gave her a wry look. "I wouldn't be surprised, actually."

"You're going back?" Jack asked Kaye, the material question of the moment.

She gripped his arm, tight. "I can't think of another way. Let me explain, and then I am open to suggestions."

"This should be fun." Jack sat back. Violence replaced his brief contentment. He needed her full reasons so that he could crush each one. She wasn't going anywhere. This was his little war: Him against Kaye. Light against Shadow. Had been from the beginning.

He shot a look at Laurence, who said, "Adam, how about you show me how we can best keep the lights on in a power outage." To Jack, Laurence said, *Be careful.*

Jack held Kaye's gaze for the duration of the rolling of papers, the hurried gathering of laptops, and the exit of the others. Then he started over, saying again, though an octave lower, "You're going back?"

Her polite mask dropped as soon as they were alone. "It's my world. It's who I am. I need to be inside magekind," she said. "You know that. And especially now that I've got my House wards."

"Is this decision because of your father?"

"It has nothing to do with him." Kaye stood, paced. Kept herself away from him. "I want to see him, understand some things, but no, I'm not doing anything for him. I can make a difference here. Or I can try. People died yesterday."

"And Grey?" Just saying the name made the room go

white. Her answer would only dictate the amount of force he'd exert to get her to stay. He could stand to be burned again. He wouldn't mind at all.

"My father is right about that: I'm perfectly placed between Grey and my father's group. Right in the middle. There is too much at stake to abandon it now."

The rhythm of his heart was irregular. "You can't go back."

"But I've got a plan for the future," she said.

"Dear God," he prayed. He was going to lose his mind.

She grabbed the top of the sack and lifted the heavy bundle. "I'm going to build a warded house. I'm going to make sure that seat on the Council is mine, but as soon as I can, I will hold it *without* Grey. I have to, or I'll be stuck with him forever as a spy or a pawn." Her intensity flared. "The stones are everything. I just need a damn building on top of them to be safe and strong among the other Houses."

"I'll build it," Jack said. How fast could a mage house be built?

"And with a real house, my new so-called supporters, and a Council seat, I'll have a voice in the decision as to how magekind proceeds. If need be, I can be as conniving and ruthless as the best of them. But for *peace*."

The Order was arming itself. His sword had been prepared. Generals were planning where and how to strike.

She did need a warded house. He'd begin right away.

"Because I can't plot against my kind and I can't fight yours," she said. "I can't do it. I won't do it. You, and Michael before you, ruined me."

"And you just plan to move out when your house is ready? You think Grey will allow it?" This ought to be good.

"There's an issue I intend to use to distance myself."

"What kind of issue?" His tone was mild, but the avenging angel within was bursting through his control.

"A private one."

He should just kill Grey. He didn't need a good reason. End this. It was wartime anyway, and Grey was the enemy.

"If he dies," Kaye said, as if she could read his mind, "then no mage will trust me. All my work will be for nothing. Don't do that to me."

"Do it to you?" Had she any idea what she'd done to him?

"Trust me."

"How, when this is insane?"

"I'm doing my best," she returned. "I've helped a little, I hope."

That wasn't true. She'd performed spectacularly. She had no idea how much it had tortured him.

"You will tell me everything, especially what is between you and Grey." His voice was mellow, curiously even considering he'd come up against a wall inside. It was as if the oceans had gone very still and the wind had stopped blowing and the world was slowing its rotation.

Kaye seemed to retreat. Why did she keep moving away from him?

"Stop," he said. "Stop right there."

"Bastian."

"You will answer me. You weren't alone in this. I suffered with you every goddamned second."

Now she went white.

She sat. Kept her back straight. Looked nowhere in particular. "Fine." Her breath was all wrong. But then, so was his. "Grey doesn't need his ring to draw Shadow from people. He can do that by touch. It's how he messed with Custo, but I didn't realize it until after the wolf was loose. There."

He took "there" to mean "done." So his mind cranked unwillingly to the simple conclusion. She'd been with

Grey, which meant he'd been taking her Shadowfire every time he touched her. *He'd touched her.* She'd looked ill these past days because she was ill, not because she was drinking.

Had she known when she became engaged to Grey? Didn't matter; Jack knew she would have made the same choice with Ava in the house. Damn Michael.

"I can beg off on the grounds that he's diminishing my Shadow," she said. "That I won't stand for it anymore. And I won't. I think he'll try to reason with me, say it's not his fault, or not deliberate, and give me some time to get strong again."

Jack paced to the table. He wasn't thinking, couldn't with the ice on his skin at her revelation. Diminishing her? Grey would die. Very simple.

"And I need to stay in a warded house until mine can be built," she went on, as if she didn't have other choices. Maybe she thought she didn't. "If I'm out in the open, I won't last a day. The other Houses would dispose of me so they can return to the status quo."

Kaye was mistaken. Grey would never leave her alone. Not in a million years. She was a light in the dark, and any who saw her would draw near and try to take her for their own. And she had no idea what happened to soldiers in between two opposing armies.

A valiant effort, but no.

"I thought we'd come to an agreement. A joint thing," he said for lack of better words: a pledge, a union, promises. "And then you went off on your own."

Grey would take her again and again to make a point. That's what a tyrant did.

"I didn't lie to you, if that's what you think." She pulled back again, an island unto herself.

And he understood why: She thought he didn't want her anymore after Grey. She thought she was alone again.

"No," he agreed. "You don't lie when it matters. I know why you did what you did."

Which made her tremble. But she kept her chin level.

"I'd like to make a new contract with you, if you're willing." His voice was angry, but he couldn't help it.

The thought of Grey taking from her . . . Jack didn't think the rage would ever leave him.

She lifted her eyebrows in a miserable question. *What?*

See? He could read her mind too.

"It's simple," he said. "Very straightforward so that you don't misinterpret my intentions again."

She closed her eyes, waiting.

He wanted them open. "Kaye."

She lifted that Shadow-black gaze his way.

"From this moment on to forever, there is no one but me."

Kaye concentrated very hard on what Bastian was saying, but she couldn't actually understand it. She'd thought this whole conversation had been conducted in English, but the meaning of each statement seemed to slide past the one before it. And that last bit . . .

"Wha—?" But her throat was closing up and she had that rushing feeling behind her eyes.

"You will agree," he said about as angry and terrible as he'd ever been since she'd known him. Of course, he had every right to be.

She hitched for air, but it came out like she was crying. Which she wasn't.

"Say yes." He towered over her.

She wheezed, looking up, afraid. "What was the question?"

There was no question. "You're mine," he said.

So she had heard him. "Okay?" She was shaking hard. Because he couldn't mean what she wanted him to mean. After what she'd done . . . no. . . . And hadn't she just told him that she wasn't leaving magekind? That was her place.

Her ribs hurt.

It had to be the job. That he wanted her to continue to work now that she was inside. And she would; she'd never really expected to stop. Not when he needed . . . just . . .

He growled, seemed furious, looked about, then snagged something. Held it out to her.

A tissue.

She blew her nose, which was difficult because her hands shook. She needed another for her eyes, but she was suddenly moving through the air with his mouth pressed hot on hers.

Flying. Weightless. Held so tight by his angel strength she didn't care if she was crushed against him, as long as they were one.

She fisted her hands on the shirt at his neck and kissed him back. The return was urgent, wet, roughened by his afternoon growth. She inhaled the scent of him, Jack Bastian, as much as her lungs could take.

"You're *not* going back to that house," he said, smoothing hair out of her eyes and unsticking it from her tear-salted cheeks. "I will ward you."

She looked into his eyes, and shut herself up. That look broke all plans.

"You got in between Grey's group and your father's too easy," he said. "But do you know, do you have any idea, whose support you really have? You stand between two armies now. Did you know you have one at your back?"

But . . . the implications were spinning in her mind, everything that was dangerous before, now going deadly. Especially for Bastian. "If I don't show up at Grey's tonight, he'll come after you. He'll think I'm sleeping with you again."

Bastian shrugged. "So he's smart."

A flame burst into being inside her, sparks fizzing through her blood, and she buried her face in his neck to catch her breath. He smelled so good, felt so solid. He'd been there the whole time. With his arms around her, she could feel herself growing stronger.

"Are you with me then?" he said. The anger was gone.

Her heart was going wild against him, but she managed to say, "Yes."

Tonight. If they were lucky, they could have tonight.

"All right." He put his chin on her head. "Let's go with the rest of your plan, just faster."

She thought back to the plan she'd conceived on the way over. All the puzzle pieces she'd been trying to figure out. The Council—the seat she'd hoped for was as good as lost. She'd barely touched her rear end down before the upset about the pureblood. She'd have liked to have truly acted the Council member before leaving Grey. At least she knew where the mages met.

Grey's plans for a widespread mage resurgence weren't going to go smoothly, thanks to Adam Thorne and Bastian's Order. The war between Shadow and light was coming, but the information from Grey's files bought them time to minimize the damage for everyone else.

And Mason and her father would just have to deal with her relocation. She'd meet with her father tomorrow and make sure he understood that she wasn't his puppet anymore. She wouldn't be sold to Grey for anything. Brand House, like the future, was hers.

Which left, "My House?"

Bastian nodded. "I agree that the stones make the difference. Like a seat, only the most powerful mages have them. You won't be ignored among your kind once you have a warded House in place. It's safety and power all at once. You have no idea how much power. Just ask Adam."

"Houses take time to build."

"Then we'd better start right now."

Chapter 15

Ferro paced Kaye's bedroom, missing Penny fiercely. Penny, who'd been loyal until she'd died in his arms. She'd lived a little longer inside of him, a wisp of her umbra; then that Shadow too had perished. And now he was alone.

Magekind would mock him behind his back. They'd whispered that his prick had killed Penny. Kaye's defection would be worse.

He didn't have time for this today. The world had shaken, and now the lights would go out. Watts House was in place, each family doing its part. The domino effect would begin in the Midwest. As transformer wires melted under the electrical current overload, systems would fail, spreading east from the Mississippi River to the Atlantic Coast, casting half the country into darkness.

Kaye had said her affair with the bodyguard was over. She would've had to have believed it or he would've felt the lie in Verity's Shadow. If he'd seen her for what she was, he would've known the truth. Like a *whore* she'd gone out to attend her client, that Adam Thorne of the Segue Institute. She'd met with her lover, and the romance had been rekindled. That, right there, had been Ferro's mistake. He never should have let her leave the house. He'd trusted her, and gotten burned.

She'd burned him. And without her fire, he couldn't even be sure how close the fae were. Sounded like they were snickering in his ear. Having a laugh at his expense.

Had she allied with the pureblood? Must have. Segue would be rubble when he was through—not today or tomorrow, but as soon as his plans would allow. The pureblood and that human nothing of a woman he owned would be hounded. No warded House would take them in.

He would have given Kaye everything.

Ferro paced the length of the bed. Smelled like her—expensive and sensual. He was already getting hard.

His sister, Zelda, had been right all along. If he could, he'd set a wraith on Kaye now too.

No time for this.

Was Kaye Brand worth calling in a favor? He could set retribution in motion, then get back to the matter at hand.

He pulled out his mobile phone. Dialed a number, but the phone lit up in his hand before he pressed SEND. He listened in stony silence, his skin flashing icy hot. "And when are they meeting tomorrow?"

Kaye; her father, Aidan Brand, presumed dead; and Mason, another nuisance. Select others were coming too. Probably Segue as well.

Mage children were taught from birth not to romanticize marriage. Passions were permitted, to a certain extent. Affairs begun and ended as appearances permitted. Overall, he thought he'd been very tolerant.

But this was outright betrayal.

The sun was still up, a low blood-orange glow, when the earthmovers backed away from the plot of land. The dirt was hard, but not wet. Jack led Kaye from where they'd parked to the site for her house, some thirty miles from the inn. He'd used Adam's map to make certain that there was an abundance of natural resources, that the area wasn't prone to natural disasters, and that any possible territory disputes would be minimal, should the mages in fact become lords over individual fiefdoms.

She gripped the bag heavy with Brand ward stones and was shocked stiff that all this should be done for her.

"I don't believe it," she said, shaking her head while taking in the construction. "It's so much. . . ."

"This is Order." Jack's chest expanded with pride. The actual building would take longer, of course, but they were even now mobilizing a workforce. The purchase and transfer of ownership had happened even more quickly, thanks to modern technology. A few memories would have to be altered, but the human impact was minimal. He was enjoying this more and more. The real frustration had been getting a construction company out there in the midst of the other chaos and speeding them to dig deep for her foundation. Money was not a problem, but many workers preferred to remain with their families during the upheaval and fear following the quakes, no matter how much was offered.

The sun was fire on the horizon, washing the land in gold, but they'd done it.

Once the stones were in place, set by Kaye's hand, the building would begin. She'd permit the scores of workers past the wards for the duration. Even now, massive work lights were being trucked in. Tonight he'd review the floor plans with her. Weeks of around-the-clock labor—projections ranged from five to twelve—and she would have her stronghold. This part was easy.

Adam Thorne was hollering instructions, directing the

workers to fall back. Jack relished the commotion of thought, everyone working together.

"They're ready for you," said Laurence, who'd come ahead of them.

Jack clapped him on the shoulder. His friend had been there when his heart was breaking; now he'd be here when history was made, when Order, humankind, and Shadow labored together to build. This was a momentous step. There was work to do elsewhere as well; tomorrow both Adam and Laurence would move on, but the three of them needed to be present for this: peace while their realms crashed together.

The hollowed-out earth went deep and was wide enough for generous square footage. Footings had been built, awaiting Kaye to set the ward stones so that they could be covered with concrete. The foundation walls would be framed and poured on top of those.

Kaye, Jack, and Adam used a ladder to climb down. Laurence looked on from above, and Jack's heart leaped when other angels joined him around the perimeter to witness this moment.

Kaye was beaming too, stars in her eyes from the floodlights above. "Let's get started."

She walked to the nearest corner of the foundation, took a stone from the bag, and placed it on the ground. It glowed with fire and smoked with Shadow; the earth was invested with power. She stood and smiled. He could feel her strength returning as if it were his own.

"Where do I get me some of those?" Adam murmured.

Jack grinned at him.

She moved to the next point, set the stone, and watched it glow, Shadow snaking into the dusk. She set the next and the next, magic filling the air, until she came to the last spot that would hold a ward. She held it in her hand, and the light caught her profile—proud, scarred, beautiful, and strong.

"Brand," she said, and put the stone in place.

Instantly, Shadow roared into the foundation space from all directions. It surged over Jack, flinging him off his feet and onto a slab of rock, breaking his back. His vision blanked with the pain, but there . . . the itch of recovery was already working, though fainter than usual. But his sight didn't return. Either that or they were lost in darkness.

Sounds of fighting clashed; then Adam yelled.

And a pillar of fire erupted in the dark—Kaye, eyes black and slanted like a faery's. Her fire illuminated the black pitch of her House's foundation, revealing the swirls and eddies of magic.

Right. Jack let loose his light as well, and the angel unfolded within. The Shadow wasn't illuminated; it was pushed back from his person. The burn of healing grew more fierce.

He spotted Adam—bloody, being dragged unconscious into the earth—but Kaye was there first, brandishing fire to beat the opportunistic fae back like a torch. Gradually the fae retreated into a ghostly pulse of smoke.

She dropped and felt Adam's pulse. "Alive." She looked up. "Someone help me!" Angels suddenly leaped from above into the foundation to get Adam out.

Get him to safety.

Here, I've got him.

Coming around.

Dangerous.

Jack didn't need their thoughts to know that no human workforce could be safe inside the demarcated boundary of her wards. Just looking around told him how potent the magic was here. Like Grey's house, the area was maddening with the smell of passion and webbed with nightmare. The fae leaned in from the earthen walls of the pit to get a better look.

Twilight was close, so very close.

That moment when Kaye had placed the last stone, Jack had felt that there'd been no boundary between Twilight and Earth at all. Even now, it was membrane thin, on the edge of the world. It would take a long time for the Shadow to dissipate, and not all of it would.

"Bastian?" Kaye called across the space, feathers of fire around her.

He'd thought building would be the easy part. They'd needed one easy part. But Shadow liked to break hearts as much as it broke backs.

"I'm good," he said. Not five to twelve weeks to build. Much longer.

This was the kind of building, as in ancient times, that took lives, that had blood in its mortar, bones in its walls, souls pursued forever by wicked fae. How had Grey and the other Houses managed? The answer was easy: wraiths. The fae weren't interested in them, so the wraiths could build unimpeded.

Well, wraiths weren't an option here. And Jack could allow no human near the site either. Not anymore.

Never easy.

Fine.

If humans couldn't build the house, he would. For her, anything.

Jack stripped off his jacket. Stripped off his shirt. Dropped them in Shadow as the whispers chattered around him. He'd bend the rebar with his bare hands if he had to.

The glow approached. "We'll just make another plan. I don't need a house right away. I like hotels better anyway. I've got my fire, and I've got you. . . ."

She'd come to all the same conclusions.

"Kaye," he said.

"Let it go, Bastian," she said.

"Not with what I've seen in your visions. Not with what we discovered today."

He returned to the pile of building materials to find Laurence there before him, heaving a stack of two-by-six boards onto his shoulder. Old man still had it. Jack didn't need to say anything, not even thanks, as he passed to get another for himself.

The Shadows grew brighter, Kaye revealing the entirety of the space with her fire.

Jack turned to tell her not to waste her strength. But he was shocked into silence when he saw something swing overhead. A brother angel rode the chute from a cement mixer as it descended into the murk. And above, others seemed to be organizing the job below.

Now *this* was Order. Her hard-won army was massing.

Jack lowered his gaze to Kaye again, who burned resolute, even if her expression was heart-stricken by the shift in labor.

Yes, for you, he wanted to say. She, who'd been bought and sold, braved it all, was worth everything.

He filled his gaze with her, then went back to work.

"Kaye," a careful, low voice said.

She was dazzled by flame, spinning in a kaleidoscope of hot color around her. She drank with her eyes to feed her umbra, to spark her blood, and to light the space for Bastian and the others. So many to help her. Her. Why? The magic went through her and out again in loops of infinity. Steady, constant, like she would be for him.

"Kaye, love," the voice said again. "See me, sweetheart."

She couldn't let go or she'd lose the light. Constant. She rode the heat.

"Careful," someone else said. "She'll burn you like that."

Burn whom? Why had she ever been afraid of being consumed by fire? She *was* the fire with her ward stones near.

"I'm tired, love," the careful voice said. So weary.

Bastian.

She breathed in deep and took the flame. It went down like a scaly dragon's tail and grumbled brimstone in her belly. Slowly the world came back into focus. The pit around her was now lit by strange white torches, the light akin to Bastian's angel glow, pushing the Shadow back. When had those arrived? Men and women worked around her, but Bastian looked exhausted, streaked with dirt across his bare torso and haggard around his eyes. Laurence was seated on the ground, leaning against the dirt wall, also looking the worse for wear.

"The torches will keep the Shadow at bay," Bastian said. The night sky was the black before dawn, the stars dimming. "You've done enough, and I'm past ready to go back to the inn."

She couldn't just leave while others worked on her behalf, but he was listing to the side with exhaustion. His jerky, uneven progress up the ladder made her even more worried. Another angel darted under his arm and added his two legs to Bastian's stumble toward the car. Packed him inside. Belted him in.

She drove.

Fifteen minutes down the country road, she felt angel light shimmering across her skin, raising hot goose bumps. She glanced over to find him inhumanly beautiful, severe in his hard gaze, and yet beat up, sweaty, filthy, his defined muscles still swollen from exertion.

She felt a nervous tingle in her belly. She'd never been nervous around men in her adult life. Not like this. Which was very strange because no one knew her better than Bastian. And he'd made it clear that he still wanted her, still cared for her, in spite of everything.

"I couldn't heal while trying to hold back all that Shadow," he said. "Those ward stones are powerful, just like the Brand line."

She blushed. Powerful. She might have the fire, but he of all people had to know she was faking her swagger among the others. "Feeling better now?"

She could see he was. It was she who was quivering, though she had no idea why. He was beside her. She had nothing to fear.

A slow grin spread across his face. "Yes. Much. Every second. As we build higher, the Shadow should thin, so I'll hardly notice it when I go in and out."

Her blood rushed at the thought of a future of him around her every day, safe, of him in her every night, so dangerous. She was scared. She concentrated harder on the road to hide her response. And changed the subject. "So the, um, Order, is now building my house?"

"Yes." He stroked her with his voice, patient, as if he was humoring her and this turn in conversation.

"And that's okay with everyone?"

Maybe she was anxious because by now Grey had to know that she wasn't coming back. He'd be planning some retribution like his sister, Zelda, to make it clear that he thought Brand wasn't good enough for Grey. Zelda had set a wraith on her when Kaye had refused the marriage. What would Ferro do?

Bastian cocked his head forward to see her better. "Is it okay with you that The Order should build a mage house?"

She glanced over at her angel, bright and terrible. She

didn't know what Grey would do to her. Or worse, to him. That wasn't why she was nervous.

"I'm both honored and scared at what that means. But you'll have to help me find a way to thank them." She could barely wrap her mind around this turn of events, how things could get better when they should be at their worst.

"You're missing the point. There's no need to thank them," Bastian said. "I, on the other hand . . ." Want rolled off him in great cracking waves, like lightning to dry tinder.

She drew a ragged breath. No, it was something about that look he was giving her that made her jumpy. All day long she'd sent quick glances his way—glimpsed the flex of his jaw, his big shoulders rolling with his exertion, his taut expression of concentration, the knowing in his green-flecked gaze when he'd caught her staring. His able hands. Sweet Shadow, his hands.

Bastian chuckled, reading her mind again. Had to be.

But the last man to touch her had been Grey. Though she'd chosen the course herself, she couldn't quite move beyond the fact that he'd been inside her and preyed upon her during the intimacy. He'd weakened her. She felt used. She'd hurt Bastian the same way. She wasn't altogether easy about jumping into bed now, even if it was with the man she loved. She had to get past what had gone before, but she didn't know how.

The inn was lit up with activity when she pulled into the parking lot. Upon entering, Kaye could hear Adam's voice beyond the far double doors where she'd met with the group that morning. She started in his direction to apologize for what had happened, and see how he was, but Bastian caught her firmly around the waist and altered her trajectory toward the stairs. "He's fine."

Her heart beat harder.

He hurried her next to him as they topped the stairs and started down a long hallway. His expression had taken on that stern glower of endurance—that he'd held on just about as long as he could.

"Maybe you should eat something." Their history was mostly bad. Could they really build something together? An old, familiar instinct was kicking in, telling her to run.

Suddenly he was bracing her up against a wall, his hard body molding to hers, trapping her. Arms caging her at either side of her head. "You promised me. Forever," he said.

She begged into his eyes. "But—"

She'd had sex with men before, much of it heartless. Everything had been different since she'd met him.

She could feel how perfectly they fit together. How her body recognized and fitted back, while another part of her clamored in distress. She arched for breath, but he stole it with his mouth. He tasted her, rubbed her tongue with his, and she yearned to be filled with him and shaken to pieces at the same time.

He drew back a little, his free hand working at the handle of a door. Open. He shifted one side of his body to block her escape, the other side, near the door, pulling back to show her the way to go. Shadow help her, she entered. Of course the place would have a four-poster of dark, spindly carved wood. Patchwork quilt. At least there was a fireplace, which exploded into flame.

"Come on," he said, close behind her. The feel of his warmth and breath over her shoulder sent a wave of something exquisite down her body to beat at her sex. He must have felt it too because he gathered her close, his strong arms around her waist, and pressed his mouth—she loved his mouth—up and down the column of her neck. She could feel how much he wanted her at the small of her back. His embrace tightened, the night scruff of his face on her skin.

She couldn't get away. She didn't want to. Trouble was, and she got it now, she'd compartmentalized what had happened with Grey, a very handy trick . . . until it wasn't. She'd separated what she wanted from what needed to be done. Her heart from her mind, her body from both of those. And Bastian, the bastard, her safe place, would not settle for parts. She was pretty sure he wanted all of her at once. But things were going to get bad, ugly, when everything mixed together.

"Shower," he said, moving them forward again. He bypassed the bed, kicked the bathroom door open, and set her on the sink counter, her legs straddling his hips.

He left her cold for half a sec, then was back by the time the shower water burst from the head. Thick clouds of steam wafted out from the claw-footed tub.

Her clumsy fingers unfastened his pants. He was deft at her blouse's buttons, slipping the silk from her shoulders, and efficient at the side zipper of her slacks. He pulled her off the counter, and slid her underwear and slacks to the floor. She climbed inside the tub, his hands low at her waist keeping her steady. The water scalded her skin, and she had just enough time to tilt her head back, to wet her hair out of her face before he was with her, his mouth on her shoulder, his hand slicking between her legs.

As a rule, Jack didn't like the modern world's conveniences, but showers were a genius that even he couldn't deny. And the way the water made her skin so slippery, erotic, made his arousal that much more acute, a blood beat that was earthy and wild with chaotic sensation. He'd never get used to it.

He roughed his mouth over her shoulder. Her skin was hot to the tongue, yet sweet to taste. He stroked her heat and she leaned against him, her back to his chest, a whimper in her throat.

She trembled, an emotion surfacing. "I'm so sorry—"

The hot water pounded down. "I'll make it better," he promised, knowing what she had to have endured at Grey's hands. "Let me make it better."

A sob broke out of her, and she braced herself, a hand to the wall. He knew the fear of the past days had shaken her. She'd carried it all, braved the darkness. She must have been terrified to feel herself growing weaker, yet know she was powerless to do anything about it. She must have been frantic to be at the mercy of the man who'd ripped her life apart more than once.

They'd betrayed each other. He'd set her on a terrible path, more ruthless than any mage, and she'd walked it even after they'd agreed on a different course. He wouldn't debate the ends and means. He would simply make it right. He'd reach deep and make it right.

She turned in his arms to face him, black eyes full of dark thoughts. "Please," she said. "I don't know how. . . ."

He drew her into a kiss, the water hissing as it hit her skin. Again he thrust with his tongue to fill her mouth, to share one breath between them, syncing the drumbeat of his heart to the double flutter of hers. She twined her fingers in his hair and clung to his back to bring him close. He could do better, so he lifted her up, reveling that his strength could be used for this too, and fitted her to him. She cried out but wrapped her legs around, rolling her hips to stroke and clench.

His control strained against the swell of immediate gratification. He knew he could bear down on the desire, find the iron rod of his resolve. But that would not serve either of them now. He went with impulse, with reckless desire. He intended to exact revenge for her betrayal on her body. When he was finished, every nerve in her body would know him, every inch of silken curve punished with pleasure. And then the assignment would be behind them.

He braced an arm against the tile and took her, pounding deep to reach her core, that umbra of her mage power, and stoked it to a blaze. Burn him, burn them both, he didn't care, as long as nothing of the past was left.

Her mouth snagged his ear, teeth grazed his cheek, lips shaped the words of a spell against his jaw. Magic, clashing, crashing. Passion. She was a star inside, flames within flame, the primal elements churning together. When the first shock wave moved through her, he couldn't stop the roar that ripped out of his throat. It was a supernova of Shadow and soul, exactly how new worlds were made.

Chapter 16

"I have no clothes," Kaye said. She lifted the ruined silk of her blouse in one hand, the crush of her slacks in the other. She could locate only one shoe. "I can't meet my father in a robe."

"What do you need?" Bastian, on the other hand, sitting comfortably by the fire, looked magey in Shadow-gray jeans, a black slim sweatshirt, a black coat folded over his knee. He smiled with deep satisfaction. His angel light was stuffed down inside him.

She did an up-down gesture indicating her body. "Everything."

"It's a good look."

"Bastian!"

"Good thing the world is wired," Bastian said. "After the meeting between Grey and Segue I was hopeful you'd leave him, but knew the circumstances might be difficult. I wanted you comfortable, so I took the liberty of having your accounts accessed. I reordered as many of your recent purchases as possible, though, for the record, spending six hundred dollars on a single pair of shoes is obscene."

The boxes were waiting outside their suite's door. The

red cashmere sweater would do, and she had to go uncharacteristically casual in jeans as well. The other pants needed hemming. And why he had ordered a gown was a mystery. Yes! Her gorgeous boots. She felt powerful again four inches taller.

"I've decided against telling my father about the house." No makeup. Good thing she had backup mascara in her bag. "The most I'll say about it is that I'm looking at some land."

She waited for Bastian's reaction. They'd talked about everything from the Lakatos key, now tucked in a dresser drawer, to her conversation with her maybe friend Gail. He seemed to be waiting for her to get around to the heart of the matter.

"Okay, I'll mention Grey's touch thing." It didn't scare her to say his name. She didn't get that tight, no-breath feeling either. She only felt slightly ill at the thought of herself at his mercy at the age of fifteen. "I need to know if my father is aware that Grey can do that. I need to know if my father knew back then, or if the marriage contract was simply a business arrangement that they rushed because of infighting among the Council members."

"If he asks, how will you introduce me?" It was a practical question.

But Kaye went warm all over again inside. "As mine."

Jack had kept his mind closed for privacy, so he was surprised to meet Khan, composed like a crow in a black seethe of Shadow, at the bottom of the stairs in the inn's main entrance. Why hadn't the others there—Adam or Laurence—warned him of the mage's presence?

Jack felt Kaye's arm slip around his waist, her body fitted to his, and enjoyed Khan's none too subtle glower.

"I'm going with you to meet these mages," Khan said. He looked displeased with his angelic company, then shifted his gaze to Kaye. "I'd like to meet this Mason, who made a false wraith, and your father, who seems little better than Grey."

Jack felt Kaye's hold on him grow tighter. She asked, "Why?"

"I won't aid The Order, but if Grey shook the earth, then he will do worse. And it's my fault he has the Shadow in the first place to make his mischief. This other faction may be better. We will see."

So *now* he thought to become involved? Jack wasn't so sure. "Our aim is to organize the chaos that is coming, not stir up more contention among them."

"Organize," Khan sneered. "Smacks of Order. And Order does not comprehend Shadow. Never has."

Jack almost laughed. "You can use *comprehend* and *Shadow* in the same sentence?"

"Look." Kaye raised a hand, which Jack guessed was to shut them up. "This is my meeting. My business. I say what goes, and nobody else. Got it?"

Khan's eyes narrowed dangerously, but he said, "Understood."

"Bastian?" She wanted his agreement too.

"Yes."

They stopped in to say good-bye to Adam, who still looked a little worse for wear, but was working as usual.

"Adam," Kaye said. "Set aside some square footage in the house for you and your family. You never know when you may need a warded refuge."

Adam looked at her for a long moment, then he nodded, short, with feeling. "Thank you."

Then they headed out. The drive was a couple of hours, around the Beltway and back out into farmland on the other side. The chatter on the radio was now broken by music as the shock of the simultaneous earthquakes became old, though still frightening, news. The tone remained dark, given to rumor and conspiracy, as though the radio announcers also felt that worse was coming.

When Kaye pulled into a wide meadow of dead grass, Jack was glad they had Khan with them. Several cars were arranged in a wide semicircle facing them, doors opening as Kaye came to a stop.

"I thought this was just going to be you, Mason, and your father," Jack said.

"Me too."

They got out of the car, but instead of walking at Kaye's side, as he'd intended when he met her father for the first time, Jack walked a pace behind, sending a different kind of message of support. And God help him, when Khan took up the other part of the triangle, also behind Kaye, Jack resolved to like Death, in spite of everything that had gone before.

Kaye walked before them, tall, confident, unafraid.

The waiting group began to murmur, connecting the rumor of Khan to the vicious, black-haired pureblood beside Jack. Jack recognized a few in the group, including one from the meeting Segue had had with Grey. And there was that Marcell Lakatos, whom he'd beaten in the sculpture garden. His nose wasn't going to heal straight. And almost concealed, but visible to Jack's practiced eye, a woman in the back shifted her arm, her hand loose, ready to draw some sort of weapon. Not everyone was a friend here. Maybe none of them.

The mage who had to be Mason—Jack was unfamiliar with both the name and face—came forward. A terribly scarred old man stood beside him, hairless, his skin like molded and pocked putty—someone who'd been in a fire.

He could only be Kaye's father, Aidan Brand, who didn't have anywhere near the Shadow Kaye had within her to protect him from their element. Still, he'd lived, while everyone else had perished as Brand House burned down.

"Hello, Dad," Kaye said. She sounded tired.

"My daughter walks with the pureblood." The burned man pivoted slightly to the group. He was proud of her. "That's why she left Grey."

"Don't think you know me," Kaye said. "You know nothing about me or my allies."

"I like what I see," Aidan answered back. "I always said Shadow flowed thick for Brand. We'll rebuild our House together."

Jack tried very hard to remind himself that Aidan had attempted to scare the Little Match Girl so that she wouldn't be caught up in the intrigue and danger. He'd saved the ward stones for her. And, according to Kaye, there was a moment when he'd even tried to protect her from the wraith attack when she was fifteen. No one was all bad; he loved his daughter in his own magey way.

"Why Grey in the first place, Dad?" Kaye had kept her tone light, but Jack knew the turmoil underneath. "What did he want with a fifteen-year-old when he could've had anyone? Why me when back then I had so little Shadow to show for myself?"

Jack didn't like the mage woman with the weapon. Though she stood among the group in front of them, something about her made him want to look over his shoulder.

"Brand is an old and strong family," her father answered. "You had every promise—"

Kaye cut him short. "No, I didn't. Back then you said I was born to 'breed power,' which I understood to mean bear his children."

Aidan frowned. "That's the primary purpose of a

marriage contract. Alliance first, then offspring of the mingled Shadow. A blood bond means safety and strength for both Houses."

"Did you know then that he draws Shadow out of every mage he touches?" Her question was barbed with longtime pain.

But Jack knew to keep his focus elsewhere. The mage woman in the crowd seemed to inhale slightly and his memory sped back through the ages, recalling other mage attacks. She flung a blade, aimed straight at Kaye's heart, but Jack trusted his instinct. This was a mage trick of perception. He reached, angel quick, *behind* Kaye, and caught the blade midair. The metal cut into his skin and blood dripped to the frozen ground. He was so angry, he didn't feel it at all.

"Bastian?" Kaye turned, her gaze flicking from the knife to his expression to understand. The group went silent as Jack wiped the blade on his pants. He was shaking with rage. Mages. Never a head-on attack, just a knife in the back. If he hadn't had the thousand years' experience fighting them . . .

The mage assassin took off into the forest, as if there were any place on Earth she could hide. No, that one was going to die. Jack could pursue and kill her, but he'd reveal himself as an angel. Luckily, he had an unexpected ally at his side. "Khan," he said, with exquisite calmness. "If you will . . . ?"

"Certainly," Khan answered. "No one lives forever." He raised his palm and black Shadow boiled into the frigid air, a compact tempest of death to throw at the fleeing figure. Shadow grumbled, rolling to a frenzied acceleration.

"Stop," Kaye said. She put an arm out to her side, palm facing Khan, fire blooming in her palm and battering the pureblood's Shadow back. Jack almost staggered with the realization that her firelight was a match for Khan's despair. "She's mine," Kaye said. "She has to be mine. It's the mage way."

With one hand, Kaye held Khan's Shadow back with her fire.

Khan hissed. "I know what you are now."

But Jack didn't think she was listening. Her head turned slightly to track the assassin's progress through the woods. The running mage was getting farther, probably having that whizzy feeling of hope that she just might escape. Jack saw Kaye blink, and the assassin screamed as she went up in flames.

The gathered mages were loosening, backing to their cars. The few brave remained in place, to carry on the discussion. "She wasn't one of ours," Mason said. "I swear it."

Kaye didn't seem to think it important. She regarded her father again. "You were saying?"

Her dad looked flustered, so she helped him out. "Did you or didn't you know that when Grey touches another mage, he draws on their Shadow? He weakens them and assumes their power, the strength of their umbra."

Kaye was grateful for Bastian and Khan behind her because she was so furious, so hurt, the faraway screams so irritating, that all she could really concentrate on was her father stuttering for an answer in front of her.

"But even you just said you didn't have much Shadow back then," her father finally answered. "I didn't think I was risking much in that regard, yet giving you safety and power. Grey wanted heirs, but none of his partners could conceive because of his touch. A young woman, just reaching maturity, full of vitality, might have a better chance."

Kaye was going to be sick. "So you didn't sell my Shadow, you sold my youth."

"I paid for that decision," her father said. "I pay for it every day. I wanted to protect you."

A couple of cars were starting to pull out of the field, heading for the access road, mages who'd seen enough and didn't want to stick around for more fireworks. Kaye was glad to see Gail remain behind, her maybe-friend, though she hadn't expected to see her among this group.

Kaye raised her hands again—the mages flinched back. "Look at me, Dad. If you had waited just a little while longer, like, say, until I was seventeen . . . if *you'd* kept me safe, none of this would have happened."

"I know it," he said. "That's why I gave you the stones. I gave over Brand to you because of what happened. The power of our name, the bonds of our vassals, the mantle of our heritage. I gave it all to you."

He might have done all that, but . . . "Yesterday I was told not to squander my position with Grey."

"We had no idea you had made other friends."

They were going around in circles, Brand-Kaye-Brand.

"This is not the reunion I was hoping for," Mason said. "We don't have time for family feuds. Can we come to an agreement?"

Kaye couldn't stop looking at her dad. The scars from his burns were awful; the pain must've been excruciating. They were both scarred, father and daughter. But his eyes were the same. Same color, same set, though the shape of one was smudged. That night the wraith had charged at Zelda's command, and her father had pushed her out of the way and stood between them.

"We can agree not to do business with Grey," Kaye said. She wanted that final.

"Works for me," said Mason. "It's a good place to start. How about we take the next step, and you introduce me to your friends?"

The plural on the end of *friends* was what swayed her to agree. Mason wasn't discounting Bastian, just because the big bad Khan was next to him. Of course, Bastian's snatching a knife out of thin air suggested he was pretty special too, though Kaye wouldn't be the one to tell Mason why.

They approached each other—Kaye, Bastian, and Khan meeting in the middle with Mason and her father. None would shake hands, which was only smart, but the introductions were made.

"I had no knowledge that anyone here intended to kill Kaye," Mason said. "That mage, Kyoko, was included as an emissary from the Eastern Houses. We've been in careful talks with them for the past year, but I think, obviously, their position has changed."

Kaye shook her head. The Eastern Houses had their own Councils, just one more faction with its own agenda.

"They've also been in contact with Grey," her father said. "We'd hoped this meeting would sway them to our side. I don't understand why they'd want Brand killed instead. Would've been nice to question her."

Mason looked at Bastian and Khan. "Regardless, your daughter has formidable protection."

"She doesn't need my protection," Khan answered. "Knock her down, and she will only rise again. It's her nature."

A swell of feeling rushed Kaye's breast that he should think her powerful when she was quivering in her boots.

"So the two of you are associated with Segue?" Mason asked, and the conversation turned to wraiths and Segue's mission. Bastian was dodging the necessity to lie, which made her smile, and Khan was enjoying himself by entangling the angel in more untruths.

Kaye excused herself to say hello to Marcell, who looked so alone among the group.

"Once I build, you are welcome in my house," she said.

"I won't live there," he answered. "I only came to let you know that I'm going away for a while."

"You're going away?"

"If I have your permission." He didn't like asking.

"I didn't mean it that way," Kaye said. This whole vassal thing was uncomfortable. "You can go whenever, wherever you want." He was young, twenty at the most, but then, she'd been on her own since she was fifteen. "Do you need anything?" She didn't offer money.

"Not from you." He turned and stalked into the woods.

She watched, vowing to keep an eye on him. Keep him safe, for his father's sake.

"Angry kid," Gail said.

Kaye turned, a smile ready. This one was for her. Then she'd have to make the rounds with Mason and her father to at least meet the mages who had remained behind before returning to check on the construction of Brand House.

House. Vassals. Mantle. Assassin. It was a lot for one day.

"How are you?" Kaye tried for a warm voice. A woman friend. It would be good to have one of those.

"Better." Gail smiled back. "My aunt didn't want me anymore, so my cousin took me in."

Kaye looked to where Gail pointed. "Mason?" Then he couldn't be that bad. The aunt sounded like a witch. What was it with mage families and their young?

Gail did a surreptitious look around, then leaned in, as she had in the kitchen when she'd warned Kaye about

Grey. Kaye leaned in as well. Innocent gesture until Gail took her hand.

Suddenly, Kaye had no will to pull out of her grasp.

"Gail" hovered on another face, so that two women gripped her: the one she liked, and someone else familiar. One of the many mages she'd been introduced to—but when, where?

"You will do me no harm. You will do Grey no harm. You will return to him at your earliest opportunity, when no one will notice you missing. And you will tell no one of this meeting, or of me."

Kaye almost laughed. Like hell she'd return to Grey. She'd never leave Bastian like that again, not while she was living. And she'd burn up this bitch and inform Mason that he had two traitors in his group today. And, yes, soon, she'd deal with Grey too. She'd make it quick, and then everyone could move on with their lives.

But she was doing none of those things. She tried for fire, found it smothered. Tried to step back, but she kept leaning forward, as if listening pleasantly. She tried to yell, but her voice wouldn't cooperate. All the while, her mind went mad.

Lorelei Blake, that's who it was, the lure whom Grey himself had warned her about the night of her welcome back party. And hadn't Grey also cast an illusion in the cellar? An engagement ring, Kaye remembered, a token of his affection. It was the Shadow he'd stolen from Darshana Maya. And the illusion now made everyone see Gail and not Lorelei.

Someone had to have been watching when Kaye had spoken with Gail that night at Grey House, and Grey had found out about their tentative friendship. The assassin with the knife had belonged to the Eastern Houses, an unsettling thought, but Lorelei Blake absolutely belonged to Grey.

And now Kaye did too.

The drive back was quieter than Jack anticipated. Kaye was sunk deep in her thoughts. Khan had taken his direct route through Twilight to the inn and Layla, always astonishing, and Jack had to wonder again what power Kaye could have to keep the Shadow of Death at bay. Fire was just as elemental, but . . . ?

Beside him, Kaye seemed troubled—they'd discovered new dangers today, but he'd be by her side to counsel her and to catch the knives at her back, literal and metaphorical. The sad tension around her eyes had to be caused by thoughts of her father. Jack wanted to question her, gently, about how she was doing, if she'd considered taking her father into Brand House when it was completed, or if she'd leave him to the mercy of someone else's wards. But those discussions were for later, when she had distance from the encounter.

"What did you think of Mason?" he tried. The drive was smooth, the afternoon sun just cresting the sky.

She shrugged. "I think he's like the group he had with him today."

"Indiscriminate," Jack agreed. "He was shifty regarding his House too. Some mystery there."

"Houses are hard to take sometimes," Kaye said and looked out the window again.

Silence lapsed until Kaye indicated a preference to go to the building site first, and Jack thought that actually might help her. It was built on the Brand legacy, yet was her own. The past was easier to deal with when the future seemed bearable. Jack knew from experience. His memories of war hadn't bothered him for days.

They parked and walked across the property, a new driveway having been bulldozed earlier that day. The turned earth was dark, smelled fresh in spite of the industry beyond. Steel girders were being craned into position to frame out the interior. Shadow reached upward from the foundation like octopus arms to grasp the lengths of metal and hold them in place while others worked. The thoughts among the angels building were hopeful, satisfaction and pleasure in a job well done and the promise of what such collaboration between a mage and an angel might mean.

Jack looked down at Kaye beside him, who still seemed forlorn. *You sold my youth* echoed in his mind, so he put his arms around her. "It's quite something to see how much progress they've made, isn't it?"

He meant, look ahead. Imagine tomorrow.

"I'm amazed," she agreed.

Still not quite there.

"We could help out for a while. Might make you feel better."

A fierce emotion overcame her features, but she nodded. He wanted to get his hands dirty, hammer the nails himself for the place that would shelter her. Feel that body exhaustion that came from building, not cutting down. And then enjoy rejuvenating later.

She was called to examine the blueprints. Her "whatever is good" answer didn't cut it with anyone.

"At least come see," said the foreman/angel.

"You know how particular you are," Jack chided. She didn't have to be shy because The Order was building her house. When had she ever been shy? He'd actually enjoy her bossing them around a little. Let them see her fire. He hoped they'd made her closet very small.

Chapter 17

Kaye dug her fingernails into the plywood table set up for examining blueprints and felt her manicure splinter with the strength of her grip. The wind was gusty, carrying blasts of cold, but it was nothing compared to the force that yanked at her to leave the site of Brand House and travel to Grey. Every time she'd tried to speak of the compulsion, no words would come out. She couldn't scream, she couldn't gesture, nothing that would communicate the dictates of the lure. She'd hoped, prayed even, that the ward stones might help, which was why she'd agreed to come here and not the inn. But the lure's magic had ensnared her umbra, put it in a birdcage of her will, and carried it away by a hand of Shadow.

For the first time in her life, Kaye saw her penumbra, her foregoing intention, in a dirty trail that led north. She might grip the table until her fingers bled, but she knew she would eventually follow that path of Shadow. Her flesh was nothing, incidental. The umbra inside was her life, and it was caught on a very long hook. Deep inside, her umbra thrashed as she resisted.

She was battering herself by resisting. Doing damage and weakening her Shadow.

Then go? It was the only other alternative.

Face Grey strong.

But would that only give him more power when he touched her? Because that's what he was going to do. Kaye was sure of it.

And yet, just this morning she'd only had to blink to kill the assassin from the Eastern Houses. And she'd held back Khan's death Shadows. Maybe she was strong enough to break this. Or break Grey. Either was good.

She let go of the table. Her umbra beat against the bars of her rib cage.

She looked to find Bastian, but he was so far away, down in Brand Shadow. No good-bye. Again.

She'd just have to make it back. She'd promised.

"Just calm down for a minute, Jack," Laurence was saying.

"I need keys!" Jack shouted. And he had to drop by the inn to pick something up before going on to Grey's, though it would cost him time.

She had been going to look at blueprints. Jack knew she'd been unhappy about her father. The revelation had been difficult, but the more he thought about it, the less he believed it was the root of her melancholy. She hadn't expected much from her father. The knife in her back? No, she'd barely batted an eye, which meant she was completely confident in herself, in him, in Khan as well. Mason or the others? They were unreliable, but not dangerous. Yet.

Then Grey? How?

Too many ways to count.

He wished he had time to go to The Order's headquarters, arm himself properly.

Laurence commanded the angels to put down their tools. A very bad sign. But then, Grey sat in the High Seat of the Council of Mages. A strike against him was tantamount to a strike against magekind. War.

It was always going to come to war. They were ready.

"Is there any reason she might have taken off on her own?" Laurence didn't want to fight again either. Once it started . . . "Could she be on her way back to the inn?"

Jack didn't even need a moment to think. "No."

"Hello, darling," Ferro said. He clasped his hands casually in front of himself, lightly touching his ring with his opposite thumb and middle finger to keep himself in check. The key was to hold on to his good mood, even though he'd itched to slap her from the moment she'd entered his house. But some of the Council members were there—Maya, Wright, Terrell—witnesses to her betrayal. Such things were necessary. "This way."

He led the Council members into the small chamber next to his office. Wraiths brought the Brand bitch along and forced her into a chair in the center of the room. She sat at ease, as if at any moment someone would bring her a cup of coffee. She liked it sweet, with lots of cream.

Part of him still loved her.

Kaye's black eyes laughed up at him. "You're going to die."

The lure had done her job well. Nothing was on fire.

Ferro waited while the others took up more comfortable seats. He took a wingback so as not to appear as though he was lording his possession of Kaye over the gathering. He was, though. Kaye was his business. She'd embarrassed him for the last time.

"Let's begin." He smiled to seem friendly. "Kaye Brand,

I'm very troubled by a report I received today. I have a witness that places you in negotiations with a rogue faction of mages, mostly strays, but with one or two other Houses in attendance"—he looked up at the Council members—"whom we'll deal with shortly." Back to Kaye. "You were given a seat on the Council, and now, it appears, you plot against us. Do you deny it?"

"I don't plot against the Council," Kaye said. "Just you."

Ah. "I am the High Seat."

"You shouldn't be. Everyone here knows it."

Ferro looked at his fellow Council members, all loyal. They had generous stakes in the new world and were in positions to weather the shift to darkness easily. They all called him Ferro. Ferro, meaning iron. Pharaoh, meaning Great House. He'd been born for this.

"Ms. Brand. Your House has burned; you stand alone now." Didn't have to be this way. She could've been right next to him, burning into the Dark Age. "I move for the Council to deem you stray. We cannot have unallied, or suspiciously allied, mages among us during these trying times."

"Maya will take her," Arman said. "I can control her. My wards are open to Brand."

Kaye stared at Arman, surprised.

So was Ferro. She'd made a friend. He counted on his fingers. Gail. Arman Maya. That was two. Good for her. She'd made some allies in his House. But was she in or was she out?

. . . in in in in in in in . . .

Ferro smoothed his tie, ignoring the whispers. "You can't even manage your own daughter, Arman. You're certainly not a good patron for someone who burned her own house down." Ferro looked to the two others. "What say you?"

. . . fire fire fire . . .

"I was told she held back the pureblood's Shadow," Wright said. "We may need her, and soon. The Wright House wards are open to Brand."

Ferro's belly soured. As usual, Kaye's fire brought things to light, this time treachery within his own Council. Had he been outmaneuvered? Impossible.

The woman actually had the nerve to smirk. "Your spy reported correctly." She spoke to Wright, but she looked at Ferro. "I did hold Khan's Shadow back. You should've been there. I was a little fabulous."

He used to like her vanity. Now, however . . .

"Terrell?" He could count on his vote. They'd been in this game from the beginning.

"Stray." Raiden's shifty eyes looked to the door; he wanted out.

Good. "Two votes for, two against, but since I am the High Seat, the vote is official. Kaye Brand, you are declared stray, at the mercy of the elements, humanity, and Order. No mage will shelter you."

She smiled, gorgeous and bright.

He would've taken care of her. Given her absolutely everything.

"I make five thousand dollars per second," Kaye said, "and the people who cross me burn. I think I'll be okay. You, on the other hand, are looking older."

Bravado. She wouldn't be leaving his house. Though she was correct about one thing: He hadn't been able to replace his angel. Usually he had one lined up before the other died. He *was* getting older.

Ferro stood. "I think we're done here. If you all don't mind, I have a few things I'd like to say to my fiancée in private."

Raiden exited quickly, didn't even look behind him.

Wright rose, adjusted the sleeves of his suit jacket. "This is a mistake," he said. To Kaye, "I'm sorry." Then, he left too. A problem with the alliance, there.

Arman said nothing, but then his daughter was upstairs, and Lorelei was with her.

Still, Kaye had managed more support than Ferro had thought possible.

"Well done," he said when he and Kaye were alone. "You haven't rested a moment, have you?"

She lowered those thick lashes halfway. Her skin glowed, that generous mouth stretching into a curl.

He warmed, just looking at her. "In spite of everything, I'm still entranced. I would have given you the world."

She made a *tsk* sound. "You couldn't even touch me without stealing."

"I can't help that," Ferro said, "any more than you could help burning your house down."

She made a face conceding his point. "Still makes you a parasite."

The lure had bound her well. Her fire was checked; all she had left was attitude.

He walked a circle around her, slid his hand down the front of her shirt to rest on the silky skin of her breast. Her heart was pounding like mad. "Afraid?"

A delicious wisp of her fire entered him, though nothing like the surge he got when mounted on top of her.

"I'm a little afraid," she said. "They will come for me, and I don't want anyone to get hurt."

"Who will?" Ferro brought his hand up to her chin. Tilted her head back so she'd have to look at him. "Your human lover?"

"I'm thinking they'll all come."

All. The pureblood. The human. Maybe that angel-fae monstrosity. Mason and his strays?

He pushed her head away from him and circled back around. "I'm in a warded house."

"They'll wait."

"I have years' worth of food and supplies."

"They'll wait years." Her voice caught a little; she was overemotional, like a human.

Sweet Shadow. He'd have liked to fuck her one last time, but she might just be right. Her allies could be coming for her. He had allies of his own staying at Grey House, of course. Raiden could kill with Shadow.

"Huh. They care about you that much?" Ferro took her hand in his and turned it palm up. Loosened his ring.

She smiled, though her eyes were filled with pain. "I was as shocked as you are."

"Then I'd better arm myself, eh?" And he pressed the iron circle into her palm.

A thick wave of Shadow blood flowed into him, sweet, potent, and true. The world around him wavered, as if it were a heat-induced illusion. The whispers of the fae sharpened and he saw the outlines of strange creatures prowling the room, predators looking on, yet another reason that he should take her into himself. Hers was indeed a power above all others. And now it was his.

She slid off the chair in a loose-limbed collapse. Her eyes remained parted, so she gave the impression of still being somewhat aware.

"If you could hold back Death," Ferro said, leaning down, "then now I can too."

Whispers woke Kaye. Her eyes wouldn't open. Her cheek rested on a rough surface, but the rest of her was numb. Fire. She tried to lift her hand, find her hand, but her mind fuzzed, and the voices faded.

. . . *Kaye Kaye Kaye Kaye* . . .

Something licked her nose. Instinct made her recoil and swat. She shifted to one elbow, which shook with her weight, then lurched up, her palm braced on cold stone. She was blind, amoebas of light swirling in her vision. Squeezing her eyes shut intensified the effect. She was in utter darkness.

A scurrying sound.

She turned her palm upward and tried for light. The spark came from within, but the Shadowfire that feathered upward, gold-orange-red, was fed by the fuel around her. Shadow.

Ferro's cellar flickered into sight, a rimy tomb for slow dying. A rat-thing from faerie cringed in the corner. The place smelled wet and earthy.

. . . *Kaye Kaye Kaye Kaye* . . .

Kaye breathed deep. Strangely, her mind was clearing. Either that or she was experiencing some deprivation-induced euphoria. No. She was feeling better, which was very strange because she was parched and cold and hungry and her body was weak.

How long had she been down here? Her heartbeat kicked up.

Bastian would know she was missing by now. He'd be frantic to reach her, but the Grey House wards wouldn't let him pass.

As he and she had been from the beginning, they were each on separate sides of a magical line, Shadow on the one side, Order on the other.

And when Ferro was ready, he'd use her own Shadow to destroy her warrior angel.

How long? Would it really be years? She had seen the end-of-the-world supplies firsthand.

Kaye could feel her temper rising.

In spite of everything, she kept coming back to this same place. The cellar, under Grey's power, an angel in torment, she not knowing what to do. It was a puzzle she couldn't solve. The first time, she'd been a stupid kid far out of her depth. The second time, she'd tried to do the right thing. And now?

The fire burned steady in her hand, but she was the one locked up. The Little Match Girl never had much of a chance. She died huddled alone in the cold, peering into visions of home and comfort.

Not going to happen again.

The Match Girl was starved and weary, but Kaye had Shadow in abundance at her fingertips, a significant difference.

. . . burn burn burn . . .

She could burn Grey's house down around her. She'd burned one down before; she could again. Fire wouldn't kill her; her father had survived it, and so would she.

But the lure would keep her from harming Grey, which meant she couldn't set fire to his house. She was good and angry and stuck.

Bastian. Years?

Dark figures moved in the layers of light cast by her fire. The fae.

The irony of the situation was that while angels would be weakened by this much Shadow, Kaye could feel herself growing stronger. The night of her trial against the wraiths she'd almost burned herself out, and Custo had brought her back by filling her bedroom in the town house with the dark stuff. Ferro had trapped her in his cellar, close to his wards. She had all the Shadow she could ever want but couldn't use it against him.

Ferro would figure it out eventually. He'd keep her captive, shut away, use her Shadow and eventually her body, exactly the situation she'd have been in when she was fifteen.

Years. The world would be dark before (if?) she ever saw it again.

Bastian.

His name made the flame burn brighter. The cellar turned gold with the heat. The outlines of the onlooking fae took on three dimensions, rounded parts of their features illuminated—a cheek, the set of a queer eye—but the rest of their faces absent in darkness. The rat-thing darted through the wall.

The fae were that close, all the time. She'd known it on some level, but witnessing how permeable the boundary was firsthand made her buzz with awe and apprehension. The world had no idea what was coming. If magekind was capricious and cruel, the fae would be wilder still.

Bastian.

Her Shadowfire leaped. The stone walls turned semitransparent, infinite darkness beyond. The fae beckoned, phasing in and out of visibility. A silvered outline of great trees, magic trees, glimmered in the distance.

. . . come come come . . .

Could she?

She pushed the blaze higher, hotter, brighter, so that she no longer needed to hold it in her hand. She was the fire. She was on fire.

This was her vision, the one she'd been afraid of all her life. Maybe deep down she'd always known that fire would save her. And if Khan and Custo could cross Twilight and reenter the world elsewhere, then maybe she could too. Khan had been cryptic about what she could do. Maybe this was it. Magic was everywhere.

Bastian.

She opened herself, as if unfolding great wings, and burned. The trees of Twilight, old with magic, exploded into impossible color all around her. The jewel-toned hues made her eyes tear. Their scent was dark and sensuous, tangling with emotion. A wind moved through the trees, rustling across her and filling her ear with an old song in a language she seemed to have forgotten.

A beat of small, rapid footsteps.

She cocked her head and peered at a human-faced animal. In the reflection of its narrowing black pupils, she saw the strange, fairy-tale shape of a firebird.

Jack vaulted over the perimeter fence to Grey House. A wraith met him halfway across the expansive lawn, but Jack put a little angel force into bringing it down. Broke its neck. Another charged as he reached the entrance portico. Jack impaled it on a pointy iron post, a decorative element that now had function.

Jack made it to the door. They all had to know he was there by now, but they didn't know he could get inside.

He drew the skeleton key from his pocket, the Shadow-laced bone. A thin hand of darkness emerged and reached toward the door. The fingers moved like spider legs. The front door swung open. If Kaye was right, the wards were passable now too.

Ferrol Grey himself was descending the staircase, a leg poised midstep.

"Where is Kaye?" Jack asked from the threshold.

Ferro smirked at him, then came the rest of the way down to the landing. "This is very sweet, but really, a mage has no business with a human."

Jack stepped through the wards and let his angel light roar to the surface so that Grey could see that he did not contend with a human. Again, he said, "I want Kaye."

* * *

As Ferro watched the angel cross the threshold of his house, he trembled at the revelation. Kaye had never really lied to him. She had not allied with any other House or human. Always ambitious, to get what she wanted she'd done the unthinkable: allied herself with Order.

Mr. Bastian's penetrating gaze lasered his way, but Grey wasn't scared. He'd fed off angels for years. Shadow brought them so easily to their knees. But because this one came for Fire, that's exactly what he would get.

Ferro raised his arm and searched for the Brand within him, found it sparkling like fairy dust. He moved his umbra to coax the spark into fire and pushed for a Kaye-like bloom on his palm.

A high, woman's scream ripped from his throat as his arm and hand blackened to char. A spindly finger broke and the iron ring fell to the floor.

"That's what you get when you steal another's Shadow," Mr. Bastian said fiercely.

Ferro spotted Raiden Terrell behind the angel, his eyes going black.

"You have some of her fire, but your body wasn't born to wield it," Bastian continued. He moved forward to finish the job, but a cyclone of Shadow lifted him off his feet and crashed him into the staircase.

Raiden, saving his liege lord.

Mr. Bastian fell in a heap.

Ferro gripped his burned arm at the elbow, blinking with pain, unable to move with the shock of it. "Angels aren't so unbeatable, really." He looked at the ruin of his limb. "Magekind are the ones to fear."

Raiden went to check the body.

"If he's alive, we need to bind him," Ferro gasped. It

appeared his angel replacement had come to him. "If I can draw light, I can heal." He might just get out of this alive.

Raiden crouched, felt for a pulse, then shouted when Mr. Bastian grabbed his arm. The wind circled hard again, but this time both were lifted, whipped, and flung. Their bodies cracked the front wall and busted the front door, revealing daylight.

Raiden fell to the ground, blood oozing from his ears and nose, coating his mouth.

"You're not ready to fight The Order," Mr. Bastian said disdainfully to Grey. "The ancients at least knew what they were doing. This one knocked himself out."

"We will learn," Ferro promised. He shook with pain and went down on his knees. "We're learning right now. There's no way you can beat us. Eventually we will reign."

"Tell me where Kaye is," Mr. Bastian said over him. "And I'll let you live."

"I, for one, will never help Order."

Jack stalked across the office to where the secretary, Camilla, hid behind Grey's desk.

"Where?" he demanded. He'd searched these back rooms, finding nothing.

A moment later he ripped the cellar door off its hinges. He could smell Kaye now; she'd been there recently. He took the narrow steps—dark, claustrophobic—in two stretches. This had to be where Ava had suffered too. He pushed the heavy Shadow back only to find more Shadow.

Where was she?

Jack whipped around to illuminate the rest of the space. Only then did he notice a heap of Shadow that didn't move.

He'd been looking for color—for her red hair, her perfect skin—but what he found was a whisper-fragile likeness of Kaye, so real, so rich in expression, that he knelt before her expecting her to see him. Expecting her to move. And she did, each grain sliding together, into a pile of ash.

Ferro couldn't believe his reprieve. The angels were weak in so many ways. Saved by sentimentality. How had they ever beat Shadow?

He pushed himself up and the room spun around him as sweat dampened his face. He leaned for support on what was left of the banister, panting for breath and straining to stay conscious.

Somehow he'd been granted this extra chance. Wasting it meant he would have to face the angel again, and after Mr. Bastian saw Kaye's condition, his soft feelings might harden to rage.

Run. Get as far away as possible. Hide, then return later.

He looked toward the hole made of his front door.

A line of angels stood on the front lawn, their breastplates a shining wall of gold. All of them had vengeance in their eyes, but the wards kept them out.

Fine. He'd hide inside the house until Mr. Bastian left with Kaye.

. . . Kaye Kaye Kaye . . .

He spotted the smoky bone on the floor and crushed it with the heel of his shoe. No more in and out of *his* house. His arm was cauterized. He had no choice but to wait until it was safe, and then seek medical attention. Upstairs. His dark room. He'd shroud himself with the illusion of Maya House. No one would be able to find him. Only Camilla knew to look for him there. In spite of his injury, there was hope for survival.

He panted as he sought within again. This power was

silky, not hot. It swept over him like cool water and made him invisible. Now, to hide.

He turned to find Arman behind him.

Ferro stopped breathing so that he could pass the other mage without him noticing that he was there.

But Arman smiled directly at him, and Grey understood that Arman couldn't be fooled by his own Shadow.

Arman drew a black blade. "If not for Kaye Brand, I would have lost Shana. You draw too deep."

"Never again," Ferro said. "I swear it. Maya will be great."

"Never again," Arman echoed, nodding agreement, and he planted the blade in Ferro's belly. As he died, the illusion faltered and he was once again exposed.

The angels outside looked on.

A commotion battered Jack's mind. *Power's failing through Ohio, Pennsylvania, and New York.* With Grey dead, the wards were down and the angels gathered reported what transpired. All their efforts for nothing. Grey was gone, but as Kaye had warned, others were happy to step into his place and strike during the turmoil. Before too long, there would be kingdoms of Shadow everywhere.

"Jack," Laurence said from the stairs behind him. "We haven't the time to grieve now, friend. We have to stop them while we can."

Jack hovered a hand over the ash, not wanting to disturb. Love, beauty, hope. A numbness stole throughout his limbs, freezing his bones with its cruelty, trapping a scream inside, warmth forever gone from his soul. Every day henceforth, blood, until Shadow swallowed him.

A mage war, all over again. And they'd already lost.

Chapter 18

Kaye ran through the trees, and when her feet wouldn't carry her fast enough, she flew, because in Twilight anything was possible. She was still ablaze, but now it seemed her natural skin, like she was always meant to burn. That she could, for once, be serene and alive with passion simultaneously.

"There you are," a man shrouded in Shadow said to the sky. "I've been waiting for you."

She circled. Peered into his dark face, which was almost familiar, but not quite.

Moving felt better. Up was exquisite.

"Do you know who I am?" he called. The words meant something, but she was slow to find their meaning and to shape the answer.

She circled again. "No." Strange, closed little word.

The man lifted a brow, quizzical. "Has Shadow confused a mage's mind?"

Mage sounded familiar too. Did she care?

"There's an angel named Jack Bastian—"

She shuddered with pain and loss, though the dark one kept talking.

"—thinks you're dead," he said. "He's a different man now."

Jack . . . "Bastian?" The trees wailed with her.

"He's alive and commands the host that moves against the Council of Mages."

Her memory finally stirred. "I came into Shadow to find a way back. Can you take me back?"

"I won't take a phoenix into the mortal world."

She keened, and the colors of forever blurred around her. She felt mean. She would tear him apart. "I'm stronger than you."

"Yes, as is resurrection to death. If you want to go back so badly," he said, "you know how."

Kaye was a quivering nerve, zapping with lightning pain. The one shock became two, which burst into a hundred, and a thousand, until her mind was full of agony and light. She stretched, unwilling, beaten by blood and bone and gripped by corded strands of muscle that tied her into a body. When she cried out her suffering, the fae answered.

. . . *fly fly fly* . . .

Taunting her because she was lashed to Earth.

. . . *fly fly fly* . . .

Or urging her to hurry.

Bastian.

She struggled to her feet, found herself naked. Didn't care. She ran, unsteady, up the stairs and into the room where she'd been cast out from magekind. Beyond that, the offices were trashed, and the front hall was a scene of destruction, the curving staircase blasted in half. And when she turned, she found that part of the front wall of the house had been destroyed as well.

Bastian had been there. And now where? Khan had said the Council of Mages.

"It's all right, honey," a man's voice came from above. "You're safe now."

Arman Maya and his daughter, Shana, started down what was left of the stairs. The girl looked much better but was staggering in his grip. Kaye forgot her nakedness and ran up to help him, afraid they'd fall on the fractured staircase.

Arman seized with alarm. "Who are you?"

"Kaye Brand," she said, trying to take one of Shana's arms. "You're the illusionist here, remember?"

"Where are your scars?" he demanded, keeping his daughter back.

Kaye put a hand to her cheek and felt smooth flesh and a pang of disappointment. "I guess they didn't come back when I was reborn."

He looked at her a long while, considering. "I've got her," he finally said. "You get some clothes on. The Council is meeting, and we'd better be there to say our piece."

"We? I was declared stray."

"The grounds were erroneous, and you know it," he said, descending. "You have vassals and supporters aplenty, and ward stones to keep your House strong."

"You played both sides," Kaye said.

"No," he said. "That was part of my illusion. I am loyal to one side. When the angels come, your fire will be more useful."

We do not strike first. Jack instructed a host of angels a hundred strong on the rules of engagement. *We deliver our demands, and then we leave them to their Council. Don't be tricked into a false attack.*

But be vigilant, Laurence added. *We've never left a parley without bloodshed.*

Look for decoys. Jack belted the breastplate in place. It was polished to a silver-gold shine but would not remain so for long. The sword was too familiar, an extension of his arm. At least he'd be able to cut down wraiths in a single strike; the blade had been honed by Heaven. It went into a scabbard at his side. *The Council members will be protected by their vassals. Don't be so intent on the mage before you that you don't see the one attacking from behind.*

This was always what he'd been sent back to do. First, an attempt at negotiation, a futile gesture considering the human and angelic lives already lost at the hands of the mages, as well as the coordinated attacks on major cities by earthquake and loss of power. Second, in the likely event the first measure didn't work, more bloodshed. He'd fight Shadow, but he didn't think he had it left in him to survive.

We have one chance here, Jack said, *to get some of the heads of the Houses. They aren't aware that we know where the Council meets.* That was the one piece of information that had actually been valuable, it seemed. *So they won't know we're coming.*

If they have created drones out of humans, Laurence continued, *cut them and their mage puppeteers down. All wraiths are considered hostile.*

Jack gripped the burn on his arm to take what little strength he could from it, but it just hurt. He leaned into Laurence, "Did Adam say whether or not Khan was going to assist us?"

Laurence shook his head. "He said Khan thinks he's helped enough."

Jack wasn't surprised. Everything had fallen apart. All goodwill and alliances, gone.

If any one of the mages appears weak or begs for

mercy—he'd have to be satisfied with some mage-learned ruthlessness—*know it for a lie, and cut them from the world anyway.*

Kaye clamped down on her revulsion as she walked from Arman's car through the small army of wraiths amassed outside the Council building. She'd dressed in the smartest clothes she'd left behind at Grey's house. She and Arman flanked Shana, who was shaking with fear. A woman was on her knees on the ground chanting. Kaye's umbra responded: It was a call for Shadow to shroud the land. To lend them cover for secrecy. To darken the minds of humanity.

Shadow answered and smoked on the ground. The overcast sky dimmed and the air quieted.

Kaye didn't have the heart to tell them that she'd already informed The Order where they met. She couldn't tell them that she'd be the instrument of their destruction. She couldn't bring herself to warn them that the angels were coming, and to run while they could.

Because she hoped that Bastian would be among them. That he'd be cool reason when her guts had gone weak and her heart was failing.

The wide hallway was empty, though she heard raised voices from inside the Council chamber. And she fancied she saw the strange, insubstantial form of a fae with its ear to the door. Arman didn't seem to notice. His hand passed right through it to grasp the handle.

They entered into the midst of an argument. The room was full of power. Webb, Hall, and Martin spit harsh words at Wright, Heist, and Terre. A few mages stood solitary, wrapped in their thoughts, while others sneaked near the walls to watch and listen. There was Mason. And on the far side, Gail, whom Kaye would not embrace. She looked around and spotted her father too. And Shadow moved like a snake among them all.

The table at the far end of the room was occupied, two seats vacant, the one she'd taken from Arman with Grey's help, and Grey's High Seat.

The gathering parted to allow them through, surprise at her appearance hushing the group to breathy whispers.

Bastian was coming. Any moment now. Bastian would be there, and if the mages were moved to violence, then no one would survive.

"Brand," Martin addressed her from the Council table. "Do you foresee an imminent attack by Order?"

Kaye stopped before the table, while Arman went ahead and took her hard-won seat. Son of a bitch. His daughter sat on the floor at his knee.

"I do," Kaye answered. "They're moving now, but I hope not to attack."

The crowd was murmuring around her, and the fae were weighing in too, in their own rippling words.

"And how do you have this information?"

"The pureblood told me." Not quite a lie. Khan *had* told her.

"When?" Martin demanded. "Where? We understood you'd burned to death in Grey's house."

"I had actually crossed into Twilight," Kaye explained. "Khan and I conversed there."

She'd been delirious with magic at the time, but they *had* gone back and forth a bit. Martin looked pensive for a moment. "I do not trust fire—it is too unpredictable—but your worth is undeniable: We've learned that you have House wards, with vassals aligning with Brand fortunes. You've won the respect of other Houses as well, and in so doing, Grey has fallen. Further, your power is greater than that of the pureblood who used to be Death. And you know more about what's to come than any of us here." Martin continued, "Please take your seat and address magekind so that we may prepare."

Kaye looked over at Arman. He'd told Ferro to his face that the Maya House wards were open to her. She was not going to return the favor by unseating him again, and in front of all these people.

Arman subtly inclined his head toward the center, as if he had a momentary crick in his neck.

Oh. Kaye slicked with sweat while her mouth went dry. She lifted her chin and stalked around the table. She wasn't dressed for *this,* the only perk that would make this nightmare bearable. She angled her hips just so and lowered herself into the High Seat.

She breathed shallowly so she wouldn't throw up and looked over the assembly. What was an outcast like her doing sitting here?

"The Dark Age is ours," she said, her voice echoing in the now silent room. "We all know this to be true, and I have it on good authority that The Order knows it too. Our Houses are thick with Shadow, and will grow even more so. I have seen this in many visions, and have witnessed personally just how thin and porous the boundary between this world and Twilight is."

So far, so good.

"Therefore, the recent attacks on humanity are unnecessary." A murmur began in the group again. If they didn't like that, then they were going to hate this. "As is the use of wraiths to protect us and the capture of angels to feed them. These practices must stop."

The murmur turned to sounds of dissent. This was not going to go well. She caught only a few words—angels, slaughter us—but she got the point.

A wraith shriek cut through the lower noise in the chamber. The mages stirred, pushing toward the perimeter.

Another shriek lifted and was cut off midcry. And then came the sound of marching footsteps in the corridor, so regular they could only be those of The Order.

Bastian, please.

Some mages darted behind the Council table; others hid in the Shadow along the walls. Several primed themselves to fight. Kaye stood, fire in her hands. She hoped for Bastian with everything she was, but she wouldn't let her kind perish at the hands of others either.

The Council door was flung open by two angels and Jack strode inside, his light parting Shadow into two churning waves. He was unconcerned with the shifty-eyed mages he passed. Their cruelty was in plain view at the far end of the room.

Kaye Brand. This was a weapon of the mind, an illusion meant to torment.

He would not let it. She didn't even look like herself. His Kaye was scarred.

Hold your ground. Do not be swayed.

"I am the voice of The Order," he told her. "I have specific demands regarding the treatment and preservation of humanity, as well as the capture and murder of angels."

"I'll consider them," the false Kaye said. She was smirking, a very good reproduction of Kaye's own expression. Someone had paid attention. "Why don't we arrange a meeting later to discuss the matter in detail? All this pent-up energy in here is just going to get someone hurt today."

A dodge to let the mages get away and plan mayhem later, when they were safe in their Houses.

Be on your guard.

Kaye's gaze shot over his shoulder. She snapped her fingers and hollered, "Hey!" to get someone's attention. "Put down the black blade," she commanded. "I'm talking here." Her gaze settled back on Jack. A bright, satisfied smile. "Forgive my irritability. My temper's not so great on the best of days, and today I was reborn out of my own ashes, which hurt like Hell. And then I got the big chair, and I really think if we don't wrap this up soon, one of the mages in the back—"

She frowned, eyes shifting back again. "I *will* burn you."

"—is going to act without the Council's consent."

Jack gritted his teeth, but that didn't stop his heart from pounding. This was witchcraft. *Reborn out of ashes.*

I'll be damned, Laurence observed. *Everything new.*

"The real concern," she continued, "should, of course, be the fae. When I was in Twilight recently, most seemed benign. With the exception of Khan, of course, though he's no longer fae, is he?" She shrugged. "Regardless, the darker the world gets, the more access the fae will have to it."

Jack felt himself breaking. She was seducing him, again, but this time by making sense. And she was enjoying herself.

"How does next Tuesday work for you? Say we meet back here? Let's all agree not to kill each other until then." She glanced at his sword. Her mouth stretched in appreciation. "Impressive."

"Kaye?" It couldn't be she. He shook his head while his blood rushed and he choked for air.

"Yes, Bastian?" That lazy drawl again.

Ten years ago he'd carried her wraith-ravaged body from the site of her burning house, and now she stood before him, the High Seat of magekind. A thousand years' worth of tours watching Shadow's ebb and flow, and he was shocked by the magic before him. An age of Shadow, like Kaye, would be dangerous, frightening, rapturous with pleasures. But he, like the earth, needed it—*her*—badly.

"The world darkens, Mage Brand," he said. "Will you light the way?"

Epilogue

Jack leaned in the bedroom doorway and took a big, morning bite out of an apple. Kaye was up, her hands working to whip and twist her hair into a loopy ponytail. He wanted to snag it right out again, and would later, but was overcome by a feeling of contentment. His girl was wearing a paint-splattered sweatshirt and jeans. She shoved her feet into work boots, sexy as hell. And he'd discovered, to his delight, that she was never more dangerous than when wielding a hammer.

Their inflatable mattress was sagging for air again, a continual struggle during the night, but they'd been too eager for a night in the house to wait for a proper bed. The main construction was complete—structure, plumbing, electrical—the angels off to other employment. Jack was assigned here, would stay here anyway "to pursue peace." He and Kaye still had a long way to go, but they had a warded roof over their heads, albeit one creeping with dark things in the shadows.

Kaye buckled on a work belt, slung low on her hips. "This place is going to take years."

Jack took another bite. "One room at a time. Bedroom first."

She didn't seem at all worried that Houses were aligning to remove her (violently, if necessary) from the Council for her very close association with an angel. She had too much support, from too many unexpected directions, to be cast out. And already whispered among the Fire-enchanted and disaffected alike was a new idea, dangerous and fraught with conflict: an Order of Shadow.

She sauntered over, hammer in hand, and hooked the claw end to a loop of his jeans. She pulled him to her, and he went willingly, lowering his head for a deep kiss, Light and Shadow coming together much more peaceably, though still buzzing with passion.

When she drew back, she licked his chin, apple juice and all, and looked up into his eyes.

What she saw there made her shake her head. "No," she said. "I hate that bed. I hate it more than anything in this world."

He felt a smile start way down deep inside. "Don't worry. You won't even touch the ground."